To Roy and Pat
Hope you enjoy it!

Nels Parson

A mon petit Engoulevent
Que j'aimerai toujours

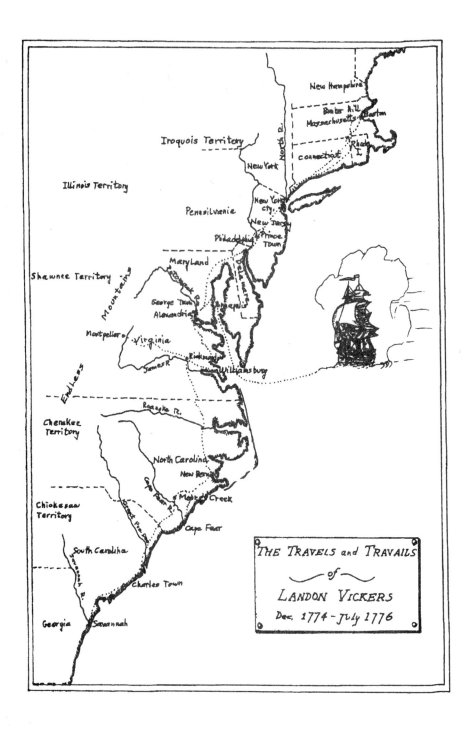

New Hampshire

Bunker Hill
Massachusetts
Boston

Iroquois Territory

Connecticut
Rhode I.

New York

North R.

Illinois Territory

New York City

Pennsilvanie

New Jersy

Prince Town

Philadelphia

Maryland

Shawnee Territory

Mountains

George Town
Alexandria

Annapolis

Montpelier

Virginia

James R.

Richmond

Williamsburg

Endless

Roanoke R.

Cherokee
Territory

North Carolina

New Bern

Chickasaw
Territory

Cape Town

Moore's Creek

Cape Fear

South Carolina

Charles Town

Georgia

Savannah

THE TRAVELS and TRAVAILS

— of —

LANDON VICKERS

Dec. 1774 – July 1776

THE COMPLEAT JOURNAL
of
LANDON VICKERS
A memoir of the days leading to
AMERICAN INDEPENDENCE

by Nels A. Parson
with illustrations by Rex Slack

Iberian Publishing Company
Athens, Georgia
1996

copyright © 1996
Iberian Publishing Company,
Athens, Georgia

ISBN: 0-935931-90-2

Printed and bound in the United States of America

order from
Iberian Publishing Company
548 Cedar Creek Drive
Athens, Georgia 30605-3408

PREFACE

When I, a new cadet as West Point in 1941, stood with upraised hand and swore to protect and defend the United States Constitution, I did not really appreciate the document to which I was referring. For more than fifty years and throughout three wars I have seen young people taking the same oath, suspecting they had only a vague notion of our national values and their origins.

When I retired from active duty, I was determined to find a way to remind new generations how unique it is to swear allegiance not to a king, a president or a political body but to a composition of writing, and to the values therein and their origins. I turned to fiction based solidly on actual events so that the authentic message would be delivered.

Over a period of twenty years I spent many hours in the Library of Congress, the National Archives, the Smithsonian Institution and in the colonial capitals studying books, letters, newspapers and journals of the era.

The result is *The Compleat Journal of Landon Vickers*, a memoir of the days leading to American independence. It addresses the beginnings of many aspects of our national heritage which have since found their way into the constitution—freedom of speech and religion, emancipation, and women's rights to name a few.

This book is the secret journal and associated letters of a young Englishman who is ordered to the American colonies on a dangerous intelligence mission. This character is a composite of several journal writers of that era. The young lady with whom he falls in love and his companion whom he frees from slavery are also based on real people who lived then.

Almost every event depicted actually occurred. From the day he arrived in America until the Declaration of

Independence, from dining on tongue-and-udder to attending the ball in Williamsburg, from originally considering George Washington a criminal to struggling with his own loyalty, he reveals in his journal authentic historical detail. The intrigue, espionage and violence of the most critical time of the Revolution are woven into this suspense fiction.

But most fascinating are the origins of the national values the founding fathers wove into the Declaration of Independence and the Constitution. These enlightened men were well aware of the Glorious Revolution a hundred years earlier in Britain, French political philosophy and ancient Greek and Roman concepts of government and selectively adapted them to meet the unique needs of America. The result is the most enlightened government of, by and for the people on earth.

I am grateful for the criticisms of friends and family and especially those of Jennifer Davis McDaid, historian, in the creation of this work, a passion in my life.

N.A.P.

Charlottesville, Va.
July 4th, 1826

*W*elcome Reader:

The Compleat Journal of Landon Vickers lies finished, fifty years after the U.S. Declaration of Independence. Though in the winter of my life, I journeyed here for a foreword from the author of the Declaration, Mr. Thomas Jefferson, who alas, expired this very day. His passing renders me all the more determined to make my revered friend's remarkable tale known to posterity.

Landon was but a pawn in an unholy atmosphere of hatred and international conspiracy when Lord Chatham sent him to America. The Compte de Vergennes, French foreign minister, detested Chatham and was obsessed with revenge for the humiliating peace terms he imposed upon France eleven years earlier. To destroy British power in America Vergennes secretly encouraged and supported American independence. When he learned that Landon was an envoy of reconciliation between Britain and the colonies, he directed his agents to thwart Landon's efforts and, if necessary eliminate him.

Landon's secret journal, written during the 18 months prior to the Declaration of Independence, reveals his search for his true identity, faith, and country. He suffered the painful anxieties of a wounded conscience, of murderous enemies and of a frustrating love. By his own judgment he failed at times both his beloved and his King.

He wrote in a little known shorthand and stored the journal in a strongbox found only recently. This manuscript is faithfully transcribed from his original entries and associated letters.

Randolph Ewing Howard

London, England
November 1, 1774

To all Officials of His Majesty the King:

Know ye all men by these presents that we, William Pitt, Earl of Chatham, and Landon Chichester Vickers are held and firmly bound to our sovereign Lord, the King.

Whereas the bearer of this Letter of Introduction, Landon Chichester Vickers, is my personal emissary to British America and is entitled to the protection of the King, his proper representatives should offer assistance to this gentleman's laudable and patriotic efforts.

His mission is to determine and report to me the views of provincial leaders and representative assemblies regarding the more exacerbating abuses of the rights of British citizens in America. He is to transmit to me any reasonable proposals by these parties for reconciliation with the British Government and for restoration of peace and harmony.

He should be provided the courtesies and amenities due an English gentleman; I will bear the burden of the cost.

In the name of His Majesty, King George III:

Acknowledged and accepted:

William Pitt

Landon Chichester Vickers

Earl of Chatham

Scrivener and Witness:

Randolph E. Howard
Randolph Ewing Howard

JOURNAL FOR DECEMBER 1774

December 21st, 1774 - County Gaol, Annapolis, Maryland

Here beginneth my sojourn in British America, here in gaol! I, Landon Vickers, emissary of Lord Chatham, had been ashore but one hour when assaulted and then had a barred door slammed in my face! The stench in here is abominable. Damn them all. I am in the right and would lash him again if given the chance. My body is throbbing with bruises, my clothes are muddy and my head is cold for lack of wig or hat. Where are some responsible authorities?

As a much abused and sorely vexed English gentleman on official duty, I hereby record today's events for future action in the courts. Failing any satisfaction there, I shall obtain it directly from the asses who assaulted me.

This unseemly day began when the *Sophia* dropped anchor in Annapolis Harbor, delayed by the frightful hurricane that brought on near mutiny and almost cost us our lives.

Captn. Carmichael, unusually articulate and knowledgeable for his station, but incurably cynical, appeared at my cabin door. Our conversation as I recall it:

"Ready to go ashore?" he asked, then looked at me and laughed outright. "You're dressed to the life, from buckled slippers to powdered peruke. Has the voyage made ye daft?"

"An Englishman dressed as a gentleman will be treated like one."

"You'll be a target for urchins with horse manure."

"I'll take the risk, sir. Can you get me ashore now? I want to see all the colonies."

"You're welcome to them. You'll be entering the land of the slothful, who were either failures or religious heretics at home."

"But Lord Chatham has sent me to....."

"Lord Chatham told me of your mission; a heavy responsibility for a lad of four and twenty," he snorted. "I've had commerce with these blackguards. You'll find them to be avaricious land speculators like that scoundrel George Washington, who started a war with France in an attempt to get a British commission. And there be smugglers like John Hancock and Silas Grover and maniacs like Gadsden of South Carolina. They'll tar and feather you, if they don't kill you. What do you write?"

"A journal about my experiences and the people I meet."

"You'll meet a few wealthy exploiting the many poor and the pitiable slaves. It's an accursed unhappy country of fevers and foul diseases, papists here, rogues and whores down south and daft religious dissenters to the north. This land is so unhealthy, neither people or animals reach full stature after a few generations." He lowered his voice. "And God have mercy on your carcass if any of those blackguards get their hands on your journal. They'll make a eunuch of you."

"Captain, I write in the new Byrom shorthand. No one in these colonies will be able to read it."

Carmichael shook his head and pulled out his spyglass.

"I'll show you what you're facing," he murmured. "Take a look at that sloop unloading casks. They're being put ashore below the main wharf to avoid customs. And it's gunpowder; I saw some spilled. Has an unusual yellow tint in the sun, like it was poorly mixed, but it's gunpowder. The blackguard supervising on shore is Silas Grover, a smuggler and slaver. The likes of him—and the no-trade-with-Britain madness —are ruining the business of the likes of us. With this season I am finished. By springtime I'll be in Boston, bring aboard my wife and depart for England forever."

I looked at Grover only to discover him sighting through his glass at me.

"I shall report this lawbreaking to the authorities. I know the law on matters such as this, Captain."

He snorted and dispatched me ashore in a dinghy with an unfriendly fellow passenger bearing the unlikely name of John Miller. He looks foreign and watches me too much.

I stepped on the wharf at dusk, profoundly happy to be off that wretched ship. For eight weeks I endured hard biscuits, dried fish, stale grog, churning stomach, the smell of vomit and a cabin too low to stand in and too odorous from the indentured below to sleep in.

It was chill and windy on the wharf, moreso than I ever knew in England. I procured my two chests and hired a field wagon to take me to an inn in town. Hardly the proper conveyance of a gentleman but the shivering misery of my body spoke more strongly than the pride in my spirit.

Difficult to express the exhilaration of stepping ashore. For the first time in my memory I was free from Lord Chatham and a career in the clergy which he tried to force on me, free to explore a new world and to find my own faith. But my freedom was short-lived.

Just as the wagon started to move, a tall man in dirty osnaburg clothes suddenly seized the reins and another rogue mounted the wagon and demanded to inspect the contents of my chests on the authority of the "Association of the Continental Congress and the Committee of Anne Arundel."

Assuming the blackguard's authority to be a hoax and myself the victim of a robbery attempt, I shoved the fellow sprawling, seized the whip and attempted to lash the horses into action. But the tall rustic, though feeling the whip too, retained his grip and began shouting for help.

Other men ran to the wagon, swarmed aboard and seized me from all sides. Bewildered and most assuredly concerned, I struggled to free myself, but ended up flat on the ground,

Other men ran to the wagon and seized me.

less my hat and wig. Then I was lifted to my feet and marched straight to this fecal-floored cubicle.

Oh merciful God, I had been trapped for nearly two unendurable hours,* shouting and pounding on the door when two men appeared, one of them the smuggler, Grover. This conversation:

"Young man, I am John Shaw, member of the County Committee of Correspondence and required to enforce non-importation of manufactured goods from England. Do you have anything other than personal items in your possession?"

Expostulating with all the indignation I could summon:

"I, Landon Chichester Vickers, of Westminster, London, am under charter to his excellency, the Earl of Chatham. As his emissary I am on an official mission and have nothing among my belongings that would be of interest to you."

I produced my contractual letter with Lord Chatham and his demeanor promptly changed.

"Mr. Vickers, please accept my apologies! We had no idea you represented Lord Chatham. As Prime Minister he was a friend to the American colonies and is still a powerful influence in our behalf. There is no man in Britain for whom we have more affection and respect. But now I must concern myself with illegal imports from Britain."

"I assure you, sir, I am importing nothing illegally but that man is—gunpowder!"

The committeeman continued to be apologetic but politely insisted, upon Grover's urging, that he inspect my chests. His reasonable demeanor prompted me to pocket the affront and unlock my chests, containing merely clothes and

---

* *One of the reasons Landon left Divinity School was his irrational loathing of solitary confinement—for minor infractions.*

equipment for my sojourn. There appeared to be nothing of interest to him; tea was mentioned and I had none.

Grover was clearly disappointed that Shaw found nothing illegal. I suppose I have gained Grover's enmity but I will see that the Law deals with him.

Nature has disfavored this intruding fool with abated height and a repulsively bloated carcass. A flat, freckled, flushed face is punctured by small close-set reddened eyes, probably from an excess of spirits. His own sandy hair escapes from an old hat on the back of his head and he slouches about in ill-fitting garments and with a heavy cane which likely contains a rapier. His thumb and first finger nails are of eye-gouging length. Sinister and uncommonly ugly is this disreputable creature.

Now someone comes to release me from this ignoble chamber; sitting here alone in this stench and with these thoughts has been but poor amusement.

Thus I complete my first journal entry, including two conversations faithfully retained by the Byrom Shorthand. Mr. Boswell would be proud of me.

December 22nd, 1774 -Golden Swan Inn

Smoked Buzzard Inn would be a more fitting name. With annoying vapors, dirty windows, tobacco-stained floorboards, low beams and sooty ceilings, it is scarcely an improvement on the gaol.

Last evening wagoner Turner brought me to this inn with both chests but neither hat nor wig could be found. On the way we drove by the spot where Grover had been unloading his illegal munitions. The casks were still there, guarded by two rogues who watched me with lowered eyebrows and raised muskets.

Exhausted, frightened and lonely on this first night ashore, I examined my bed, found small creatures awaiting me and slept on the floor.

Though shaken by my first experience in America I was determined to report the customs violation but found no authority the least interested. I did learn from wagoner Turner, a free Negro, that Grover whipped him recently because he refused to carry contraband.

I felt a sense of affection for this African who, though probably racially inferior even to the Irish, is succeeding in an honest trade. He dresses neatly in hempen homespun and wears leather shoes which he made himself. The toes are as square as the end of a box.

Finding only faces of fear, hostility or indifference in the Province House, I finally decided to drop the matter and not raise the blackguard's ire any further.

Had some soup and bread, then pleasured a walk through Annapolis. Despite my prejudice against those who gave me bad encouragement, one of whom was following me, I enjoyed the scene. Annapolis is surprisingly well ordered for a colonial seat of government. There's a remarkable quality of architecture and engineering. The streets, some earthen, some cobblestone, lie straight and true, projecting from the Province House at the center like spokes of a giant wheel. The Province House itself, having lost its copper roof to the same terrible tempest that nearly sank the *Sophia*, is under repair.

Supposedly, wild game is plentiful and gardens were bounteous this year, so why did I have to sup tonight on dried fish and old cabbage, boiled together and poured over black bread, after weeks of little else on shipboard?

Four long tables with benches and wooden dishes were the only facilities. How to move the aging victuals from plate to mouth was for me to solve. The kitchen wench proclaimed the Liberty Boys had taken all the plates and utensils to force the owner to sign "The Association" (supporting non-importation) and had not yet returned them. For a spoon bought from another diner, paid two pence.

But the food was not nearly as foul as the company. Silas Grover and the parcel of arrant blackguards who accosted me on the wagon swaggered in. All dipped their paws or pieces of bread into a large common bowl of the same fish and cabbage stew I tried to consume.

Under their filthy coats, shirt fronts revealed evidence of their eating for months in the past. All had tobacco stains about their mouths, dirty hands and greasy hair, adding stench to the already odorous room. The one-eyed peasant was wearing my wig.

I concentrated on the local weekly newspaper, the *Maryland Gazette*, which announced that the infamous Continental Congress just met with treasonable intent and open rebellion is imminent.

Then Grover belched his way to the door, peering at me with those strange little eyes and I knew I was a target for mischief. The old fear of confinement flooded my soul as I looked for routes of escape. Windows were shuttered from the outside and the kitchen door was behind the men. Front door was near me but bolted. A row of wall pegs held nothing but coats and a wagoner's whip. Now the drunken one-eyed rustic with my wig stood up.

"Hear about the *Peggy Stewart?*" he loudly queried.

"No, what?" came a chorus from the table.

He described the burning of the brig because a ton of tea was aboard.

"And that," belched the rogue, removing my wig and wiping his mouth with it, "was a true sacrifice to liberty. Don't ye think so, Marster Vickers?"

He replaced my wig on his head, fixed his one eye on me and lurched toward me like the mythical Cyclops. Quickly oversetting my table in his path and causing him to fall, I made for the bolted door. Unable to open it fast enough, I seized the wagoner's whip and lashed across the room at my onrushing antagonist.

The end-weighted whip caught him under the ear, wrapped around his neck and bit into his cheek under the empty left eye-socket. I was as surprised as he but jerked the whip and pulled him off his feet again. Cyclops hit the floor heavily and stayed down this time. His companions stared in amazed and respectful silence as I, with great pretense of calmness, took my wig, unbolted the door and retired to my chamber, my whole body quivering.

Despite the stench of an ill-used chamber pot, I bolted both door and window. Why am I such a target?

December 23rd, 1774 - Black Horse Inn - Upper Marlboro

Schmidt's lodging is some improvement but Smuggler Grover and his rogues still intend mischief against me. Last evening I heard stealthy exertions by someone to open my door. Though the bolt held the door secure, I drew my saber so quickly the steel sang in the air and the intruder hurried away. This event unnerved my stomach; the cabbage I ate became a cud the whole night.

My immediate objective is Alexandria in the Virginia Province, where I am to be the guest of my uncle, Mr. John Carlyle. Wagoner Turner will deliver me and my chests to the Potomac River bank opposite Alexandria.

Had a misbegotten breakfast of boiled tongue and udder at the Golden Swan; that establishment is unprepared for gentlemen. Meanwhile Cyclops and his cadaverous companion loitered outside.

But the attraction was across the street. One John Parks was forced to burn a chest of tea in his possession. However a gaggle of rowdies thought the Committee measures were inadequate to the transgression and are breaking the doors and windows of his house. Amid this distraction Turner arrived and we left with expedition.

Rode out of town past a harbor crowded with people, provisions, horses and wagons. Shouting market vendors and two drunken sailors fighting captured my eyes and smells of fish and horse manure alternated in my nostrils. Slaves rolled hogsheads of tobacco down cobblestone roads and onto gangplanks before a forest of tall ship masts.

The gunpowder was gone but I saw the strange Miller and Grover talking there. The two were eyeing each other with the virginal innocence of a pair of slave traders. Whoever Miller is, he is involved in Grover's devilment.

Upper Marlborough is a trifling place but has better accommodations. Over a reasonable supper of beef, potatoes, beans, apple tarts and mead and proper utensils, I met Mr. John Smyth, a tobacco planter, who appears to be as loyal to the Crown as anyone I have met. A fierce-eyed red-cheeked fellow, sprouting briar patches of hair from his eyebrows, ears and nostrils, he was most garrulous and gesturing.

To gain some intelligence I asked him his views on civil liberty.

"Of course I am in favor of civil liberty, but we have it now. The Stamp Act was a mistake, but it was repealed when protested. Neither a despotic nor a Republican government could have achieved that."

I knew the term from debates in the *Puritan Club,** but naived: "Republican government?"

---

* *Our secret and most unpuritanical parcel of students at Oxford which discussed every subject imaginable. R.E.H.*

"That's what these rebellious asses want, a government without a monarch, one which would place all society at the same level and have them exercise supreme power by electing all government officials. All, mind you." His eyes widened; he leaned forward with meaningful low tones: "A dangerous, unpatriotic, atheistic concept, certain to produce anarchy. Can you imagine ignorant plowmen and indentured servants electing a government? They would elect their own kind; those naturally endowed by heredity to lead would be discarded and civilization would end. That's Republicanism!"

He leaned back with arms folded to let me contemplate that.

"Mr. Smyth, how can I determine the Americans' views?"

"Americans, you say? No such people as Americans. These colonials are a hopeless, helpless, hapless mixture of peoples differing in every way possible."

"But Lord Chatham desires that I evaluate their grievances and likelihood of reconciliation. How to do it?"

"Nationality, religion, race, political temperament and property all vary in each province. You must evaluate each one individually. Virginia flirts with independence; the Carolinas will have none of it. All this agitation was started twenty years ago by an inept Virginia provincial named Washington. But it will dissipate with time."

At my insistence he elaborated on the man Washington. According to Smyth he led a band of Virginia militia in an ambush of a French patrol escorting an ambassador to parlay with British representatives, killed the ambassador and several others and precipitated the war with France.

"This avaricious warmonger participated in one military disaster after another," added Smyth, "trying to get a British commission. He was turned down, of course, and still sulks while gaining his fortune in other ways."

Thus this Falstaff opined—as I recall it.

December 24th - Alexandria, Virginia

Christmas Eve but I am sick with the horror of what I saw today. I arose early but found neither Turner nor his wagon anywhere, nor were the two villains in sight. Finally, when the Baltimore stagecoach came by with two ladies already aboard, I joined them.

Then the execrable horror. Outside the town was a bloody quarter of a Negro, his leg chained to a tree, cruelly executed by being pulled apart alive.

"For the murder of his overseer," read a sign above it.

Oh, unmerciful God, I knew whose leg it was by that square-toed shoe. They had murdered Turner, probably because of his befriending me and seeing too much.

Later I saw his wagon with two others, loaded with Grover's gunpowder and en route to Alexandria. Unable to contain my thoughts, I began to tell the two women about it, but they remained quiet.

The younger is a lovely creature, age perhaps twenty years. She has dark hair, a pretty, somewhat Latin face that breaks into a charming smile, straight back and full bosom over a slim waist. Her ladylike demeanor and poise was such that when they had a bit of food, not a crumb escaped her lips.

We reached the Potomac River, the broadest I have ever seen, boarded a packet-boat and crossed to Alexandria. As we moved away from shore I could see the three gunpowder wagons approaching a pier where another packet lay. I swear to almighty God, I'll make Grover regret that cruel murder.

During the crossing I introduced myself and the ladies returned the courtesy. They are Miss Watkins and Mrs. Heyward, her aunt, from Charles Town, South Carolina.

We landed at a great tobacco house where coaches were waiting, exchanged goodbyes and they were gone. What a strange influence she had on me; I very nearly followed her.

She reminds me of Miss Martin at Gresham's School. What a fool I am; I am witness to a murder and may be their next victim, yet savoring a young female as though nothing had happened.

The town, although newer and smaller than Annapolis, is even better situated and organized. The streets are mostly earthen, but absolutely straight, either parallel or perpendicular to the magnificent Potomac River. Maritime industries line the bank, producing everything from hawsers to sea biscuits. The water is clear and blue like a lake and holds vessels of considerable burden.

I was somewhat apprehensive as I approached my uncle, for it was my first opportunity to learn something about my parents. Justice Howard wrote that when he sent me to England to become Lord Chatham's ward, neither of them knew my mother had a brother in Alexandria.

Mr. Carlyle welcomed me most warmly. When I told him about Miller and Grover and Turner's death he merely shrugged and said that I should stay away from Grover, an avaricious and dangerous man. Miller he does not know.

He also knows little about my parents. He met my mother, his half-sister, only briefly just before he sailed for Virginia. Her English mother died when she was young and she lived with an aunt in Kent.

I joined my uncle and his family at dinner where we supped on oysters. Later we went out on the balcony overlooking the garden and watched Negro slaves sing and dance with a fervor that is beyond my understanding. These pitiable creatures reminded me again of the foully murdered Turner. In the harbor beyond, ships' lanterns reflected on the water and I shivered with chill and loneliness. I will never return to Oxford or Kent; my parents are buried in North Carolina. With friend Randolph in London, there is no one to confide in and I feel a great depression of soul—if I have one.

If God exists and knows of me, or the murdered Turner, He does not care. The Church is not only irrelevant, its hierarchy is rotten to the core. Randolph agrees, but he also said the freshness of American freedom and the new approaches to God in America would refresh me. I do not find it so.

Uncle John just handed me an epistle from Lord Chatham confirming my mission and reminding me as ever of Duty, Integrity and Country. Damn his virtuous admonitions. Letter appended hereto.

At midnight many candles were lit to symbolize the new light of the Christ child, but it did not relieve my despondency. Finally retired to my bed chamber. By this lone spermaceti candle I write these bitter words and end my first day in the colony of Virginia.

--------- ⟶•••◦◉◦••⟵ ---------

Hayes, Kent
October 28th, 1774

My Aberrant Landon:

When your parents perished in North Carolina and I assumed responsibility for your upbringing, I decided that training for the Clergy would be proper for you. I could not foresee nor understand why you would become so diverted by your desire for travel or your property in Carolina that you would abandon the calling of the Church.

Even so, I have offered you this employment to support your venture. We have discussed the task before you. The British Government is embarking on a ruinous course which could result in the loss of the American colonies. I am convinced that meeting the legitimate complaints of these free-spirited people will bring about reconciliation and, until recently, communication with my colonial friends has been gratifying. But now there is little response to my queries.

I must know the current views of the colonials, hence my employing you as my personal emissary. Go to their next Continental Congress and to their provincial assemblies. Report to me any possible avenues of reconciliation. In addition, watch for the sinister munitions conspiracy we have discussed.

Remember you are going only as an observer. Restrain your inclination to make quick judgments and take impulsive actions. Such demonstrations will only be deleterious to your mission and to your safety. Discreetly maintain a daily journal with details of conversations, impressions and cultures and correspond with me fortnightly.

Finally, Landon, act with utmost discretion and when tested, remember your Duty, your Integrity, your Country. I bid you Godspeed.

William Pitt, Earl of Chatham

December 25th, 1774 -Alexandria, Virginia

This first day of Christmas started with gunfire. I had been dreaming of the wagoner's death and thought I was being shot, but it was only for celebration of Christmas. Strange custom.

In better cheer today. Lord Chatham's support of the colonies in Parliament is widely known and I am well accepted. However, I was a fool to reveal my interest in the illegal import of munitions. Now Turner's murderers may be after me. The one-eyed rogue I lashed is in town and so is Miller. But who is he?

Went to the morning prayer at Christ Church, but found no comfort in the ritual. It was a typical exercise in prayer book reading followed by sermon reading, so dull and detached from the times that many slept through it. There has to a more felicitous way to reach God and find one's own faith.

During his preachment, I read a broadside entitled *A Sure Guide To Hell*, and very helpful it is, if one so desires. I fear I have already taken the first steps.

The congregation was well dressed, not unlike a London congregation. The gentlemen wore colorful waistcoats, either wigs or their own hair well dressed, lace, and shoes with silver ornamentation. One wore a gold-trimmed hat. The ladies, a little beyond London, were trussed up from their bosoms to their hips and drawn so tightly could scarcely move. One stout crimson-faced lady looked as though she would explode, were she to fall or be pricked by a pin. Very few common people were at the service but they were reasonably dressed in osnaburg or other homespun. The dark-haired Miss Watkins, who was on the ferry, was there with her aunt. The young lady and I exchanged smiling glances several times. She does capture my thoughts but I shall not allow her to divert me from my mission.

The Carlyles dined at four o'clock in the afternoon with a surprising elegance and choice of foods. There was native turkey, venison, pork, and fish, a wide assortment of vegetables including Indian corn, and several pies and puddings. We ate with silverware commemorating on the handles the repeal of the Stamp Act. Thence we retired to the drawing room for singing and merrymaking with newly arrived guests.

Among those who appeared were Miss Watkins and her aunt, Mrs. Heyward. We laughed outright to see each other.

But hardly had we spoken when Uncle John asked Miss Watkins to play the pianoforte.

She responded with a most comely smile, revealing dimples in her cheeks and friendliness in her eyes that would win any man's heart. She turned and moved with the grace of a young deer, revealing dark hair and erect head, unswaying shoulders and straight back which led my eyes to a delightfully slim waistline and full skirt. She sank to the bench with captivating grace and began to charm the entire company with her playing.

Fragments of Bach, Vivaldi and Handel came out of her head without a scrap of printed music before her. Her last piece was an old English lutesong which she sang and then taught us.

"Since first I saw your face I resolved to honor
    and reknown ye,
If I be disdained I wish my heart had never known ye,
What, I that loved and you that liked,
Shall we begin to wrangle?
No, No, No; my heart is fast and cannot disentangle."

Her eyes met mine several times with a smile. I cannot remember music affecting me so. She's truly talented, but I wager she has some Mediterranean blood in her veins.

The party evolved into an informal ball. Negro musicians appeared and for a bit the company danced a minuet with reasonable grace—for colonials. Miss Watkins joined in with another partner and I flattered her aunt, Mrs. Heyward, with talk in order to be next. Remembering Captain Carmichael spoke of a Charles Town revolutionary, Gadsden, I inquired about him.

"Christopher Gadsden is an advocate of Republicanism (she spat the term) and independence, an irresponsible malcontent who organized ignorant townspeople of like mind to resist British suppression. Can you imagine? Suppression indeed."

They are returning to Charles Town after a summer in England where Mrs. Heyward disposed of some inherited Hampshire property. They will be visiting Williamsburg and New Bern en route. Despite Charles Town's apparent charms, their return is a delayed one and, I sense, with a deliberateness akin to avoidance. She made a chance remark about precipitate arrival being undesirable.

"Aunt Elizabeth" Heyward is clearly playing the role of mother to her. This attractive bluestocking lady has culture, education, adequate means and a mind of her own.

Unfortunately, the ball degenerated into vulgar jigs, reels and country dances with instructions monotoned from the fiddlers. The rapidity, the grotesqueness, the sheer peasantry of the dancers' actions is indescribable, but even Miss Watkins joined in. I was tempted to approach her but knew none of the deplorable dances and she enjoyed them all.

Uncle John pulled me into a political debate, advising me to listen only. Introduced as Lord Chatham's aide, I was immediately a friend to all.

But how haughtily and jealously Virginians do talk! They are fond of law discussions to an extreme. They extol English law, swear allegiance to the King but curse the Parliament's "repressive" measures. They have placed the terms "Liberty" and "Freedom" on pedestals to be worshiped and savor every law that supports them. And this often mentioned military failure, Washington, is a hero to them. All seek high-sounding phrases to express their exalted sentiments, quote Greek and Roman discourses on government.

The hypocrisy is amazing. Uncle John, once a tax collector, is now against any tax collection for the Crown. Some slave owners now oppose slavery, faithful church members resist state support of the established church, and apparently better class men reject "stratification of society." All are filled with self-pity for "how the Government is treating us." What a maudlin gathering. I do not share Lord Chatham's compassion for these whimpering colonials.

I pocketed these thoughts, however. The discourse reminded me of *Puritan Club* debates during which Randolph praised the goodness of the freedom movement in America. But here the reality is different.

That Charles Town maiden does captivate me, but no more useless thoughts. I must not allow female diversion.

December 26th, 1774

Preparing for travel. Will leave most baggage here.

The shorthand is working; By capturing a key word of each sentence, I can remember and record complete conversations. My journal shall be in shorthand and be most personal. Observations about old men and young ladies, scoundrels and saints and innermost thoughts will be known only to me. May truth ever be my goal.

This profound loneliness remains. Have I abandoned my faith? And what do I believe about American independence? What is going to happen to this vast possession of Britain? There is no one in whom I can confide, but I am determined to proceed with this mission.

December 27th, 1774

Impatient to travel. I would like to meet the governor and perhaps a few other prominents. Then I shall course southward to escape the winter, find my property and see Justice Howard. Must purchase a horse and some equipment and Uncle John promises to help.

Visiting warmonger Washington today.

December 28th

Yesterday Uncle John, young son George and I rode to visit Mr. George Washington. To my uncle he is a well known plantation owner, land agent, entrepreneur in general, and the most prominent political leader in Virginia. In spite of leg chafing, I managed the borrowed horse fairly well but packed the saddlebags poorly. On our return, every item within got wet from rain and my notes were destroyed.

Mr. Washington's seat, called Mount Vernon, is very large; he has several hundred slaves and indentured servants and many outbuildings. He has acquired a vast estate, I suspect, by a combination of marriage and acquisitions (of doubtful legality, says Smyth) of land to the west.

This obviously capable man has absolute authority over a virtually self-sufficient kingdom that produces and prepares for market wheat, corn and pork, provides housing, clothes and victuals for all. He breeds his own herds of animals and slaves alike.

The slaves sorely discomfort me. They are captured in Africa, brought here in chains, sold at auction and worked and recorded as livestock. Uncle John purchased one from Washington, a ten year old boy, as a gift for his son, also ten. The young slave was orphaned by a swamp fever epidemic and will join an uncle already owned by Uncle John.[*]

The Washington seat is singularly attractive, offers a delightful prospect over the river, and the occupants are masters at receiving visitors. Mr. Washington, addressed as colonel, is in his forties, a tall dignified gentleman with

---

[*] _George Washington did not separate slave families. He never moved a slave unless the slave was willing and arranged for the freedom of all of them upon his death._

impeccable manners. He has a rather Roman nose and large hands and feet, but a commanding presence. His laugh reveals some missing teeth but he has handsome features. He may not be well educated but he is well informed and evidences considerable experience.

But he has a closed mind on politics. No argument changes his pout. His Congress-mandated "Association" will surely be more injurious to the colonies than to the homeland and may bring him a collar of hemp rope.

We remained for the night and returned today in a cold drenching rain and through two deep fords, but far worse to endure was the unhappy young slave riding behind his new owner. The miserable African child wept silently all day.

Today a leather-worker sold to me for ten shillings a light-weight, watertight secretary's bag. Made of pigskin, it lies flat, holds paper, quills, and an apothecary's bottle for ink. Future writing should be better protected.

Cyclops just walked past the house. I'm going to become the pursuer and see where he leads me.

Safely back in my chamber. The oaf led me to munitions being loaded in the Georgetown packet-boat and overseen by Grover and John Miller. Why Miller?

December 29th, 1774 -Alexandria

A servant awoke me this morning, busy with the fire, chamberpot and lantern. My comfortable bed-chamber is on the second floor with four others. The entire house is made of stone and balconies extend from both floors around the rear toward the river and provide superb promenades. Designed and undertaken by my uncle himself, it serves his purpose well. There is a magnificent view from my window.

Purchased a horse today, an action denied to me in England. Old Chatham often said that giving a horse to a young man will turn him into an ass and horses and asses do not mix well.

Having agreed to meet Uncle John at his office at noon to assist me, I left a little early for a closer inspection of the harbor and perhaps a sight of Grover and the packet.

There he was, the unmistakable silhouette of Silas Grover moving toward his rope walk, where hemp is converted into hawsers and *(illegible)*. Overcome by curiosity, I followed. He paused a bit and watched the apathetic slaves walk and twist, walk and twist, many miles in a day, all within a shed not a hundred feet long. Grover spoke to the supervisor and he made the poor creatures increase their pace. Then Grover limped down the long wharf and went into a non-operating distillery, up for lease.

Curiosity possessed me to follow but I hesitated at the door. Then a huge man suddenly appeared from the shadow.

"Like to see it, sir? A very good opportunity to lease it. Harper is my name, of Harper and Hartsborne."

He squinted nearsightedly and moved even closer until his foul breath nearly overcame me. I declined his tour and hurried past the mystified man to find Grover. The huge shed was dark and quiet, but I could hear voices below. I crept closer and looked over a balcony to see Grover talking with Miller. At first the language was French but I could understand "L'Insurgente en Fevrier" because the fellow repeated it to Grover several times. The *L'Insurgente*, a French frigate I have heard of, is probably delivering another cargo of munitions to Grover in February.

Then Grover angrily shouted "Let's be rid of him."

"No no," Miller answered with French accent, "Chatham will accuse Vergennes of murdering his ward and there will be repercussions. Not until we have to do so."

Then they boarded a bateau and the oarsmen, French sailors in appearance, deposited Grover on the George Town packet and delivered the other to an unidentifiable sloop.

My murder they were discussing! Must leave here.

Joined my uncle, not mentioning the distillery incident, to purchase a horse. A two-year-old mare named Mysty was my choice (at £10-15s). She's just a cocktail but who needs a purebred? Worth perhaps £5, but she is large, compact of body and handsome of face.

To George Town tomorrow. Uncle John travels there on business and will let me accompany him to look for a rifle he insists I should buy for protection. I also intend to gather more evidence of Grover's activities.

First letter to Lord Chatham—no copy saved—a recitation of the abuses encouraged by the Confounded Congress, the resistance to taxes and the ominous spread of Republicanism by such as George Washington. Also informed him about Grover and Miller.

His letter of October 28th dwells on our painful differences over my avoiding the clergy, but my epistle ignored them. How can I convince him that the thought of consuming the remainder of my days reading prayers and preachings, churching and baptizing, publicly rebuking and burying, pigging and gardening for sustenance sickens me?

How can he be made to believe that the masters of theological training were slothful, self-indulgent and even corrupt? Appointed for life, they had little moral incentive and resorted to every vice known. And how can he not understand my desire to have my own land and my own freedom to do with my life as I please, as he has? No sight of Miss Watkins today. Not that I was looking for her.

December 30th, 1774 - George Town, Maryland

Gave my letter for Chatham to Capt. Rogers of the *Bexley*, sailing today for London. I pray he is loyal. Six oarsmen rowed us in a flat-bottomed river-boat to George Town today, about eight miles up the river, under swarms of geese, a magnificent spectacle. George Town is on high ground just beyond a small tributary, aptly named Rocky Creek, on the left bank and below the rapids. This modest brick village is older than Alexandria, but may soon be overtaken by the latter in size.

We were met at the dock by Thomas Johnson, attorney, and John Ballendine, canal builder. They plan for opening navigation of the Potomac by building a canal and water gates around the falls just above George Town. We spent most of the day looking at the sites.

We went to a gunshop, but Uncle John recommended against buying anything they had.

There was no sign of Grover, yet there lay the George Town packet he boarded at Alexandria and on the wharf, hardly disguised under a wooden shelter, was a large stack of gunpowder casks, same type I saw at Annapolis. I was prevented from approaching the stack by none other than two of the strangers who followed me into the inn at Upper Marlborough. No doubt Turner's murderers, they fingered their muskets so nervously I retreated.

We're spending the night in Mr. Johnson's comfortable town house on Bridge Street. Oh to get that gunpowder.

December 31st, 1774 - Alexandria, Virginia

Cannot believe what I did in George Town last night, but this morning the missing munitions shelter and nearby shattered windows proved my unseemly mischief was not a hallucination. Has my judgment abandoned me entirely? With some trepidation I record the adventure. Truth must ever be observed.

Last evening my couch was near the rear door on the back porch but I could not sleep for thinking of the gunpowder and Turner's murderers. Finally I arose, dressed in some rather foul working garments hanging by the door, because they were dark and I'd be less conspicuous, and crept cautiously to the gunpowder shed half a mile away.

The two murderers who were supposed to be guarding it were asleep by a waning fire before the wooden shelter; astonishingly careless to have a fire so near. Behind the shed was a single empty cask but there was enough gunpowder in it to make a small powder train to some firewood against the back wall.

Thence I summoned all remaining courage and crawled between the snoring rogues to the fire for live coals to ignite the powder.

Someone was coming! I remained squatted, pulled a hood over my head and watched the fire as though I were one of the guards. My heart pounded as the night walker continued past us. When I could no longer hear his footsteps I rolled a few coals into a bucket, took them to the powder train, lit it and ran as if Satan were after me.

I was back in my bed, heart still pounding, before I heard the explosion. Oh, it was magnificent! The entire household rose to see what had happened. We heard that the shed had been set on fire accidentally by the guards, but they escaped before the gunpowder exploded. I had not killed them and that knowledge both relieved and frightened me. I now realize I am capable of murder too. Unmerciful God, you seem more remote each day.

There is one odd aspect of that gunpowder which Capt. Carmichael had also noticed: its color. I had made the powder train with my fingers and before washing this morning I could see tiny flecks of yellow in the dark powder on my hands. They have to be sulphur.

Did not dare share my secret. At breakfast in Suter's Tavern, the occupants could talk of little else.

Mr. Johnson saw us off on our return boat. As we pulled away from the pier I could see a small crowd inspecting the blackened hole where the gunpowder had been.

Needing to confide in someone, I opened my soul to Uncle John tonight on deserting the clergy and my misgivings about the task Lord Chatham had given me. He listened quietly and opined that I probably took the correct action with respect to the clergy. Would that I could make peace with the Creator as easily. He also suggested that I give up the role of Chatham's emissary.[*]

The year 1775 and my own 25th is upon me. What shall I do with it? I cannot embrace this treasonable fetish for independence. A kingdom of God was supposed to have been established here by the Puritans and others, but there is little purity here. Republicanism, like Christianity, is an attractive but unrealistic philosophy of life. But I must seek faith in something, else life is, to quote the Bard, just sound and fury, signifying nothing.

Is anyone down on the street now, watching for me? Plan to imbibe at the City Tavern tonight.

---

[*] *This confessional prompted Mr. Carlyle to write my father at New Bern (letter attached) knowing Landon was going there. Father put the letter in his strongbox. Eventually other letters and Landon's entire journal were stored there, to be found by me many years later.*

Meanwhile I shall follow a bit further the instructions in the *Sure Guide To Hell*. Plan to imbibe at the City Tavern tonight. Premonitions or not, I am walking out of this house.

———————————

The Honorable Justice Martin Howard
New Bern, North Carolina
Written December 31st, 1774

Sir:

   Permit me to introduce myself, John Carlyle of Alexandria and uncle to one Landon Vickers, whom you nurtured in his early years. He speaks of you with great warmth, as a young man might of his father. Therefore I write hoping that when he comes to visit you, you may be of some assistance to him.

   Be pleased to know that at four and twenty he is nearly six feet tall and weighs perhaps twelve stones. He is well proportioned and featured and demonstrates an agile mind.

   But Landon has abandoned one profession and undertaken another which he should also abandon. I do not know your political views but let me describe his situation. It appears that until he rebelled and returned to America, Landon made few decisions for himself. They were made by Lord Chatham, who pushed him toward the Clergy, Headmaster Martin at Gresham School, who disciplined him unmercifully and Bishop Coucher at Oxford, who disillusioned him. They chose his career, what he should believe, speak, even wear.

   Landon tells me he was sorely disappointed with many of the Oxford faculty. Encouraged by Bishop Coucher, Landon had taken a vow of celibacy "to achieve a higher level of grace" but the Bishop's pretension of celibacy was as false as a street prostitute's. He and others pursued not only women but the young clerics. Coucher often made merry by drinking to excess, exposing himself, even attempting more than once to lie with Landon. Ecclesiastical standards of piety and service were a farce.

Landon has escaped it all but his desertion of the Clergy haunts him and makes him determined to succeed in his new mission. He is engaged in interviewing Colonial leaders on Lord Chatham's behalf to determine whether any accommodation with the British Government is possible. Now that he is free, his relish for travel borders on vagabond.

His task is not only impossible but dangerous. He is at cross purposes with a sinister element here which puts his life at risk. Perhaps visiting you and finding his property will return him to his senses. I have become quite fond of this personable but vulnerable young man and will assist him in any way I can, but perhaps you can better influence him.

Your servant Sir
John Carlyle

COMMENTARY

Curious Reader, Landon's first journal entry reveals remarkable detail, even dialogue, a practice he continued. He planned well for his chosen method of keeping a journal. He sought the advice of James Boswell (journalist and biographer-companion of Samuel Johnson) who urged him to "write with the style of a gentleman and avoid stooping to terse bookkeeper's notes." Boswell also strongly recommended attaching letters received and copies of those written.

Mr. Boswell taught Landon how to record dialogue and suggested he mimic the famous diarist Samuel Pepys with some *form of shorthand.   Landon and I studied together the new Byrom Shorthand for nearly a year for use in his journal entries and our encoded correspondence.   We encoded the shorthand by rearranging the symbols through the windows of stencils.   Using shorthand in his journal saved space and rendered his entries secret to all except those few who could transcribe.   (With this skill I qualified as a scrivener and obtained a position with Mr. Arthur Lee, American agent in London.)*

Landon purchased pens, graphite pencils and a dozen cleverly bound journal books for making his entries.   The journal covers were made of cloth and hollow, making it possible to hide the stencils within them.   He also had small scrivener notepapers on which he could discreetly record and transfer later to the books.

My transcriptions are faithful, even to spelling Charleston in two words as we all did then.   I have used American spelling, e.g. harbor rather than harbour.

Landon was prepared for journal-writing but not for the hostile environment.   He came into the American colonies just as the "Association" passed by the Continental Congress began to take effect.   All trade with Britain was to be avoided and imports of tea were particularly forbidden.   By 1774 Silas Grover, former slave trader, found that smuggling munitions to American rebels was more profitable.   French agents were his conspirators and suppliers.

R.E.H.

JOURNAL FOR JANUARY 1775

January 1, 1775 - Alexandria, Virginia

The City Tavern was my diversion last night, for which I am exceedingly sorry. The early part of the evening was pleasant enough. My relationship with the revered Earl of Chatham gave me amiable drinking companions and we debauched the year out.

We were enjoying whist and conversation until Cyclops walked in. To taunt me he decided to read the Congressional petition to the Throne, a copy of which was displayed on the wall with the other broadsides of that arrogant gaggle.

The ignorant ass could barely read the words, but when he got to the phrase, "We ask but for Peace, Liberty, and Safety," I, feeling my spirits, belched a loud "Amen."

The brutish kern spat, "What think you of that, Tory?"

I stood up and shouted, "God save the King."

"God damn the King!" he shrieked and began to curse me in a most scurrilous manner. I walked over to him and emptied my mug of grog in his face, stood before him with hands on hips. Cyclops responded with a knife, but others stopped him and transferred us both to the courtyard to settle the scrap "Virginia Style."

After we stripped off our clothes above the waist on a freezing night (revealing a long scar across his ribs), the unpolished clown who is called Goose O'Neil circled about me for a bout of boxing. Observers quickly made wagers, mostly in his favor, before the first blow.

Then, as this one-eyed oaf maneuvered clumsily, I saw he was no heavier than my 12 stone. He was so drunk the left eyelid hung over the socket and, being Irish, less intelligent, so my courage gathered.

He made the first move and struck me with such ferocity that I lost my footing and fell. Next he kicked at me but missed and sprawled from his own exertion. Then the vulgar rogue grabbed my legs and overset me, seized me by the genitals with one hand and attempted to gouge out my eye with the other. I bit his hand until I could stand the pain in the groin no longer and nearly broke the fellow's elbow with an arm lock. These struggles threw us apart.

Furious at this foul play, I presented him with such a flurry of blows that he fled into the night. However, the pain in my groin left me scarcely able to walk and blood was flowing from my right eye.

Trembling from excitement and the agony below, I was helped by the barmaid and stable boy up the stairs to a room on the third floor where other drunks had been deposited. Then my young assistants giggled into the next room for mutual pleasure. Bacchus overwhelmed me and I remember no more.

This sinner missed church today—had hoped to see Miss Watkins again—but heard that the parson was also drunk and unable to attend.

My hand resists any further writing tonight. My knuckles hurt, my left thumb is sprained, my face is clawed and my right eye is disgusted with me. Showed it to a doctor but he only gives me powders of willowbark for pain.

January 5th

At breakfast, I endured Uncle John's counsel about raking and fluttering away my income. When I blurted out my experiences with Grover, he offered:

"I don't know where he gets the gunpowder but Silas Grover is an avaricious shipowner who'll transport anything that will fill his pockets. You've brought him to public attention and he's a very secretive and dangerous man. As for your visits for Lord Chatham, you're wasting your time."

After much argument he reluctantly agreed to write letters of introduction to those I wish to visit.

Then in a low serious voice he added, "I must warn you of the dangers involved in your employment, especially if you are considered a spy. The feeling against Tories is high." And my spirits low.

January 6th, 1775 - Still in Alexandria.

Despite my wounded eye being swollen shut this morning, I went to my uncle's office for his letters of introduction. His sloop had just returned from delivering provisions to Boston and Captain Marshall was telling of his voyage. He reported the whole Province of Massachusetts is in revolt.[*]

When Uncle John introduced me, the sun-browned captain raised his bushy eyebrows.

"Ye be informing on Silas Grover?"

"Lord Dartmouth instructed all governors to arrest...."

"Oh he was arrested, to be sure, but freed for lack of evidence. Then he lost his shipment of gunpowder in George Town and he be seeking your scalp."

Dispatched the attached letter to Randolph in London.

---

[*] *The British Army had occupied Boston and closed the harbor to all commerce. The threat of famine in the city produced generous gifts of victuals from the other American colonies to nearby ports and overland to the beleaguered. The British action had served only to unify the colonies. R.E.H.*

6 January 1775

My Ignoble Friend Randolph:

Greetings; here is the first letter, encyphered as we agreed. Mr. Byrom's shorthand is indispensable to me. Moreover, his recollection system works. As people talk, I make pencil notes on a scrivener's pad, a napkin, my cuff, anything. Later I can recall and record entire conversations in the code.

Randolph, I am appalled at the widening disloyalty to the Crown over here and I am obliged to tell you that the atmosphere of freedom and liberty that you promised does not exist. The execrable "Association," is a rebellious Congressional document leading to the most vulgar abuses. These excesses will lead to civil war if the Parliament does not do something other than send troops over here.

How is your position with Mr. Lee? Is there enough commerce to justify his employment as a commercial agent, and yours as his assistant? Here every possible effort is being made to eliminate commerce with Britain.

You cannot imagine my relief to be free of the cloistered life of Divinity School and able to travel. I will be riding south as soon as I acquire a rifle and learn to handle my newly purchased mare. I shall go to New Bern as soon as possible to call on your father and I vow I will not discuss with him your odd political views. I am trying to ignore them myself. If the colonies are not part of the British Empire, they will be part of some other empire. They are too weak to stand alone. I suspect the French are already scheming to transfer ownership by smuggling munitions to the Independents.

And Randolph, I have made the acquaintance of a young lady who is not only unusually comely but of considerable refinement, education, and talent. She affects me so, she's diverting me from my wanderlust. Does that amuse you?

Please write either to Philadelphia, where I will eventually go (The City Tavern is recommended as an address) or to New Bern, through your father.

> *With warmest friendship and affection,*
> *Landon Vickers*

There is a ball tonight and I am preparing for it as best I can. My new lace cuffs were damaged and best wig ruined in my encounter with those Irish dullards in Annapolis.

I had thought the rout might not be held since the Association urges an end to all unnecessary entertainments. The religious dissidents of New England, who consider dancing sinful in any case, must be influencing such a prohibition.

The ladies are inordinately fond of balls; it's their chief diversion. Virginia is a drinking, dancing, racing, gambling province; what a sacrifice to the cause will be the denial of these.

Downstairs a French dancing master named Mirabeau is rehearsing dance steps with some visiting young ladies who travelled to Alexandria to attend the ball. He is pounding an ill-beat drum and bellowing like a corporal at their every turn. This itinerant is a professor of French and Latin at the College in Williamsburg who tours the countryside and provides dancing and archery lessons when not engaged at the College. I spied on them. With their hair up in papers for proper curls this evening, the cavorting young females look silly. Tonight I shall discover whether the training has any value.

Will Melinda Watkins be attending?

January 7th, 1775

Ten o'clock and raining and I have just arisen. The ball lasted until nearly two in the morning and I am truly exhausted, knocked up, as Randolph would term it. That delightful young Charles Town belle was there; her energy would not diminish and I was determined not to concede she was superior in stamina. I must record this remarkable evening.

The occasion was Twelfth Night. Mrs. Hawkins, the proprietor, had decorated the hall on the second floor of the city tavern with evergreens from the forest and extra candles were livened with bits of glass or colored paper.

There were perhaps forty ladies (fewer men) dressed and powdered to excess. Most wore small-waisted rustling dresses. Some were rather handsome of face and displayed their contours fully, yet modestly. However, except for a few, such as Melinda, who have had the advantage of social intercourse with English gentlemen, they are seldom accomplished, unequal to any refined conversation. They make no attempt to keep the body vertical when dancing and when seated often cross their legs, even ankle on knee.

The gentlemen's dress varied from imported English material to locally and somewhat crudely produced. Most coat tails were shorter than usual but with tight breeches and stockings the legs were fully displayed for the ladies to admire.

The dancing began with reasonable propriety. I summoned my courage, asked Melinda to dance and discovered she is an excellent dancer. It was a delight to see her curtseying low in the rhythmic minuet, displaying her figure to fine advantage and moving easily to the music.

But my fortune began to fail as English decorum faded. The informal dancing increased until the minuet was abandoned entirely. There's a great lack of taste in these deplorable jigs, reels and country dances. The men whirl their partners, move them back and forth, sway from side to side and even collide frequently and amorously. The Negro fiddlers sang movement instructions and appeared to enjoy themselves as well as any.

Somewhat abashed, I held back at first, but Miss Watkins came to my rescue and smilingly offered to teach me some of the movements. Oh, she is a sparkling creature with dark hair, charming figure and delicate manner of speech. Fortified with spirits and urged by this vivacious partner, I entered into the fray with complete abandon.

She grasped my hand and pulled me to the center of the room where a great circle was forming. When someone tried to join the circle between us, she clung to my hand tightly, assuring we remained partners. As we swung into the various maneuvers I could think of nothing and see nothing but her. She twirled before me, around me, and close to me while I stumbled about as best I could but savoring every moment. Faster and faster the music went and we were both laughing and panting for breath by the time it finally stopped.

We stood in the middle of the room holding hands, looking at each other, and for a moment became serious. I watched her sweet bosom rise and fall as she regained her breath, the quizzical look on her face as she searched mine. A flicker of a smile brought dimples to her cheeks, then faded. I led her into an anteroom and we sat down on opposite sides of a small round table.

I was nervous in the extreme but so caught up with the moment that I was determined to express my feelings. I fingered my punch cup and the tablecloth but could not raise my eyes to look at her.

"Miss Watkins," I finally blurted out, "I must tell you that, since the first moment I saw you, I have been attracted to you. I cannot account for it."

I hesitated, looked up, and she smiled encouragement.

"When I was a lad in Gresham's School in England, once or twice a fortnight, Headmaster Martin's daughter, a half-dozen years older than I, would acquaint us with the world of music. She was attractive, talented at the harpsichord and most gracious in her demeanor. I have imagined ever since that I would want someone like her for my....But that cannot be the situation here. I confess I do so admire your grace, your charming manners, your ....loveliness that I am overtaken by it." (Verily, I said these things.)

"And why isn't that the situation here?"

"Such a delightful person as you must be spoken for and I have a compulsion to travel ... and a binding obligation to my employer. So I harbor no thoughts of any... intimacy with you. But I....am profoundly affected by you."

Embarrassed and stammering like a child, I abruptly rose. She stepped up closely to me and quickly kissed me on the left side of my neck. When I turned toward her she stepped back quickly and raised her hands, perhaps embarrassed at her own boldness and concerned that I might take advantage.

"Just a kiss of friendship, sir, an old Charles Town custom."

"A custom I like, but I'm not about to seize you. I don't want you to be afraid of me."

"I am not afraid of you."

The music recommenced and she pulled me into the next dance. Shortly after midnight, a fight developed between two debauched buffoons and Melinda's aunt escorted her out. I saw them both to their carriage with a great dumbshow of boundless remaining energy, retrieved my saber from the door clerk and started for the Carlyle house only to find myself facing two knaves.

"That's 'im," one whispered, "they's fifty quid on 'is head."

When they maneuvered to seize me from opposite sides I drew

saber and slashed at the one before me in one motion. The blade cut his hand and I whirled to the one behind me, but he was showing his heels. (Learned that maneuver in the *Puritan Club*, not Divinity School.) Both scoundrels ran and I hobbled home to soak my feet in salts water.

But she IS a treasure! Not just her attractiveness that fascinates me. She is highly intelligent and classically educated.

She said she would sail to Williamsburg and New Bern en route to Charles Town. Perhaps I could see her at these places. But no more of it; she's leaving today anyway and I had best do so too. To Leesburg!

January 8th, 1775 - Leesburg, Virginia

The Red Fox Inn here is pleasant enough; built of hewn logs, but there's warmth and a shank of venison roasted.

Before I left Alexandria, Uncle John warned me again of the unprincipled Grover and reminded me that I should buy a good rifle, dispense with the wig and dress in more common clothes. My apparel marks me a Tory.

Hence was I more than a little interested to learn from a dissident preacher, "Reverend" Norman by name, that some hunting rifles, clothing, and other equipments are for sale at West's Ordinary near Leesburg. They belong to a Mr. Geo. Mercer, a loyalist who could no longer tolerate "patriot" harassment and moved to England.

Methodist Norman and I departed for Leesburg yesterday; do not believe anyone followed us. This congenial but unlearned zealot spends his life in the saddle riding a circuit and preaching to the ignorants in the west.

The Established Church is ignoring these settlers, as it did the poor in England. I remember well we, student-clergymen, standing at a window in Bede's Tavern, chewing on pork ribs, while watching the populace drive the poor out of town so as to reduce the poor-tax. Only the Methodists ministered unto them. God forgive us.

Out of courtesy, I attended Norman's meeting in Leesburg, a remarkable but discomforting service. The preacher used Bible quotations quite erroneously to justify the rebellious viewpoint in Virginia.

"The indentured knave is as worthy as the Governor," says Norman, "and has the right to seek God as he sees fit, without direction from the Church of England or mindless mouthing from a printed prayer book."

He cleverly inserted the golden words of freedom, liberty and equality into religious phrases as though the ancients had proclaimed them. Exceedingly low stuff.

Supposedly, the Baptists are even worse. In addition to near drowning new members, most refuse to pay taxes to the Established Church and preach radical ideas. No surprise that some ended up in gaol. Both sects appear to be bent on destroying pleasure in every form, yet there is a simplicity and purity in their beliefs, however odd and inflexible.

After the meeting, I found West's Ordinary and bought one of Mr. Mercer's excellent "American" rifles (cost £5) and a map of the southern provinces.

The American rifle is so-called because it was invented over here. The interior of the barrel has twisting grooves, called rifling, which impart a spinning motion to the elongated ball as it exits. The weapon is long, heavy and slow to reload, but it has great range and accuracy. The confounded ragged crews called independent companies springing up everywhere are armed with them, but their military drill is quite ridiculous because the rate of fire is so slow and there's no bayonet. It's a good hunting rifle, but if it ever comes to war, the British regiments will slaughter its bearers.

Saddle weary in the extreme tonight.

January 9th, 1775 - Alexandria, Virginia

Mysty returned me to Alexandria today in a long and foolhardy ride of 40 miles. My legs are pitiably sore, skin rubbed away in places, and Mysty is footsore. Just wrote Lord Chatham that all events demonstrate a deepening animosity between Britain and the colonies. Saving no copy.

Leaving in the morning if my legs can tolerate it.

January 10th, 1775 - Fredericksburg, Virginia

Departed before daylight and rode hard all day because of the cold and to lose any possible pursuer. There might have been one. A lone man on horseback followed for several miles, but Mysty's stamina finally won out and we left him.

My map is almost useless, it is so wanting in accuracy and information. Thrice it failed me.

At noon an ordinary in Dumfries sconced me 4s for a neck of lamb, tarts and ale.

Late afternoon, being chilled, lonely and low-spirited about my loss of faith, I turned in to the Potomac Church Glebe for a warming of soul and body. However, Clergyman Reston was so wrapped in his problems, he could not hear mine. He has an annual income, established by law, of 1600 Wt of tobacco and should be happy but fears he'll soon be dismissed from his church.

The unfortunate animosity began when, after a poor tobacco crop raised prices greatly, the Virginia Assembly directed the clergy be paid in money rather than expensive tobacco. Instead of appealing to the Assembly, the clergy sent a protesting representative to London where the Parliament repealed the law. Humiliating the Assembly and thwarting the will of the people created much ill will.

Mysty brought me into Fredericksburg after dark, thoroughly chilled and hungry. Riding must be punishment for past sins; my saddle blisters have become sores. A shopkeeper directed me to Weedon's Public House and stable where I retired after a supper featuring pig's face, which I detest. 'Twas a pig's face Oxford students placed on my pillow one night. I awoke to find this face staring at mine and endured the name Piggy for a time after.

Now I must sleep on straw in a room already occupied by all manner of strangers, none of whom smell the best.

January 11, 1775 - Todd's Bridge, Virginia

Left Fredericksburg at dawn. It is a handsome little trading center, stands well above the Rappahannock River, yet provides good rolling roads to the ships and access to farms in all directions. The roads in Virginia are, on the whole, so miserable that ships sail as far up the rivers as possible. Along these water courses, reaching inland like giant fingers, lie elegant family seats and plantations.

Near the center of town was the slave auction block, now silent on this wintry day. Among the notices on the wall behind it, I read and decided to copy in part:

WANTED

Runaway slave named Nick, recently whipped and has many fresh marks on his back...his fingers much marked by being often cut. £ 3 for return or 40s in any jail, so that I may get him again...a clear mulatto 25 years of age, 5 feet 9 inches, speaks and walks very quick, reads a little, has scar over one eye...So very artful he will escape; by trade a mill-wright. Ran away recently and hired himself as a freeman.

BENJAMIN HARRISON

Why should this poor wretch not run away?

Reached Todd's Bridge Inn by supper time. The spiced-mutton stew and straw-mattressed bed in a chinked log curing room (reckoning: s 2p) were adequate, but my associates were discomforting. Drysalter Todd's stuffed animals watched me from shelves on the back wall, their glass eyes reflecting from the candle. Are these the eyes of souls I as a priest could have saved or those of devils waiting for mine? I turned them all to the wall. This chamber suggests confinement, but I verified I could not be locked in.

This northwest wind will surely bring more frost. Drysalter Todd's stuffed animals watched me from shelves on the back wall, their glass eyes reflecting from the candle. Are these the eyes of souls I as a priest could have saved or those of devils waiting for mine? I turned them all to the wall. This chamber suggests confinement, but I verified I could not be locked in.

This northwest wind will surely bring more frost.

FORTUNATE READER:

By a stroke of good fortune, Madame Jane Austen, English novelist, kindly returned to me some thirteen letters written by Melinda to Jane's mother, CASSANDRA, during the period of Landon's journal. I had learned of and asked for them. They shed revealing light on both Landon's and her experiences. Following is the first. R.E.H.

Alexandria, Va.
January 7th, 1775

My Dear Friend Cassandra,

Our thoughts are full of you. Aunt Elizabeth and I do not pass a day without discussing the lovely summer we had in Hampshire. I had wanted to visit the Mother Country and you made it possible. Our gender finds it more difficult to travel, yet we have equal curiosity and judgment about affairs other than domestic, right?

Especially do we remember the times with you and the Reverend Austen at the Steventon Rectory. It is a lovely spot and you are gracious hosts.

We are safely returned to the American Provinces but the voyage was on the whole unpleasant, even frightening. Adverse winds lengthened our crossing intolerably and a great tempest and shortage of provisions forced us into Annapolis. The miserable ship was swarming with rats which first fattened themselves on unprotected stores and finally became a source of food themselves. Some below paid up to eight shillings for a rat.

The dress materials we purchased in London arrived without damage. We so appreciate your accompanying us to find them and to see King George ride with great fanfare to open the Parliament. It was a splendid spectacle, rendering us proud to be British.

I must confide that I have made the acquaintance of a young Englishman named Landon Vickers from Kent. He is more than a little interesting and he appears to have some interest in me. He sometimes projects a patrician and arrogant attitude toward colonials but our private conversations reveal a shy—even uncertain—young gentleman who needs a little encouragement. He is a welcome diversion—as opposed to the Bennett McKee I discussed with you. The latter would use marriage to me for the *most foul reasons; to improve his financial situation. I dread to confront him again.*

I confess I hope to see Mr. Vickers again. We embark tomorrow for Williamsburg. The captain declares that if even one rat appears our transit is without cost! I shall endeavor to communicate monthly but disturbing political events may not allow it.

With undissembled affection,
Melinda

January 12th, 1775 - New Kent County, Virginia

More than a little discouraged tonight. Crossed Todd's bridge about nine in the morning, restored at Ruffin's Ferry and made a great exertion to reach Williamsburg. However, Providence was not to will it. The unrelenting wind was so frigid, my extremities were in danger of frostbite. I retreated to the nearby seat of one Colonel Bassett, a gentlemen of compassion, even if politically daft about independence. He considers George Washington a hero!

Servants had to lift me from the mare and help me into the house. Only now is feeling restored in my legs, ugly with saddle sores. Everyone has been most solicitous and I now sit encoding these words before a cheerful fire in a small log guest house not far from the mare's stable.

January 13th, 1775 - Williamsburg, Virginia

Here at last at Raleigh's acceptable Inn, but I have foolishly become involved in the slave trade. Last evening I went to the Bassett barn to inspect Mysty one last time before retiring. It was intolerably cold and she was grateful for a blanket, but when I started from the building a spectre rose the hair on my head. A pair of eyes in the corner reflected from my torch. When they did not move I ventured closer and there was a Negro man scarcely able to speak or move. Since he was not of great stature and apparently near starvation I gathered him up and bore him to my quarters.

Not regarding the hour, I summoned aid and we labored over this poor wretch until past midnight. He was not only frigid but badly beaten. I perceived that this was very likely Nick, the runaway slave I read of yesterday in Fredericksburg. He acknowledged as much and pleaded with me in tears and short bursts of almost unintelligible speech, to let him die rather than return to the torture of Mr. Harrison's overseer.

Overcome with compassion for this man, I asked Col. Bassett if he would tend to the pitiable fellow and arrange for me to buy him. Furthermore I wished to free him if that was possible. My host agreed and I left an assurance of £5 and written intent behind. Now I am probably a slave owner!

January 14th, 1775 - Williamsburg

Arose tardily this morning. Afflicted with saddle sores and a fever, I had no interest in breakfast; went looking for Messrs. Patrick Henry and Thomas Jefferson.

I walked straightaway to the Capitol, the meeting house of the Colonial Assembly. The exertion affected my chest and created some vascular uneasiness but the sights in this agreeable town distracted me. Williamsburg is a tolerable seat of government. The entire town is organized on a plain around a handsome square in the center and a long earthen street. There is a College and a Capitol of reasonable architecture at either end.

My eyes also beheld two men and a woman being hanged for murders. One of the men, oddly enough, cried "Vivre la

France" before he dropped to his death. For the woman, Suzannah by name, the execution was especially cruel. When she dropped, her slight weight wrought little injury; she writhed and twisted in strangulation until I had to turn away.* Several in the crowd said she was innocent. May God forgive her and give her happiness in Heaven—if it exists. Why doesn't God intervene for such as she and the murdered wagoner Turner? And who was "Vivre la France?"

Arriving at the Capitol, I found the abominably cold building closed and learned Jefferson and Henry had long since departed the town. A pale thin clerk huddling over a small fire told me the homeseats of the two gentlemen were called Scotchtown and Monticello, but blanched at my suggestion that I wait on the Governor. Showed him my charter with Lord Chatham and the timid soul finally proposed that I see him on Monday next, at ten. When I went outside, the wind struck me as uncommonly cold and my entire frame shook. I hurried to the Inn and trembled to my room. All the symptoms of colic seemed to be upon me. I was full of wind, escaping in all directions, and when I vomited, the belch was bilious.

By supper I thought I had calmed down enough to take a parcel of lamb stew, but it made me ill again.

---

* *SHOCKED READER, by British law more than a hundred offenses were punishable by death and in many forms. Irish nationalists were slow-hanged, had their bowels cut out and burned before their eyes before they died. The Eighth Amendment of the Constitution aimed to eliminate cruel and unusual punishments but failed to define the term. Whether any execution is cruel and unusual is in debate. R.E.H.*

January 15th, 1775

Another Sabbath in America, my fourth, but not a happy one for me. Attended no service for fear of aggravating an already wounded conscience. Also, despite a generous dose of Anderson's elixir this morning and Harlem oil this afternoon, I am still flatulent. The medications were supposed to carry off this insufferable wind in my bowels. Harlem oil is a Dutch specific for flatulent colic but I do not prefer it. It goes off without warning and causes severe caustiveness.

A gentle puke and a good bleeding is needed but there's no one to come today. My blood is feverish, purging inwardly for want of proper evacuation, and the products are collecting in my head and flowing copiously from my nose. Had the same difficulty at Gresham's School once and the bleeding helped then.

Is Miss Watkins here?

January 16th, 1775

With a prodigious headache and dry sore throat, I stood before Governor Dunmore in his well appointed office. He is a short, stout, affable Scot of forty or more.

His manner was not affable at the outset. He queried me exhaustively about my purpose and frowned over my letter from Lord Chatham at length. Assuming his probity of character and benevolent disposition, I described my sojourn in America thus far, to include the unlawful activities of Silas Grover.

My monologue had the desired effect. Dunmore promised a warrant for his arrest and rang for an Indian servant. The handsome young native, dressed in black osnaburg, deposited a bottle of Madeira and retired quietly.

I remarked I did not know the colonials used Indians as slaves. He replied that Pitch is a free manservant, not a slave, raised by the Governor when the native was orphaned. Dunmore calls him Pitch because he creates wooden implements and stains them with pitch to preserve them. He stains his arrows too and can hit game at amazing distances.

This gave me an opening to mention Nick. When I asked him if he could free Nick, he must have interpreted my question as doubting that he could do so. With some irritation he seized a quill and began to write.

"I'll show you I have the authority of manumission. What's his name? You have a receipt for purchase?" He signed with a flourish. "Have the clerk record this." In a moment I was holding Nick's freedom in my hands.

"With regard to French support of the rebellion....."

Allowing me to record a tutorial, Lord Dunmore began to speak rapidly and frankly.

"Vickers, the French strategy is to destroy the British Empire in America. Eleven years ago at the Treaty of Paris, the Compte de Vergennes and I were both witnesses to Lord Chatham's humiliation of a defeated France—an arrogant imposition, I must admit. The loss of Canada and India was particularly painful to the French. When Vergennes, an aide at the scene, blurted out his resentment, Chatham coldly asked:

'From whence cometh this goddam little frog?'

"To this day the French call us the goddams. By the time the little frog Vergennes became foreign minister, he had established spies throughout the American colonies and Britain, to include a member of Parliament, and initiated an elaborate conspiracy to drive us out of America."

"And are the spies here now? I suspect I'm being followed."

"I would be surprised if you were not being followed. The one we hanged for murdering one of my customs officers, the one shouting "Vivre la France," had been spying on us for eight years.   Vergennes won't allow Chatham's peace overtures to succeed and to them you're just a miserable goddam, an expendable pawn. They're dangerous, Vickers, and they'll not suffer the likes of you."

January 17th, 1775

The governor did invite me to a ball Wednesday next. He has three grown daughters, needs gentlemen to dance with them and Miss Watkins is a guest at the palace as well. I accepted, but feeling poorly, sent for a doctor.

A tall man with large snuffed-stained nose and protruding ears below a scabby bald head bent over me this afternoon and solemnly introduced himself as Doctor Joseph de Sabbe. After much deliberation he bled me.

I disliked it and couldn't watch lest I faint, but the bleeding was essential. Should there be a brisk vomit or hearty lower motion prior to bleeding, it may throw the disease upon the brain or burst some blood vessel.

Dr. de Sabbe suspects a pleurisy or cancer in my infected mouth and swollen throat and has prescribed a decoction of pleurisy root and Seneca snakeroot boiled in water. I am to down three tablespoons every fourth hour until it produces a plentiful sweat. If that is not successful he will apply a blister under my chin to draw out the poison and put leeches under my tongue as well.

Meanwhile I am to accompany the medicine with plentiful drinking of flaxseed and barley tea. I am much attending to myself in order to go to the Governor's ball.

January 18th, 1775

Embarrassment is my lot. Feeling somewhat refreshed, I decided to discontinue the doctor's cruel prescriptions. This parasite thinks me a gentleman of means and cheerfully plans to extend the period of my illness. Whatever his motives, he is either ignorant or a fraud. I am no more with pleurisy-cancer than with child.

Lord Dunmore's new daughter, the ninth child, was christened at the church this afternoon and the ball followed this evening, in honor of the Queen's birthday. Though a trifle unsteady this morning, I was not unduly miserable. Took a broth only and felt better for it. Then proceeded to a clothier, purchased stockings and lace cuffs to prepare for the rout.

At the governor's palace, an elegant edifice, the ball was performed in a salutary, essentially English style. An indentured quartet produced the music. They come to the colonies to be auctioned off as seven-year slaves. French dancing instructor Mirabeau stood by approvingly.

As in Alexandria the ladies discreetly displayed their bosoms, the gentlemen their tightly dressed legs. But the young ladies were somewhat more cultivated in their conversation than those in Alexandria. Then Miss Watkins appeared!

The happy surprise and smile on her face left no doubt that I should ask her to dance. Despite my fever, I did so at the first opportunity. As we danced, this graceful lady turned, curtsied, sashayed and teased her way back into my heart.

She's a person of surprises. Her demeanor can be that of a lady whose upbringing has been tenderly conducted. Then suddenly she will play the impish child. Just before the Virginia style intermission (refreshment with a partner chosen by chance), she discreetly asked for my shoe, then pretended to find it in the pile of gentlemen's footgear placed in the center of the ballroom. Each lady was to take one randomly and find the owner. Thus, by conspiracy, she was my intermission partner.

Regrettably the imbibing and exertion increased my fever until, while executing a half-gypsy in the celebrated Dance Wellhall, I fainted and sank to the floor.

Awakening in a guest room in the palace, I perceived several solemn-faced people in the room and Melinda bending over me solicitously. Contemplating death might be near, I lost control of my emotions and blurted: "My dear Lady, I have the strongest desire to be pleased by your person indefinitely, to be mine in marriage, should I survive!"

All present were amused, including the object of my affection. They are all departed now but Melinda remains a house guest. I have no ability to rise and am scarcely able to record this day's events on my pad, remarkable though they be. What am I to do about this bewitching lady?

January 19th, 1775

Finding myself still in a guest room in the Governor's palace this morning aroused neither pride nor pleasure. I was diverted from my intended travels, had publicly made an ass of myself and inflamed the ailments of the head and chest. My throat is burning raw.

Verified from last evening's entry that I did in fact make a thoughtless proposal of marriage to that young damsel. Must have been delirious or drunk and shall not mention it again. But she has an intoxicating influence on me. When she speaks in that soft accent, I am entranced.

Doctor de Sabbe appeared this morning. His grave countenance implied that he had given me over but he eventually proposed with a false eloquence the application of *hirudo medicinalis*, Latin for leeches.

He applied five of the blood-sucking worms under my tongue, to which they fastened themselves immediately. Then he left beside my bed some roasted figs to be placed under my tongue when the leeches dropped off and some laudanum for my dysentery. Finally he produced a most painful blister under my chin with a hot coin, put an aromatic plaster on my chest, and left. I decided to terminate his services.

Thus in agony and mortification I received my next visitors, Lady Dunmore and Melinda. I must not have appeared too ill to either of them for they were exceedingly pleasant. Melinda glided about the room, opening the curtains and adjusting the pillow. When they left the room, I left the bed and, staggering about the room, extracted the leeches, scraped the plaster from my chest, hurled it into the chamber pot and hurriedly dressed. Finding myself able to descend the stairs without too much difficulty, I paid my respects to the surprised hostess and laughing Melinda behind her and departed. Though attracting some attention in my evening dress, I made directly for the Inn and fell into bed.

Awoke about midnight from a nightmare involving Melinda in some distress and I could not help. Made today's entry to get it out of my mind.

January 21st, 1775

Somewhat relieved this morning from most difficulties except the large blister under my chin, planted there by Quacksalver de Sabbe. I should like to return him the hot coin on his posterior.

Escorted Melinda to a demonstration at the College of how to produce rum from pumpkins and thus avoid buying British rum. But the true reason for her going was to discuss advancing her education in music, French and other subjects, perhaps by tutoring outside the College. When I questioned the idea of a female attending college while professors ogled over her, I opened a hornet's nest. She said sharply:

"Read the life of Charlotte Lennox, New York novelist educated in England; if she can do it, why not I?"

Thus chastised, I returned her to the Palace and to her approving and friendly aunt, a lady of some good judgment. Also apologized to Lady Dunmore for my abrupt departure.

I decided to forego payment for Dr. de Sabbe's dubious services. Rather present him with a blow between the ears.

Sinfully diverted tonight at Anderson's with several others on half a buck, many pennyworth of bread and cheese, and a keg of strong ale with no gastric complaint. At midnight Anderson desired we retreat lest he be fined for violating the Sabbath. Which we did most noisily.

January 22nd, 1775 - Col. Bassett's, New Kent County, Va.

Being Sunday, I attended Bruton Parish Church in Williamsburg because I knew Melinda would be there. The parson presented a lame discourse, asked us to examine our consciences but adroitly avoided taking a stand himself.

He also administered a court-ordered public scolding of a woman for some unrevealed sin. The ritual brings to mind the rector at Kent reading at church, as directed by law, the silly act of Parliament against profane swearing. State laws and church admonitions should be separated.

My eyes wandered over the congregation and found Melinda smiling at me. I sought her out after the service and told her of my plans to strike for the West.

She volunteered that after her Aunt Elizabeth attended to an inherited home and flour mill at Williamsburg, they would next be in New Bern, then her home, Charles Town, South Carolina. She gave me two Spanish oranges and her Charles

Town address but was hesitant about something and I could not entice her to tell me what it was.

I carried my belongings to the stable and was saddling up when I realized Melinda was there. She walked up quite close to me, offered wine from a bottle, and struggled to remove the cork. She invited assistance but held it so firmly to her bosom I could neither avoid touching her lovely self as I did so nor did she try to prevent it.

When she held up the wine to me I seized her hands instead and let the container fall to the ground. Then, overwhelmed by her loveliness and encouraged by her smile, I took her in my arms and kissed her soundly. Pressing her tightly against me, I stroked her delightful back from neck to waist, a waist is so small could reach around it and touch my own coat.

This went on much longer than it should have; I was almost out of control. Only when Mysty put her nose in my back did I recover my senses. The lady broke away, turned back with an unhappy tearful face and started to speak, but hurried off. We both forgot about the wine. She's become an illness with me, but what did she want to tell me?

A sinister figure followed me out of town and passed on by when I turned in at Col. Bassett's farm to get Nick.

Nick is much improved; his back is healing and no limbs were damaged by the cold. He appears to be much taken with me; how genuine his affection I do not know. I will take him to his former owner tomorrow and negotiate a settlement. According to Bassett, Harrison considers Nick already sold. I consider him freed.

What should I do with him? Perhaps retain him as a hired servant. His major flaw is a deep hatred and fear of his Negro overseer.

These are long entries to my journal, but how can I reduce them when so much should be recorded? And what else is there to do with my evenings?

January 23rd, 1775 -Berkeley, Charles County, Va.

This morning Col. Bassett sold me (for Nick's use) a bay gelding, a pair of saddle bags and two blankets, all for £4-10s, and bid me farewell. He is a gentleman, but I am near penniless.

Nick was most apprehensive about approaching Berkeley, the country seat of Benjamin Harrison, his former owner, and fell into a fit of trembles and stuttering when the Harrison mill came in view. Nick had labored and been tortured there by his overseer. He was once lashed to the mill wheel so that his head would pass under water with each revolution and his back would feel the whip upon each emergence. If he had drowned, Harrison would merely have had to pay a small fine.

Nick didn't fear Harrison himself but was ready to show his heels if his primary torturer or any attempt to confine him appeared. Mr. Harrison took Nick straightaway into the kitchen and turned him over to an older servant woman making bread before a great open fireplace.

This woman lifted her hands out of the flour, turned towards him, gasped, hobbled across the stone floor into Nick's arms and burst into a mixture of tears, moaning and hysterical laughter as only a mother would. She hugged handprints of flour all over his back and face. I confess to a welling of the eyes myself. Why does God permit this pernicious institution of slavery?

Harrison made it clear Nick was to remain there unmolested and any interloper would answer to him. Nick's mother is quite black but he is clearly a mulatto. And who is the father, Harrison?

We returned to the house through a connecting service tunnel filled with food stores and two hurrying servants who both stopped, flattened themselves against the wall and nodded their heads as we passed. My host grumbled about slavery all the way to his library, cursing both the government and the Royal African Company, but the hypocrite did not suggest he would free his slaves.

I presented Lord Chatham's letter of introduction and the names of those I intended to visit. He laughed when I mentioned Patrick Henry. Then I boldly invited the portly gentlemen to explain his objections to the Government and he allowed me to record them.

He holds the Government's only motivation is avarice and it is responsible for the slave trade, the shortage of money, high taxes and the denial of manufacturing and exporting of goods. Even trade between the provinces is forbidden. But slavery is the heaviest millstone.

"What have the colonies done to end slavery?"

He whirled on me in righteous indignation.

"Both Virginia and South Carolina endeavored to end it; Georgia has too. But their acts were rendered void by royal command because the slave trade was very advantageous to Great Britain. The Ministry directed that no laws injuring the interests of slave traders would be enacted."

He stopped to get his breath and regain his composure.

"Why are you going to see Patrick Henry?"

"Uncle John recommended him."

"For what purpose? To teach you how to be indolent, how to tell stories, to incite the mobs? If he hadn't taken a case opposing the clergy when they refused money in lieu of tobacco, thus catching the attention of the most common people, he'd still be tending bar and fishing. He's a good example of the dilatory poor who would level us all to be equally poverty-stricken and uneducated. We have justified complaints, but his levelling Republicanism will bring us trouble. We have quarrels with the Government but our loyalty to the Crown must be preserved."

We were interrupted by a handsome supper of sauced lamb, vegetables and tarts. Thereafter I was shown my quarters in the "Bachelor's House," a guest building identical in exterior appearance to the kitchen-domestics house but on the opposite side.

January 24th, 1775 - Berkeley, Charles County, Va

Mr. Harrison had a political meeting this morning. For the occasion this stout gentleman, who must be near his 50th year, was dressed and powdered to the life. He arrayed himself in a most luxurious blue and cream colored suit, black boots reaching his knees, and a long queue tied up with a black ribbon.

He invited me to listen to the proceedings in his ballroom but out of sight because some of his neighbors were so fearful of being associated with the rebellion.

With great affability he greeted his guests and had little difficulty convincing them that they should support the Congress and the Association. Even to the suggestion that resistance could be a dangerous step leading to the noose, the stout fellow replied in jest:

"Those that fear hanging lack my advantage. For me it will be over quickly. You who have neglected your middles will doubtless swing for half an hour before you expire."

Then MY name arose. One of the visitors stated with a foreign accent he had seen me at the governor's palace, recording military intelligence in a secret journal and strutting about in Tory clothes. This questioner, a man I could not see, asked if I had been here; said he desired to find me.

Mr. Harrison explained my connections with Lord Chatham, but did not admit he had seen me. He made a diversion of me, saying I was not to be taken seriously.

Never did see the person wanting to find me; grievous mistake. I know not what he looks like. Any man walking up to me could be my enemy. Harrison told me later his name is Cartier, a farmer about 40, bearded, medium stature and usually clothed in buckskins.

January 25th, 1775 - Cover's Tavern, Hanover County, Va

Before departing Mr. Harrison's manor, I could not refrain from relating the malicious deeds of Nick's overseer to his owner and the latter promised to see to him.

By mid-afternoon we reached Cover's Tavern, near the Henry home, and stayed for the night. Cover volunteered that Mrs. Henry is mentally ill and my overnight presence at Scotchtown, as Henry calls it, might be an inconvenience. Nick saw to the horses and my room with enthusiasm. He is so useful he's already become a necessity. Despite his recent travails, he is recovering rapidly.

According to Taverner Cover, Henry is apparently convinced that reconciliation is beyond all hope and is preparing for war. He personally organized the Hanover volunteers, each armed with a rifle and a tomahawk. This is the wild man with whom I must discuss conciliation tomorrow.

January 26th, 1775 - Scotchtown

At Patrick Henry's door, a comely lass, no more than 20, introduced herself as Martha. Five more faces, closer and closer to the floor, appeared. Their father had gone for a walk in the woods and Martha appointed the boy John to take me to him. As we walked I inquired of the health of his mother. With somber face the lad replied that she was very ill in the mind and confined to the basement.

The air being chill, I was startled to hear violin music. We came over a rise and there sat Patrick Henry on a rock beside a stream. He appeared to be serenading a cork which was trying to escape downstream from its fishing pole captor. His dress was backwoods and his music was the country jig variety I detest.

As he spied me, he nodded and continued to play with comic fiddling, teasing eyes and tapping boot.

When he finished the rustic piece we talked. Without success I tried first one approach and then another to reach this slothful troubadour with Chatham's offer of conciliation. He was patient with me but his mind was locked and despite his obvious lack of education he was remarkably astute. To him British actions for the past decade were abridgments of liberty and freedom and that was the whole firkin. This wild man has chosen for independence from Britain and its Church and is prepared to fight for it.

Further political discourse was hardly warranted and I departed. On the hill, I looked back and he was still dawdling in the creek.

Ill again at Cover's, several days. Finally wrote Melinda. (Fair copy attached as Boswell advised)

                              Cover's Tavern, Scotchtown, Va

My Dear Melinda,

It is a faltering epistle I write for I know not how to express this feeling in my heart. Yet I am bold to attempt it, for the emotion is strong and I flatter myself that you have given me some encouragement.

For more than a week I have dwelled on your kisses at the stable and at the twelfth night ball in Alexandria. How vividly I remember our dancing at both balls until I was actually exhausted! When you took my shoe as the one whose owner you wished to share intermission, when you allowed me to dance with you endlessly could I assume, would I dare think there is a place for me in your heart?

You must have thought me delirious when I proposed marriage in my sickbed, but I am quite recovered now and the notion does not leave my head. Would I be too forward if I renewed the subject at some time in the future?

Both my work for Lord Chatham and my longing to see you again, dear lady, will bring me to Charles Town, God willing. I am now obligated to visit a Mr. Jefferson near Charlottesville, but will travel southward thereafter.

We meet in troubled times and I truly fear the possibility of war. My charter and my sense of duty demand that I attend to that possibility and do my best to assist in diverting it, however insignificant my efforts, but my emotions regarding you have no lower priority.

If I may be candid, I suspect someone has already spoken for you (how could such a lovely person not be?), but I come, nevertheless, in the hope that you will see me again.

                            For I am your honored admirer.
                            Landon Vickers

Richmond Virginia - date uncertain

We arrived at this little village in time to find a clothing merchant and outfit Nick; the reckoning: 8s/6p. An apothecary tended his hands and provided a healing salve which I apply to his festered whip scars. Nick is so unaccustomed to compassion, he is bewildered, but beginning to relax. He is interested in reading, even asked to look at an old newspaper, but used it only to identify simple words he knew and could pronounce aloud. There was no understanding of sentences.

Richmond is a frontier village of perhaps 500 souls situated at the head of navigation of the James River. Most streets are canals of mud and, other than St. John's Church and a few dwellings, the buildings are crude. It must be on the edge of the civilized world, yet out in that wilderness to the west, Thomas Jefferson lives. How could anyone so remotely situated have any influence on political affairs?

We're spending the night in Gretchen's Inn with the bed against the door and Nick in the hallway to avoid surprise entry, but I detect no sign of Grover's villains. Every bearded man in buckskins could be my assassin.

In the Wilderness

Know neither the date nor my location. Coursed westward today toward the home of Thomas Jefferson with Nick as my guide because he's been to Michie's Tavern and Monticello is presumed to be somewhere near there.

For our lodging tonight Nick was seeking a certain farm but could not find it. The mist laid so low all day that I no longer have any sense of direction and have no compass. I sense only that we are wandering deeper and deeper into a wilderness of rugged slopes and stagnant swamps hiding under a primeval forest that admits to no trails. Except for an occasional stand of pines, trees are bereft of any sign of life, standing leafless or leaning against one another in death or decomposing on the ground.

We're obliged to bed down out in the elements without adequate protection and it is unmercifully cold.

But Nick is resourceful. He flint-started two warming fires on the sandy creek bed and opposite a rock wall that shelters us from the wind. We are huddled between the wall and the fires and are not too uncomfortable, but we're very much alone. As I record the events of this wretched day in "the style of a gentleman," as Boswell termed it, I imagine every sound in the dark to be either an Indian or one of Grover's scurvy knaves after my scalp. Why such a premonition of danger?

———————

(ATTENTIVE READER: Melinda's 2nd letter to Cassandra.)

January 31st, 1775
Williamsburg, Va.

Cassandra my Dear,

Both in England and in subsequent epistles I have confided in you with innermost thoughts and your counsel has been invaluable. Now I must admit what I cannot even tell Aunt Elizabeth, that a young man named Landon Vickers affects me beyond reason. He not only fills a lonely void, he is a gentleman and loyal to the Crown. So many men in British America are neither.

Shall I describe him to you? He is a special envoy of the revered Earl of Chatham and highly regarded by loyal citizens.

Age four and twenty, he stands six feet tall, and is pleasant of face, has blue eyes, ready smile, is fair-haired. He is strong-limbed and handsomely proportioned and sensitive to others' feelings.

Landon has endured a cloistered schooling and I suspect has had little experience with the ladies. In other than the more formal dances he is reticent and even boyishly clumsy but that endears.

Dare I use the term affection to describe my emotions toward him? No, less intimate epithets such as esteem or friendship must suffice for the present. Our acquaintance has been too short. Yet I was wont to tears when we parted—I so feared I would not see him again. He does promise to come to Charles Town. Do I dwell on him too long?

Aunt Elizabeth and I have enjoyed innumerable civilities as guests of Lord Dunmore, Governor of Virginia, and depart tomorrow for New Bern and Charles Town on the Swallow. Thoughts of my final destination give me premonitions of sadness. I must find a way out of these unwanted shackles.

Until Charles Town,
Melinda

JOURNAL FOR FEBRUARY 1775

February 2, 1775 - Michie's Tavern

Yesterday commenced poorly enough before dawn, when Nick awoke me with a quiet caution not to move. Then with a piece of firewood he struck repeatedly between my feet at a large coiled snake, rattling its tail and striking back at every blow until no longer able. I leaped to my feet only to see a second snake disappearing into a crevice.

Finding ourselves over a den of rattlesnakes, driven out by the heat of the two fires we were sleeping between, we abandoned the site with little ceremony.

Last night was spent in the barnloft of a backwoods pig farmer named Jamison. This tall fellow had a cud of tobacco in his cheek and kept chewing and spitting as long as he was awake. His house was a one room log cabin filled with a common-law wife and half a dozen dirty pock-faced children. He told me he bought the indentured woman for 120 pounds of tobacco, a pound of sot-weed per pound of flesh. They were illiterate, had never heard of either King George or the confounded Congress and had never seen a clergyman, much less been wed by one. But they were proud and refused compensation for our lodging or victuals, venison stewed in pumpkin sauce and Indian bread.

Michie's Tavern appeared after two days on the poorly marked trail. This modest outpost includes an ordinary, (fine haunch of pork and plum pudding tonight), tavern, ballroom and a crude bath house. I have my own chamber and Nick a teamster's loft.

The keeper is the sole literate person about, but his views are distorted by seditious newspapers and by the general wildness of the frontier. There is no evidence of any government whatever. The people here are coarse in appearance and vulgar of speech. Most have cuds of tobacco and rotten teeth like Jamison. This Jefferson must be even plainer than Patrick Henry, who was formerly a bartender here. (With this entry my first journal book is filled.)

Am I being followed? None pays me any attention.

February 3, 1775 - Monticello

Mr. Jefferson's homesite is not a little surprising. Near a muddy frontier hamlet called Charlottesville, I was unprepared for the scene that opened before me. This Thomas Jefferson is transforming the top of a hill he has named Monticello into a magnificent country estate.

His personal servant, Jupiter, met us and led us to the house. There stood Mr. Jefferson, high on an unfinished brick wall, telling an assistant in explicit terms what he wanted. Seeing me, he smiled and climbed down to greet me. He is at least six feet tall, rusty haired with blue-grey eyes and rangy athletic gait, but his demeanor was shy at first, even awkward. He knew of my reason for coming but all political talk had to wait for a tour of the house and gardens.

The main residence is a two story brick building with grand entrances front and back and symmetrical wings. Two large L-shaped terraces extend from each wing and turn forward like a giant horseshoe to define the upper level grounds before the house. At the lower outside level, the terrace walls contain a series of service rooms and stables. The plan is ingenious.

Also met his family. Mrs. Jefferson is a comely lady, has two little daughters, aged one and two years. She invited me to dinner so earnestly I could not refuse. His neighbor, Doctor Mazzei, will also be there.

At last we entered a small brick building at the far end of one L-shaped terrace, the first building, he said, of the entire plantation. The omnipresent Jupiter quietly appeared, revived the fire, and disappeared. I sat down and shorthanded his comments, spoken with the greatest clarity.

"Mr. Vickers, your employer, Lord Chatham, has a virtuous motive, to preserve the rights of the American colonies and to save the British Empire. He seeks a peaceful political solution and I applaud that quest."

"Aren't you the author of the *Summery View*, sir?"

"Aye, I prepared it for the August meeting of the Virginia Assembly but a copy went on to England and procured for me the honor of having my name inserted in a proscription and perhaps my neck in a noose."

"Might I see a copy of this, sir?"

"Yes, but let me tell you about it. It's simply an address to his Majesty laying before him our grievances, claiming our rights are derived from the laws of nature and not as the gift of their Chief Magistrate. It states that kings are the servants, not the proprietors, of the people and begs him to open his breast to liberal and expanded thought."

And then he read a portion, most arrogant and presumptuous, addressed to our Sovereign King. I must acknowledge this man's articulate grasp of affairs, clarity of thought and definition of problems are remarkable. But his radical proposals are impracticable, even treasonable.

He rose and excused himself for plantation duties. He invited me to remain there, read his pamphlet and several other papers and prepare for dinner. I accepted with some hesitation because my only respectable clothes lay wrinkled in a saddlebag. Nick pulled them out and ran to the kitchen for pressing irons. What a necessity he has become! Jupiter has given him accommodations tonight.

February 4, 1775 -Monticello

Awoke this morning to find myself on a magical ice-covered peak above a white sea. Distant peaks protruded from this ethereal sea and on my island every twig had turned to flashing crystal in the morning sunshine. A freezing rain had transformed my world overnight but alas it was transitory. By noon the thin ice had melted and the white sea of clouds below me had disappeared.

Last evening was remarkable as well. Another dinner guest was Dr. Mazzei, an Italian immigrant neighbor who added much with his wit and philosophy. He too is a political radical, an advocate of Republicanism who escaped from his own land. Mrs. Jefferson charms me with her knowledge of literature and skill at the pianoforte. But Mr. Jefferson is the most remarkable of all. The variety of subjects he can discuss in depth are endless.

After a generous dinner of goose roasted, varieties of beans, root vegetables and a rich raisin pudding, we retired to the parlor. Mrs. Jefferson chose to come with us, a bit surprising in view of so many other indications of her good breeding and genteel manners, but her husband appeared to welcome it. First there was excellent conversation, breathtaking in its range of subject matter. We wandered from the geology of the Blue Ridge to the excavations of Pompeii, from Homer to gardening. There were exchanges between Mazzei and the host in both Italian and English, as each learned the other's language.

Mrs. Jefferson was very much a part of it and eventually suggested we turn to music, the most delightful portion of the evening. She played the pianoforte, he the violin, and Dr. Mazzei the flute. Having neither instrument nor ability to play one, I sang when there were words. One was Melinda's favorite, *Since First I saw Your Face.*

She is a lovely and remarkable lady, much like Melinda. I had been led to believe women in the colonies are coarse and domineering of their husbands.

The evening was as remarkable for its location as for its quality. There cannot be another pianoforte within a hundred miles; indeed there is not now even a lighted window to be seen in any direction from this hilltop. Yet amidst this barbarous wilderness, I have pleasured an evening of food, conversation and music unequaled.

When I admired the simple graceful pewter cups they used for wine, he presented me with two saying, "Have a toast with your young lady." (I had mentioned Melinda.)

Politically he is incomprehensible. His Continental Congress has petitioned for relief of grievances and now it is time for the Government to answer. Even this man of apparent fine breeding and education holds that Philadelphia pigsty and its "Association" sacred.

He goes to Richmond tomorrow and I shall accompany him.

The Jeffersons did not invite me to the house tonight except for a brief supper. The younger daughter is ill and he went to fetch a female slave for her breast milk.

February 5, 1775 - Elkhill, Gouchland County

Mr. Jefferson and I rode in his phaeton to another plantation of his and stayed the night.

February 6, 1775 - Richmond, Virginia

We made our way again to this nasty little town, sited amongst a series of unnecessary hills that will forever inhibit its growth. I shall miss Mr. Jefferson and his phaeton. He nearly overset my opinion on almost every subject and left me curious about his religious beliefs. The subject never actually arose, but his quick mind welcomes all enlightened thinking. Unfortunately he is an idealistic Don Quixote.

Tonight I am in the same miserable inn (Gretchen's) used when travelling west. After Monticello, it is particularly odious. A cesspool somewhere annoys the air and I so suspect my bed of vermin that I sleep on the floor. At the bottom of a long hill on the outskirts of town, the inn stands beside an unaccountably rough portion of road. This fieldstone trail renders downhill vehicles nearly out of control and turns uphill traffic into a bedlam of rattling, groaning wagons;

cursing, lashing drivers; and horses blowing unpleasantly from both ends. I pray the cacophony will cease before I retire.

If I should make some charitable comment, it is that the victuals are not too dear. A cut of beef with bread and peas and two pence for the waiter cost a shilling, my last. Coins are unobtainable. Another example, says Jefferson, of British indifference. Thousands of half-pence coins have been stored in Virginia for a year awaiting Government authorization for use.

Thoughts of Melinda and my weak faith are obsessing me.

February 7, 1775 - Richmond

For an indifferent pack horse and a blanket for Nick and some tobacco in return, paid £3. Traded the tobacco for a small ham and a pair of saddle bags.

I shall not be at ease until I depart Richmond. I am regarded with suspicious looks by more than one bearded man, but which one is after me? I now dress like a backwoods rustic and my rifle is my constant companion.

February 8, 1775 - Petersburgh, Virginia

Someone, or the Almighty, is pursuing me again. A chimney fire ignited the inn last night and trapped me in my upstairs room. Though log chimneys are outlawed, this primitive building had one, plastered to conceal and protect the wood, and it began to burn when two drunken yeomen built a large fire in the tavern fireplace. One of them was bearded, could have done it deliberately.

A bell ringing somewhere awakened me and every dog in town. Finding a raging fire in the hallway and opening the window to find it barred, an overwhelming sense of entrapment nearly overcame my rationality.

Then resourceful Nick came with all three of our horses harnessed to a hawser which, from the top of a ladder, he lashed to one of the bars. In a few seconds the animals lunged to his whip and tore out the entire window. I threw my belongings to him, came down the ladder and dressed in the chill night.

Then the fire company began straggling down the hill. First came a half a dozen men behind a heavy suction pump wagon out of control and unable to stop at the scene of the fire. They turned it into a haystack where it came to rest undamaged, but by then the fire was out of control.

Volunteers appeared with monogrammed leather buckets, formed a line between the creek and the re-positioned pump wagon, and began to pass water-filled buckets to the wagon tank. Four men pumped the water into a nozzle aimed at the fire. The pitiful stream exiting the nozzle had all the size and the effect of a cascading horse.

It being a full moonshine, Nick and I saddled up and rode out. As we left the landlord was thrashing one of the debouchers who started the fire. The other rustic, bearded and in backwoods attire, watched me strangely as we rode away. Cartier? We rode east, then waded in a creek to the south to lose any followers. There seem to be none. My appreciation and respect for Nick grows daily.

Eagle Tavern has a scrupulously clean dining room with scrubbed pine tables, white sand floor and generous display of candles. Dinner was savory roast pork and legumes.

February 9, 1775 - Oliver's Racon Tavern, S. Virginia

Last night's dreams trapped me in that burning room incessantly; hope not to repeat tonight. Taverner Oliver is a big, muscular, stupid fellow; must be Irish. He is going to Alexandria to observe George Washington's militia on the

18th, then the oaf plans to organize a "licit" company in this area.

Oh my God, it's good to be free!

February 10, 1775 - Hallifax, North Carolina

Arrived in this town at dusk, heartily tired, but free of the leg sores. Nick is teaching me how to be a better rider and remains curious about reading. He studies the few road signs at length and attempts to pronounce the words. It's amusing to watch him.

It's bed and breakfast in the home of a Mr. Obediah Miller. He has six noisome children who are supposed to be sleeping. A pouting servant girl just appeared and chased them into their bunks. No rural coquette, she is doubtless a virgin and invincible.

Not that I contemplate conquest. The Almighty knows there were times when my animal spirits might have prevailed, had I the opportunity. But even if sheathed with sheepgut, I would not enter a trull and have no courage with others. I have always been too reticent around maidens of quality. It always amused Randolph that I would not pursue females, but my ill-chosen profession and vows interfered.

February 11th, 1775 - MacMillan House

Arrived in a heavy rainfall with a limping pack horse. The inn has beds but no ordinary. Nick resourcefully shoed the left hind hoof of the packer and baked our little ham in the farrier's leftover coals by protecting it in a jacket of clay. That with 2p of cornbread constituted our supper.

February ...*(Entry illegible from water damage.)*

February 13, 1775 - New Bern, North Carolina

Here finally, my childhood home. Arriving here tired and thoroughly chilled, I reached Justice Martin Howard's home just before darkness fell. What a joy to be in this excellent abode where I spent four happy childhood years, where the King is still revered and I am welcomed. His son Randolph and I were inseparable here.

The portly justice immediately included me in a dinner honoring the Reverend James Reed, rector of Christ Church. Scarcely having the time for a proper toilet, I washed and changed into clean attire, which Nick again had pressed.

The Rev. Reed is quite deaf but handsome and amiable, as is his wife Hannah. Typical of the conversation this evening was the Rev. Reed, speaking loudly to hear himself:

"Landon, you were scarcely taller than a firkin when your dear mother and father came here from Charles Town to escape the yellowjack. We all had the fondest hopes but within a year the fever took many here too, including your parents, and the rest of us nearly starved. Now I'm being pressed to swear allegiance to the Association."

"These are troublesome times," Jst. Howard interposed, "but the Carolinas are loyal to the King. Unlike Virginia, only a few are causing the agitation and they will lose out. If they do not, I will be for England. I admit the court is already being ignored. Criminals are not arrested nor brought to me for trial. One jackal named Marchaud, probably a French spy, was caught selling illicit gunpowder to Indians known to be hostile, but he went free."

"You would return to England?" I asked. "Randolph plans to come here."

"I hope he returns with more sense than that with which he left. You know of course that after Lord Chatham arranged his and your acceptance at Oxford, Randolph got

himself dismissed for brawling.   That ended Chatham's
obligation. Randolph does seem to have matured somewhat
since his year in France; studied history and French. Does he
still argue for separation from Britain?"

Do not remember my answer but I was evasive.

Jst. Howard changed the subject to my inherited property,
told me my mother named it Whippoorwill Plantation because
she learned to whistle an imitation of the little night birds, to
which they would respond.

"Creighton brought the property title and survey here for
safekeeping when they fled from the epidemic. John Harvey
holds these papers and you shall have them tomorrow."

They returned to deploring current events; except for the
Justice, they are all melancholy pessimists. As for Governor
Martin, he is away so I cannot see him. Justice Howard did
not urge me to abandon my mission for Chatham but gently
suggested my efforts were probably irrelevant.

No news of Melinda having been here.

February 14, 1775

Trying to comprehend my own beginnings, I asked Jst.
Howard and put to pad with graphite pencil his response:

"You should know the truth. In partial payment for the
properties in Kent that he bought from your father and me, he
agreed to sponsor you two lads through a university. William
Pitt, or Lord Chatham if you prefer, virtually forced us to sell
to him to order to enlarge his estate. In 1753, your father and
I decided to come to the Carolinas, he to the south. He had
scarcely bought his property when the fever came."

So there is the truth. Pitt forced my parents out of their
home, obliged them to come to the Carolinas where they lost
their lives. How could he so manipulate? What was their
social status? Am I just a peasant's son supported out of his

sense of obligation? Why does Jst. Howard not tell me my father's livelihood?

Called on Mr. John Harvey, speaker of the Assembly, to obtain my property papers. The Rev. Reed proclaimed him to be the wildest revolutionary here but Harvey was not the least difficult. He is a gentle old gray-haired man who shuffles around, toes pointing outward and arms dangling like a puppet, appearing quite harmless. But he has a brash tongue when the subject is independence.

He ambled out of his office and led me across the street to lunch with the most conniving malicious gaggle of conspirators I have yet seen. The most treasonable of them is Doctor Alexander Gaston, a surgeon who owns 2,000 acres bordering the Trent River. He claims to be an acquaintance of George Mason and wants North Carolina to adopt some of Mason's ideas about independence. He is scheming to raid armories to steal weapons and disestablish law and order. Tall, about 35 and unmarried, he imagines himself handsome with his Scandinavian hair and athletic figure. Clearly most dangerous, he should be jailed expeditiously.

But I did enjoy an excellent repast of veal fillet roasted with morellos and truffles. And with the yellowed inheritance papers came a surprise, a little money box my poor Mama kept for me, my name on it, in which there was a guinea, two half-crown pieces, a small Spanish coin and fourteen pence.

Thence went to the graves of my parents, who died only a month apart. They were marked with crude gravestones with only the names Creighton Vickers and Maria Vickers and 1754 cut into them. I found myself weeping with loneliness for this pair whom I never really knew but will always revere.

Did God take them or was He too busy elsewhere to notice? My only recollection of either is my blessed Mama running her fingers through my hair as she sang to me. And I remember, after their deaths, sitting before these stones and talking to them as though they could hear, telling them about my childish interests. I would sometimes shed down to my skin nearby and with Randolph slip into a backwater pool, hoping they could see me playing there.

I also recollect being transported from this scene to an English school with more capacity for learning than love.

During a walk around the harbor, I imagined seeing Miller and Marchand together at a distance. My mind is taking leave of me.

A single candle illumes these last notes. Melinda, where are you? I need you.

February 15, 1775 - Trenton, North Carolina

Melinda is already betrothed! I would not believe Gaston, who told me this, but Howard confirmed. Melinda was in New Bern before I arrived, when her ship laid in for provisions, and told Mrs. Howard of her betrothal to someone in Charles Town. Why did she deny me the truth?

Another letter to Lord Chatham, describing my visits and the probable presence of French spies. Told him that Virginia's reconciliation with Britain is impossible without troops to enforce it. The epistle is enroute by a loyal ship's captain; no copy made. Melinda's news is wounding.

February 21, 1775 - Georgetown, South Carolina

Foul accommodations and foul mood. So weary I crabbed at Nick when he did not deserve it. The hurt in his eyes shamed me into begging forgiveness. Most difficult to do. I had traveled for six days in silence, wrapped up in my selfish thoughts of Melinda, my mission and my miseries.

This depressing course has been through pine barrens, fetid swamps, and multiple stream crossings, every one a trial with Mysty—she panics at running water! Inns were rare but I do admit private home owners have been hospitable. Charles Town is yet sixty miles away and the horses are losing their flesh for want of good provender.

Even so, each morning I flee my last abode revelling in my freedom and the trail ahead. Nick is less enthusiastic.

No Cartiers or Marchauds appear to be following me. To Perdition with them.

February 23, 1775 - Charles Town, South Carolina

Here at last but very late. We had a devilish time obtaining passage across the bay at Haddrel's Point. Four men with a large flatboat eventually rowed us across after dark for a Spanish dollar. We went forthwith to an inn but I do not know where I am in the town. Nick is preparing my clothes for tomorrow and has already tended the horses.

February 24, 1775

"Chatham Inn" my accommodations are remarkably called, on the north side of the town near the green. The man's reputation precedes me and makes me welcome when I reveal our connection. More crucial was finding Melinda.

The inn's scout knew nothing of Melinda's livings but gave me directions to those of Christopher Gadsden. I rode into a delightful little city resembling a painting I have seen of a West Indian port. Elegant homes are close to the streets. Some have delicately designed balconies the full length of the buildings and often wrapping around the sides. There are high-walled gardens with ironwork gateways and the light colored plaster walls are interrupted by jalousied doors and windows. (Looked for Melinda at every one.) Great oaks with grey-green beards of moss and smaller colorful trees abound everywhere. Smart carriages driven by coachmen move about as in London and there is a statue of Lord Chatham! He is more the colonies' champion than mine.

I found Mr. Gadsden's residence soon enough but not the man. "Down at the Gadsden's Wharf," the neatly attired doorsman told me, but more importantly: "Miss Melinda Watkins? Why, she and her aunt, Mrs. Heyward, just arrived several days ago. They be at the Heyward house on Church Street, third house from Tradd."

I ran to Mysty and went off at a dead gallop down a long sandy street to Tradd, turned right, avoided a vendor's wagon, right again and reined up so abruptly in front of the third house that I failed to note the slick cobblestone surface there. Mysty's hind quarters dropped as she sat down on her rump, with forelegs still straight. Then I slid backwards and found myself on the cobblestones on my back behind this ridiculous looking animal which sat for an instant like a dog. In this mortifying position, I looked up to see Melinda observe me from the second floor and burst out laughing.

"Do the English always dismount in this manner, sir?" she called mockingly and disappeared before I could conceive of a reply. I tethered Mysty and went to the door. A servant opened it and Melinda stood before me. I had almost forgotten how comely she is, was undone by her graceful form and laughing face. The dimples in cheeks, the dark hair, her whole being made me stand speechless.

"Do come in Mr. Vickers. Take his coat and clean it off, Jasper."

I gave the servant my coat and, though feeling a bit undressed to be calling on a lady, followed her into the parlor. Regaining my wits, I managed to laugh at my diverting display of horsemanship, inquired of her sea journey, told her of mine through the Carolinas, asked about the town, and finally came

"Do the English always dismount in this manner, Sir?"

to the subject on my heart. The conversation so burned in my memory I can record it exactly.

"Miss Watkins," I stammered, "Miss Watkins, have you received my letter?"

She became serious. "Yes, oh yes, you honor me, sir, but there is something you must know. I tried to tell you in Williamsburg. I'm not free to, to, to....."

"Then it's true. Why couldn't you have told me?"

"I tried, oh I tried. But I feared that once you knew I was betrothed you would....." she hesitated, then she whispered, "You would go away." She sat down, covered her face with her hands, bent over and did not speak.

My whole body trembled at seeing her unhappiness. We were alone and I found myself kneeling before her. I ran my hands under hers and held her sweet face between them. She raised tearful eyes to me and stared into mine.

"I need you," she whispered, and then began to weep silently. My own eyes filled, I cannot deny it. Neither of us could say anything until she regained her composure.

"My life has been laid out for me by my elders...more recently a...I can't discuss it. Then the betrothal..."

"When?"

"Last May. That's why I took the trip to England with Aunt Elizabeth. I knew the betrothal was wrong."

"But why did you allow what you felt was wrong?"

"I don't know, I was frightened, I guess. There was no one else and I was afraid for my father; hounded by my mother, who wanted it; afraid of Mr. Trammel because....." Then she was silent.

A long pause ensued and she would not look at me.

"Landon Vickers," she said in a low unsteady voice, "you're very attractive to me, but you're virtually a stranger. I've already told you too much."

We heard footsteps on the stairway at the end of the hall and stood up quickly. An older lady, who proved to be Melinda's mother, swept into the room. I displayed my best manners but to no avail. Her icy greeting chilled me.

"Mr. Vickers, you are alone in the parlor with my daughter and half undressed at that!"

Jasper entered with my coat and retrieved the situation somewhat, but Melinda's reddened eyes and my embarrassment only stiffened her mother's resolve to see me out.

Between Jasper and her, I found myself on the street again, attending to the mare. Then just before I mounted, Melinda came out with an invitation to return and offered her hand. In taking it, I was slipped a note from her palm which read, when I had a chance, "Come to White Hall."

Later learned this is the plantation home of the Heywards and Mrs. Watkins, Melinda's mother, is Mrs. Heyward's sister.

I turned to the task of finding Mr. Gadsden. As I approached the wharves, more of the commerce which makes Charles Town wealthy began to appear. Heavy wagons from back country, loaded with deer skins, lumber, naval stores, wheat, corn, pork and barrels of other produce creaked down to the ships. Barges laden with rice and indigo floated down the Ashley and Cooper Rivers for export.

It's a thriving port. Perhaps I could abandon this impossible political mission, develop my holdings here, and win my whippoorwill.

Mr. Gadsden was there indeed, on his wharf. He was dominating the scene with nervous shouts and pacing on the wharf. Apparently the ship's captain was anxious to leave with the tide and the loading was not finished. Gadsden is short, wears neither wig nor gentleman's clothes, has dark hair and brown eyes, carries a round stomach. He is mounted on legs which constantly move the long-waisted body around but with no seeming connection with what the upper half is doing. The legs turn and take the man away while he is still talking and gesturing to the workers.

I interrupted this scene only after waiting for the ship to cast off and for him to calm down.

"Mr. Gadsden, I'm Landon Vickers. Lord Chatham......"

"Yes, yes, I received a letter of introduction about you." He squinted at me. "You're very young for so impossible a mission, but no matter; too late anyway. Are you Irish? My mother was Irish, father half Irish."

"No sir, my parents, now dead, were English."

"Well it can't be helped. No matter. Suppose you dine with me this evening and we'll talk about your sojourn in America. Bring your belongings and your manservant and be my house guest," he called over his shoulder. "But I have no space for your horses. No matter; leave them at Conklin's Stable." His arms waved vaguely to the north.

The innkeeper's wife says Mr. Gadsden is a widower in his early fifties, has been married twice and now has four children, two still at home. He is a successful merchant, factor and planter, member of the South Carolina House of Commons and for more than a decade has been a leader in political mischief. He speaks better than he listens.

I reached his house about six.

"You're late! But no matter. Go find your room."

I did as I was told. He commands handsome livings, three floors of rooms, all well finished. Mine is on the third overlooking an enclosed garden. It has a balcony and outside fire ladder; no sense of confinement here.

At dinner, some of the wild conversation I recorded:

"The Tories say I have a maggot in my brain. Did you know that? That ass across the street, Laurens, with the elaborate boxwood and cauliflower gardens, started it. He's President of the Provincial Congress, but cold to independence—and avaricious too. For stud services with his prize stallion, it's 20 shillings the single leap, twice that for the season and still more to ensure. If we ever resort to arms, the first thing I shall do is shoot him."

"Is there any accommodation the governor might make?"

"We have a house of commons and the Governor has little to say about what we do. And what we're doing is separating from Britain."

"But hasn't the Government protected you from seizure by the French?"

"No, Mr. Vickers, it has not. British troops came over here all right but their officers treated our militia with contempt; wouldn't give our officers any authority, yet we had to fight the Cherokees. That arrogant British Lt. Col. Grant humiliated our Col. Middleton until a pistol duel ensued. They both missed but Middleton's message didn't. We will not be treated as inferiors by the asses the British send over here and we will not suffer infringement of our right to have a militia and it to bear arms."

"But the Army..."

"The British Army is trying to starve the people in Boston into submission as well as prevent the newspapers from advertising it. We are collecting provisions for them now. In a few days the *Sophia* will sail for Boston laden with a hundred barrels of rice, fifty of Indian corn and fifty firkin of salt pork."

Thus he thrust and I fruitlessly riposted all evening but I have it recorded. He is an opinionated, irascible fool and so energetic as to be dangerous, but a man of the first consequence in S. Carolina. He is for independence and I cannot touch his reasoning.

I do like his accommodations. But what is Melinda's secret? Is she with child?

February 25,1775 - Whippoorwill Plantation

Found the property today; perhaps I will name it Whippoorwill, now that I have seen it, but I neither saw nor heard any of the little birds. Nick says it's not their season. My parents' crude shelter at the foot of the hill serves as bedchamber tonight.

Mama, Papa, I feel your presence so strongly. When I was a child and talked to you beside your graves, I believed you were in the arms of Jesus. Now an emptiness engulfs me and I know not what to believe.

This is a beautiful site. The thousand acres has both virgin forest and pasture, a little stream with several pond sites. The hundred acre bounty grant is adjacent to it and has the 500 foot ridge Jst. Howard mentioned.

This land is mostly pine barrens with some fertile soil here and there. On the little hill there are some oaks, walnuts and other trees. My father partially cleared the ridge, but no house has been started. I found only a large rectangular stone serving as a bench in a little pine glade. It is an outdoor chapel, this little glade, and I shall never change it.

February 26th - Charles Town

We left Whippoorwill at first light, intending to return with equipment to explore the property and mark the bounds. I went straight to Gadsden's wharf. He would know where to find the tools I need.

A horrid scene was what I found, a slave ship unloading its miserable human cargo. Several hundred dejected men and women stood shivering in the chill wind while corpses of those who did not survive were carted off. Except for a square foot piece of blue cloth to cover their loins, the Africans were naked.

A second shock was the appearance of Melinda and her friend Ruth Craig with the St. Cecelia mercy wagon. This concert society is also a charitable organization. The two osnaburg-dressed ladies proceeded to give a blanket to each chilled victim while the Heyward servants offered water. The blessed women worked rapidly, for the irritated owners were anxious to move their property to the auction block. While the wide-eyed Nick held the horses, I assisted them.

We did not fail to hear the guards swear most horridly in undertones over the delay, but Melinda and Ruth worked with a deaf nonchalance and would not be deterred. Fair haired Ruth is a little shorter than Melinda but no less energetic and no less ripe for a mate. They patted the cheek of every female, spoke to them tenderly though they understood not a word.

Their task completed, the two angels of mercy bid me good day—with a reminder to come to White Hall—and rode away in the wagon. May God bless them.

Gadsden then appeared and loudly demanded the slaves be removed and ordered the owners never to use his wharf again.

As passed me:

"Fustilarians! Come have coffee with me Vickers."

I did so after assuring the fearful Nick I would never allow him to go back to such a life. Told Gadsden my plans for my property.

"Excellent idea, Vickers. Mark your property well. What do you know about the Irish?"

"I know little about the Irish, sir."

"Except that they are stupid, right? Mike O'Donnell and I attended the prestigious Oxford and outscored them all. The fair-haired long-headed Irish who have not been contaminated by English rapists are superior in every respect and we will not allow them to tyrannize us here."

He abruptly rose and left as he called back:

"There's a message for you at the house."

This man oversets my opinion of the Irish, an opinion based on myth. He is truly brilliant, admits it himself. But all say it is true. That is why he is so dangerous.

A sealed message at the house directed me to call on a Mr. Trammel without delay. I did so and found an ill-mannered factor in his office who thrust at me a letter from Lord Chatham. With the rudest clarity, Trammel announced he would not be an intermediary again and bid me good day. Is this the Trammel Melinda mentioned?

Lord Chatham wants me to leave immediately. I answered his discomforting letter; both are attached.

House of Lords
January 3, 1775

My Wandering Landon:

Not knowing your precise whereabouts, I have also dispatched this same confidential message to your uncle and to Jst. Howard. I must be brief. The Dover, is weighing anchor.

I have intelligence that open conflict threatens in Boston and large shipments of gunpowder are en route to the rebels. Also, certain munitions factories in France have never been busier and munitions ships are leaving European ports and returning with American products. With whom are they trading and where? What do you know of this most illegal and dangerous trade?

Go on to Boston promptly. Throughout your journey look for signs of gunpowder imports. Inform me of what you learn and do not fail to approach the Massachusetts leadership with the message of reconciliation.

I remind you to seek this munitions information with the greatest discretion.   I have openly accused the French ambassador of hiding a conspiracy to provide military aid to the American rebels and I fear you may appear to be my source of intelligence.   Last month the body of one of Ambassador Stormont's undersecretaries, named Gaylord, was found near one of these mystery ships in Le Havre with his throat slit!

Finally Landon, I prevail upon you to reconsider resuming your career in the clergy after completion of this mission.   You have some obligation to me and with the talents God has given you, that pursuit would best serve the ideals of Duty, Integrity, Country.

*William Pitt
Earl of Chatham*

———◦◦◦●◦◦◦———

*Charles Town, S.C.
27 February 1775*

*The Honorable Earl of Chatham Hayes, Kent, England
Sir:*

In answer to your secret letter of January 3rd, I leave this reply with the Governor's secretary and pray he forward it through a loyal ship's Captain.

Sir, I beg of you to appreciate what you ask of me. More than forty days I have been traveling to the south and have been in Charles Town only three days. Now you direct me to return immediately through the wilderness to Boston.

I shall do so but I am not encouraged that much can be learned. The intelligence you seek is elusive. I suspect European merchants rendezvous with rebel privateers, who then bring the munitions ashore and I am convinced there are French spies in all provinces who are dedicated to separating them from Britain.

You have asked me to determine those abuses which most disturb the people here. In Virginia there is a passionate endorsement of English Civil Rights and the right of the taxed to consent to taxation. They resent any limits being placed on their authority, their trade and manufacture and on their diverse practices of religion. In the Carolinas there are loyal Scots in the highlands and a loyal populace in Charles Town. However a radical few such as Christopher Gadsden want nothing less than separation from Britain. I have not yet been granted an audience with either Governor Bull or Mr. Laurens, president of the Provincial Congress.

As for the clergy, I shall never return to it, for reasons already discussed, and I respectfully suggest that any obligation was yours for forcing my parents from their livings in Kent and off to a land where they lost their lives. I shall write again from Virginia.

> *I remain your most obedient and humble servant,*
> *Landon Vickers*

February 27th, 1775 - White Hall

A written invitation came from no less than Melinda's aunt to attend a charity ball at White Hall (to aid the suffering Boston citizens) and to ride there on the Heyward riverboat. I presumably have more rapport with her than with Melinda's mother. The latter, fortunately, had to return to the Watkins plantation.

I was delighted and met the two ladies at their boat, again at Gadsden's wharf. Nick is following with the horses and he and I depart from White Hall.

Before the ladies arrived, I watched Gadsden bickering with a backwoods man over a wagon load of deerskins. When the yeoman finally began to unload, Gadsden turned to me, complaining all commerce is down by one-half.

"Because of interference by your rotten government, everything must go to Britain and prices are poor there. In France or Holland that load of deer hides is worth twice what I get in Britain. We've protested but we're IGNORED."

Happily the ladies appeared and this old bachelor curmudgeon turned to the production of politeness. They apparently found his manners agreeable enough but I found them odious. He looks at Melinda too much.

We boarded their graceful craft, made of three huge cypress logs, joined side by side and hollowed out until the hull is nowhere more than an inch thick; then pinned together with oak ribs. The portable cabin and slave crew wore matching colors; red top and jackets, white curtains and trousers. There were ten oarsmen, doubtless selected for their strength and ability to sing. Wearing white straw hats with red ribbons on top and white grins underneath, they sang almost endlessly. The stroke of the oarsmen set the pace, the helmsman entertained us with solo verses and the remainder did the choruses.

But I had eyes and ears only for Melinda and she didn't appear to mind. Mrs. Heyward turned her back on us and alternately read a book and watched the scenery; she gains more of my gratitude with every encounter.

An approximate recreation of our amorous diversion:

"What are they singing?" I asked, touching the back of Melinda's hand.

"Roll Jordan, Roll." The hand moved a few inches away.

"Are they as happy as they appear?" I caught up with the hand and closed mine over it.

"I suppose. At least it keeps them out of the rice and indigo fields." No attempt to escape this time.

"There must be more slaves than free here." I put my fingers between hers.

"Three times as many. Uncle John says up to fifty times as many on some plantations!" Turned her palm up.

"They could revolt with such an advantage in numbers." I dawdled with her fingers.

"Not if treated properly," she gently scratched my palm with her fingertips. I slipped my arm behind her and stroked her lovely back from head to waist.

"Would you like some Portuguese wine?"

"I wouldn't mind."

"If you don't mind drinking them from pewter cups. Mr. Thomas Jefferson of Virginia gave these to me. A craftsman makes them in Charlottesville."

"They're very graceful."

"A toast to our friendship."

And so it was for the afternoon. One can adventure only so far in such a situation but it is no less exciting. And I will now admit to some familiarity with her hair and back. She does not stop me but I do not want to lose her by being overly amorous.

White Hall is a handsome three story country house with white columns across the front. Before it is a pecan grove and behind it the outbuildings. There must be several thousand acres of rice fields around it and several hundred slaves to work them. It is an evil society that preaches liberty and freedom, has great wealth for the few and lifetime bondage for the many.

Met Mr. Heyward this evening. He will represent South Carolina at the Continental Congress but is noncommittal about his political views. He will not discuss the subject with me, anyway. Clearly Melinda deplores all moves toward independence and wishes he were not involved.

Meanwhile my abode is an attic room with dormer; the ball is tomorrow night. Oh, just to touch her back again!

February 28, 1775

This is the last day tea is to be drunk on the continent, "by an act of the Continental Congress", and I am attending the rout honoring the occasion. I wager there will be nothing served as weak as tea. As for my dress, I have neither silk stockings nor satin shoes. Cotton and leather will have to suffice. The shoes being reversible, I will switch them to put the worn leather to the inside. At least my cravat is fresh linen.

The ballroom is one entire wing of the ground floor designed for concerts, plays, and balls. There's a small stage and on it is a pianoforte not unlike Mrs. Jefferson's. To my delight that darling Melinda and I spent the afternoon there. She played the instrument for me, one charming rendition after another. She is a treasure of talent and loveliness, most tenderly educated.

We talked of many things, from religion to politics. She is remarkably well informed for a female and thinks as I do, especially about loyalty to the Crown.

"But for our British protection," she said, "the American colonies would have been divided between France and Spain and we would be subjugated forever."

And we agreed that to reject British protection of our civil liberties and set ourselves adrift with some strange form of Republicanism, conjured up from some ancient Greek republic that failed, is worse than treason. It's self-destruction.

With respect to religion, she has a strong faith which I truly admire. I told her how Lord Chatham decided that I should become a priest. I even admitted that I had run away from Gresham twice and from Oxford once before this final departure, each time talked into returning and enduring solitary confinement and threats of enrollment elsewhere.

She commented most tenderly that my fear of confinement would fade and my faith would be renewed in time.

Unfortunately, underlying her views is a premonition of war and unhappiness in her personal life. Twice this afternoon, lapsing into melancholia, she quietly told me to "Go home," meaning that I should leave this land and avoid the catastrophies she may experience.

Several times She referred to—and I suspect has been profoundly influenced by—a Mary Wollstonecraft,* a young

---

FEMININE READERS: I would not offend your gentle sensibilities, but Mary Wollstonecraft became a most perverse woman. She was revulsed not only by bullying and brutal husbands, beginning with her own father, but by more gentle masculine insistence on women being "submissive, frail, malleable but beautiful creatures kept in slavish dependence on their masters." She viewed marriage for most women as subjection to a lifetime of petty tyranny.

Genuine equalityof the sexes became her passion in life. Her book, Vindication of the Rights of Women, proposed that women should pursue careers in politics, business, farming, medicine, law and other activities beyond their station and natural abilities.

A small but growing number of American females such as Abigail Adams endorse these ideas, exploiting the term "Declaration of Independence" in a fashion unintended. R.E.H

English friend of Cassandra and apparent despiser of men. Melinda vowed never to subject herself to Bennett's "martial tyranny." One wonders what became of this Mary.

One unhappy development was the unexpected appearance of her betrothed, one Bennett McKee, in a gooseturd green militia uniform. The only bright side of this event was that both Melinda and her aunt were as disappointed as I.

"A braggart, a revolutionary, and a dullard," Mrs. Heyward snorted, revealing to me for the first time her own views of both Bennett and the independence movement.

He is a bit taller than I, perhaps older too. An agreeable looking man I suppose, but red-haired, thick waisted and I suspect he pads his calves below the gaudy knee-buckles designed to draw attention to his legs.

Now to prepare for the ball.

———————•••◐••••———————

Whitehall, S.C.
February 28th, 1775

Cassandra my Confessor,

How elating to discover your epistle waiting for me when I arrived. Indeed I have posted two letters already. I pray you have received one by now.

I fear my communications dwell too much on this young man who obsesses me. I write at the end of an entire delightful day with Landon. First we rode together by flatboat to Whitehall, Aunt Elizabeth's plantation, with her in attendance. I had thought her rather prudish until today when she sat in the bow for several hours, leaving us alone and unobserved in the stern. Landon and I shared in lively conversation and harmless little intimacies in which only the virtuous engage. It continued in the ballroom at the pianoforte and in the garden in the most delightful way, as we became acquainted with each other.

This evening the ball included every charm which would render such an event successful. Its purpose, to celebrate the end of tea drinking, and the presence of Mr. McKee failed to detract from my propensity to enjoy life to the fullest.

The evening ended with—shall I confess it?—a sweet but all too brief rendezvous with Landon for an intimate goodnight kiss. Have no fear; he is a gentleman and I am quite safe and comfortable with him.

Landon came into the world in America but—orphaned early—became a foster child of Lord Chatham and matured in England. He has been educated for the clergy but has no calling or interest in that regard.

Unfortunately his duties take him away from me again—perhaps for months this time—and I shall be fending off Bennett's matrimonial plots. Even my mother presses me toward this unseemly liaison. I truly believe, however, that overcoming all such efforts will be the affection and trust that Landon and I have for one another.

The Charles Town atmosphere has worsened. I sense far more people are colluding with that dwarfish Christopher Gadsden than did so before we left for England. He offers nothing but disagreeable animadversions on the British Government and preaches revolution.

Returning to America saddens me in another respect; the necessity of living with the abominable existence of slavery. This pernicious practice has avarice as its only motivation. Slave traders and plantation owners exploit these human beings as animals. Another 400 ill-clothed wretches were unloaded today and stood shivering on the wharf waiting in numb despair for a life of penal servitude. Six who died since docking were carted off *for disposal. Ruth Craig and I brought water and some charity blankets as usual.*

Even so, there are ways to raise our spirits; by helping where we can to ease the pain of slavery and, with respect to politics, by being an example of loyalty to the Crown for those who waver.

Happily amidst all this turmoil the St. Cecelia concerts continue. Music is so essential to human existence, don't you think? It brushes off the soul the debris of commonplace living.

Old friends still remain. Charles Rutledge (the Governor's nephew) is a regular caller on Ruth now. She is my closest friend in Charles Town. We used the first of the London materials to make gowns for the ball—she the cut velvet and I the brocaded silk. It is nigh to dawn and I remain sleepless. I have dressed and plan to bid Landon farewell, a wretched pastime. Despite all, know that we are well and still relish our memories of the summer in Hampshire.

Affectionately

JOURNAL FOR MARCH 1775 *Melinda*

March 1, 1775 - Black River Crossing

An appropriate name for my black mood. Again, as when I left Jefferson's, I plunge from elegant surroundings to a crude lodging not deserving description. More depressing is separation from Melinda with no prospect of early reuniting.

Last evening deserves a memoir to relish. What better use can I make of my time in this decrepit habitation?

When the ball commenced, Bennett assumed at once the role of Melinda's escort. I did not accept this assumption but when the music started I hesitated an instant and he swept her away at once. As I watched them with the vehement flame of jealousy, I could see that he does indeed pad his calves.

And so do a few others. But the quality of dress exceeded that of the previous balls. Many gowns and coats proclaimed by style that they were made in England.

Fool that I am, I found myself paired with some female whose teeth and feet are both rather outsized. One cannot help God-given features but the former never stopped talking and the latter constantly got in the way. After we stumbled through the first dance, I more clumsily than she, I feigned a chill and need for the warmth of the fireplace. The great firebox radiated heat dozens of feet but I edged closer and closer continuing idle conversation until my back was nearly smouldering. Finally she could stand the heat no longer, excused herself and left me to burn; whereupon I made for the door and the outside chill to recover.

When the country dances began I reintroduced myself to the scene. The ladies began snatching men and I hurried to Melinda for capture. She glided by the disbelieving Bennett McKee and grasped my hand. I took it and we allowed no one to break that grip the remainder of the series.

A crisis came with the charity minuet. Each couple was to commit itself in turn to a gift for the people of Boston by placing a note of intent in a large silver punch bowl. There being no normal method of determining social status in America, Aunt Elizabeth arbitrarily assigned double-couple positions.

"Landon, we're placed in eighth position with Charles Rutledge and Ruth Craig, but you will be expected to defer to Bennett. What shall we do?"

"Take the position Aunt Elizabeth gave us."

"Do we dare?"

"I am her special guest from England. I would not offend my hostess." I offered my arm and walked her to position eight in the gathering line.

"Aunt Elizabeth's special guest," she murmured to Bennett as he approached us. "Must not offend."

"Sorry," I added. "You won't mind this time?"

Bennett's jaw dropped in stunned silence.

When our turn came some other jaws dropped as well. I could see older ladies behind fluttering fans asking who is the young Englishman escorting Miss Watkins.

We danced properly through the minuet and reluctantly pitched in a reckoning for a firkin of salt pork—doubting the tales of Bostonians suffering. Meanwhile Aunt Elizabeth managed to introduce Bennett to other ladies, obliging him to dance with them.

After a few more formals we went into some of the American dances to which I was exposed in Alexandria.

And oh, I touched her many times as I guided her through the salacious movements. It was a delicious but genteel hop.

When the ball finally ended, Bennett was purple with rage. When told by Aunt Elizabeth all of her overnight accommodations were filled and that he would be obliged to go to a neighbor's, I thought he would explode. He departed for Charles Town instead, after midnight.

The prospect of his future actions generates unease. But I will marry her, by the Almighty, I will.

Upstairs after the ball, wanting in courage to go to Melinda's room, I did meet her in the darkened hall at the water barrel which supplies our chamber pitchers.

At first we were both shy of touching but the necessity for close whispering led to the temptation for intimacy I could not resist. I put down my pitcher and took her in my arms, called her my whippoorwill, and kissed her soundly.

How sweet to hold her close to me, both of us clad only in nightgowns! There is no language to express adequately the excitement of it. Her arms about my neck, her slim waist tight against mine, her warm bosom and her sweet kisses all maddened me with desire.

Alas, only our fear of discovery provided any restraint. I know not what I might have maneuvered otherwise. When we heard someone coming, she slipped away.

I snatched my pitcher, accidentally and noisily struck the barrel with it and retreated as well. Grasping the offending crock with both hands and holding it before me, I followed it to my chamber, believing I had left the door open, which it was not. Again the clatter was fearsome and, concerned about discovery, I went straight under the covers, not realizing until motionless that the pitcher had come to bed with me. Lest another sound be made, I kept it there. Fortunately no water in it.

But all was silent thereafter and sleep finally came. I am more familiar than ever with her features. Take care, you fool. You may lose her if you take improper advantage.

This morning Nick joined me with a disturbing tale. He had followed me from Charles Town with the horses, but just after dark two men accosted him. Nick assumed they were trying to steal the horses or him for resale. They spoke a language he could not understand and he was truly alarmed. He had my permit for him to travel alone, but when they attempted capture, he maneuvered Mysty with a turn-and-kick which flattened one rogue and he brought the rifle to bear on the other. When that one drew a pistol, Nick fired and struck him in the leg as the pistol discharged harmlessly. Leaving both on the ground, he applied the whip and escaped. Strong actions for a Negro but if renewed slavery threatens, he is desperate. I shall never expose him to such again.

This employment is both absurd and dangerous. I had only just arrived in Charles Town, now must travel overland the length of the continent and look for gunpowder smuggling en route. This is arrant nonsense.

I employed an indentured carpenter to repair the Whippoorwill cabin roof while I am gone. I would prefer indentured to slaves if I should live there. Slavery is not only unspeakably cruel, but unreliable. One Rodney Buchman moaned at the ball that his costly purchase of twenty healthy young males from the Niger was disastrous. Eight of them hanged themselves rather than submit to the life.

Two early judgments on Charles Town remain lucid in the strongest light of afterthought. One, the city is loyal. Its people briskly trade with and imitate London, send their sons there for education. There is some dissatisfaction among the gentlemen but neither loose tongues nor my own observations reveal the smuggling of gunpowder. Most of the influentials are too comfortable to seek change.

The other judgment is that Gadsden is a dangerous exception. His name is whispered with conspiracies to enforce the Association, seize forts and armories, manipulate the Provincial Congress.

As for my Charles Town whippoorwill, she is no house decoration behind a fluttering fan. She is an intelligent and ambitious person determined to chart her own course, but frustrated and tortured by some unrevealed family obligation. Taking leave of her was most disagreeable employment. In our last private moments, she again urged me to leave her forever, quit the continent for my own safety and go home. If I could take her with me, I might.

March 11, 1775 - New Bern, North Carolina

Rode into New Bern last night, most heartily tired and melancholy. The only relief has been imagining Melinda as my wife, building a house for her, being at concerts and balls and abed with her. If that's lust, the Church be damned.

Attempted an audience with Governor Martin but he will not see anyone for fear of his life. After he published a proclamation condemning the North Carolina revolutionaries, some assassin fired on him but missed. His proclamation only encouraged the Republicans to engage in more sedition.

The Howards were happy to see me again and took me in as though I were the Prodigal Son. Supper tonight included a generous parcel of lamb, a dish increasingly hard to find. It has become patriotic to raise the lamb into a wool-producing sheep, use the wool to make clothes and thus avoid purchasing them in England.

I watched Jst. Howard and his wife at dinner, revered them for their care of me as a child and admired them for their loyalty to King and Country despite the great ocean that separates them from the Homeland. They are perhaps in their fifties now, but their faces seem little changed from the days when Randolph and I were children here.

The Howards proudly showed me Randolph's letter to them with a gift of riding spurs for me. The spurs were but a disguise for Randolph's first coded message in the wrapping. It's content gives me little cause for joy. (Attached hereto)

London
27 January 1775

Piggy, you Rascal,

Remember when we called you that? It has been three months since you departed and I shall not be at ease until you communicate. Do you know that another British agent, Gaylord, has been murdered in Le Havre?

Here is ominous news that may affect you. Lord Chatham gave the Parliament a tongue-lashing they will not soon forget. The poor gout-ridden old gentleman pleaded with the Government not to misadvise the King lest his kingdom be undone, but the speech was in vain. Then he accused the French of shipping munitions to the American colonials. The French ambassador demanded an apology. I fear you may be blamed as the source.

Mr. Lee, in his position as "American" trade representative, is exploring most delicately and discreetly munitions trade with France. Do not pass on this intelligence to anyone. Meanwhile a French agent of King Louis, named Beaumarchais, is in London engaging in blackmail to prevent the publication of a slanderous book about the King's Marie Antoinette. We have approached Beaumarchais and he is amenable to supplying us.

Have you heard of the precarious position of Mr. Franklin? He was publicly rebuked before the Privy Council, accused of being a thief and of plotting an American revolution. Then he lost his situation as Postmaster General for America. Oh, they bloodied his derriere! I suspect he will soon leave.

I realize this news is disturbing, Piggy, but I applaud it. Forgive me for my candor in our diverse arguments.

I regret you cannot meet my Agatha, a not uncomely Scottish lass recently arrived for education—which I am happy to augment.

Anxiously awaiting news from you, my friend.
Randolph

March 12, 1775

Hoping to learn something from loose tongues about any munitions trade, I attended the last performance of *She Stoops To Conquer* by some traveling players, a pastime now frowned upon. They should retire; they sconced me a shilling for a mean production and I gained no intelligence.

My chests have safely arrived and are stored in the Howard's cellar. He encourages me to maintain my journal and in the detail Boswell suggested. Often difficult to do because of sheer slothfulness on my part.

Jst. Howard told me Marchaud is confined with an injury. Nick do it? The Jst. avoids telling me my parents status in Kent. Why the mystery? If I am the son of peasants, that does not change me. It might in Britain, but not here where no social structure appears to exist. Tomorrow for Richmond.

March 20, 1775 - Richmond

Entered with some temerity the city where I was nearly cremated, but there is no indication of anyone following me.

The illegal meeting of the Virginia House of Burgesses is the reason for returning here. Delegates are obviously gathering to plan rebellion; for what other reason would they not meet in Williamsburg?

Uncle John sent through a delegate, Judge Tucker, this letter from Chatham (attached). John noted that it had been opened by some spy before he received it. That means some murderous blackguard may know the *Dorchester* is coming to Boston and that a Mr. Bradford, who is aboard, brings secret intelligence to me.

Chatham now addresses me as esteemed!

House of Lords
25 January 1775

My Esteemed Landon:

Greetings from London; I pray this letter finds you well and in no danger. The political atmosphere here continues to deteriorate. I enclose two parliamentary speeches defending the American points of view, which I hope you can use to advantage. The first I just delivered in the House of Lords and the second is an even more conciliatory speech which Edmund Burke will present in the House of Commons. Use these speeches to show the good intentions of the Parliament and perhaps to prevent rash action there.

I remind you to proceed at once to Boston. Report to me what is happening and what might be done to relieve the tension between the troops and the townspeople. Report directly to General Gage any intelligence you gain on our special subject.

I am convinced European death merchants are violating neutrality. A British Man-o-war recently boarded a Dutch merchant ship off the coast of Spain and discovered bottles labelled Spirits but filled with gunpowder. The British captain was forced to allow it to proceed, but to Spain? I think not.

New instructions and intelligence, as well as additional funds will await you in Boston, delivered by one Gustavus Bradford. He should arrive in April on the provisions ship Dorchester and will be employed in the Governor's office. Approach Bradford discreetly and take utmost care in all your actions. Foul play is quite possible. Gaylord was probably murdered in Le Havre because he learned too much.

I have not as yet received any reports from you. I pray for your safety and enjoin you to remember your

Duty , Integrity , Country
William Pitt , Earl of Chatham

March 21, 1775

Today's Assembly meeting offered little to two newspaper representatives and me. In a small observation chamber they slept through most of the session. One has a bad eye which never closes when he sleeps and both were flatulent. My discomfort was remaining in the cramped space and forcing myself to overcome the daft compulsion to flee. Melinda having pointed out my disorder, I am determined to defeat it.

The real meetings are not taking place here anyway, but in taverns and homes, where little circles and big tankards loosen tongues. All is correct and polite in St. John's, but without substance.

Jefferson and Henry came with Judge Tucker to Cooley's Tavern tonight and the judge invited me to join them. At first opportunity I told them of Chatham's and Burke's conciliatory speeches but it accomplished little.

I excused myself and retired. Beloved Melinda, what are you doing tonight?

March 22, 1775

Judge Tucker invited me again to lunch, making me privy to a remarkable political sermon by Mr. Jefferson. Tucker says Jefferson is too reticent at the Assembly meetings and will not be a representative to the Continental Congress. He should be thankful that he is not going. If this Congress were to declare independence, he would be obliged to sign such a document and for that would surely be hanged.

When Jefferson joined us, we fell to discussing education. I chanced a remark that, with so few titled families in the colonies, it must be difficult to know who to educate for positions of responsibility. This began the preaching which he invited me to shorthand.

"Mr. Vickers, we must eradicate every fiber of aristocracy which is based on inheritance and replace it with an aristocracy of virtue and talent, discovered by general education of the populace."

"Educate everyone? Impossible!"

Jefferson smiled and continued. "Every government on earth has traces of human weakness, Mr. Vickers, some germ of corruption and degeneracy. Therefore it will degenerate when entrusted to the rulers alone. The people themselves are the only safe depository of government. So it follows that they must be educated."

While listening to this idealistic nonsense, I looked out the window at the people in the street, at the peddlers, artisans, poor farmers, indentured and slaves, most ill clothed and dirty, ignorant and illiterate, reeking of their work and sweat. Are these improvable creatures?

"Mr. Jefferson, you would put government into their hands? That is Republicanism!"

"Their minds must be improved first."

"But the cost and uselessness of educating every common yeoman....."

"And common slave, once freed. Prove it to yourself. You have a manservant and have considerable opportunity to educate him. Teach him to read and write."

"To what end?"

"To increase his understanding and participation in society."

"But how," I asked, "can exposing everyone to a little knowledge create anything but anarchy? Look at the strange religious dissenters it's already created. The Church itself is threatened."

"Look here, we've inherited a state-supported church to which non-members must pay taxes as much as members. Heresy is still, by common law, punishable by burning."

"But these severe punishments are little observed....."

"Almighty God has created the mind free; all attempts to influence it by any punishment whatever tend only to beget habits of hypocrisy. Our civil rights have no more dependence on our religious opinions than on our opinions in physics or geometry."

My mind's awhirling.   This man advocates a total restructuring of society, church, and government. His remarks could be labeled treason and heresy, yet I find them just sentiments to a point. But polite education for all is beyond reason. Cost alone would preclude it and few of the plebeians could absorb any of it. However, I shall try his experiment on Nick, teach him to read and write—if I can.

The backwoods arsonist at Gretchen's I have seen twice, always at a distance and feigning not to be watching me.

March 23, 1775

Another closed meeting of the conspirators today, but I learned the rustic Patrick Henry delivered an impassioned harangue which created the very opposite atmosphere that Burke and Chatham were seeking. Henry proposes war and now.

March 24, 1775

Today's session was delayed until the sheriff led a father to the altar and forced him by law to marry a woman he had impregnated.   The new husband acted nothing like a gentleman. Could Melinda be with child; would she have to marry Bennett? Cannot imagine her cavorting with him.

Not permitted to attend today's meeting either, but Judge Tucker said they are considering formation of three regiments, manufacture of gunpowder and implements of war. Idiots, they will all be hanged. However, for my military ledger I have identified a total of three regiments and ten independent companies about to be recruited in Virginia.

Where is Melinda now? I still fantasize her in my arms by that water barrel.

March 25, 1775

Little more to report from the Assembly. It approved resolutions of the first Confounded Congress and debated hotly without decision over whether to propose independence.

March 26, 1775

At St. John's Church today, I sat with many delegates and listened to them read prayers for forgiveness of sins, as well they should. And the preacher should be deposed for his treasonable sermon on "Render unto Caesar". His Caesar is the President of that Philadelphia Congo. The service gave me neither peace nor comfort, only renewed my skepticism. Damn them all.

March reckoning to date: (transferred to account book)		
Victuals and lodging	-	£ 7/10 s
New boots and shirt	-	/8 s
Nick's clothes	-	/7 s
Pack saddle	-	/9 s
Provender (3 horses)	-	£ 2/2 s
Spirits	-	£ 1/2 s
Total	-	£ 11/18 s

Must ask for a larger stipend.

Visited Triplet's ale-house but soon retired. Randolph would not; once in a tavern, he never retired until want of pence intruded upon his gaiety and obliged departure.

Wrote Melinda and saved a fair copy. I suppose Randolph would sneer at my more tender emotions, but I care not a farthing for his opinions on love. For him, the thought of lying between a woman's legs is only that; a fair thought to be put into action whenever possible.[*]

Richmond, Virginia
26 March 1775

My Dearest Melinda:

You are constantly in my thoughts—I need so much to talk to you—I had hoped to avoid going on to Boston but new urgent orders from Lord Chatham oblige me to do so. The potential for explosion there is very high. If the people around Boston resort to military action they will be crushed. I am to find whether such action is imminent and thus my returning to you is delayed.

We are faced with serious problems but none is more frustrating for me than my inability to be with you. I want to touch you again, to hold your sweet face between my hands, kiss those smiling lips, to take you in my arms again. Oh, gentle lady I pray my boldness does not offend, but should I not share with you my most intimate dreams? I confess they are dreams of a lifetime with you.

---

[*] *SHOCKED READER, I must protest this characterization. My tales of erotic prowess were far more robust than actual performance and I reformed markedly upon marriage. R.E.H.*

Is there no undoing your commitment to another? Is betrothal so binding that you must take an unhappy course the remainder of your life? I do not believe it; this is America, the fount of liberal thought!

As for the political climate, the unhappy events unfolding now are quite beyond our control. Virginia is mobilizing thousands of troops and North Carolina may soon follow. I pray these activities will not prevent my coming to you, sharing my life, my land, everything with you some day.

Dear Lady, please write to me in Boston; send the letter to the Governor's Headquarters and I will get it. Tell me of your affection, that I might endure our painful separation.

I remain your faithful, loving
Landon

March 28, 1775 - Berkley

Bid farewell to Richmond after the final session of the Virginia Assembly. At the very last, someone realized Peyton Randolph could not be a representative to the Continental Congress if Governor Dunmore ordered him to call the House of Burgesses into session. So the delegates elected the shy Thomas Jefferson to be his substitute at Philadelphia. I pray his influence and association with that gaggle will be nil.

Mr. Harrison invited me to ride with him as far as his home and spend the night here. Gratefully I did so, to avoid an ambush on the trail, but did not dare reveal to him my thoughts on the meeting just ended. Neither did he reveal his, but something happened back there to create an atmosphere of war planning.

I taught Nick to write his name today in four carefully printed letters. This experiment will have more diversion value than utility.

March 29, 1775 - Williamsburg

Obtained an immediate audience with the Governor tonight, but a wide-eyed James Parker, Assembly delegate from Norfolk, was already there. According to Parker, it was a melodramatic speech by Patrick Henry that changed the course of the assembly, a speech which opened by his calling the King a tyrant, a fool, a puppet and a tool to the ministry and closed with the flush-faced vein-throbbing Henry screaming with arms outstretched as if on the Cross itself, "Give me liberty or give me death."

When Parker finished, the governor stood at the fireplace for a long time, staring at the flames. Then the Scotsman turned to us with contorted face and muttered:

"We are undone." If I were you, I would leave this town with discretion and expedition. Have Pitch lead you out; he knows secret ways."

So advised, I am remaining in the governor's palace. Filled with nine children of all ages it was a bedlam in the early evening. But for French professor Mirabeau, who was giving dancing lessons to the older girls, it would have been worse. Apparently he has insinuated himself into the palace with his abilities to teach French, dancing and archery and has complete freedom of the house. Surely Lord Dunmore has investigated his background and is confident of his character or he would not give the professor such access. I did note that the "Frog" and the Indian Pitch have little to say to each other. Jealousy over their archery skills?

Nick paid that dunning Dr. de Sabbe for me and is meeting me with the horses at the rear entrance before dawn. The knot of fear in my stomach won't go away.

March 30 - Todd's Bridge

Most cruel habitation yet. Indian Pitch launched us early on a little used trail, then departed elsewhere as a decoy to fool anyone following us.

The ruse failed. We were challenged by the arsonist I saw in Richmond and another maggot-brained knave. Escaped their ambush by firing and bolting. But they follow.

Rode hard all day to Todd's Bridge. Pack horse does not look the best. Hiding under bridge for the night. Raining.

Huddling under my cape and writing this entry to a feeble candle is nothing but miserable. Would James Boswell make a "gentleman's entry" under these circumstances?

March 31, 1775 - Fredericksburg

Nick exercised his evasive genius today and led me along a creek and into the forest to evade any pursuers. We soon heard panting horses pass, pushed to their limits. We pushed ours to their limits too and often left the trail to avoid a potential ambush.

Eventually arrived here and stabled the horses in a tobacco barn by the river where they will not likely be seen. Nick is with them, nursing the packer. He says it has maw worms and we may have to put it down.

I slipped into Weedon's Public House from the rear for victuals. The establishment is befouled by rats and chamberpot dumpings in back and heavy tobacco spittings up front. Will never stay here again. Bought some bread, hamhock and ale for our supper and returned to the tobacco barn where we shall stay.

Blockheads are rattling their chariots here too.   The Fredricksburg company of militia, which I added to my military ledger, was drilling on the green before an admiring audience. But from a distance I discerned two men wandering through the crowd, looking over the bystanders. Looking for us?

Nick does not understand why I am being hunted like a criminal. Difficult to explain.

Now for Alexandria, if we are not ambushed en route!

(At least a week of entries, water damaged and largely illegible, not included. R.E.H.)

JOURNAL FOR APRIL 1775

April 1st, 1775 - Alexandria, Virginia

"Only four hours ago," Uncle John fumed, "four rogues burst into my house, demanded 'the Tory spy Vickers' for questioning by the Committee of Safety and then searched the premises without explanation or warrant." He was livid with rage.

"Violated the very civil rights we claim the British deny us! What mischief are you involved in, Landon? What are you doing to endanger yourself and now my household as well?"

"Sir, Silas Grover has a price on my head and they would have delivered me to him to collect it, not to the Committee of Safety. He will use my guts for garters if he gets his hands on me."

"But why did those four blackguards break in here? How did they know you were coming when I did not?"

"They tried to intercept me when I left Williamsburg and followed me here."

"But they were here first."

"Near Dumphries we turned into the woods to evade them. One of several times we did it, but this time the wretched pack horse revealed maw worms grievously. The miserable creature had to be shot. But that and finding another packer allowed those murderers to get well ahead of us. They must have assumed I was here. Where are they now?"

"In gaol for breaking and entering, but not for long. They'll be released in a couple of days and you'd best be off for Boston by then, if that's where you want to go. I can't imagine why you seek intercourse with those people. They would export their levelling and rank Puritanical beliefs to all of us if they could. Get some rest first. You'll be safe here in the cellar for another day. Servants are guarding the house—we nearly shot you sneaking in at midnight!"

"Is Nick safe?"

"Yes, he and the horses are in the warehouse down by the ferry. But you stay here and give me no more grief!"

With that he left me confined with my abominable thoughts. My body is aching all over and my spirit is in trepidation. Neither I nor Chatham nor God Almighty are going to turn the rebels away from independence if they want it, but why should these fiends want me? Wearily to bed.

April 2nd, 1775

No attending church today, but I thought of Melinda when she was in the pew, in the ballroom and at the pianoforte in Uncle John's parlor. How I miss her.

Now for Boston. Uncle John is toting Nick across the river tonight with the horses and I'll join him before dawn tomorrow. Dare not discuss my business any further with my uncle. He is an honorable gentleman but is leaning toward independence and is out of patience with me.

April 3rd, 1775 - Upper Marlboro

Had a pleasurable ride through this largely Roman Catholic countryside. Maryland's a fair province; peach orchards and little white-flowered dogwood trees are blooming. The rain has rinsed the roadside dust from the wild flowers and renewed their color as well.

No followers in sight.

At the Black Horse Inn again. Bought a pair of pistols for 15s from innkeeper Schmidt and gave one to Nick. Now I am teaching him how to use it as well as read and write. He is very proud of his weapon but takes a poor aim.

Trying to erase the memory of wagoner Turner's murder here. Nick is in my chamber with me for mutual protection. Began teaching him to read tonight. He has said nothing about our dangerous situation but he must be considering whether or not to continue with me.

April 7th, 1775 - Gresswold Farm, New Jersey

While ferrying the Delaware this morning, the new pack horse panicked and threw Nick into the water. We pulled him aboard after some delay; both air and water were fair cold and Nick is not recovered yet.

We're in the sturdy log cabin of Quaker Gresswold, overlooking the river and Philadelphia on the other side.

Wrote Melinda but kept no copy.

April 8th, 1775 - Trenton, New Jersey

The lodging in this town is in a tavern formerly called the King George, then Liberty, but nameless now. Differing rogues tore down each sign and the proprietor fears to replace it.

We took advantage of a Scandinavian practice the inn offered and baked ourselves in a scalding hot room while our clothes were being boiled, both to heal Nick and to rid ourselves of an infestation of fleas. The taverner did not mind my taking Nick in with me but it was odd to sit there naked with someone beneath my station. But what is my station?

Nick remains ill and the pernicious cold weather does not help. The local doctor will not treat him; suspects him to be a runaway slave, I wager. I shall press for Prince Town tomorrow and find a recommended Doctor Thornhill.

———

Charles Town
April 8th, 1775

Dear Friend Cassandra,

I have your epistle of February 15th including the disturbing news that the Parliament has declared Massachusetts in a "horrid state of rebellion." This surely means more troops to Boston. We had prayed that conciliatory measures would be adopted.

Landon has been gone for a month now and I have received only two letters from him. I had urged him, despite my own desires, to quit the continent for his own safety. His response was that as soon as he could, he might well do so. He is conscientious but naive and may be in more danger than he realizes.

I cannot bring myself to tell him as I have told you the terrible dilemma I am facing. I love my father and I detest the unreasonable law that would imprison him, but I do not accept that I am stock to be bartered for property and my parents well-being.

We are experiencing shortages in certain foodstuffs and clothing materials. Some items are no more to be found. Ruth Craig just returned from St. Augustine with no cloth of any kind. She was looking for common osnaburg which we intended to make into clothes for the slave children we are teaching to sing. We expect a prohibition on purchasing anything from Britain.

I suspect my parents and the McKees are inclined toward separation from Britain. I know Bennett is. I shall never be of such a mind. The American colonies are threatened by the Spanish from the south and the French and Indians from the west and we will be destroyed if we do not remain under British sovereignty and protection.

Forgive me; you do not deserve a moody letter such as this from me. But I cannot mask my concern.

> *With eternal affection from*
> *Melinda*

April 9th, 1775 - Prince Town

We arrived at nightfall to find the only inn filled. So after supper (excellent Harrico mutton), we had to look elsewhere.

Innkeeper Cranston, an abolitionist assuming me to be one also, told me privily that bounty hunters were outside inquiring whether anyone was harboring a runaway slave. Cranston advised me to go to the dissenter's college and Dr. Witherspoon would hide us.

Nick being seriously ill, I played the abolitionist role and went straightaway to Dr. Witherspoon's attractive home by the main building. He was immediately compassionate, took Nick to a bed in the servants' quarters and sent for Doctor Thornhill.

He also assigned me to an unoccupied student room in the main building. Called Nassau Hall, this huge stone edifice of four floors contains the entire college. I am invited to join the students at meals and any other activities I care to observe. The whole lot of them are rank Presbyterians, but treat us decently in spite of it.

Dr. Thornhill was quite willing to minister to Nick but his experimental methods concern me. He called Nick's difficulty a prodigious cold and prescribed only soups and bed rest for a few days. The man presents a good image of intelligence and competence, yet refuses to bleed Nick.

This being Sunday, the students gathered in the chapel at six this evening for worship. I listened to the boys' singing and Dr. Witherspoon's sermon, his third today for them. He's a staunch "Patriot" and Presbyterian, is guiding at least half of them into the ministry and a rebellious one at that. If war comes, the Lord will send His angels and Dr. Witherspoon to assist them.[*]

---

[*] *Dr. Witherspoon, a signer of the Declaration of Independence, was once a member of the Scottish General Assembly and was imprisoned by the British. He escaped and came to America an uncompromising independent, denouncing both the British Government and the established church. As President of Prince Town College he educated James Madison, creator of the Constitution, and many other young men who became prominent leaders in young America. R.E.H.*

This delay is vexing but I will not abandon Nick. I was his sitter-up all night and he is somewhat improved.

April 10th, 1775

There's a price for staying in this Prince Town College: the schedule. I was not at all prepared for the five o'clock rising bell and servants pounding on bedroom doors. I found myself on my knees at prayer with a hundred others in the chapel by five thirty. Then back to rooms for an hour of study. At breakfast they sat at long pine tables and ate dark bread, butter and coffee.

From nine to one, recitation, followed by a hearty dinner of boiled beef, vegetables, cider and pie. Then freedom until three, two more hours of study, more prayers, and supper of more bread, aging apples and chocolate. At nine another hour of supervised study, then to bed.

Nick little improved. The doctor gave him a vomit and enema but these measures exhausted him. He is fearful that I may leave him behind.

Believe I have escaped my pursuers, but what awaits me in Boston?

April 12th, 1775

Nick is much better; I spent the day advancing his ability to read—and with some success. I shall wait one more day to take him, but I must go. Suspicious students know I am recently from England and these walls are creeping closer every night.

April 13th, 1775 -Newark, New Jersey

We escaped the Presbyterians only to find ourselves tonight amongst a den of Methodists who offer bed and breakfast. In the past few days I have passed from Anglicans through gaggles of Catholics, Quakers, Presbyterians, Lutheran Swedes and Methodists and each is convinced the others err in some manner. I am told there is a Jew's synagogue in New York, Boston is Congregationalist and Rhode Island dissents in some other way. With such religious dissension, how can these provinces possibly unite on anything? Their only common doctrine is fear of the Church of England. Verily I believe the establishment of an American Bishop would bring on armed rebellion.

Nick is himself again; a most loyal servant. He learned to write the entire alphabet while ill and is beginning to form simple words.

April 14th, 1775 - New York

We crossed the commodious North River into this well compacted city—staying at Hull Tavern. New York is a remarkable peninsula port, protected from the sea, yet close to it. Streets are absolutely straight. One could fire a cannonball down one of them to maximum range without ever striking a building. Very considerable trade here; the import ban is not enforced.

No indication of munitions imports but there is controversy. A statue of King George is a target for filth. The city cleans it and rebels desecrate it with dung and the most foul words.

There's also a statue of Lord Chatham here, standing on a pedestal clothed like a Roman orator. That man haunts me; to the French he is the original Goddam.

Several gentlemen of substance dine at the tavern, where I had my first lobster in America, with bread, cheese, plum pudding and ale. Reckoning 2s/6p.

April 17th, 1775 - Boston, Massachusetts

Boston, finally Boston! This last day I fell in with a dozen oxen-drawn wagons with provisions for Boston. Their source is North Carolina. When we approached the city on a narrow neck of land guarded by British sentries, some of the militia gave their arms to comrades and led the wagons into the granary. The sentries searched for arms but my precious Chatham charter allowed me to keep mine.

The Granary Committee oversees distribution of the charity provisions. One can either buy wheat there at 6s/bushel or earn it by digging wells, making bricks, paving streets, etc. To accept provisions without earning them is unacceptable to givers and receivers alike.

With darkness approaching, we hurried into the city but immediately became lost. Found myself on a lengthy commons called The Mall, where a lamplighter showed me the Green Dragon Inn. I could not get my bearings until I saw a map on this tavern wall. The area depicts two islands trying to escape the mainland, but each is still connected by a narrow isthmus. The larger contains Boston and, across the Charles River to the north, the smaller holds a village at the foot of a hill that overlooks Boston.

The Green Dragon Inn is my lodging for one night only. I am in the midst of something sinister. Suspicious eyes follow me everywhere and somber-faced men come and go quietly from a back room. Directly beneath my chamber, the room becomes quiet when I enter mine. Why? Neither French agents nor Grover's knaves could possibly know I am here.

April 18th, 1775 - Boston

Mrs. Stedman, a forthright woman and local midwife, let me a chamber with breakfast, reckoning: 2s/6p. She also quarters a British grenadier named Gibson and his provincial wife, but against the landlady's will. Bostonians fiercely resent this mandatory quartering. Her dilatory sloth of a husband is a cooper and the proud owner of an Encyclopaedia Britannica, the contents of which he imposes on anyone who will listen.

Midnight

Oh God Almighty, in what venal conspiracy has Chatham involved me? I am abandoning this dangerous employment. Bradford is dead, coldly murdered and I may be next. With curtains drawn I sit here in the corner like a trapped animal, watching both door and window with a loaded pistol in my lap, and flinch with every suspicious sound. A bewildered Nick is sleeping before the door with his pistol nearby.

Must record today's events for explanation of my resignation. As I struck out to find Gustavus Bradford, who was supposed to have a secret message for me, my first sight of Boston was thrilling. The city is as crowded with soldiers as the harbor is with warships. British flags and regimental colors, the pennants on the ships and the elegant uniforms all served to elate me. How could the rebels entertain any hope of defeating such military power?

Finding Bradford's ship, I approached the deck officer, a lad who could not yet be twenty. The young officer was looking for some postponement to answering when a sailor in the rigging shouted:

"Mister Bradford was killed when the bloody privateers raided us and sconced all our hogs, but we gutted him and stowed him with the ballast in a barrel of vinegar. We promised full passage and we gave it to him. Want the corpse?"

The embarrassed officer intervened and told me Bradford's remains are in the customs house. The victim appeared to be a special target. One of the blackguards with a French accent asked for him by name, shot him on sight, and took all his clothing and personal belongings with him. Left the bloody corpse naked.

"Did Bradford have something for me?"

"Oh yes. He had a packet addressed to you in the captain's strongbox, but we didn't tell those murderers."

Soon he was back, without even verifying my identity, gave me the packet and excused himself because they were casting off.

And cast off they did, to allow space for the warship *Somerset* to leave. It moved slowly out into the harbor, trailed by several longboats secured to her stern, and joined other warships with longboats at their sterns.

My mysterious packet from Lord Chatham had the attached letter inside.

Hayes, Kent
March 1st, 1775

My Courageous Landon:

This is another confidential letter. Treat the contents with care; your life may depend upon it. I note your expenses. Keep an account and I will pay them. Enclosed are six more monthly stipends, £ 90.

Also enclosed are letters of introduction and safe passage for you and Gustavus Bradford to General Gage, commander of British troops, and to John Adams, his leading antagonist in

Boston. Mr. Bradford also has a conciliatory letter from the Prime Minister. Go to them and arrange a conference to relieve the causes of tensions. Bradford will remain in Boston to further this intercourse, but you go on to the Continental Congress to see if some variation of the Galloway proposal is acceptable.

Now Landon, study with closest attention. Lord Stormont is trying to verify that gunpowder is being shipped from France to the American colonies. His agent at the gunpowder stamping mill at Harfleur is adding an extra amount of sulphur to the mix late in the process so that the yellow crystals will not have time to dissolve.

The specks of yellow color are noticeable only in bright sunlight. By this means we can identify the source of that gunpowder wherever it appears. Gaylord traced it to the merchantman St-Jean-de-Monts but lost his life in doing so. We want to know where it is going; watch for signs of it but with utmost care.

My gout and headaches have driven me home for an extended rest. Do your Duty, Landon, maintain your Integrity and serve your Country but do not risk your life. Destroy this letter lest it destroy you.

William Pitt
Earl of Chatham

Addressing me as courageous now, Chatham wants me to be his spy but I will collect my own intelligence. I am returning to South Carolina anyway; may well burn all such material.

Despite instructions to destroy it, I encoded his letter and attached it to today's entry. But what in all of Purgatory is the Galloway proposal and where would I find yellow-tinted gunpowder? Merciful God, already have! Grover's powder at

Annapolis had a yellow hue in the sun and I saw it again on my hands at George Town.

Grenadier Gibson's wife is in the next room, still weeping at this hour. Her husband departed this afternoon in full field dress and she is heavy with child.

Some military action is brewing. While midwife Stedman attended to the girl, the sly husband hurried (I discreetly followed) to the Green Dragon Tavern. It must be a rebel intelligence link and that scoundrel a spy.

April 19th, 1775

God help us all; there has been grievous bloodshed. This morning grenadiers and light infantry crossed the harbor by longboat and marched to Lexington to seize some rebel arms, only to be cruelly bled in a continuous running battle all the way back to Boston. At least fifty soldiers are already dead and more than 200 wounded, some grievously. The rebels had been warned and ambushed the raid.

Grenadier Gibson is back but a mutilated man. He has been shot through the belly and thigh and is in agony. So are many others and the wailing and moaning of the wounded and their women is indescribable.

I went to the suffering Gibson this evening to try to comfort him. A doctor had attended to him, but was of little help. Mrs. Stedman was spooning into the pitiable fellow a decoction of some drug to reduce his pain.

When I asked him what happened:

"They're cowards, savages, beasts! Not once did they stand up to us. From Lexington and Concord to here they skulked behind trees, stone fences and buildings, thousands of them, and shot us up fierce. And then they scalped the fallen. I seen one scalped on the bridge myself. Leave me."

I left after offering my condolence to his young sobbing wife in the parlor. I tried to walk beyond the sounds of unhappiness but it was impossible. On the edge of the city, soldiers would let me go no farther.

Finally went back and served as sitter-up with Gibson while his sick wife rested. When I gave him over as dying, I awakened her and recited an absolution and commendation as though I were a priest. It was presumptuous of me but brought some happiness to his face. May God forgive me.

Gibson died in a pool of blood about an hour ago. When the death cart came by to take him to a common grave, his wife, in a fit of emotion, went into travail.

So help me God, I must stay the course and help Chatham to contain this disaster. Events demand that I do my duty, act with integrity and serve my country, whatever the risk.

April 20th, 1775

More horror and death. Not only are many of the wounded dying but widow Gibson birthed her child stillborn. The sound of church bells announcing the passing of another soul is constant.

Much confusion now. Thousands of rebel militia have Boston surrounded and the city is under siege.

April 21st, 1775

Chaos! A squad of most unruly soldiers burst in the door this morning and searched the entire house. They broke open the cellar door to find empty moonshine containers and some spirits, seized the spirits and departed with Stedman. Lord Chatham's Charter saved me from molestation.

Soldiers also raided *The Green Dragon*, charged the barkeep and Stedman with being spies. (They probably are.)

But the British Army had not reckoned with Stedman's wife. She rolled a barrel down to the Commons, stood on it and began to protest their treatment publicly. Soon she collected a sympathetic crowd of several hundred, a crowd growing increasingly restive. Then an officer approached her, told her to get down and be quiet and that her husband was about to be tried by court-martial for treason. She responded by kicking him so sharply just under the ribs that he fainted for want of breath. The mob proceeded to strip him naked, then revive him and ran him off the Commons.

A company of grenadiers appeared with fixed bayonets, dispersed the gathering and took her barrel but oddly did not arrest her. Remarkable woman!

And Stedman himself was dismissed by the court-martial and returned home. Perhaps fear of riots?

No more church bells allowed; all tolling ordered stopped by General Gage. The Widow Gibson's right breast was so swollen and discolored that midwife Stedman decided to cut it. Her husband and I restrained the girl while Ms. Stedman opened the screaming female's breast with a freshly scalded razor. After an ugly flow of fester, Ms. Stedman sewed up the breech with silk thread and the pitiable girl seemed relieved.

April 22nd, 1775

Still cannot get an audience with General Gage but did get permission to visit the mainland and negotiate the return of wounded. My real purpose is to find this John Adams and present him with Lord Chatham's proposal for negotiation, but this hostile atmosphere does not encourage me. I leave tomorrow alone and unarmed. Perhaps my senses have taken leave of me but I must try.

How did such a slovenly mob defeat the British?

April 23rd, 1775 - Braintree, Mass.

Rode out under a flag of truce, across the Boston neck and through the rebel militia. This gathering of armed farmers has no uniforms or apparent authority over them. Soldiers call their elected officers by their first names and obey or not as the mood strikes them. Obviously there is no upper class to provide any leaders.

These unwholesomes relieve themselves everywhere, have no tents, little food and many have no weapons. I watched for yellow tinted gunpowder but saw none. Cannot imagine how such a slovenly mob as this defeated British Regulars.

A Reverend William Gordon, who escorted me to see Adams, is very proud of this militia and stupidly recited the number and strength of many units.

Gordon and I are bedding tonight under guard at a neighbor's in order to see the infamous Adams in the morning. He is not well and his wife would not let me see him tonight.

Upon asking Rev. Gordon about his religious persuasion:

"Independent Congregationalist. Ours is a new holy commonwealth, where neither Papists nor Episcopal Bishops dare enter. America is destined to be the moral and political leader of the world."

I wearily bid the oaf goodnight.

April 24th, 1775

"Come on lad, this is your chance to see Mr. Adams." Thus the Rev. Gordon awakened me with a shout and a slap.

I ran over to the Adams porch with impatient Gordon. A handsome woman who introduced herself as Abigail Adams allowed only a short visit in his bedroom.

We nodded assent and entered. There he sat in bed, big of belly and short of hair. I presented my letter of introduction and relayed Lord Chatham's plea for peace, for any measure to avoid war and separation from the Mother Country.

John Adams eyed me for a bit, smiled a humorless smile and quietly talked as I shorthanded.

"My young friend, I hold your Lord Chatham in high esteem. Would that he could have been prime minister these last years, but it's too late."

"Sir, Lord Chatham earnestly implores you to indicate some desire for reconciliation. Even Lord North has...."

"How can we discuss reconciliation when Wednesday last the soldiers of a despotic government sallied forth into the countryside applying the torch and the sword, killing, looting, raping? For General Gage it may have been just an unsuccessful raid; for us it was an assault on our right to have a militia bearing arms in our own defense. More than that, it was an assault on the whole continent of America."

"But shouldn't we avoid a revolution if we can?"

"The revolution began with the first plantations in America and was effected fifteen years ago. The war upon us now is no part of the revolution, only a consequence thereof."

"Is there any hope that I can take to General Gage?"

"He has my hope that he'll withdraw from Boston and return the troops to England, but Lord North won't allow that. He will have his war and shed our blood; however, we'll be victorious—and independent."

I finally added the only thing I could.

"Lord Chatham directed me to deliver his petition to the Continental Congress to offer one more plea to the King for reconciliation. Would you give me safe passage?"

"Certainly. I'll not stand in the way of a peaceful acceptance of our independence."

He wrote an authorization to visit the Congress and Mrs. Adams ended the conference. Gordon escorted me back through the military lines.

Mrs. Stedman wants me to return Gibson's hysterical widow to her home. She lives to the west somewhere but cannot go there now, not alone.

April 25th, 1775

A reluctant aide led me to General Gage's office with a caution that I had only a few minutes.

I was wanting in nerves to meet the man who had just ordered such a bloody raid. I presented Lord Chatham's request but he said he had already offered reconciliation.

"As for this unfortunate skirmish, you can tell Lord Chatham these rebels have been openly drilling militia for battle, collecting munitions and other supplies. I was forced to make a show of might."

"But it's only worsened the situation. We're now a besieged town denied necessities from the countryside."

My remark was a mistake. He reddened in the face and turned his back on me. In less than a minute I found myself again in the street.

April 28th, 1775

Delayed my departure three days in order to escort Widow Gibson back to her home in Worcester. Her breast surgery is apparently healing.

When I asked Stedman if he thought the Lexington debacle was fought over the right to have an arms-bearing militia, he agreed but posited security against unwarranted search and seizure to be equally important.

The outspoken Mrs. Stedman added to that the right to speak her piece in public, to refuse to quarter soldiers and to refuse the religion of the Church of England. She actually believes the next and larger raid will include seizing churches and placing Episcopal priests in them to collect tithe-audits like taxes. No argument, including the unavailability of such priests, affects her irrationality.*

April 29th, 1775 - Cambridge.

Widow Gibson, Nick and I easily passed through the lines and reached Cambridge before nightfall. An attic loft is the room tonight and I had to feign the girl was my wife to get it. She invited me to stay with her but I declined. In her state fornication is neither her intent nor mine but I prefer to sleep outside in my greatcoat and guard the horses and provisions with Nick. Thieves are everywhere.

---

* *PERCEPTIVE READER, the first major battle of the American Revolution was a tragedy for the British in particular. It accelerated a two-way flow of unity that could never have been anticipated. The flow to the north was one of troops, munitions and foodstuffs, led by General George Washington. The flow to the south was one of ideas. New Englanders had long entertained two notions which spread southward, that:*
Their freely chosen religious beliefs, however diverse, were blessed by God and superior to a monarchial state-mandated church; Civilization and the center of world power was moving to the Western side of the Atlantic. A unified America was destined to lead the rest of the world in morality, law and civil rights. The essence of these notions remains today. R. E. H.

April 30th, 1775 - Worcester

God help me, I'm a prisoner again! I had just left the widow at her home when I came upon a large body of men beside the road. We tried to pass quietly but were seized and marched to the nearest house. They took me into the cellar where one of them told me I was being held until a certain military campaign, which I was now privy to, was completed. All protests ignored. I shall go mad in here.

———————————

Charles Town
May 5th, 1775

My Blessed Cassandra,

I am so very sorry that you have been ill but since you believe you are with child, is it not a blessing? By the time this epistle arrives you will probably be in confinement. How frustrating it must be to retire from public view, but what else can a lady do?

I must acknowledge that in some cultures here pregnancy is neither embarrassing nor hidden. The so-called sandlappers—a term I abhor—to the west are out and working as a matter of necessity until the child comes. The pitiable slave women sometimes drop their young in the field like livestock.

My world is ever deteriorating as our fortunes fail. Our townhouse is already sold and soon our slaves will belong to the McKees. Fortunately they can walk to the McKee plantation daily and do not have to lose their brick dwellings here. My father is the only person in South Carolina who built brick houses for slaves.

I had hoped they would all be freed in my lifetime but now I have no control over their destiny. I live at the farm now and have undertaken some of the labor—while enduring my mother's unending censure for not sacrificing my happiness to the shackles of marriage for the family's sake.

We have learned that on April 19th last a terrible conflict erupted near Boston between Army troops and rebelling militia. I know not how much to believe but my premonitions are ominous.

My gallant is probably still in Boston now and may be in danger. He wrote he plans to meet with the treasonable John Adams on behalf of Lord Chatham—I cannot imagine why. My thoughts flee to you and the adventure of creation ahead.

> My prayers are with you,
> Melinda

JOURNAL FOR MAY 1775

May 26th, 1775 - Cambridge

What a farce and waste of time these four weeks have been. Resuming my journal for the first time in a month. I have had neither the means nor permission to write anything, except in teaching Nick. To divert myself, I turned to that. My jailer, one "Captain" Mott, let us scratch words on the plastered cellar walls and Nick and I used every square foot. Then we turned to the sand floor in the wood bin, where we could erase a lesson and start again. His progress is the only redeeming aspect of this maddening imprisonment. And oddly, he was allowed to come and go as long as he stayed on the property, tended to the horses, brought me food, etc. But I was confined!

Mott professes to have never heard of either Grover or French agents, but I have been his prisoner while, without firing a shot, a drunken band of rioters and looters, led by two glory-seeking asses named Ethan Allen and Benedict Arnold, captured Fort Ticonderoga, then seized three British garrisons, at least 150 cannon, two small ships, and innumerable stores. This is as Mott told it to me.

If this abominable tale is true, the British forces involved in these actions have been a grievous disappointment. The surrender of the Fort itself was disgraceful and the absent governor of the area, Major Skene, was so depraved he had not even buried his dead wife, so as to continue to receive her annuity as long as she remained above ground.

Meanwhile my compulsion to escape grew more intense until Nick and I executed a departure which we consider more than a little clever.

First, Nick went to a nearby village and, with money I gave him, hired two boys to come on horseback to divert Mott when we escaped. They were happy to do so, having some resentment of him for an earlier mistreatment.

When Nick brought me breakfast, I laid down in a shallow trench I had dug in the sand floor of the woodbin. He covered me with a canvas, covered that with sand and smoothed the surface until it looked normal. I lay on my back breathing through a clay pipestem. Just lying there immobile, under the weight of the sand was the greatest exercise of self-control I have ever experienced.

Nick then went quietly out to the barn, saddled the horses, put our cargo on the packer, and waited.

When Mott came downstairs, he found the cellar empty and an apparent escape route between two window bars which we had pried apart. He and the guard ran out to see the two hired boys ride off to the west. They mounted up and gave chase, leaving the house empty and the cellar door open. As soon as the pursuers were out of sight, Nick came to the house with the horses, retrieved our weapons and called to me. I pushed away my cover, ran up the steps and mounted up. Coursing for Boston, we did not stop until we got to Cambridge.

We arrived here safely with all three horses, most equipment and sand in my hair. Someone condiddled Nick's pistol. Will reenter Boston tomorrow to inform General Gage about the rebel Ticonderoga campaign and dispatch the same news to Lord Chatham.

May 27th, 1775 - Charles Town

Am obliged to remain overnight in this little Puritan village across the inlet from Boston because the stock transport for the horses did not arrive. Remembering that Capt. Carmichael, who brought me across the Atlantic last winter, said his wife lived here, I inquired for and found the lady (for whom the ship *Sophia* is named) packing for departure to England. I was seeking a courier for my letters, but heard a remarkable tale I must record.

"Several years ago," she related, "when I was younger and perhaps more comely, Capt. Carmichael sailed in on a Sunday after a long absence. When I ran down to the wharf to greet him, he embraced me with such enthusiasm and affection that some onlookers were offended by such an indecent act in public, profaning the Sabbath."

"Hardly a crime. What came of it?"

"He was required to appear before the town magistrates, who decided he had committed a crime and ordered him to be publicly whipped. After forty lashes were administered the magistrates forgave him with many expressions of Christian piety and considered the matter ended. "However," says she, "the Captain has yet to expend his indignation."

She added that he is here now and I am invited to go aboard to a farewell party day after tomorrow.

May 28th, 1775 - Boston

We left Charles Town at dawn and crossed the inlet without difficulty. Hundreds of loyal citizens, no longer safe in the countryside, were coming into the city with me.

Even more "patriots" were streaming outward. What a sad spectacle; both groups are abandoning homes and belongings and tearfully fleeing without even knowing where they will sleep tonight.

At General Gage's headquarters I wrote a memorial on what I had heard about the Fort Ticonderoga attack and was ushered directly to his office. Most preoccupied and serious, he wasted little time.

He read the memorial for a moment with deepening frown, then threw the document down in disgust.

"How am I to offer amnesty and pardon, which I am ordered to do," he fumed, "and at the same time demonstrate the futility of resisting the British Army, when I have the likes of Lexington and Ticonderoga on my hands. I am willing to pardon; this proclamation proposes pardon for all except Samuel Adams and John Hancock, both traitorous criminals. But no response"

"Get out," General Gates ordered. "But don't leave Boston until I've seen you again. Breathe not one word of what you've heard here or you'll find yourself sitting on a lance, the point of which will be tickling your throat from the inside." He moved so closely to me I could see the hair in his nostrils. "Not one word!"

Staying at the Stedmans again, can scarcely tolerate this confinement either.

May 30th, 1775

Never imagined I would ever desire to board the *Sophia* again, but I would not have missed Captain Carmichael's farewell celebration for any consideration. In an apparent gesture of Christian charity, he invited aboard the same magistrates who had him whipped in the past and two others who had accused him of profaning the Sabbath. There was much conviviality and generous offerings of sirloin of beef roasted, plum pudding with orange sauce and negus.

At the rout's conclusion, the sails were lofted and the anchor was apeak for getting under way. The Captain led his guests on deck, assured them he should eternally remember them and wished to recompense them this very day for their civilities toward him.

He then ordered his crew to pinion them and strip off their shirts. One at a time they were brought before the Captain, where the boatswain laid on each forty lashes with a cat-o-nine tails. He also bid farewell to me, sparing the lashes, and put us all on their boats. Then he shouted after that he forgave them all with Christian piety and forthwith sailed for England. The language employed by these gentlemen as they painfully rowed to shore was hardly Puritan.

May 31, 1775

Wrote letter to Chatham and now I am going to escape Boston. If I can just get to South Carolina I may abandon this mission and let the independence movement do what it will.

Charles Town, S.C.
May 10th, 1775

My dear Landon:

It seems so long since I saw you last; I miss you. Recent news and events are frightening. We have learned that several thousand British soldiers marched into the countryside west of Boston without provocation and killed, looted, burned and generally ravaged the land. Is it true?

The atmosphere in Charles Town is frightful. We fear the possibility of a naval assault on this fair port and most able-bodied men, including Mr. McKee, have joined one militia or another.

All activity not essential to the war is ending. We are obliged to fill a schooner with provisions for the people of Boston. The theatre and all other forms of artistic endeavor are in a state of collapse.

I and my "sister Americans" have not drunk tea, bought new clothes, attended parties of pleasure, nor enjoyed other frivolity since hearing of Lexington. We dare not. We are learning to knit, to make clothes and engage in other "patriotic" endeavors to avoid total ostracism or even expulsion from the community.

How can that villainous Congress in Philadelphia impose such tyranny and oppression on the provinces? Many here are still loyal to the King, sincerely wishing for reconciliation and praying that he will reverse this course of events, but I am not encouraged.

My life is full of uncertainties, as is yours. You are uncertain of your faith, but it will return when you rid yourself of your guilt. The only thing of which I am certain, dear Landon, is that I miss you. Each day, like geese flying northward, my thoughts take wing and soar to you.

Melinda

JOURNAL FOR JUNE 1775

June 1st, 1775

Finally a letter from Melinda. She addressed it to General Gage's Headquarters as I proposed, but someone there has opened it. What a distorted version of the Lexington-Concord skirmishes she describes. Truth is not a virtue of American news papers.

How deeply her writing affects me. Her calligraphy is so feminine and regular and the content makes me ache for her. But what of her mysterious obligation to marry McKee? Did she submit to him—she with child?

June 2nd, 1775

General Gage sent an officious young aide to remind me with some arrogance that I am to remain in this house. Am I under house arrest?

June 4th, 1775

A grenadier stopped me when I started for church this morning, so I am under house arrest. The soldier professes to know nothing except that I am to remain in the house. He says the church is a stable now anyway and the pews have been cut up for firewood.

The grenadier is to occupy the deceased Gibson's room and brought a firkin of rice, from the *Amantha*, he says, for his rations. So Charles Town's provisions for the people are being issued instead to British troops.

June 6th, 1775

The moonshine becoming very fullsome and facilitating night travel, Stedman has been looking for a visit by his smuggler. Last night the moonshiner appeared with tubs of gin and brandy which Stedman asked me to help bottle forthwith. We worked until nearly dawn and then went straight into brewing a hogshead of beer. I assisted him so that he might, feeling some small obligation, help me escape.

June 11th, 1775

Nothing these days but waiting and teaching Nick to read.
Some mischief is pending; Stedman is often gone now at odd hours and not peddling his brews; he has a most serious manner. Last night he quoted a rumor that General Gage is planning an attack on the mainland next Sunday. If Stedman knows it, the rebels know it too.

June 13th, 1775

Smallpox on the next street now. Stedman opined that the rebels may attack before the Army does. Each morning a loyalist volunteer battalion rehearses bursting out of homes and gathering on shore to repel invasion.

June 15th, 1775

Today General Gage declared martial law and hanged a deserter.
All is in readiness. I dare not tell anyone that we leave before dawn. Fair copy of letter to Melinda (attached).

Boston, Mass.
16 June 1775

My Dearest friend:

It is late, so very late. In a few hours I shall leave Boston; my situation is untenable here. Should such dangerous activity prove to be my undoing, this letter will reveal my innermost thoughts about you and the national tragedy now unfolding.

I am tormented by my desire for you and by your commitment to another. Yet I am honored, even elated, by your response to my love.

I do not deny my physical desire but my affection for you, dear Lady is based on more than that. When I remember your graceful walk, I love you. When I recall your hands at the pianoforte, creating beautiful music, I love you. When I observe your warm friendliness to those about you, I love you. When I see your compassion for the less fortunate, I love you.

The military situation here is desperate. The skirmish at Lexington involved only a few hundred men, but it was a disaster for the British and a rallying event for the rebels. Boston is now under siege and so is my faith. These tragic events suggest that God has little interest in what is happening. Yet I am willing to be shown otherwise.

Forgive me for my boldness. I do not know what tomorrow will bring and my emotions are affected by the hour. God willing—or ignoring—I shall dispatch this letter from Philadelphia. Please write soon; send your letter to my Uncle John's address in Alexandria. I will likely go there after Philadelphia and then, I hope, back to you.

I am, my charming love, yours
Landon

June 17th, 1775

Lord God have mercy; the war has begun. The rebels moved first last night and were eventually driven back today, but at frightful cost. The whole city is mourning now and there is no escaping the sound of wailing as the magnitude of the slaughter is realized. The shock after Lexington was nothing compared to this. Stedman said the only reason it was not worse for the Army was that the defenders had only enough powder to fire two rounds each.

Not knowing this battle was about to eventuate, Nick and I slipped out before dawn to the north of Copp's Hill and coursed toward the Boston Neck. We had scarcely cleared the shipyard at first light when we heard cannon fire, a warship firing on Breed's Hill across the bay. The rebels had occupied the hill, created an earthen fort overnight and were still feverishly digging.

Then cannon on Copp's Hill behind us began to fire at the fort, directly over our heads, and the horses went wild. Trapped at the foot of Copps Hill and looking directly at the object of the firing, we blindfolded the animals and remained as quiet as possible. One loyal citizen, a member of the new volunteer battalion planning to fight beside the British troops, ran out of a nearby house with musket to join his unit, only to killed by a British soldier who thought he was a rebel. Soldiers ran everywhere as regiments began to form up on the Common and more ships commenced to fire on the rebel-occupied hill.

The most incredible part of the scene was the apparent efficiency of the rebels. I could easily see their leader calmly strolling along the fresh parapet and directing the digging whilst the remainder pitched the soil. The artillery fire was inaccurate and appeared to bother them little. But at the foot of the hill, Charles Town, which I had recently visited, was soon set afire.

It was half-past-one before barges began to row the soldiers across to the shore of the fortified hill and after three before they began a slow ascent behind an intense barrage. They looked clumsy and vulnerable with their heavy packs and red coats in the bright sunlight and they marched straight into the face of the defenders. But the rebels neither fired nor fled.

People came out from all over Boston to watch, as though it were the Roman amphitheater. Some looked worried but many were joking, eating and gambling on the time the rebels would bolt. Peddlers moved about in the hot sun selling food and drink in a carnival atmosphere.

Then the cannons became silent, as did the watching crowd. Finally, just as the attackers closed with bayonets lowered, the defenders fired a volley—and another.

Merciful God, the smitten Army fell back, those who could, leaving the hillside covered with fallen soldiers. Forming again, the red lines started up the hill once more. Still with heavy packs, still slowly.

The artillery fire renewed and Charles Town became a sea of flame. The church steeples were spears of fire above the streets into which rows of burning houses collapsed.

The redcoat lines closed on the dirt fort again and the people here were horror-stricken; the carnival atmosphere changed to one of foreboding and lament.

A second time the soldiers were hurled back, slaughtered by murderous volley fire at very close range. But after falling back, the Army ordered a third assault, this time without the hundred-pound packs. Whose merciless stupidity led them into that wall of death again? Was it impossible for Gage to imagine himself in error? People about me were then frightened and weeping. One woman ran away screaming she could not watch her husband being killed.

The red lines advanced over hundreds of their fallen comrades, directly into the rebels' muskets again, and that time they prevailed. Apparently out of ammunition, the defenders fired weakly and retreated. The red coats poured over the parapet like a ocean breaker of blood, bayonets flashing, and the defenders fell back. Deus misereatur!

But the defenders fell back in good order. There was little firing, both sides having empty muskets and no time to reload. It looked rather like herding cattle as the rebels tried to stay out of reach of the bayonets. They passed out of sight over Bunker Hill and the battle was over.

But not the results. The grassy slope behind them was covered with the dead and dying. At this distance the motionless red coats suggested red wild flowers decorating a field in the spring, but it was the flowering of war.

We returned to the Stedmans. I do not dare try to leave Dystopia tonight. God have mercy on us all, Amen.

June 18th, 1775

My grenadier guard is back, confining me to my room this time, with instructions that I am to report to a board of inquiry tomorrow. Fills me with trepidation.

It is Sunday but no church services, just funerals. Stedman says more than a hundred officers' bodies have been returned for burial, but the men's are being dumped in the long ditch the rebels dug. A thousand wounded have been returned and in a field hospital down the street, amputation victims moan incessantly. Half will die of fester or, in their weakened condition, of some disease. Behind the hospital is a growing pile of limbs and a loaded burial cart. I must escape this carnage and that board of inquiry.

And how would the Trinity faculty explain God's role in this event? An act of God or one just permitted by God?

Punishment of sinners and devout alike? Perhaps it was such an insignificant event on a minor planet, so remotely located in the universe as to not even be noticed by God.

In the *Puritan Club* Randolph and I could only agree that there has to be a creator; the infinite universe is too complex to be accidental. We often debated the meaning of tragedies in the abstract, but here before my eyes is a shocking example; indescribable suffering and death for young lives. God has to be compassionless.

June 19, 1775 - Thompson, Conn.

Laudate Dominum! Never believed I would feel free away from the protection of the British soldiery. We escaped yesterday morning by the same route attempted on Saturday; had no difficulty passing through.

The American militia around Cambridge are in a more disorganized state than ever. They too have been hurt by the battle and they fear further attacks. A more plebeian mob I have never seen, feared for my life as I rode among them. Most important, I saw gunpowder being issued from a munitions wagon and a newly opened keg showed yellow flecks in the sunlight! Those sulphur crystals pronounced, as surely as words, "manufactured in France."

Will try Middle Post Road for Hartford tomorrow.

June 21st, 1775 - New Haven

Found lodging in the house of one John Trumbull, who has rooms to let. A deranged Republican poet ill from smallpox inoculation, he harangues with great emotion for liberty and civil rights.

Another guest is Mr. Hopkins, a daft religionist from Newport, Rhode Island. At supper he was bursting with news so odd that I shorthanded it:

"Massachusetts may be the first to declare independence, unless North Carolina does. By the time the constipatal Congress does anything but flatulate, anything at all, it'll be too late."

I diverted the daft fellow with: "What brings you to New Haven?"

"Certainly not to get the smallpox inoculation; illegal in Rhode Island, you know. Inoculation is interference with God's plan for the disposition of mankind. I'm here to publish a tract urging the suppression of Deism, Infidelity and Quakerism. That atheistic Newport Mercury refuses to print it. And I'm printing a broadside to stop all slave importation."

"I thought Silas Grover's slave trade is based here."

"No more. We've denied Grover the right to enter any Rhode Island port. That avaricious man has violated all standards of decency with his slave and gunpowder trading and victual stealing. We'll send our own ships to Statia."

With the mention of Statia, Trumbell hushed his guest. I lied that I knew about Statia but that I did not think all of Grover's activities are known to the Carolineans.

"We hope to thwart his commerce with this broadside describing his traitorous practices," Hopkins added and handed me the tract. "This lists every one of his ships by name, description and captain commanding and recommends that patriots seize them and make their own voyages to Statia for munitions. We've posted copies to every colony. Want one?"

I accepted several. So now I have the connection. The transfer of munitions to the likes of Grover is at the West Indies island of Statia! French merchantmen, and probably Dutch and Spanish too, are sailing there.

Nick is very quiet today. He will not even respond to my "What does it say?" game.

June 22nd, 1775 - New York

At the Hull Tavern again where I was invited to join a convivial gathering of men of commerce at a plentiful supper of rabbit smothered with onions, a neck of mutton boiled and a goose roasted. There were several Dutch and French sauces to flavor them, reminding me of Randolph's complaint upon returning from Paris to London, that Britain has a dozen dissenting religions but only one sauce. There were also vegetables and a currant pudding followed by spirits, coffee and tea.(The ban on tea ignored) After many weeks of frugal fare and unfrivolous piety, the repast was most welcome. Took a large platter of the victuals to the wide-eyed Nick, which I often do.

There's great excitement here over the fight at Boston, now entitled the Battle of Bunker Hill. New York fears it too will be occupied. (Many would welcome it.) Perhaps the greatest resentment here against the Government is that the Parliament denied the owner of a mill, just erected, the right to manufacture nails and other iron implements. New Yorkers must buy ironmongers' wares from Britain. That is indeed stupid and avaricious.

There is intelligence that "General" George Washington is en route to Massachusetts to assume command of the rebel "army" there. He'll be appalled to see the unruly mob they are calling an army. Have pocketed all my thoughts and do not even admit I have been in Boston. I did find a loyal ship's captain, however, and entrusted to him a letter to Lord Chatham describing the battle and informing him the tainted French gunpowder was reaching Massachusetts through The West Indies island of St. Eustatia. Kept no copy.

June 25th, 1775 - Philadelphia

Rode hard again these three days in heavy rain; everything is wet. I finally got in Nick's head and he is complaining for the first time. So much travel puts him in a strange bed, and often no bed, each night. I must amend.

This accommodation on the north side is a mineral bath house of a Dr. Kearsley, reputedly good loyalist. I'll be obliged to use it until I can find something closer. Nick is well cared for here but not yet the happiest.

June 26th, 1775

Awoke this morning to a knocking on my door and someone entering. Must record this amusing conversation.

"I'm Dr. Kearsley," a voice boomed, and I sat up in bed to see at eye level a doctor's cloak unsuccessfully trying to cover an enormous hairy belly. My eyes raised to the top of this pear-shaped body to find a black-thatched head with piercing blue eyes, between fat cheeks, squinting at me.

"Understand you arrived last night," he continued, "and wish to go on into the city. But are you prepared for the city?"

"Prepared?"

"For the hazards to health such as the bloody flux that comes with Springtime. Drink this water as a specific for venereal diseases and to prevent the bloody flux. And have you have been inoculated for smallpox?"

"No, I don't think I want to..."

"Three hundred people died of smallpox in Philadelphia last year, one out of every seven who contracted it.

"The mercurial inoculation death rate is a hundredth that of the natural infection. I never lose any and the sore is small. My inoculation hospital is the finest."

"I'll keep it in mind, sir. I must go to Philadelphia today."

"Of course," he smiled, "but inquire elsewhere and you'll learn you had best do it."

Thus advised, I set out for the city alone, leaving Nick to rest and repair equipage. First I made for the port to put Melinda's letter on a mail packet.

Philadelphia has to be the largest city in America. Coming down the Delaware River bank, I saw a hundred wharves extending into the river before I reached the mail packet. I counted at least twenty ships under construction and saw more than I could count anchored in the river. And there is a great marketplace that must be a mile long.

On one wharf several hundred Irish bonded, just disembarked, were waiting to be sold at auction as indentured servants; a pitiable sight. But for circumstances, that lot could have mine. I must look upon the Irish with more compassion and respect. Saw no munitions anywhere.

One coasting vessel caught my attention because there was a sign on the mast inviting the people to contribute to the suffering people of Boston by leaving stores on deck. But the vessel, named *Janus*, was strangely quiet; hatches battened, no crew in sight. The name seems familiar though.

The Pennsylvania Hospital did indeed verify that smallpox was spreading and that I should be inoculated. Also, Dr. Kearsley has an excellent reputation and is loyal to the Crown. His fee of 7s plus 5s per day of confinement is also considered normal but I still do not fancy to it.

At the State House I presented my letters of introduction to the Secretary, Mr. Charles Thompson. From him I learned that Mr. Benjamin Franklin, Lee's superior in London, has returned from England and is a delegate to the Congress. I met Franklin once in London; must see him.

There is no respectable lodging nearby at a moderate price. The City Tavern is too costly and others are too cheap.

I finally settled on the Indian King, operated by John Biddle, at 25s a week, available Friday.

Back to Dr. Kearsley's where I'll take the smallpox inoculation if my courage holds. Nick not willing.

Midnight: the thought raised me straight up in bed to light a candle and look at the Grover Broadside. One of Grover's ships is the *Janus*, docked here in Philadelphia. Forthwith I dressed, returned to the offending vessel and placed one of the broadsides condemning it on the notice board directly before the sloop. No one saw me do it.

June 27th, 1775

With gravity and decorum but without pity a buxom woman rolled a small instrument with four razor-edged wheels across my arm, cutting four gashes about two inches long. My head reeled with faintness as she lifted this instrument of torture, stopped the welling blood with a heavy yellow inoculation salve (which is nothing more than pus from smallpox sores added to some concoction,) and bound the wound with a cloth. Feeling ill, I left the hospital immediately and went to my chamber.

Unwilling to do anything for the rest of the day. The cuts smart feverishly.

June 28th, 1775

Nick picked up two letters waiting for me at the City Tavern. One was a discouraging letter from Randolph (attached) boasting about his wenching as usual, and the other was instructions from Lord Chatham to return to the southern provinces after doing what I can in Philadelphia. He hopes in vain the reluctance of South Carolina and Georgia will prevent independence. I burned that one.

London
19 March 1775

My Long Lost Landon:

I received your first letter, of January 6th, more than three months later. I had almost given you over. The decoding works magnificently! I have your complete letter before me, perfectly readable. I shall inform Mr. Lee of its content and then destroy it.

News for you. Mr. Franklin sails tomorrow for Philadelphia and with him go any remaining hopes for reconciliation with America. In total concession to the Hawks, he has abandoned hope of a peaceful settlement.

Meanwhile, in a secret session of the Parliament, Prime Minister North outlined an address to the King declaring Massachusetts in rebellion and to be put down, and proposed a naval blockade and other outrageous measures. (We learned of this secret session from the French agent M. Beaumarchais. We suspect this scoundrel owns a member of Parliament.) Now the rumors are wild that Great Britain will make war on her own colonies.

So a lady has caught your eye! She must be remarkable indeed. Landon, if she is as you suggest, unusually attractive, refined, educated, talented and takes a fancy to you, you should by all means have nothing further to do with her.

I am enjoying myself immensely, especially with the London ladies! No sport exceeds that with females! You should meet Isabel, daughter of a prominent MP and a lady of first consequence. These are exciting times, perhaps more for you than for me. I envy you, but take care lest your Tory inclinations do you mischief. Bathe in American logic at every opportunity and they will eventually wash off.

Your rebellious friend,
Randolph Howard

June 29th, 1775

Just read Randolph's letter again. He has not changed; he is my impetuous, rebellious, earthy, but reliable friend. I once took him to a holy Eucharist service, which he was most disinclined to do, and in which he disdained to participate. Christians are cannibals, he said, no better than savages in the jungle, to eat the flesh and drink the blood of their Savior! He diverted thus merely to shock me, knowing that I was preparing for the clergy, but if his father were to hear such blasphemy it would break his heart.

The issue with Randolph, however, is that he should be able to have this or any other dissenting view of religion. He is even beyond John Locke, who wanted religious freedom for all except Roman Catholics and atheists. In his independent America, even those views will be permissible.

Doctor Kearsley says I have the illness only lightly. He lies.

June 30th, 1775

Nick cancelled my appointment with Mr. Franklin for me and paid for my chamber at the Indian King until I am well enough to remove to there. With my permission Nick is helping Mr. Dunlap, stable owner and printer, at both of his establishments. Nick is particularly fascinated with the forming and production of words on the press.

Too sick to do anything; Melinda, I need you now.

Charles Town
July 6th, 1775

My dear Friend Cassandra,

My thoughts and prayers are with you as you approach your travail—all say it need not be severe. Have you gone into confinement yet and are you employing Mary Wollstonecraft to assist you as planned? Her views on abusive husbands and the inherent rights of women obsess me when I contemplate marriage to Bennett.

Surround yourself with good books—even novels, despite the Reverend's opinion of them. Reading is enjoyable and increases the child's intellect.

The news papers tell us the situation around Boston continues to ferment. Frankly I pray the Army will come to Charles Town and put an end to the Gadsden-generated conspiracy. Landon is apparently in Philadelphia and out of danger. His affectionate epistles fill my soul with joy. Lest I sound too passionate, have no fear that I will become his leman—unless marriage should unite us.

I have donned the osnaburg and am helping in the rice fields whenever possible. I resent my father's absence. He writes he cannot return until our financial situation is improved, but he does nothing to improve it. I conclude he has abandoned us and I deplore the lender who caused it.

You inquire about Bennett's overtures toward me. Fortunately his exercising with the local militia has engrossed him. I absent myself to the plantation where he comes less frequently. To the consternation of my mother, when he does come I appear in soiled osnaburg and field hat.

I must tell you of a delightful respite from our worries. The recent St. Cecelia concert—at Aunt Elizabeth's home to avoid the ban on entertaining publicly—extemporaneously expanded its repertoire to include dramatic sketches. Charles Rutledge and

Ruth Craig performed an hilarious love scene in which he used some Shakespearean lines of Romeo and she a parody of the Biblical Ruth entreating Naomi. The alternating misfits of passages were highly diverting. Ardent affection and congenial virtue distinguish this lovely pair—I predict their marriage.

Despite my voluntary commitment to the rice crop, we do maintain civilized standards of conduct and dress when appropriate. However, virtually no quality velvet, silk, satin, or linen is to be found here. What were the ladies wearing to the Mozart concert you mentioned? And is this lad, Mozart, truly a genius?

My prayers reach out for you and the child in this blessed event to come.

Melinda

JOURNAL FOR JULY 1775

July 6th, 1775

Sores on my hands and feet have prevented my writing or walking but I am one of the favored few who is not seriously ill from the inoculation. My face is little affected and the fever is diminished but I still feel poorly.

Today the Congo (as the loyalists here call the Congress) approved a "Declaration of the Causes and Necessity of Taking up Arms." Do not know its content but the very title is ominous.[*]

The weather is warm and heavy. The oppressive air and perspiration aggravates my sores and my soul.

July 7th, 1775

Mr. Franklin will see me tomorrow. Nick was my messenger and handled the task very well; he can read street and office signs now and is becoming quite confident of himself in the city. Mr. Heyward has not yet arrived from Charles Town. I pray that he can reveal Melinda's mystery.

---

[*] *Written a year before the Declaration of Independence, the words (Jefferson's) are as stirring and include:*

"Our cause is just. Our union is perfect. Our internal resources are great...We most solemnly, before God and the world, declare that...we will...employ them for the preservation of our liberties; being with one mind resolved to die freemen rather than to live slaves." R.E.H.

July 8th, 1775

Oh God Almighty, local Sons of Liberty seized the *Janus* Tuesday last and found provisions documented for the British Army in Boston. Two crew members were captured but others escaped. Thus Grover loses one more ship and he may give me the credit.

The Indian King Inn became my lodging this morning, but I registered as Reginald Garrick as a precaution, then called on Mr. Franklin.

En route I noted the brick-paved streets are quite regular, high in the center with gutters on the sides. Footways on either side stand above the gutters and provide safe dry walking with little befouling from windows above. There are street lamps to light the way at night. I have seen few streets of this quality in England and none elsewhere in America. The public buildings I passed are large, some even elegant, and there are a number of splendid townhouses.

When I reached Franklin's three story house on Market Street, a manservant led me to a disorderly drawing room. There my eyes beheld a well appointed chamber overlaid with debris of all sorts. Scientific apparatus for mechanical and electrical experiments, books, newspapers, drawings, clothes, tools, piles of manuscripts and other items all lay intermingled wherever there was a table or chair to leave something on. Behind a littered desk sat Franklin, amused by my wandering stares and my readied pad and pencil.

"Clear off that chair, Mr. Vickers, and sit down. Welcome to Philadelphia. I remember meeting you in Lord Chatham's home. I am the courier of his letter for you."

I started to read it but he asked:

"So William Pitt would have us talk to General Gage. What would he have you do now?"

"Report the proceedings of this Congress and return to the southern provinces. Sir, is the Congress actually seeking independence?"

Mr. Franklin stood up and walked to the window. He is an older man, rather rotund. He gazed out the window for a moment, then turned to me.

"The Congress is a bundle of weak nerves. There's considerable disagreement as to what we should do. The middle provinces and South Carolina—despite Gadsden—are balking at the thought of separation. Georgia is so disinterested, it hasn't even sent representatives. Our communications to the South are grossly inadequate."

"Perhaps, Mr. Franklin, if the Congress sent a conciliatory message to the King..."

"Already did so. But I am concerned about yourself, Mr. Vickers. Your mission could be exceedingly dangerous."

"I appreciate your warning, sir. I honestly do not know what to do now. Lord Chatham wants me to go south again. How can I continue to report events to him and not be hanged as a spy?"

Mr. Franklin pondered that question for some minutes, then brightened with an idea.

"Why not report events to me as well? After you've spent some time here, continue your travels. Tell Lord Chatham what you observe, here and elsewhere; send your letters through me. We want him to know and to understand, but do it as my emissary. You cannot continue to travel openly working for the British."

I hesitated, wondering if what he was suggesting was duplicitous or any less dangerous. Could I maintain my INTEGRITY, as Lord Chatham lectured, and be an informant to two potentially opposing parties?

"Mr. Vickers, I'll give you written authorization to act as my liaison to the southern provinces. We need someone down

there and we need to know more promptly what they're doing.
It takes a month to hear from Charles Town. You have my
assurance that Lord Chatham will receive everything you send
me."

"I had best think it over, sir. See you tomorrow?"

"Why, yes. If you don't want it though, you'd better plan
to return to England while you can."

Thus instructed and scarcely knowing my own mind, I
repaired to the inn.

July 9th, 1775

My inoculation invited me to remained quiet today, but I
did go to the City Tavern for supper. There I saw none other
than Major Skene, the British lobby-walker who kept his dead
wife's body above ground so he could illegally collect her
annuity. He's restricted to the tavern inn until the local
authorities decide whether to hang him or exercise Tory
Riddance—a street term for deportation.

July 10th, 1775

Last night was miserable. The inoculation sores itched
unmercifully and I fretted with Franklin's offer until dawn. But
there is only one choice; in order to continue on Lord
Chatham's mission I must accept Franklin's employment.

Called on Dr. Kearsley first for reassurance on my health
and to arrange a meeting with Mr. Galloway, author of the
compromise plan of union with Great Britain. They are old
loyalist friends. He assured me of my health but told me two
seafaring men were looking for me. Not preferring their
demeanor, he told them nothing. (From the *Janus*?)

Franklin sent me to Charles Thompson, Congressional
Secretary, for an authorization to act as his agent. I sat down

apprehensively in Mr. Thompson's office. He eyed me a bit, then began to write with a flourish.

As he wrote he peered at me alternately, jutting out a strong long chin as he did so. Finally, he gave me the document and allowed me to read it with widening eyes, to his amusement. It makes me every bit as much an emissary of Mr. Franklin and this Congress as I am of Lord Chatham. But if captured with it by British authorities I could be tried for treason.

July 11th, 1775

Still suffering from my inoculation, I forced myself to rise and go to the City Tavern again, this time to have lunch with Mr. Galloway and Dr. Kearsley.

Galloway was accompanied by his wife and an attractive niece with the biblical name of Naomi. She looked me over not altogether contemptuously and I did not ignore her blooming femininity either but the ladies, who profess to be Quakers, departed and we went in to dinner. We retired to a small but richly furnished private room and enjoyed a sumptuous feast of delicious meats and seafood, vegetables, fruits, cheeses and wines for two hours.

Galloway shows all the signs of a distinguished gentleman. He is educated, articulate, sensible and a loyal British subject. He, like Kearsley, deplores some British policies but resists any move toward separation. He believes the American colonies are on the brink of disaster.

His remarkable view: George Washington once strutted about the Congress in the uniform of a Virginia colonel. Now he is "General" Washington and will surely turn the Boston confrontation into a general war. I shorthanded these words:

"And what if he is successful—which is unlikely—and we separate from Britain?" Independence could result in some

European power, probably France, seizing the country. Or if there is a longer period of independence, there will be a disastrous war over slavery. The Abolitionists will win but the nation will be so bloodied and exhausted it will again be vulnerable to domination by another nation."

I excused myself from his gloomy forecasting with a visit of dysentery. Remained here for the rest of the day, despite the heat. Something at the feast has poisoned me, brings frequent salutary evacuations.

July 12th, 1775

Staying in my chamber with a dolorous stomach, I read in the newspaper that the Congress authorized ten companies of Virginia, Maryland and Pennsylvania frontiersmen, armed with their long rifles, to reinforce the troops in Boston. The Virginia companies marched the entire 600 miles to Boston in three weeks. Added this to my enemy troop ledger.

July 13th, 1775

The arrogant Congress is establishing a Continental currency, the "dollar," to replace the British pound, the most stable currency in the world. Incredible folly.

Nick is in good spirits, responds again to my "What does it say" game. This Quaker city is so opposed to slavery, some abolitionists will have no commerce with merchants who have them. So Nick walks about a truly free man, unmolested by anyone. He has adopted his former owner's last name and proudly signs his name as Nicholas Harrison. He is serving as ostler at the stable and works in the stable owner's printing house as well. He also admits to having found a female friend.

Franklin is arranging my meeting with the S. Carolina delegation. Knowing my intent he is but amused.

July 15th, 1775

Being Saturday and the Congress not meeting, I made for Dickenson's handsome townhouse and entered, I believe, without being seen. He is obviously a successful lawyer, but cadaverously thin and topped with a too-large wig that gives him the appearance of a shrunken head. And he is harassed by a mother who suspects my motives and wants him out of the Congress, lest he be hanged.

No need to record his remarks. In fact, he made few; he is a writer, not a conversationalist, but his position is clear. He is a liberal-minded patriot who believes in rights for the colonials but who is opposed to separation. And he is trying to persuade others to stand with him. His advice to me: "Cultivate the South Carolina delegation, Mr. Vickers; they may be crucial in avoiding war."

The only S. Carolinean I want to cultivate is Melinda.

July 16th, 1775

Mr. Galloway invited me to attend church today with his wife and odd niece, Naomi. (She professes to be a Quaker but reveals few of the attributes.) I am being attentioned by them for some reason.

Christ Church is a remarkable building. There is a ceiling beneath the roof and a tiny window in each, placed so as to create a stream of light on the great Coverdale Bible open before the altar.

The service was less remarkable. The Rev. Jacob Duche, rector and Congressional Chaplain, despite being Established Church, lashed out unmercifully at the Government. The holy oaf has a warped mind. Galloway was angered by the sermon but Quaker Naomi was incensed and flagrantly walked out in the middle of it.

The Galloways took me for a pleasant carriage ride and picnic after. Naomi was very charming with her Quaker use of Thee when addressing someone. Not an unattractive person and revealingly dressed for a Quaker (doubt she is one) but she does not compare with Melinda.

Some rain tonight, the first moisture in a week.

July 19th, 1775

Today is the "First National Day of Prayer" despite the fact that this land is hardly a "nation." Again I heard the Reverend Duche thunder sedition from his pulpit while the great Bible illumed by the shaft of light silently protested. Is God listening to any of us? Deus misereatur.

Naomi was there and met me after the service. She ranted about Duche's hawkish remarks and threatened that if he did not cease, she would humiliate him somehow. She is a most unlikely Quaker.

After she left, I approached Duche despite his political viewpoints to discuss my religious dilemma. His demeanor in private was congenial, not unlike Jefferson. A learned man of perhaps fifty years, he discerned by my questions and some knowledge of the Bible that I had clerical training. Finally I confessed my abandonment of the calling, the guilt that action produced and my search for a new faith.

He was most understanding and encouraged me to pursue the truth, yet I wish I had not confided in him. Someone who advocates separation from Britain cannot be the best Christian.

Letter from Melinda! (attached) Just want to see her.

Charles Town
June 18th, 1775

My Dear Landon:

At the suggestion of Aunt Elizabeth and believing you to be in Philadelphia by now, I shall dispatch this to the City Tavern.

Do I overstep propriety if I plead with you to return soon? You cannot imagine the change of atmosphere and the momentous events here. The Provincial Congress has formed a government which is nothing less than rank Republican, has adopted an Association which all men must sign, declaring they are ready to sacrifice life and fortune to "secure the freedom and safety of South Carolina."

There are still many loyal gentlemen in Charles Town but any expression of that loyalty presents them with danger. James Dealy and Laughlin Martin, members of our St. Cecilia Society, were tarred and feathered like criminals three days ago for criticizing these actions. Both are in the hospital and will be deported under the outrageous "Tory Riddance" scheme as soon as they recover. Our new governor, Lord William Campbell, arrived today but was shocked to be coldly received, taken to his residence and subsequently ignored. Lacking means of enforcement, he can do nothing.

Charles Town is readying for war. Privateers have not only been dispatched to the West Indies for gunpowder, they have resorted to thievery. At St. Augustine, they captured a munitions-laden ship in the harbor and are now distributing the gunpowder here.

Rumours persist that the British are arming Catholics, slaves and Indians to turn on us but there is nothing to support this. The many slaves and the few others nearby are being *treated cruelly as bands of ruffians try to substantiate the false tales.*

My only encouragement comes from your letters. How can our affection be anything but strong, dear Landon, when our beliefs about the events around us are so similar? The situation here is so dismal. I need you.

Goodnight, my charming swain,
Melinda

July 21st, 1775

Wandering dispiritedly through the city this morning, I was torn between Lord Chatham's orders that I stay with the Congress until adjournment and Melinda's need for me now. She so occupies my mind I can think of little else.

Nearing Dr. Kearsley's house, I saw a noisy crowd gathering before it. As I approached, the doctor opened the door and two ill-dressed militiamen seized him. After some exchange of words I could not hear, the angered doctor shook himself loose and turned to re-enter the house. When one of the young idiots lowered his bayonet and thrust it at him, Kearsley deflected it with his hand and received a deep cut below the thumb. Then they forced him onto a waiting cart and hauled him around town in a humiliating fashion, displayed with a sign reading, "Object of the resentment of the public."

Dr. Kearsley was livid with rage and indignation, and completely fearless. He stood up in the cart, hatless and his wig askew, bloody from his wound, and cursed the mob about him until he was hoarse and perspiring.

I followed this outrage at a distance, wanting in nerves to do anything to help him.

At one street corner, when Dr. Kearsley asked for some punch, I could refrain no longer and brought a bowl to him. He drank it in noisy gulps, so great was his thirst and discomfort. Since he was barely able to stand, I asked the wretches to release him, a true servant of the sick.

At my insistence, they returned him to his doorstep and the carting was over. He strode in the door and slammed it shut. The drunken idiot with the bayonet then turned the blade on me. I drew saber, parried the thrust and put the tip of my blade at his throat in an instant. Others intervened and the crowd dispersed.

This is the anarchy that Republicanism produces.

July 22nd, 1775

Today another opportunity to cultivate loyal subjects and another encouragement to resign my position with Lord Chatham. Mr. Galloway invited me to join him and Mr. Jay of New York to see a stage play and have dinner. This "Synagogue of Satan", as the Quakers term it, is located just outside the city limits (being illegal and sinful within) in Southwark. Shakespeare's "Midsummer Night's Dream" was the sinful drama and agreeably well done.

We returned to Peg Mullin's Beefsteak House where Mrs. Galloway and Naomi joined us. All oppose independence but Naomi is too outspoken for one of her sex. She is more an ally of the Quakers than an actual one. The Galloways invited me to visit their country seat tomorrow.

The new encouragement to resign my position with Lord Chatham was a rifle ball embedded in the brick wall opposite the window in my chamber. It had passed through my cloak which I had hung with hat to dry before the window. The silhouette was obviously mistaken for me.

Decision! to escape these assassins I shall accept the opportunity to leave the city with the Galloways but upon return, leave for the south and take Melinda with me to England—if she will come.

July 23rd, 1775

Today the Galloways, with Naomi and I, went to Bucks County for a picnic and to see some country dances, but there was a larger purpose in the event. At the dances, barefooted young lasses in rural dress bobbed and spun about with their partners to fiddle music with the greatest of freedom and joy. Both braids and bosoms bounced enticingly.

There is a certain freedom of action among the females here not found in England. Even the young ladies from the city waded a small stream by removing shoes and tucking petticoats above their knees with the greatest indifference. Naomi flaunted bare shoulders until her aunt spoke to her.

With the picnic came a delicious portion of ice cream which we were obliged to earn in pairs. Whilst I labored to paddle an ever-stiffening mixture of milk concoction and crushed peaches, Naomi exercised a rocking device which moved the container up and down in a larger pot of salt and the last of the summer's ice storage.

Later the men gathered in Galloway's library for the purpose of planning tactics to thwart the independence movement. One gentleman by the name of Dr. Bancroft opened with a strong profession of loyalty to the King and led a toast to our Sovereign. The remainder of the conference was discussion without decision, but it was comforting to meet such able gentlemen and hear such quality of thinking. As an aside Bancroft spoke to Galloway about Naomi, referred to her as the "wench led astray by novel reading."

The Galloways stayed for the night but asked me to return Naomi and the coach to Philadelphia. Naomi is a fine blooming and affectionate girl but her Quaker beliefs are non-existent. First she sat very close to me and went to sleep on my shoulder, then slid to the horizontal and put her head in my lap. When we passed under a village street lamp, I could see she had loosed the strings of a tight bodice and the garment had fallen open to reveal more than a little of her well-rounded breasts.

The situation was altogether pleasant. The stars above and fireflies below gave the night a magical, sensual quality. Merciful God, the flesh nearly overcame the spirit. Am I not mortal? I should have deviated from my manner of sober regularity and really become a rake, but to enjoy her unsheathed risked an unwanted marriage or other unhappy complications with this bizarre female. Besides, it is Melinda I want.

July 24th, 1775

To thwart any assassin, last evening and again tonight I am in a different room and have a blanket covering the window until I extinguish the candles.

Nick and I spent the day working on horses and tackle. I wanted to have Mysty bled but Nick insists that it only weakens her. Bleeding would have prevented Mysty having another tantrum; she broke off a loose shoe and piece of hoof, right front. So Nick made a shoe, square rather than curved at the forward end, to fit the unusual hoof until it grew out. He's a clever man.

Moreso is the Irish blacksmith, O'Brian, who helped him. That gentleman can quote Shakespeare and read German and the Latin. The most foul circumstances forced him to choose between debtors' prison and seven years indenture here. In three more years this thrall plans to establish a school and send for his family. Melinda has said I am wrong about the Irish and the laws that suppress them and she is right.

July 25th, 1775

Ill winds flow into the newspapers from everywhere. The Continental Congress now has a "Continental Army," commanded by George Washington, and there's anarchy in the south. The S. Carolina delegation is unavailable, closeted, awaiting instructions from Charles Town.

July 26th, 1775

Two gentlemen, identifying themselves as Quakers John Roberts and Abraham Carlisle, came to my room this morning with Naomi and suggested I include in my letters to Lord Chatham information on American troops, military stores and other intelligence. I politely refused; I am in enough difficulty. With the knowledge of no one else, I'll continue my own military intelligence ledger and tell Chatham what I choose.

But how did they know of my letters to the Earl? Galloway must have sent them. There's a sinister mood here and the Congress is about to adjourn anyway.

Attempted a departure call on Franklin, discovered he has a secretary now, a Mr. Bingham. This nervous shifty-eyed fellow promises to be more nuisance than useful. He promised with secretive tones to tell Franklin I am gone.

July 30th, 1775 - Upper Marlborough

These four days have brought me here again to the scene of Wagoner Turner's murder. Nick suspects we are being followed again and I am wanting in nerves.

Merciful God, I am a prisoner again! This unhappy entry
I write on a scrap of paper by the light of a single candle in a
small windowless cellar. Only the Almighty knows.

———————⊷•◦◉◦•⊶———————

London
8 June 1775

My Romeo Landon:

*I trust you are successfully resisting any further advances of
this S. Carolina lady. She sounds most dangerous! As for my
female sport, I fear I erred somewhat in my affairs d'amour. I
had not entirely disengaged from Agatha when Isabel arrived on
the scene and they learned of each other. Now neither will
communicate with me in any way!*

*The news of bloodletting in a village named Lexington has
aroused Britain beyond all previous levels. The Parliament, the
news papers, the people everywhere talk of war. Britain is not
unlike a female animal which has delivered thirteen young, but is
unable or unwilling to sever the now superfluous cords to the
mother. The Parliamentary hawks do not recognize what has
happened. They cannot accept that the Massachusetts umbilical
is cut and the rest are soon to follow.*

*Mr. Lee is ecstatic. He believes this event and the British
reaction to it will bring foreign aid to American shores, if not
direct war on Britain itself.*

*A new development on the French spy Beaumarchais. He
wrote and presented before King Louis a popular play, The
Barber of Seville, which ridiculed envious nobles. They attempted
to be rid of this court intruder by involving him in a duel with one
of the best swordsmen in France, but Beaumarchais killed the
fellow. Then he returned to London to avoid prosecution.*

Mr Lee is in communication with this jackal, who may have been sent here by Foreign Minister Vergennes to arrange for military aid to the American colonies, and is filling his ear.

Keep me informed, Landon. I fear for your safety with those agents of Vergennes about. I remain your counselor en l'amour et politique.

Randolph

The Honorable Justice Martin Howard
New Bern, North Carolina
Written August 3rd, 1775

Sir:

Knowing your interest in Landon Vickers, I feel an obligation to present you with a memoir of a calamitous event, as reported by his manservant, Nick. I repeat this bizarre tale at length in the hope that you can offer some explanation for such an event.

On Monday last (July 31st) Landon and Nick were approaching the Potomac ferry landing when suddenly assaulted by four highwaymen, one of them the one-eyed "Goose" O'Neil. Nick put the spurs to his mount and escaped with the pack horse carrying Landon's rifle and journal entries.

But they captured Landon and led him, blindfolded, off to the east. Nick galloped the two horses at a dead run until he realized no one was following him. Then he reasoned that if he crossed the river to tell me, the trail might be lost. Behind him was the man who gave him freedom, nursed him when he was ill. He had to help him.

Nick tethered the pack horse where no one would notice it, took the long rifle, powder and ball and a knife and carefully followed his own tracks back to the ambush spot. No one was there but the trail of the rogues was clear.

Nick followed them discreetly until they reached a small log farmhouse and took their captive inside. Finding no way to approach the building unseen, he tethered his mount back in the forest, returned on foot to the edge of the clearing and waited.

As soon as it was quite dark the faithful servant slipped up to the cabin. O'Neil showed him where his master was by raising a cellar trap door and drunkenly starting down a ladder with a whip.

But the others, shouting they wanted to keep Landon alive for a reward, dragged the one-eyed blackguard back up.

Nick could find no outside entrance to the cellar, so he began to dig quietly with a shingle and his knife to tunnel under the loose stone wall. After about an hour of tedious labor in sandy soil, he saw a horseman return. The three others went out to greet him and Nick crept to the corner to listen. The message was that the smuggler, Silas Grover (whom you may have heard of), wanted to see Landon down by the river in the morning. Then they were to drown him and dump the body midstream.

They returned to the cabin. Nick heard his master moan from a kick and saw the four reassemble on the main floor to indulge in a jug of spirits.

The loyal servant dug furiously and silently in the sandy soil until he found the base of the wall and tunneled under it. When Nick reckoned the tunnel was big enough, Landon started to enter it the very instant the trap door above swung open. Landon sprawled over the hole to keep them from seeing his escape route. O'Neil stood above him laughing and foully cascaded on his back!

After the door slammed shut, Landon tried the tunnel but with leg irons it was impossible. Nick enlarged the hole, then came inside and dug into the dirt floor like a madman. It was *nearly dawn when they finally emerged. Nick picked Landon up in his powerful arms and carried him to the woods edge.*

They had to remove the leg irons. With an axe and an iron wedge found at the cabin, Nick straightened the pin and freed Landon with a single blow. The ring of metal reverberated throughout the forest but no sound came from the cabin.

When Nick insisted on returning for Landon's mount, Landon whispered "You simple black jackass. You'll get us both killed."

Nick told me he answered: "If I be simple black jackass and get away from them, come back save you, what that make you?" A point well taken.

The impudent servant returned to the cabin. Landon took the loaded rifle to the edge of the clearing to protect him. Nick slipped over to the horses, singled out Landon's, still saddled, led her away.

But they were discovered. O'Neil was at the corner of the cabin quietly watching Nick. Landon put his sight on O'Neil and when the blackguard raised a musket and aimed at Nick, Landon fired. After the smoke cleared, O'Neil was on the ground, not moving. They mounted and galloped off to the Potomac ferry and across.

For three days now Landon has been recovering here. His whole body is bruised, his ribs pain him with every breath and a twisted arm still aches. He was nearly killed and may have killed a man himself.

I send you this confidential epistle with a trusted packet boat captain. Perhaps Landon will share with you the reason for this assassination attempt. He will not share it with me and he is in extreme danger.

Your Servant, Sir
John Carlyle

Nick found the base of the wall and tunneled under it.

JOURNAL FOR AUGUST 1775

August 5th, 1775 - Alexandria

With Nick's blessed help, I escaped some venomous hoydens hired by Grover to kidnap and kill me. Nick saved my life and I told him so. He is not at all simple; he is exceedingly clever. Do not care to dwell on it.

For three days now have been recovering at Uncle John's. Although my bruised body is not ready, I leave tomorrow for South Carolina. Will be traveling with four Scottish highlanders. Erroneously believing Virginia was loyal to the King, they came here to purchase munitions and Uncle John is reluctantly allowing them to hide in the cellar tonight.

Encoded letter from Randolph, attached, indicates all this is hopeless anyway. As for his tale on Beaumarchais, like Chatham, I view Beau as just another goddam little frog. But how can I get the frogs from jumping on my back?

Lord Chatham agreed to pay for my expenses as well as salary and sent another handsome £ 90 to increase my reserve. I wrote a response and left it with Uncle John to dispatch. To look more "American" in homespun clothes, I bought two osnaburg shirts, one pr. buckskin riding breeches and two diaper towels for 10s.

August 11th, 1775 -Charlotte, North Carolina

Nick and I rode out of Alexandria with the Scottish Highlanders like a band of robbers escaping the law, and stayed with them all the way to their home in North Carolina. Pursued by four mounted rebels, we rode to the west until we reached a village named Washington because young George the surveyor laid it out. I wager that after he's hanged, nothing will be named after him.

The rebels were gaining on us, so the Scots deployed an ambush at a grist mill without the village and told me to ride on. I did so and looked back to see all four riders shot out of their saddles. Then I saw the red moustached Scottish leader stab to death two still alive. God Omnipotent, where were you? This cruelty sickens me.

From Washington we rode south through much wilderness until we reached Rowan County. I have never ridden so hard for so long. I suspect these men are not Carolina Scots but British soldiers. When one called the red-moustached leader "Sergeant McDowell", he was instantly silenced with a pointing finger. This man has an unconfinable baseness. When they commandeered a ferry, the machiavel even clubbed the owner with his musket butt for no reason. May virulent consumption catch him.

Fine generous Scots in Rowan County, highly desirous of supporting the King. Some mischief is brewing too, but they will not discuss any of it with me. Several times I overheard the name of their secret leader, Donald McDonald, and tried to get an audience with him, but they will not even admit he exists.

Housing, food and clothes are somewhat plain here but it is certainly not a land of rogues and whores as I had been told. There is some dependence on wild meats and fruits but they have gardens as well. One staple I cannot entertain a taste for is an Indian corn product, hominy grits. The most vexing nuisances are the oppressively hot days, unwholesome humidity and insects. By mid-day man and animal are drenched in sweat and blood-sucking ticks and stinging mosquitoes harass us. The nights are so shrill with unceasing insect noise, I sometimes want for sleep.

From the loyal North Carolina stronghold, Nick and I rode on to this town of Charlotte, in Mecklenburg County, where the political climate is the very opposite. This mob of rustics declared its independence from Britain more than three months ago and is preparing for war against its neighboring loyalist counties with a demonic fever.

I dare not express my thoughts except in this shorthand code. Franklin's charter saved my life again today.

And my proof of purchase of Nick probably saved his.

This inland route causes me to miss New Bern and Jst. Howard. I wanted to leave some journal entries in his strongbox and press him for more information about my parents. But even if I am a peasant's son, am I not still a gentleman? A man's status in America is what he makes it.

August 18th, 1775 - Charles Town

Damnation, Melinda's not here! She is in the country attending a funeral and should return tomorrow. Late last evening I arrived and lodged at Holliday's Inn, a public house with fair victuals, some choice liquors and a few inferior travelers who always seem to infest inns. I do have a private chamber with a pleasant breeze passing through opposing windows covered with kenting to keep out the insects. Charles Town is insufferably hot in August. This chamber with breakfast costs 7s per day.

Two execrable incidents today reminded me of what a foul and brutal world we live in and how little God intervenes. Holliday's was all whispers and furtive glances when I returned. Eventually Doctor Mulligan, loyal surgeon to the Province forts and garrisons, arrived and sensing our political kinships, allowed me to follow him to the cellar. There lying on a bench was a poor man in a most horrible condition. He was naked and remnants of tar and feathers were all over his body. Someone was shaving his head and my own Nick was spooning some broth into his mouth.

Holiday explained that this simple gunner at the fort made the mistake of expressing his loyalty to the King. Sons of Liberty led by Bennett McKee tarred and feathered him. Only evidence is the tar pot found still warm in Bennett's courtyard.

The doctor began to peel hardened tar from the poor man's loins, trying to save his genitals, while others held him steady. Although he had drunk a pint of rum to deaden his senses, he trembled with agony.

I ran outside, nearly vomiting. Holliday followed me looking a bit pale himself.

"Mr. Vickers, Doctor Mulligan is in grave danger himself. We've got to get him and the poor gunner aboard the King's ship before they are subjected to 'Tory Riddance.' With your papers you could safely escort him to a small boat that will be waiting tonight."

I was wanting in nerves to do it but agreed. Could not force myself to return to the room where they were operating on him. I wandered instead toward the outskirts of the town, wanting only to escape reminders of human cruelty.

But they could not be escaped. I came instead upon an even more tragic scene, a Negro standing on a scaffold. He was about to be hanged and then cremated in a huge fire already blazing nearby. The terrified victim was moaning and staring at the flames as a crowd pushed and squirmed to better witness the wretch choke to death.

An onlooker told me he is a freeman of some property and has been a symbol of hope to slaves and of rebellion to outnumbered slave owners. Whites are outnumbered 50 to 1 out in the country and fear a Negro insurrection. So they are going to hang him on some trumped up charge and burn the body to destroy every trace of him.

"But this is in violation of the law!"

His answer: "The Tories overlook the law when Negroes are involved. This man had no jury, no right to confront his accusers or produce witnesses, and is being subjected to a most cruel and unusual punishment. With independence will come genuine rights for the accused, even Negroes. God knows they need them."

I recorded this astounding answer that independence cures all ills. When the poor man began to wail piteously, I could not bear this scene either and fled.

God in Heaven, if you are there, why do you allow this? Where is the compassion Jesus Christ is supposed to have taught us? What is the meaning of mercy, of Christian love for one another, of Christianity itself? These warped practitioners of justice are criminals themselves. Is there no limit to our cruelty? It is mindless, boundless.

August 19th, 1775

Just after midnight I escorted the burned gunner (barely alive and carried by friends), Doctor Mulligan and his family to a small boat and safety without incident.

At the Heyward house this morning I found Melinda's blue-stocking mother and Bennett McKee, but Melinda had not come downstairs yet.

They received me quite coolly, did not even offer me a chair. I sat down anyway in one of the dining chairs with handsome carved back. Bennett wore a mourning arm band for the recent loss of his brother and, although remembering he had tarred the poor gunner, I expressed my condolences. He acknowledged my remarks and told me his older brother had died of the Yellowjack.

Mrs. Heyward entered and provided the only warmth to the scene. Attempting to extend the conversation, I asked her if she knew where I could inoculate Nick against Yellowjack. It is the scourge of the back country in the summertime and Negroes are said to be especially susceptible. I had it when a child and am now immune, but Nick has not. She took up the subject willingly but wanted to ask her husband.

The Gazette presented McKee with an opportunity to ridicule me. I had placed an advertisement in the news paper for sale of my boxwoods at 5s per foot of height but the printer had carelessly offered them at five per square foot.

Clod McKee taunted:

"Tell me, Mr. Vickers, why do you sell your boxwood by the square foot? An English custom?"

Knowing he was exploiting the editorial mistake to render me the fool, I replied with a mask most serious:

"Oh that's a very satisfactory method. Boxwoods are somewhat spherical and cast a circular shadow on the ground. I measure the diameter of the shadow and calculate the shaded area."

His mouth hung open a moment. "You jest."

"Not at all. However, their shapes being essentially spherical, I plan to sell them next year by the cubic foot. Now what would be the volume of your three-foot hemispherical tar pot? Would it be enough to cover a man with the boiling liquid?"

His face blanched, but when Mrs. Watkins suggested I return later, McKee opened the door for me and I had little choice but to depart.

Do not know why I do such things; they only create trouble for me. But did Melinda not appear because he had rendered her with child?

The bigoted bachelor was leaving as well. He followed me out and strode off to the green toward the uncertain sound of newly acquired drums. More of their silly drills with assorted weapons were in the offing.

After noon I returned to see Melinda but received a note instead that she would meet me secretly at a little cemetery at nine tonight.

I found the spot in daylight, not far from the river, then returned well before nine. It was a clear moonlit night and a fresh wind off the water kept us from being mauled by mosquitoes. Off to the west a lonely whippoorwill sounded. Melinda appeared with a servant woman—who retreated to a discreet distance.

I had not seen Melinda for five months; she was lovely in the moonlight and certainly not pregnant.

"I had almost forgotten how pretty you are."

She laughed at my remark but quickly became serious. She was shocked to hear my stories of yesterday's excesses and McKee's role in one of the crimes. When I discussed the possibility of our fleeing together to England, She rejected that but did explain that her parents have a plantation in the back country adjoining the McKee's and are trying to force her to marry him. Her father is absent, seeking a fortune near Fort Pitt, and she and her mother live with the Heywards when not working at the plantation.

The Watkins plantation must be in need of better management, but there's something else she's not telling me. Why doesn't her father return and tend to affairs here?

"Oh Landon, I am so lonely and frightened," she finally cried out, "I need you; don't you leave me!" Then she wept.

I could resist her no longer and gathered her in my arms to comfort her, called her my little "Whippoorwill". Her tears glistened in the moonlight and wet my face as I kissed her. She clung to me tightly and pressed her trembling body against me. This intimacy changed me from comforter to lover and I picked her up to carry her a few yards to a more secluded spot. At that moment, among fireflies and a bright moon, we clearly heard a whippoorwill in the distance.

That broke the spell. She insisted that I set her down and leave. Reluctantly I did so. I've been a fool again.

Thus do I write with despondent pen but I flatter myself that she begged that I not leave her.

August 20th, 1775

Knowing Melinda attends St. Michael's Church, I went there also, despite the stifling heat. The service was unusually lengthy with prayers for Yellowjack victims and for deliverance from the epidemic. Unmerciful God, were you listening?

She was there with the Heywards but without her mother. When the service was over she came straightaway to my side and we walked, without speaking or touching, down the aisle, through a doorway, down a hall and outside, entirely around the church, anywhere to avoid parting.

Again and again her eyes searched mine.

She started to speak, then deliberately opened an innocent subject when the Heywards approached. Accompanying them was a thin little man with bulging eyes and inward-pointing toes who slinked about like a cat.

It was Doctor Loocock, who has an inoculation service. He will treat Nick for two guineas, including insurance.

I looked at the feline doctor. "Insurance?"

"Yes, in case he dies. Enough to buy a replacement. My method is relatively safe," Loocock purred. "I've inoculated 463 this summer and have lost only four."

I agreed to it reluctantly but Nick may not.

"Mr. Vickers, I have invited the Heywards and Miss Watkins to dinner at my home," Dr. Loocock, purred again. "Would you like to join us?"

I accepted at once, to be with Melinda, and we turned to the carriages. Dr. Loocock rode ahead in his phaeton to his Broad Street house and I joined the Heywards and Melinda in their handsome imported coach.

We arrived to find four other friends of Loocock waiting to join us. His townhouse is more pretentious than the Heywards. Drawing room, dining room and parlour are all decorated with Chinese wallpaper and filled with Chippendale furniture from Philadelphia. A portrait of Loocock's wife, now deceased, gazed gravely upon the luxurious dinner party.

The feast was almost Roman in style with a profusion of foods, wines and fruits which deserves elaboration. The first course was a large whole fish baked, a chine of mutton, chicken pie, soup, and pudding with low spice sauce. The second included pigeons and rice-birds roasted, asparagus, cauliflower, fillet of veal with mushrooms and high sauce, sweetbreads, syllabubs, and peach tarts.

The dessert was oranges and pineapples, coffee and madeira, rendering us cheerful and merry.

Richly dressed waiters served everything on finely wrought silver and china. The silver implements were engraved like the Carlyle's with a commemoration of the repeal of the Stamp Act a decade ago.

My host, who had changed into a scarlet waistcoat trimmed with gold lace, and other guests asked me politely about England and we discussed theater and the arts. There was no mention of politics, the bloodshed in the North or anything unpleasant. The scene was one of denial of reality. Everyone in the room knew this gracious life was coming to an end, yet the subject was avoided.

I had only eyes for Melinda. We touched toes under the table and exchanged glances until we must have been obvious.

After dinner the gentlemen retired to the drawing room. I had expected the conversation to shift to the rebellion in the North but the only concern of these fashionable fops was that the troubles denied them the usual summer in Rhode Island. They discussed the Yellowjack, the high price of firewood, the slovenly service of the scavengers who fail to collect the garbage regularly, the addition of more street lamps, the renovation of the ballroom in the New Exchange, complaint that night watchmen no longer have permits to sell spirits and calumnies about persons absent. The more they drank, the more they deplored minor inconveniences to their lives.

When those who could walk (one was debauched by rum) joined the ladies in the parlor, Melinda played on the harpsichord while another lady wavered with voice off-key. Never had a chance to speak to Melinda privately again.

To bed. It's miserably hot and I'm grateful for the kenting that welcomes air and refuses mosquitoes.

August 21st, 1775

Melinda discovered me at the Heyward door this morning. The funeral of Thomas Elfe, furniture maker, was today and this was also the day for collection of clothes for the poor—she repairs the garments—but we dwelled on other things.

Melinda consented to a ride with me tomorrow while McKee and her mother are at the Watkins Plantation. Her hands pull nervously at each other when she dwells on his interest in the property.

With some trepidation I have watched for any indication that I am being followed but see none. And since there is no hope of reconciliation with Britain, how can I be a threat to the French?

August 22nd, 1775

Delicious day with Melinda! With the advice of Holidays cook, made my first apple pie, then printed on the crust with sugar dressing "Je t'aime" and "Mon Petit Engoulevent." This means, according to Holliday's French wife, "I love you, my little Whippoorwill." Then added it to a picnic basket.

With a rented carriage I foolishly tried to drive Melinda to the Whippoorwill Plantation, but the trail was too rough and tedious and we did not even reach the first immigrant tracts.[*]

At noon I turned into a pleasant glade, spread a blanket, erected a tent of kenting to keep out insects and placed the victuals before her.

She was delighted. We drank a toast of madeira to the seventh monthly anniversary of my first kissing her in Williamsburg and then followed it with the pie. We talked and laughed and teased—Oh, she was lovely.

I sat behind her, leaning against a tree, pulled her to me until her back was against me and closed my arms about her. She was tense at first and then relaxed against me. For a long time neither of us moved, not wanting to disturb the moment.

I became increasingly intimate but restrained myself when she turned to me, dropped a strawberry into my hand and said:

"If I offer you a strawberry, take it; there's no harm. But if I offer you my love, take care, do not abuse."

Then she wept, said our liaison was destined to end. What's the reason for this dark despairing premonition?

I love to be with her even when she is sad. Her comeliness bewitches me but her intellect, character and wit are equally to be admired. The total emotion is love. Is there any emotion—fear, hate, envy, ambition—stronger? Love is God's gift that differentiates us from the animals.

---

[*] *To encourage back country settlement, immigrants, if Protestant, could claim fifty acres per person at no cost and receive a small bounty for early expenses. (Catholics and atheists were excluded.) R.E.H.*

Her remark about my abusing her offer of love haunts me. She read a poem she wrote entitled *Strawberries*, elaborating the point. Tis a gentle chiding sermon I cannot ignore.

August 23rd, 1775

Nick accompanied me to Doctor Loocock's hospital to be inoculated for the Yellowjack and was as reluctant as I expected. Afterwards I walked down to the Heywards.

Passing by the carriage house I heard voices within and hesitated by the windowless wall. Mr. Heyward's voice was hushed but dominant. Fragments heard and shorthanded:

"Governor Wright must know by now."

"He cannot possibly know."

"But it's obvious the mail has been tampered with."

"We have been very careful. What we need now is a courier to deliver the documents to Governor Wright."*

There was a moment of silence.

"I think perhaps I have the man," Heyward offered. "There is a young gentleman, Landon Vickers, with excellent references from Mr. Franklin, who is visiting us. He wants to go to Savannah; let him take them."

A lump of fear settled in my chest and my heart pounded. I quickly retreated and entered the house from the front. Melinda welcomed me in, but, as I feared, I was soon alone in

---

* *Unknown to Governor Wright of Georgia, his mail was passing through the hands of patriots in Charles Town and being altered. When he wrote General Gage pleading for troops and a warship to maintain British sovereignty, they substituted a letter informing General Gage that events were going very well in Savannah.* R.E.H.

the library with Mr. Heyward. He asked me, in effect, to act as a spy for the South Carolina rebels.

What else can I do?

Heyward invited me to stay for dinner and a concert afterwards. Fortunately I was dressed adequately for the events and could accept. Proper clothes for every occasion are difficult to produce when one is living in the saddle and attempting to harmonize with the community where he finds himself.

The evening would have been delightful, but for my foreboding. It was a St. Cecelia Society concert, for subscribers and guests only. The orchestra included four violins, two base violas, a harpsichord (Melinda playing) and a French horn.

Melinda and her friend Ruth Craig surprised everyone and shocked not a few by presenting choral music with some two dozen Negro children. Dressed in bright blue uniforms, these glee singers were trained and led by Melinda herself while Ruth played the harpsichord. They sang from memory three selections, including *Since First I Saw Your Face* (with a warm smile to me from Melinda), then marched out smartly.

Several of Charles Town's cultured were there and all appear to be loyal to Britain.

But Heyward is with the "patriots". Neither his wife nor Melinda appear to acknowledge it but I did hear him caution Melinda that the Sons of Liberty do not take kindly to her "fraternizing" with slaves. The Sons fear the slaves, spread rumors that loyalists are arming them.

One of the St. Cecelia members, Mr. Gifford, wants to show me some gentlemen's pursuits tomorrow.

August 24th, 1775

Nick is faring well and should leave the hospital tomorrow. He is struggling with a book, *The Life and Strange Surprising Adventures of Robinson Crusoe*, that Dr. Loocock gave him. Just another example of the loyalists ignoring the law which prohibits teaching slaves to read. Nick asks me the meaning of a firkin of words every time I see him and wants to know now if he is my man Friday.

Mr. Gifford took me today to the lush *Sign of the Bacchus* for lunch and horse races at the *Carolina Jockey Club*. Dinner was at some smoke-filled tavern on a shabby portion of Pinckney's Street.

I did not understand the choice of tavern at first. It is next to a public house for raising orphans and bastards and the debtors' prison. The independence-minded would eliminate the latter and then there would be no incentive to meeting one's responsibilities. The whole fabric of society would be unraveled.

The dining establishment is a disorderly tippling and gaming house where the ignorant are entertained and debauched. The atmosphere was, on the whole, unsavory. Then Gifford led me across the street to Mary McDowell's brothel.

The moment I stepped into that parlor of peripatetic whorearchy, I knew where I was and retreated, but not before I saw Bennett McKee himself coming down the stairs. That king of codpieces sneered some comment about sandlapper children not being allowed. I returned to my inn.

Do not understand Gifford's actions today. Was I being tested? Whatever the reason, I will not let Melinda marry that philistine. Having observed this malevolent fornicator in the strongest light, I'll kill him first.

August 25th, 1775

I must go to Savannah. Chatham's statue in the square haunts me with "Duty, Integrity, Country". That cold marble figure reminds me of a very intense and sick old man who is fruitlessly trying to hold the British Empire together and protect the rights of British Americans at the same time. I must try to do my duty, I must.

Nick has dysentery and cannot travel. Methinks it is Loocock's well water, quite brackish and unwholesome. I fetched good water from Egan's Brewery and told Nick to drink only that.

Hello! A handsome carriage is delivering a young gentleman to the tavern below. Cannot see his face but he is rather well dressed. Footsteps on the stairs; he must be coming here.

Midnight.

Alas, I did have a visitor and I nearly shot him until I realized he was Charles Rutledge, secretary in the South Carolina House and suitor to Ruth Craig.

He wanted to discuss details of my being courier of the King's mail to Savannah, then invited me to a complain lunch.

First he complained about how the threat of revolution was spoiling the good life. American fox hunting, originated here, is virtually at an end. Horse racing, cock fighting, the theater, education in England, importation of fine furniture and clothing is all but ended.

"If any pastime pleases the better families," he moaned, "it is labeled Toryism and is to be done away with."

He reflected on that a moment.

"One good effect of those silly Congressional prohibitions," he added, "is abandonment of some quite unnecessary activities, such as the establishment of a tax funded public college. Almost any urchin could have entered and learning would have become cheap and much too common. Every backwoodsman would be for giving his son an education."

"Mr. Jefferson of Virginia would do it," I retorted. "He would like to develop an aristocracy of virtue and talent based on universal education rather than of family heritage. He argues there is rich potential...."

"Nonsense. We've tried to help the poor here. Last year we committed £11,000 to public charity and ragged sandlappers poured in from the back country to live on it. They flooded the workhouse and hospital for the poor and filled our streets. We hired wagons to return some of them."

I brought the self-righteous fellow back to the subject at hand. He told me I could leave by the sloop *Sally* Tuesday next and gave me instructions on obtaining the mail.

Then a most disturbing twist in the conversation.

He asked if I knew Silas Grover.

I must have turned pale. For a moment I couldn't speak, not knowing why this man knew of him.

He explained there is a warrant for his arrest for smuggling gunpowder and some of it is coming through Charles Town. A vagabond whom Charles suspects is employed by him is inquiring as to my whereabouts! He has never actually seen the man; says his name is Hammond Gorrie.

Rutledge is gone now and I am left only with my fears. Melinda indisposed; did not see her today.

August 27th, 1775

The day began with rain but I joined Melinda at church. I am quite accepted by the Heywards now and sat in their pew.

The service included holy communion, in which I had not partaken for a long time. Did not intend to today until she started forward. I hesitated, then knelt with her at the rail for the wrong reason. I wanted to be in her presence, not God's. I glanced at her face for an instant, saw her look upward, then close her eyes as her lips moved in prayer. Oh how I loved her and yearned for a faith like hers.

When the loaf was passed she took a fragment, passed it to me and said as the others "The Bread of Life and I forgive you." May my future behavior be such that she will always forgive me.

The preacher refrained from mentioning the political chaos and concentrated on violations of the Sabbath.

A bloodbath is about to descend upon us and he is worried about commerce on Sunday!

And commerce there is.   Today loaded Conestoga wagons drawn by the biggest horses I have ever seen continued to roll in from the back country. Merchants have huge yards behind their warehouses to accommodate them with their loads of deerskins, flour, tobacco and other products. The American colonies will never collapse for lack of trade with Britain.

This afternoon the rain stopped and I took Melinda for a walk along the waterfront. We sat on a bench in silence.

Knowing I was still concerned about abandoning the clergy, she asked what progress I had wrought in "healing the painful anxiety of a wounded conscience." I confessed to little improvement and chose to tell her also about the unknown origin of my parents. She was most understanding. The rest of the conversation I remember acutely.

"But you, Landon," she finally said, "you are going away and I'll never see you again. The premonition is strong."

"Not so. I'm returning to Charles Town as soon as I can."

"And then what?"

"I'll take you away with me," I blurted.

"I can't do that. But I must avoid marrying Bennett. Where could I go to study music and French?"

"Go to William and Mary; you remember your conversation with the professors at the College. There's the organist at Christ Church and the French professor Mirabeau. They are probably available for tutoring women in private homes. I'll take you there."

"My mother wouldn't..."

"Bring Aunt Elizabeth with you."

Her eyes regularly shined with that suggestion.

"Oh, Landon," Melinda laughed excitedly, "she might just do it. Uncle Thomas is returning to the Continental Congress and I could stay with her in Williamsburg. That was her home before she married and she still has a house and mill there!"

"Then it's settled. I'll be back from Savannah in a fortnight and I'll go with you to Williamsburg. I'm obliged to go on to Philadelphia but I can easily return to Williamsburg, and frequently!"

"I'll ask Aunt Elizabeth but I think she wants to go."

Melinda looked at me with a softness of eye, with a dimpled smile that I can only interpret as affection.

"Uncle Thomas will be traveling by coach; doesn't dare go by sea. If intercepted by a British warship he could be arrested for attending the Continental Congress."

A strange man is across the street. He has dark hair and homespun clothes and he is looking at this building as he slowly walks past, but I cannot see his face. Is he my pursuer? I am going after Nick.

Midnight and Nick is here. He is still not recovered but is already asleep on a pad directly in front of the bolted door. Epistled to Lord Chatham; no copy saved.

August 28th, 1775

The *Sally* sails for Savannah tomorrow. Nick will stay with Holliday. I do not want to taunt the sea again. Cannot forget the *Sophia* breaking both mizzen yard and fore top gallant off Old Point Comfort in frightful weather.

Will be seeing Melinda this evening.

August 29th, two o'clock in the morning.

It is late but I must record my amorous experience. Called on Melinda and was pleased to find both her mother and Bennett elsewhere. I conferred with Mr. Heyward privately. When I brought up the subject of my accompanying his coach to Williamsburg, he was entirely willing. Mrs. Heyward had already convinced him she should live in Williamsburg with Melinda while he attended to his Congressional duties.

I wanted to be alone with Melinda and thought the Heywards would never retire but they finally did. We talked and played whist but we knew we might be seen from the street. When she shyly suggested we retire to her drawing room on the third floor, and remove our shoes so as not to awaken the Heywards, I removed mine so enthusiastically I broke a buckle.

She took me by the hand and led me up to the enclosed stairway on the right side of the hall, away from the Heyward's bedroom. Past her mother's bedroom (empty of course) we tiptoed through her bedroom to the front of the house where she has her own sitting room.

We had the entire floor to ourselves and no one below us, if we stayed in the right rooms. The privacy was too tempting. I took her in my arms and kissed her until she broke away and went into the bedroom. Minutes later she emerged in a simple gown. I slipped off my coat and she came into my arms again.

Bless my soul, it was as intimate as the night at the water barrel. We sank to the rug and played with the fire of passion for some time. It is a fire as strong as hunger, thirst or the need to breathe.

She murmured softly throughout and yielded to me but I dared not become more intimate, fearing she would feel defiled and reject me tomorrow. She must have sensed this herself because she gently pushed me away and rose.

Walked back to the inn in a daze. Coming upstairs, I began to feel the ache and it still has not gone away.

How dare I record these experiences? To savor them.

August 30th, 1775

Did not sail for Savannah today. This morning Nick was so wrought with fever, I feared he had the Yellowjack. When I brought Dr. Loocock to him, he gave Nick over for dead and began to discuss the insurance payment. I sent the slinking fraud out and promised to thrash him into oblivion should Nick not survive.

Straightaway I found Charles Rutledge, told him I was not going to Savannah and that he should go.

Charles protested but finally agreed to go if Mr. Charbonneau, his superior, approved. That gentleman did approve and an hour later the disconcerted Charles found himself standing in the rain aboard the *Sally*.

August 31st 1775

Melinda joined me in caring for Nick today, most abnormal for a young lady of her station. But there is little about her that adheres to normality for its own sake. She had a servant cover him with only a wet sheet and then cool him with a huge room fan hung from the ceiling. Every person about, remembering his gentle treatment of the tortured gunner, operated the fan in turn.

Despite the continuing rain, after dark Melinda took me by the hand and led me to the darkened church, where for Nick's soul and health we prayed. I was reaching for a candle and prayer book to find an appropriate petition when she chided me to "Leave the word crutches behind."

A most startling but reasonable suggestion, in spite of my skepticism that prayer is nothing but self delusion. I joined her in praying both silently and aloud until the town clock struck ten. Then we returned to Nick to find him without senses, scarcely breathing, responding to nothing. Holiday shook his head to my silent query and retired. Alone with Melinda I sit writing these words and watching a faithful servant and companion slip away despite all treatments and all entreaties to his Creator.

Charles Town
September 1st, 1775

Blessed Cassandra,

For the past two days I have aided Landon in attempting to save his manservant—sickened by a faulty inoculation which has given him the Yellowjack. Further the doctor applied a corrosive when a lenitive would have sufficed. We have worked with the pitiable fellow and prayed for him—yes, prayed for a Negro—but at this writing I know not whether he will survive.

So you have retreated from prying eyes! And when do you expect the issue? I trust you will forgive me for sharing with

Ruth your diversion that you should now ride through the Parish as Lady Godiva! You have an impish character!

I must confide in you thoughts I cannot express elsewhere. My sweet Landon has been here for nearly a fortnight and we are at last getting truly acquainted. Unfortunately the treasonable Bennett plays the role of injured cuckold, yet he is neither my husband nor have I surrendered my virtue to anyone.

Landon and I have had several private times—lovely times—together. I confess I have engaged in some intimacies which I pray my guardian angel will not record, but only shed a tear of charity.

I have not the courage to explain to him my dilemma. He knows my marriage to Bennett would join our properties but nothing further have I revealed. Landon has pleaded with me to return to England with him when he completes his duty. The dear gentleman also suggested that he and I accompany Aunt Elizabeth to Williamsburg, that I enroll with tutors from the College for the education I desire. I intend to do so; Bennett's presence suffocates me. Write to me there; address to Madam Elizabeth Heyward, University Commons.

Oh Cassandra, would that you could meet Landon and give me counsel. Mother is convinced he is taking advantage of me—that he will abuse my blind trust in him. Aunt Elizabeth thinks not. Where is the truth? These thoughts and handing him a strawberry once inspired a poem which I gave to him. I send you a fair copy. Please deplore neither my want of poetic talent nor obsession with him.

We rejoice for you and await the blessed news. I am with purist affection and anticipation your

Melinda

STRAWBERRIES

If I hold out my open palm
With a fresh strawberry on it,
Take it, take it gratefully;
And the palm? leave a kiss upon it.
For if I offer food or drink
With a kind inviting smile,
Accept it, yes accept it
And linger yet awhile.
Strawberries, food or drink are just
As transient as a dream
And leave behind just memories.
But even so they seem
To build a cord between us of
Increasing size and strength,
A cord of understanding, yes,
And even love at length.
But should I offer love in time,
Take care, do not abuse;
For love is tender, can be crushed;
Exploiting it can lose
The special thrill of outstretched palm
With a ripe strawberry on it.

JOURNAL FOR SEPTEMBER 1775

September 1st, 1775

God forgive me for not trusting in Thee. This morning at sunrise Nick startled me awake by asking for water. With the wet sheet and the cool breeze off the harbor his fever had subsided and he had survived the night.

By noontime he had taken a little soup and by tonight some bread as well. Perhaps God does care for us and does listen to our prayers—Melinda's anyway. That darling angel stayed with us the entire night despite risk to reputation, administering to him and writing to a friend in England. One drunken Son of Liberty did call us "Tories" for our efforts.

Randolph would say God placed resistance to disease in Nick's veins when he was born and this outcome is the natural result of an unnatural event, assault by disease. But why did God create the disease?

September 2nd, 1775

Tended to Nick today and saw to the horses. Melinda is at her parents' country seat with Aunt Elizabeth preparing for travel. Mr. Heyward had to precede us with the other delegates to attend the Second Continental Congress.

September 3rd, 1775 - Mueller's Farm

Nick being in full recovery but too weak to travel, and Melinda's home being half the distance to my property, I am determined to take her to Whippoorwill tomorrow.

So here I lodge for the night in the crude pine log home of Rhinelander Mueller. His 150 acre parcel lies between the

Watkins and another plantation and he employs only family members to hunt and fish and to raise corn, peas, cauliflower in uncongenial sandy soil for the Charles Town market.

His sandy environment has earned him and his neighbors the derisive term Sandlapper but he is proud of it. The wife cuts and stitches all the clothes for the six children. I see only three books in the house, an English Bible, a spelling book and a basic primer of mathematics, from which the children are being taught. They are unaware of the political struggle; time is spent in provision for the day at hand.

For a guinea Mueller is using his wagon and two sturdy work-horses to haul tools and materials to Whippoorwill and will help me repair the cabin for three days. We'll take Melinda along for the first day if she will come.

September 4th, 1775

When I appeared at the Watkins seat, a decaying farm, Melinda was outside laboring over a boiling pot of indigo blue, dyeing osnaburg clothes for her little slave singers one last time before she departs. She was a trifle ill-dressed and wood-smoke soiled, but her surprised and happy demeanor overcame embarrassment and she charged me forthwith to hanging the blue items on a hempline whilst she made ready to join me. I could hear angry voices inside but she and Aunt Elizabeth prevailed.

We found the old trail which led past the cabin and the boxwood plantation. Mueller began to repair the cabin roof while the two of us made the final climb to the glade, tarried there and enjoyed a picnic.

Melinda wore a charming bodice and skirt which displayed her figure to advantage and captured my eyes all to often. Finally she laughed outright at my stares.

"You approve of my dress, Mr. Vickers?" she teased.

"You,—you must be very lovely," I stammered with some embarrassment; then abruptly took her in my arms.

She yielded to my intimacies only for a few moments. Even then she was most gentle and sweet in her refusal. In a melting accent she whispered she desired to come to me some some day, though unlikely. Meanwhile, prove myself a gentleman. Then the silent tears flowed.

Misunderstanding, I apologized for my forwardness but the tears were about her unfortunate family situation.

Again I asked her to marry me and again she was elusive. She reminded me of her unhappy obligation to Bennett, which she seems unable to either discard or explain. She's also concerned that I'm Franklin's agent and therefore potentially treasonable. When she accused me of evasiveness regarding employment, I accused her of evasiveness about her marriage obligation and our conversation became an argument.

We sat there in silence. As it began to grow dark, Mueller called to suggest we depart.

Then we heard a distant whippoorwill begin its repetitious call. The air was warm and still and the lonely sound carried to the far ridge line of trees. It echoed through the forest and my soul as I thought of my mother listening for a whippoorwill at this very spot. I was nigh to tears when it ceased and the faint echo died. Then Melinda astonished me by placing her forefingers between her lips and imitating it perfectly with a shrill response. I looked at her wide-eyed, started to speak, but she put a finger to my lips.

In a moment it called again, this time a little closer and she responded to that. She coaxed the little bird in until it no doubt discovered we were frauds and the hill became silent again. An evening I'll not soon forget.

Returned her home after the warmest embrace and took me to Muellers.

September 6th, 1775 - Charles Town

Mueller and I labored two days shingling the cabin roof and cleaning weeds off the boxwoods. Sore muscles remind me I actually did it.

Nick is reasonably well and the horses are ready. I do pray Charles returns from Savannah before I depart. Must inform Chatham of Georgia's status.

September 7th, 1775

Alarming news: One fatigued, frightened and furious Charles Rutledge appeared at my door. His report recorded:

"You nearly got me killed, Landon Vickers. Someone on the *Sally* must have assumed I was you. I had not bothered to exchange my name for yours on the manifest and someone sought to enter my cabin more than once. When we arrived in Savannah Harbor, despite the late hour and a heavy rain, my cabinmate and I wasted no time; we escaped in the ship's dingy. It was half full of water and we bailed it out with a firkin, but the wooden cask was clumsy and someone heard us.

"He came to the ship's side with a lantern and, just as we were about to cast off, the sailor who had been watching me on board saw me. He aimed a pistol directly at my face and pulled the trigger. But as I nearly filled my breeches, the wet flint failed to ignite. Landon, this had to be intended for you!

"He then drew a long dagger, dropped the lantern and leaped on me."

"Merciful God, Charles!"

"I drew sword and raised it just in time for him to jump blindly on to it. Oh Landon, I could feel the pitiless blade pass through his body to the hilt, just before the wretch fell on me and overset me into the water.

"We went under, but I clung to the sword and pushed him off of it with my feet, a horrid sensation. Without uttering a sound or making another motion, he simply disappeared into the dark water. The thrust must have killed him outright.

"The other fellow helped me in and we struck out for shore. There my compatriot hastily bid me goodbye and disappeared. He had enough of my company and I have had enough of yours. You're a danger to be around."

"Did you ever see Governor Wright?"

"Yes, I did. He's a distinguished gentlemen, but presiding over disaster. When he finished the letters he almost wept."

Charles went on to describe the Governor's plight. In spite of his counsel against it, Georgia sent delegates to the Second Continental Congress. What audacity for that arrogant body in Philadelphia to presume it represents the entire continent.

A mob exercised "Tory Riddance" on one of the tax collectors while Charles was there. Without warning ruffians threw him on board a ship just as it departed for St. Augustine.

Meanwhile Cherokees to the West threaten the colony.

Charles returned on a rented horse from the Williamson stable but warned me that if I am a Methodist to keep it to myself. When Williamson and his wife were preparing to marry they had a terrible argument with a Methodist priest by the name of John Wesley. Wesley wanted to marry the girl himself and became such a nuisance they put the law on him. So he fled to England and Williamson detests all Methodists.

Charles left with a warning about Indian attack during our trip and I confined myself with the doorbolt.

A letter to Lord Chatham, just finished, includes these events and a recommendation that I abandon this employment.

September 8th, 1775

More compulsion to escape, but this time with Melinda. I plan to meet the Heyward carriage tomorrow morning at the Cooper River lumber mill and depart for Williamsburg.

There's a uniformed figure waiting across the street, looking at my window. Another agent of Grover? I will not wait to find out.

Nick is well and happy to leave South Carolina. He can read and write more than a little now and is very quick to learn, to understand and to calculate. He has also taught me how to control Mysty with legs and spurs so as to have the hands free, how to ride long distances with minimum fatigue and how to survive in the wilderness.

Wrote Randolph of my latest adventures. What will he think of my employment now? Someone is knocking.

Midnight

Damnation, what else does Providence have in store for me? The caller was that uniformed figure on the street. Declaring himself an officer and acquaintance of Bennett McKee, he nervously informed me that McKee is deeply aggrieved and insulted by my actions and demands a gentleman's satisfaction.

I stood there in utter disbelief that this was happening to me, but I knew the meaning of the words. My jaw was stiff with fear but I tried to continue my stalwart demeanor.

"Be more explicit? I scarcely know Bennett McKee."

The young fellow was no less nervous than I.

"Lieutenant McKee states you have violated all standards of decency and morality by your attentions toward Miss Melinda Watkins, his betrothed. He charges you have publicly humiliated him and have, in all probability, corrupted and violated Miss Watkins."

"What! That ass!"

"He understands you now intend to remove the lady from Charles Town. He insists you will answer to him on the field of honor or he will have you arrested and tried for treason, alienation of his betrothed and kidnaping."

Seeking time to think, I blurted out with some bravado and deception:

"Notify Lieutenant McKee my representative will discuss the matter with you in the morning at nine. I rather think the field of honor should be before Mary McDowell's brothel. There he will have friends to cheer him on and properly dispose of the body with which they are so familiar."

He did not know how to respond to that, but turned on his heel and marched out stiffly, collided with the door, then the stair bannister and nearly fell down the steps, almost as terrified as I.

But I am the one to be shot at or run through; there's the rub! Moreover, I am not the least concerned about the condition of McKee's pride. That's his difficulty, not mine.

As for the corruption of Melinda, I have not, I could not. Even so, that is also none of his affair, this libertine who frequents brothels and tortures loyal citizens. She should be free of him, even if her parents have arranged this. Why does her mother have such a hold on her? Such a parental arrangement is an archaic old European custom anyway. This is America.

I shall ignore McKee. By nine in the morning I shall be gone and he may think what he will. To meet him is at the least inconvenient to my schedule and at most, dangerous. I have no facility with dueling weapons and consider the pastime stupid and criminal, especially since I am involved!

As for his threat of arrest and other damages, tis a firkin of flatulence. Let him queue up with my other enemies.

September 12th, 1775 - Corbin Plantation.

Reached here safely and happy to be within a perimeter of encamped militia. Before dawn, Nick tied hempsacks on the horses hooves to muffle their sound and we quietly led them to the edge of town. We left Charles Town without incident, crossed the Cooper River upstream at the lumber mill and met the Heyward coach on the main road after they crossed. The driver told me someone followed them as far as the ferry, then abandoned them. He was also worried about rumors of Indian attack and we soon learned had reason to be.

Melinda was curious about our crossing separately, but I avoided a direct answer. I dislike being anything but candid with her, but did not admit that I had fled from a duel.

A duel with him would have been no less unnerving than this morning's experience. At Mile 46 a wild-eyed man came riding in from the west on an exhausted mount followed by a half-dozen Cherokee Indians. As we reached for weapons, the Indians quickly surrounded us but did not assault. They just waited while the distraught wretch described how they tortured his twelve-year-old nephew to death. The Indian children hurled burning pitch pine darts into his flesh until he died.

The uncle's role was to deliver the message that if the provincial government did not provide the gunpowder as agreed and keep the white settlers out, they would make war again and spare no one.

A moment of tense silence followed. I looked at their French muskets and moved deliberately to Melinda's window to see her wide-eyed and Aunt Elizabeth weeping uncontrollably. I nodded at their leader and indicated that we would take their hostage and the message to the next town. He nodded in return and turned his mount away. Others began to follow, but one rode past me to the coach, snatched ·

the door open and seized Melinda by the wrist. What he intended to do next I never learned because my instinct overcame all fears.

When I slammed my rifle barrel down on his forearm, he snatched a tomahawk and raised it to bury it in my skull. I countered by jamming the rifle muzzle into his face. Everyone expected gunfire but the Cherokee leader held up his palm in a gesture of truce and ordered the offending savage to withdraw. In a few moments the renegades had disappeared and we proceeded.

Thus have the Cherokees become vulnerable to French collusion. But my whole being was quivering when it was over and I shudder to imagine how the incident could have ended.

We're staying here because the Corbins and Mrs. Heyward are old friends and the militia is still about.

September 16th, 1775 - New Bern, North Carolina

After seven days of hard traveling, frequently through standing water, we arrived here at dusk. With four strong coachers we must have achieved a record, but both horses and riders are fatigued.

Traveling with Melinda makes an otherwise disagreeable journey pleasurable. Our overnight accommodations were often less than indifferent, but she never complained. And the necessary stops, ladies to the left woods, gentlemen to the right, she always accomplished with decorum. When a wheel nearly came off near Wilmington, she was very high spirited about it and even helped to hold up the coach as we repositioned it. And in the evenings she often answered whippoorwills with that perfect imitation of hers. Am I in such an emotional state that I can find no wrong in her? Has she no flaws? Yes, sometimes she is a victim of melancholia.

My horsemanship is improving. Unfortunately, the one time I was unhorsed, Mysty was standing still beside the coach and I had the shortened reins tightly wrapped about my fist. A big animal, she abruptly reached down to graze and pulled me down her neck before I could get my hand free. Heels over head, I ended up sitting on the ground before a curious horse and a laughing Melinda. Remembering that I slid off Mysty's rump when first in Charles Town, she gleefully suggested:

"Why don't you try dismounting off the side rather than either end!"

I generally rode before the coach with Nick but was invited a few times to ride inside until the mare and I began to smell the same. Heartily glad to be out of the fever-laden swamps and resting at the Howards.

Just before supper, I queried Justice Howard again about my parents when at Kent. He assured me they were not paupers but property holders. My father inherited a house and 200 acres from his father and was an ironmonger as well.

So I am but an ironmonger's son, a peasant.

Jst Howard is deeply concerned that an armed rebellion is imminent, that North Carolina is about to explode. The revolutionary fever is burning in a few coastal towns but inland there are many Scots who have little sympathy with Constitutional Liberty. They know only loyalty to the King and a clash with the rebels seems inevitable.

He also told me in hushed tones that Governor Martin had to flee offshore to a British ship, but is determined to prevent the rebellion. Martin has been promised several regiments of British troops and secretly has sent two loyal officers to the west to organize a regiment of Scots. I encoded this intelligence.

To take my mind elsewhere, I spent a sublimely intimate evening with Melinda. We played whist until everyone else retired. When Mrs. Heyward, somewhat ill, excused herself, she stated in the most lucid language that we were to stay in the parlor and behave—which I did but rather badly.

The Separatists have wrought an illegal Provincial Congress at Hillsborough. Do not know what they are doing. *

Posted a brief letter to Mr. Franklin, with copy for Chatham, but doubt that the information will be any use to either.

Have safely deposited all journal entries to date in Jst. Howard's strongbox.

September 17th, 1775

Rained all day. Aunt Elizabeth remained abed ill but I invited Melinda to accompany me to Christ Church where I had a sensation most odd. Knowing my mother and father worshiped in this church, I imagined they were sitting on either side of me. I could sense their close presence, yet no one was touching me. I even imagined my mother was running her fingers through my hair, but perhaps the opening door behind me to a windy day caused that. But for the first time in many days I had no sensation of stifling closeness of walls, no desire to bolt, no regrets about leaving the clergy.

More intelligence. While Melinda was tending to her aunt, I had another talk with Jst. Howard. He disclosed a secret I had already suspected. Donald McDonald is a British Army officer and is organizing the Scots in the west. They will join forces with a fleet here and restore North Carolina solidly with the King.

Then a startling proposal from this gentle man:

---

* *The Hillsborough Congress publicly burned Governor Martin's proclamations, voted to establish an army and raise money to support it. North Carolina was in rebellion. R.E.H.*

"I am taking McDonald's message of support out to the Governor's ship. That is, after I listen in on the Provincial Council proceedings in the Palace. Care to accompany me?"
"They'll never let us in."

"They'll never know we're there. If you want information for Lord Chatham, you'll get it there. We leave the house at five o'clock in the morning."

September 19th, 1775

Nothing accomplished. The Provincial Council meeting was postponed and Melinda stayed in with her ailing aunt.

Melinda has been more than a little friendly. I reopened the thought that if all other options failed, we could flee to England. She chose to pocket the idea but did not reject it. I dare not tell her of tomorrow's escapade.

But see the North Carolina "troops" I did. We were invited to watch them on parade, some 2000 of them. They gathered on the race course plain to an ill-beat drum in an amusing variety of shirts and breeches, hats and weapons.

But they were not there to amuse. When Jst. Howard's poor clerk laughed, the crowd screamed "Tar and feather him" and dragged off the poor devil to do it. But for some of the officers, friends of the Howards, it would have happened.

After their parade they performed a field exercise of attacking an imaginary enemy through high brush. By the time they had started forward, the hot sun and the constant draughts of grog and rum created a most unmartial display. Some with powder and ball fired weapons until a man was hit.

September 19th, 1775

This morning Jst. Howard and I slinked into the Tryon Palace like thieves. This very correct gentleman approached the building from the rear, walked around it through a maze of boxwoods, entered the Palace cellar through a doorway under the main entrance and mounted a remarkable stairway.

The main stairway is in the center of the building and spirals around a stairwell with a roof window to illuminate it. Between this stairwell and the rooms of the building is a hollow wall containing a narrow servants' stairway. It links their sleeping quarters in the attic with their working area in the cellar but is hidden from view.

We sat on the servants steps opposite the council chamber and eavesdropped on the meeting. With a lone candle in that dark stairway I recorded some details.

Those present included Samuel Johnston, Dr. Gaston, John Stanly and John Green. First they addressed the problem of how to form a government but could only agree that it should be based on a constitution that placed, to quote the highly respected George Mason, "all power in the hands of the people; those in authority are their trustees and servants." After long argument it was agreed to refer the composition to a committee of the Provincial Congress.

Then they took up the revision of laws. The elimination of entail and primogeniture (requiring a man to give all his property to the eldest son), debtor's prison and silly church related offenses such as profanity on Sundays was approved.

Finally, the Council took up the subject Howard was waiting for, preparations for war. A thousand man regular force is to be trained and minutemen besides. £150,000 is to be raised and supplies are to be procured. Stanly was named to establish direct munitions trade with France! No mention of French agents. (Howard said the French spy Marchaud died.) We retreated in the same manner as we came. Jst. Howard secretly took a dinghy out to Governor Martin's ship to report on the palace proceedings. I wrote Chatham a letter (no copy to Franklin) describing the meeting and Howard took it with him.

September 20th, 1775

Preparing to depart for Williamsburg. A new reason is to get away from Dr. Gaston and his logic. A frequent visitor to Jst. Howard, Gaston pleads with him fruitlessly to join the cause for independence. Though I will admit it to no one, his arguments are more convincing than those of the loyal unbending judge. I find Gaston a sincere and altogether pleasurable fellow, but I cannot accept his idea of deliberately detaching ourselves from our country.

Meanwhile, Jst. Howard is pleading with me to take important papers from Governor Martin to Donald McDonald. He has firm intelligence that McDonald will be in Norfolk soon to collect an arms shipment. I should locate Sean MacMinamin there and he will arrange for me to deliver secret messages to McDonald.

I took his sealed packet with little enthusiasm. I have had enough dangerous adventure.

September 25th, 1775 - Norfolk, Va.

Arrived here after five days of indifferent travel, unfit lodgings and frequent halts by various militia. Discovery of my enemy troop ledger between layers of saddle leather would have gotten me hanged. Nick continues to be useful in many ways and delights in responding to my "What does it say" papers. The ladies are much diverted by this.

Norfolk is a town of considerable commerce, more than a thousand people, I warrant. There are many loyalists here who have much to lose in a civil war and the primary commerce seems to be related to preparations for their departure.

While the ladies rested, I searched out Sean MacMinamin only to find he is away. His suspicious wife feigned to not know his whereabouts so I will have to return.

September 27th, 1775 -Williamsburg, Va.

After a two day trip to get around Norfolk Harbor and ferry the James River, I delivered Melinda and her aunt to their house just at nightfall. I saw to their safe arrival, attended to Nick and the horses and found a chamber in Anderson's.

Melinda has been somewhat cool toward me the past few days. Any explanation of mine would be simply conjecture but it must be related to her family situation.

This tavern is bursting with excitement and rumors. Some young officers are here celebrating their appointments today as second lieutenants in the Third Virginia Regiment. They are handsome, ambitious young men, not one of whom can yet be twenty, and they are convinced the Sons of Bourbon are coming to their rescue. Vergennes would like nothing better.

The young hoydens also say that Lord Dunmore, like Governor Martin, is attempting to govern Virginia from shipboard: he is afraid to remain onshore! Dunmore has declared Patrick Henry an outlaw and threatens to free all slaves free and to turn all towns into ashes.

Wrote Lord Chatham a letter but did not know where to post it. Burned it lest the wrong persons see it. And what should I do with this list of rebel forces?

September 29th, 1775

Melinda and her aunt went to the college with me to arrange her private tutoring. The professors involved were quite willing, too willing. She is a most comely lass and has the means to pay them; they need no more incentives. They are John Pellam, pianoforte (Christ Church organist) and Jean Mirabeau, French language. He is the fellow who also teaches dancing and archery. A secret agent?

The tutoring will have to be in Aunt Elizabeth's home because young ladies are not allowed in the College. I like not at all professors skulking about the house, but if the program keeps her away from Bennett, I should not object.

How to see Dunmore was resolved tonight by none other than his Indian manservant, Pitch. He told me from the shadows to wait for a Mr. John Conolly to escort me and disappeared before I could recover.

September 30th, 1775

I am returning to Philadelphia after seeing Dunmore, as Chatham wants, but my soul is not in it. I could be considered a spy for either side and be executed.

Then there's Silas Grover and his French conspirators to haunt me and Bennett McKee would like to kill me at my earliest convenience. And what am I to do about Melinda?

Now I must return to Norfolk and find McDonald. Howard says the message affects the lives of thousands. Delivering it may affect mine, too.

Dare not tell Melinda because absolute secrecy is necessary. She already suspects my interest lies in Philadelphia and that Congress, or perhaps in Naomi. (Made the mistake of mentioning the odd girl.)

Last night I dreamed Melinda and I were approaching the Whippoorwill ridge from opposite sides. I ran toward her and she toward me. We ran and ran, arms outstretched, but could not reach each other. What does it mean?

And where does my loyalty lie?

Duty, Integrity, Country! To Perdition with Chatham's words.

⟶•◦●◦•⟵

> *Williamsburg*
> *October 3rd, 1775*

Cassandra my Dear,

We have reached Williamsburg only to find the town in turmoil. The Governor and his family have fled and wild men such as Patrick Henry prevail.

Yet the opportunity for tutoring remains. Knowing your bent for learning, I am sure you will approve of my education plans. I have engaged tutors from the College to increase my abilities with the pianoforte and French language. The latter, Monsieur Mirabeau, teaches dancing and archery as well. Perhaps I should take up the bow!

The trip was fatiguing for Aunt Elizabeth. On September 17th it was terrifying. We were suddenly threatened by a band of Indians and I was nearly kidnaped. But for Landon's timely intervention, it might have happened. He is a courageous man as well as gentle.

En route I enjoyed several delicious and not too improper times with him. Affection, mirth and hilarity prevailed and the hours fled on swift wings. He creates in me a gay disposition without loss of discretion!

He has the most facile hands you can imagine. I have watched them control a pair of panicked horses, deftly intercept an Indian's assault and perfectly repair a rip in kenting. I have felt them close on my cheeks, so gently I could weep. He often bids me welcome or farewell oriental style by touching the heels of his hands but with palms apart as though my face were between them.

Still, there is a facet to him I do not understand. He was often absent at strange hours in New Bern and is commencing the pattern here. On the trail he frequently looks behind him and appears uncomfortable in a small enclosure of any kind. When the forest closes to the edges of the road, he and Nick sometimes halt the carriage and reconnoiter ahead for signs of ambush. At such times he has a set jaw, clenched teeth, narrowed eyes and silent tense face—he becomes another person.

I cannot escape the notion that our love will never be consummated in marriage. Last night I dreamed Landon and I were atop his hill in deep grass running toward each other. We ran and ran but could not reach each other.

I wait with great anticipation for news from you. Know that you are in my prayers.

Melinda

JOURNAL FOR OCTOBER 1775

October 1st, 1775 - Williamsburg

Journal keeping is burdensome. May give it over.

October 8th, 1775

The influx of Patrick Henry's troops, a singularly shabby and undisciplined lot, inspires me to discipline myself and continue adding to this rag. But who will ever read it?

Enjoyed a week of visiting Melinda while waiting for McDonald to come to Norfolk. Yesterday we witnessed a contest between Professor Mirabeau's archery students. This Frog was a model of Gaullic politeness to others but I am just another goddam to him. Do not trust him.

October 9th, 1775 - Norfolk

Crossed the bay (Hampton Roads) by packet boat this morning. Lacking a fresh breeze, I was obliged to help row until about noon. Found Sean MacMinamin, at least sixty but certainly robust and knowledgeable. But I am a virtual prisoner while awaiting an audience with McDonald.

October 10th, 1775

Met McDonald and he raises my spirits. He looked as brawny as a bull and radiated total self-confidence. I was not privy to the contents of the packet I delivered, but knew from Jst. Howard that McDonald was being asked to lead his Scottish Highlanders to the coast, join a disembarking British regiment and reestablish Royal control of North Carolina. I did not know it contained a commission for his promotion to brigadier General but it fed his ego well.

He studied his commission and instructions for a few minutes and then leaned back and pounded the table with his big fist.

"We'll do it, by God, we'll do it. Where do you go now?

"Back to Williamsburg to see Governor Dunmore."

McDonald glared at me with icy blue eyes that pierced my soul.

"You will come with Sgt. McDowell and me until I have my shipment safely removed. I cannot chance that you may inform on me. It could be tortured out of you."

Sgt. McDowell ambushed and murdered the four riders at Washington Village. Prefer not to ride with him.

October 14th, 1775 - Great Bridge

But ride with Sgt. McDowell I did until we reached the wilderness. McDonald gave me no choice. On borrowed horse I was ordered to escort two wagon-loads of muskets until west of "malingering minutemen." Thence returned to the Great Bridge Inn; it took me until midnight to get here.

But for the colorful Autumn to brighten the journey, it might have been sorely aggravating. For several days, in clear dry weather, I have been presented with one spectacular vista after another. Red and yellow leaves snowed on my trail and gathered in colorful drifts in every nook. On the hillsides above the harvested fields there are maples that have turned every shade of yellow, pink, orange, and peach, all on the same tree. Sassafras, oaks, and dogwoods are in color and the tulip poplars on the far hills suggest great yellow candle flames. Every stream, from rivulet to river, contains lucid waters from which one may safely drink. The distant ridges of mountains, softened by a light blue haze, make a giant background stage setting for the tragic drama that is about to be played. America is a vast and still largely uninhabited land, but stirring restlessly. Its future both fascinates and frightens me.

October 16th, 1775 - Williamsburg

Saw to the horses and gave time to Nick today, exposing my "What does it say" papers and teaching him to write a trifle and to improve his speech. He also tutored me on leg control of Mysty as she performs the rear-and-kick. He sleeps close by across the alley, important in view of my gaggle of enemies.

Called on Melinda this evening; her thirst for learning is but remarkable. She is quite busy pursuing her music and

French and continues working with the slave children. She has not questioned my absence but she did query me about Lord Chatham.

I described him,[*] admitted I grew up a little in fear of him, he was so demanding. Told her I pursued a career in the clergy only because he would hear of nothing else. As to why he appears so contrary to the Parliament, he believes that body is losing the American colonies.

I diverted her to amusements until I had her laughing over almost nothing. It's heartening to hear her laugh. Finally she sent me away to Anderson's, which she calls my "disorderly tippling house."

October 18th, 1775

Spent these last days helping to repair the travel-worn Heyward carriage and tend to the horses. Melinda has eight little glee singers now. Between her lessons, she and Aunt Elizabeth repair charity garments, especially for those on the Judson farm, notorious for its poor care of their hands.

October 19th, 1775

Melinda is exceedingly upset over the rebels forcing the Dunmores into exile. To Governor Dunmore's ship I go tonight in utmost secrecy. I am concerned about how I am perceived at Anderson's. Two of the Liberty Boys who often come to the tavern eyed me several times last evening with

---

[*] *William Pitt was tall, slim, had intense sharp eyes. We were never close to him, never lived at Kent; visited there during the holidays. He was morose and remote, suffered from gout and melancholia but treated us fairly. R.E.H.*

less than friendly demeanor. I feign utter congeniality for independence but this pair may not be convinced. Their glances led me to hide my recent journal entries (and the rebel troop list) in Melinda's cellar—with her knowledge. Even confided in her for the first time the significance of the military ledger, told her to destroy it if there was any risk of discovery. Made an abbreviated copy of it for Dunmore and hid that in my boot inner sole.

Much levity in the tavern downstairs as they celebrate the tenth anniversary of a declaration of rights by a "Colonial Congress" that met in Massachusetts.

October 20th, 1775 - Aboard the *Fowey*

Yesterday afternoon I rode alone to the James River, stabled Mysty and joined John Conolly, the Governor's agent, in a longboat at Hampton. It was a windless night and the crew had to row much of the distance; took us until nearly dawn.

No sooner had I collapsed in sleep in this cabin than I was summoned to Governor Dunmore in the Captain's quarters.

Such infelicity! Lady Dunmore and all nine children were there preparing to transfer to a ship bound for England; assuredly no place for me.

A most agitated man, Governor Dunmore tried to confer with me, first in a corner of the cabin, then just outside the door. But she was successively cursing the squalling children, the maid, her husband, me, the captain and especially the outlaw, Patrick Henry.

Being too much of an embarrassment for the Governor, he asked me to leave and stand by until he had seen his family off.

It was late in the day before he called me back. The cabin was quieter but Lord Dunmore was no less agitated. He was in conference with several ship's captains but wanted them to hear my report on the actions being taken by the other governors. I told him what I knew and presented my military ledger of virtually all rebel troop units in the four southern provinces.

"So what should the British strategy be?" he asked. "Shorthand this, Vickers, and prepare me a letter to General Howe with these proposals:

First, since Republicanism is most virulent in the north, let us therefore occupy the southern provinces and then defeat the north.
Recruit our loyal Scots in the Carolinas and Georgia. Support them with provisions, conduct raids from Florida and encourage the Indians to attack from the west.
In Virginia, we will use Norfolk as a base and form companies of irregulars to raid the tidewater plantations. We'll offer freedom to all slaves who will turn on those masters in rebellion. Supplemented with British Regulars we can stabilize the South.
Use the loyal central colonies as a base to isolate the rebellious northern provinces. Blockade the New England coast and destroy their trade and fisheries. Attack overland from New York and Canada until they yield."

Dunmore wasted no time. He went directly into a plan for attacking Hampton, across from Norfolk, while I penned his message to General Howe.

The air is chill but I shall sleep on deck to avoid the vomit smell of this cabin.

October 24th, 1775 - off Hampton

Witness to a failed assault today. Lord Dunmore sent Captain Squires forward with a small fleet. Under cover of a cannonade, armed men in small boats rowed toward Hampton.

But the townspeople were not surprised. Riflemen all along the shore fired at the boats and they turned with a number of wounded.

Dunmore was furious. He would not talk to anyone, just kept asking for Captain Squires.

"Bombard the town," I heard him tell the captain. "Close in and bombard the town. There's enough draft. Set it on fire, destroy it."

October 25th, 1775

A disaster for Dunmore's fleet today. When the ships closed in to bombard Hampton, many riflemen were present on shore this time and with those long American rifles they shot most accurately the cannoneers, the helmsmen, and the men aloft until all ran for cover and the ships were out of control. Captain Squires ordered a retreat but two helpless sloops drifted ashore to be captured. Lord Dunmore remained in his quarters, frothing with rage. However he is sending John Conolly ashore tonight to organize secretly the resistance there. Wanting no further roles in this drama, I accompany only to get ashore.

Today I am five and twenty. Born October 14, (old style) 1750, I became eleven days older in a single day when the Parliament adopted the Gregorian Calendar in 1752. Will I ever see five and twenty?

October 27th, 1775 - **Williamsburg**

May God forgive me, I have put Melinda in harm's way and it has transformed her.

First, after much delay and confusion I was put ashore near Yorktown yesterday morning. Exceedingly inconvenient, took me until today to get the mare.

Then I found at the stable someone had disassembled my saddle and bags. Even stitching was torn to reach the space where I had once kept the rebel troop list, no longer there.

In Williamsburg the news was worse. Rogues ransacked my belongings in my chamber in the tavern and some rebel calling himself a constable and two drunken Liberty Boys broke in and searched the Heyward's home.

As they burst in the door demanding to see any belongings of mine, Melinda ran downstairs for the troop list to be rid of it. But when the constable caught her with it, she turned on him like a she-bear protecting her young. She fabricated that I had collected the information for her uncle! He was now in Philadelphia with the Continental Congress engaged in deciding whether they had enough forces to dare to declare independence. I was to deliver the list to Mr. Heyward and the constable would answer to the Congress if he interfered. The three stupid oafs stumbled out without the list.

Her ingenious fiction had scarcely been revealed to me and her wide-eyed aunt when the rogues returned to see me. Melinda's face paled but froze into a countenance of fire and determination. We met them on the porch and did not invite them in.

"Observing your return, sir," began the constable, "we have a few questions about your absence during the attack on Hampton." I reinforced her tale:

"Read my orders from the Continental Congress, signed by Benjamin Franklin. What do they say? That I am on an official mission for that body and am required to report intelligence to them. Where have I been, you ask? Gathering information on British forces and I plan to take the report to Philadelphia. If I am harassed any further by you I shall report you to the Williamsburg Committee for illegal entry and attempted search and seizure of my property, violations of the fundamental civil rights for which we are all fighting."

Perceiving their hesitancy, Melinda exploded with a diatribe of polemics that virtually blew them off the porch. She displayed a fierceness of countenance and uncontrolled temper which totally masked her usual pretty softness.

They retired but I suspect none too convinced.

Melinda is now as suspect as I am but does not appear to care. She is furious over the invasion of her privacy and the shameful treatment of Lord and Lady Dunmore and is transformed into an active loyalist. She promises that in the future if she perceives useful intelligence on rebel forces she will note it and inform the proper authorities.

I could not dissuade her from taking such dangerous actions.

The town is wild with excitement over the attack on Hampton. The effect of this mischief is exactly the opposite of what the Governor was trying to accomplish. Many fearful loyalists are fleeing and others who were wavering have cast their lot for independence.

Broadsides offering a reward for the arrest of the outlaw, Patrick Henry, are greatly in demand. Some even have his signature on them and £5 won't buy one of those.

The southern colonies are all in turmoil. At least three governors are off-shore now, exiled from their own provinces, and planning mad mischiefs to regain control. Melinda would foolishly aid them all were she able.

October 28th, 1775

Wrote a letter to Lord Chatham describing the execrable situation and entrusted its delivery to one Lawrence Kilby. (He volunteered to return to England to avoid being evicted in a Tory Riddance action.) Kept no copy.

Melinda purports to be indisposed today, but I wager she is angry with me for jeopardizing her safety. At least she knows I am loyal and she has surely saved me from a collar of hempen rope. Her demeanor with the intruders amazes me.

October 29th, 1775

Melinda and Aunt Elizabeth allowed me to accompany them to church today and listen to the most scandalous sermon that I have heard yet. Governor Dunmore is "the Devil in flesh and we should all pray for his demise," preached the rector in solemn tones.

Melinda was livid with anger; Lord and Lady Dunmore are her personal friends and she refuses to believe what she is hearing about them. I proposed again that we go to England and wait out the war. She discussed it without decision.

More foul news from the *Fowey*. An hour ago, after making the above journal entry, I opened a window to admit freshened air. I had just returned to my chair and sat down when I heard the WHSST-THUMP of an Indian arrow!

It struck the wall above my head and quivered there while I quivered prostrate on the floor. And not a sound from whence it came.

I crawled over to my rifle and lay there concentrating on the window for perhaps half an hour. I dared not move to put the candles out, but finally threw a boot at the stand and knocked them to the floor, where they sputtered out.

Finally enough courage returned to allow me to close the

window and pull the curtain over it. I lit a candle on the floor and stared at the arrow embedded in the wall.

Then I saw it had a white roll of paper tightly curled around the black shaft. Took all my remaining courage to get up quietly, break off the shaft and unroll the paper message. It read:

29 Oct. '75

Mr. Vickers:

I just received a most urgent letter from Lord Chatham which included some instructions to you, should I see you. I am giving this message to Pitch to deliver.

Lord Chatham is convinced there is a French conspiracy to aid the overthrow of the British Government in America, that secret agents are en route to Philadelphia now to offer support to that Congress. He orders you to Philadelphia to discreetly watch for indications of the French intercession. Take care; they are ruthless and determined not to be discovered. Destroy this.

Dunmore

COMMENTARY

By October momentous events unknown to Landon were beginning to shape the geography and character of America and influence his life as well. The Continental Congress reconvened but Thomas Jefferson very nearly did not return because his little daughter, Jane, had just died in her ailing mother's arms. He did finally arrive but with intent to resign from the Congress.

The stalemate at Boston featured a Continental Army (Which General Washington characterized as "exceedingly dirty and nasty people") desperately short of qualified officers opposing a British Army desperately short of fuel and provisions. General

Howe, the new British commander, was planning to abandon Boston and occupy the southern provinces.

Ethan Allen was captured in his failed attack on Montreal and the alerted British diverted troops to secure Canada. Thus did the American patriots fail to include Canada as a fourteenth member of the union declaring independence.

Most significant was the increased French support of American independence and resultant danger to Landon. A wily Caron de Beaumarchais, Vergennes' primary agent for military aid to America, had just returned from the colonies, leaving behind instructions that Landon and any other British agent be eliminated if they interfered with American independence. Until the Declaration itself I implored Beaumarchais to retract this vendetta on my dear friend—who in fact had no influence on events in America.

I never knew the effect of my pleas.

R.E.H.

———————

Williamsburg, Va.
November 1st, 1775

My Cherished Cassandra,

No news but I trust you are in good health and prepared for the travail. All say the reward for the labor is so exquisite that all else is soon forgotten. Renewed conjugal felicity and the joys of motherhood will soon be yours. I wonder if such pleasure will ever be mine?

I have just been accused of gathering military intelligence for the Government. Though not true, I dare not elaborate on the situation. I am emboldened to note such information in the

future, however, which might be useful to my country. But I
must be perceived as an independence-minded patriot.

The once congenial atmosphere in Williamsburg has
vanished. Lord and Lady Dunmore are disgracefully exiled at sea
and British warships have attacked Hampton for reasons I
cannot fathom. Yet I am wont to return to Charles Town. Here
at least I can avoid sharing the Hymenian Chain with Bennett
McKee.

Despite these horrendous events, my tutors continue to
appear and I am progressing in both music and French. Prof.
Mirabeau reveals his political views in his French lessons. He
would aid the independence movement if he could and I am
beginning to suspect he is in Virginia for more than French. He
revealed privily that as an itinerant dancing and archery master
last summer, he learned much about the rebel troops. I have also
noted he is not unaware of whatever charms I may possess and
I may well employ them —neither despoiling character nor
virtue—to learn who this French professor really is and what his
motivations are.

One of my musical pleasures is the forming of a new singing
group of slave children. They are so grateful and enjoy the
sessions. Unfortunately these endeavors do not endear me to the
Liberty Boys—who fear the mobilization of an "Ethiopian
Brigade" to fight them.

Landon departs for Philadelphia tomorrow. I pray for his
safety. I have found a loyal subject leaving for England and I
shall entrust this missive to her. She waits for this and I must
bid you

Adieu,
Melinda

JOURNAL FOR NOVEMBER 1775

November 2nd, 1775 - Alexandria

Departed Williamsburg with heavy heart for endangering Melinda. Rode by Harrison's plantation so Nick could see his mother. Now he wants me to get her to Philadelphia.

Nick is fascinated with reading. Melinda had given me a book by Jonathan Swift to amuse myself, but the amusement is in watching Nick reading it. Remarkable fellow.

Safely back at Uncle John's house but he is not happy with me. He is increasingly for independence, knows I am not.

November 8th, 1775 - Philadelphia

Happily, my room in Biddle's Inn was waiting for me. Nick is weary of travel and prefers Philadelphia where he is free, has employment and lodging with Dunlap the printer.

Coded letter from Randolph, attached, been here a month.

———————⸓⸓⸓●⸓⸓⸓———————

London
12 September 1775

Landon, you rascal!

I worry for you and trust this letter finds you well and in no danger. The news here is that loyalists are being cruelly mistreated. I have momentous news for you but it must be used with the utmost caution and secrecy. I beg you, do not decode, even into the regular shorthand, the startling intelligence I bring you. Pocket it in your head and inform Mr. Franklin, but no one else.

Mr. Lee has at last convinced Beaumarchais that British America is casting off and that French aid could contribute decisively.

As a result, Foreign Minister Vergennes has dispatched one of his most experienced agents, Julien Achard de Bonvouloir, to establish a secret liason with the Continental Congress and arrange for the shipment of munitions and other necessities of war. Bonvouloir will come posing as a merchant from Antwerp, using an alias unknown to me.

This Beaumarchais, with whom Mr. Lee is secretly communicating, is an unprincipled scoundrel and capable of any outrageous action deemed useful to his own goals, including murder, but his actions and motivations are to our advantage. I pray it does not offend to remind you of the necessity for impenetrable secrecy in these matters. Our very lives would be threatened by the placement of this information into the wrong hands.

Much is beginning to happen now; I have scarcely any time for female sport and I am disinclined to get myself clapped in a bawdy house. I will write again as soon as I know more.

remain your trusted friend and confidant.
Randolph

Your trusted friend, he writes, your trusted friend! Why does he give me the very information Chatham has asked me to seek out? If I inform Chatham of this, both Randolph and Lee will be arrested and hanged. Yet giving Franklin this message will be actively aiding the revolution.

November 10th, 1775

The Congress has gone wild with a mixture of jubilation and despair. The King has refused their petition and has proclaimed the colonies in "most horrid and unnatural rebellion," just what Adams wanted. His hawks have won.

There is no logic to continuing my employment with Lord Chatham, but what am I to do? Give Franklin this information to gain his confidence and, at the same time, inform Chatham of this hopeless situation—without betraying Randolph. My supper of cowheel sausages keep returning to be enjoyed anew.

I told Franklin's nervous secretary Bingham the essence of Randolph's letter. The suddenly wide-eyed trundle of trepidation was genuinely shocked by my knowledge. He put his hand over my mouth and then his as we whispered, as though to prevent even each other from hearing the words.

He promised an early audience with Franklin, said the man has closeted himself over his governor son's refusal to join the rebellion and lead New Jersey to independence.

Bingham then filled my ear with intelligence so critical I am compelled to inform Lord Chatham—if I can find a courier who can be trusted. (Fair copy attached)

———————

Philadelphia, Penn.
10 November 1775

The Right Honorable Lord Chatham
Sir:
I have the unhappy duty to inform you that the King's Proclamation of Rebellion has been received with unabashed joy by the independence-minded element of this Congress, but the struggle continues.

Mr. Adams, on the one hand, is manipulating events toward independence. Dickenson and Galloway oppose Adams unalterably while others appear to be in genuine torment, torn between loyalty and dismay at the King's action.

The result is that the Congress, while avoiding independence, is nevertheless authorizing the arming of ships to attack British vessels, directing the formation of Marine companies, supplying Washington's forces now holding Boston in siege, and encouraging the invasion of Canada to add that colony to their number.

The expressed grievances of the Congress and their instructions to the colonies are understandable, if confused. However, the implementation of these instructions by cruel ruffians throughout the land is deplorable. Loyal citizens are being persecuted everywhere in the most vile manner. There is little liberty or freedom left.

None of these actions would be of fatal import, however, if there were no foreign assistance. These colonies lack every necessity of war and are turning to the French (and possibly Spanish and Dutch) for aid.

My writing you, sir, now places my life in grave jeopardy. Circumstances are turning me into the unwelcome and dangerous role of double spy and I have no stomach for it. There have now been three attempts on my life and I am wanting in nerves to continue.

I shall remain here for a time. Nothing is so critical now as the actions of this infamous Congress regarding independence and foreign assistance.

I remain your loyal and obedient servant,
Landon Vickers

Loyal ship's Captain Drindell took my letter.

The Congress is holding more secret meetings. Bilious Bingham crept to my chamber tonight, whispered I was to see Franklin tomorrow and warned me not to discuss Bonvouloir's imminent visit with anyone. The language of this unctuous urn of excrement was nothing less than a threat.

November 11th, 1775

This being Saturday and the members of the Congress in need of rest—and the opportunity to cajole, threaten, bribe and argue with each other—I was able to see Franklin.

I had not told him that I was corresponding with Randolph, or that we had a secret correspondence code. Randolph's position with Lee lowered his concern somewhat but I am now privy to the most sensitive information and the old gentleman is clearly not happy about it.

I showed him Randolph's letter and impressed him with a sample of my double-encoding. Seeing that, he hinted that he might have me write a reply and perhaps even employ me!

Back at the stable, I helped Nick with the horses and tackle and to learn to read and write a little more. Around Dunlap's printing house he is gaining rapidly.

Nick wants to go to the Abolitionist Society to inquire about buying his mother's freedom. He's been saving for this purpose almost every pence Dunlap and I give him. Must help.

November 12th, 1775

Sunday, but no church. Prefer not to hear any more of Duche's disloyal harangues or even the arguments of Naomi and the loyal Quakers who protest outside. Just kept to my chamber to think and try to plan my future. I am in as much turmoil as the Congress, as to what to do and where my loyalties lie. I am on the verge of employment by this Congress I have deplored but do not want to become a sacrifice to this contest. Tried praying but doubt that God listens.

Tonight that strange Naomi and one of her friends who tried to recruit me as a spy came to my door. They are so opposed to independence and the violence sure to follow that they plan character assassinations and the collection of evidence for later treason trials of the hawks. They sought my help and were most disappointed when I refused.

Naomi must have been wearing a bosom's friend under her bodice, her chest was so enlarged. There's a freezing wind out and it takes one to enforce modest wear on that wench.

However righteous or unrighteous the cause, what are the chances of successful separation and independence? The British Government is not going to permit this loss but avaricious France will try to assure it.

No opportunity yet to speak to Heyward about Melinda. The South Carolina delegation is being courted by buzzards (the Hawks' term) at Dickenson's elegant country seat.

Wrote Melinda a billet-doux. Uncertainly to bed.

November 13th, 1775

By chance Benjamin Harrison saw Nick, learned of my presence and, seeking news from Virginia, invited me to dinner at the City Tavern with fellow Virginian Carter Braxton.

Both are understandably alarmed about events in Virginia and the likelihood of independence. They complain that the British Government looks upon the colonies as faraway areas to be exploited in any fashion advantageous to the home islands, but resist the idea of separation.

Mr. Braxton is particularly outspoken. Typical of his commentary:

"Independence will produce Republicanism, Vickers, the leveling system of New England. We will become a nation of psalm-singing Congregationalists and Presbyterians, a rank democratical government the nature and principles of which are totally incompatible with monarchy. I hate their government, deplore their religion, detest their leveling."

"And I as well, "Harrison agreed. "Maybe conciliation is still possible."

"The New England colonies do not want reconciliation," Braxton countered, "The assertion of independence is near."

Both are anxious to return to Virginia to look after their personal affairs but dare not leave lest the remainder of the Virginia delegation vote for independence.

Letter (attached) from Melinda is filled with ill news.

———————

Williamsburg, Va.
November 8th, 1775

My dear Landon:
It would seem you have been gone for months instead of days. I worry about you and pray for you. How can you, a loyalist, walk about freely in Philadelphia?

Tales of Lord Dunmore's actions in recent days have placed all loyalists in jeopardy. As much as we value the friendship of his family, Aunt Elizabeth and I are appalled at what he has done. He established a headquarters at Norfolk and began conducting forays on the countryside, stealing food, burning and pillaging.

But nothing he has done yet equalled yesterday's proclamation freeing all slaves who would bear arms for the King. He is organizing a Negro militia called the Ethiopian Brigade. Virginians have feared a Negro rebellion for years and now the King's representative has initiated one. What could have solidified Virginia more against the King?

Oh Landon, I have thought so much about your proposal to go to England until the rebellion is over. But it would destroy my parents in ways that you cannot imagine. Would we ever want to live in America again?

I am thinking of learning French beyond the basic course. Do you think I should? Professor Mirabeau says the French are becoming our very best friends in Europe. But of course he is for independence, a subject I cannot discuss with anyone. Even Aunt Elizabeth is wavering.

You are ever in my thoughts. Come back as soon as you can but do not display your loyalist views lest you invite the most dangerous consequences.

I remain, I trust, your dearest friend,
Melinda

November 15th, 1775

Even Melinda would have me play the revolutionary to save my head! It is getting too easy to do so. What does she mean, her departure would destroy her parents?

Another letter from Lord Chatham states that I may end my employment at any time and use my remaining funds for return passage. Reconciliation with the colonies now appears hopeless. He closes writing, however, that he will not give up trying. For fear that others would suspect my role, I burned the letter. What should I do?

Took a stroll along the harbor, despite the chill, looking for a likely ship from Antwerp delivering the French spy Bonvouloir. Found none but imagine I am being followed. The City of Brotherly Love has become a city of intrigue and for me, isolation from Melinda.

November 16th, 1775

While I waited on Mr. Franklin, Bingham leaned toward me with eyes shifting for unwanted listeners, whispered that Georgia has come into the Union and has dispatched delegates to the Congress. Then he leaned back with a "see what I know" look on his silly face. What a gossip; he loves to be secretive. However, of foreign assistance to the revolution, he will say nothing.

At the interview Franklin asked penetrating questions about what I had observed in the southern provinces and probed into my property and family background.

Having one of Lord Chatham's letters, he asked for an explanation "Duty, Integrity, Country." He also asked about Randolph, his parents, and about Melinda.

He then cautiously inquired about what I had seen of importation of munitions. I revealed what I had observed in general without mentioning Grover or the yellow speckled gunpowder, or appearing to be alarmed about the traffic.

My mention of shipments through Statia to the colonies in American ships did not surprise him, nor did my assumption that colonial agents were in the Netherlands. I doubt that I told him anything he did not already know, but I did not reveal everything that I have been writing to Lord Chatham either.

What Franklin wants to learn is where I stand on independence and whether Randolph and I could be trusted for secret communication with Arthur Lee in London. I assured him that with a proper courier it would be very secure. The conference ended without any commitment on his part.

The increasingly friendly Bingham escorted me back to his office and we talked another hour. Through him I learned that of the Pennsylvania delegation only Franklin is for independence. Dickenson is working arduously to stop the hawks and is entreating delegates from the other provinces to help him.

November 17th, 1775

The gaunt loyalist Dickenson shepherded the South Carolina delegates into the City Tavern this noon, looking more like a greyhound herding sheep than a delegation, and offered them a meal in return for listening to him argue against independence. Mr. Heyward saw me and waved me over.

He was more than the lanky Dickenson had bargained for; a ram the greyhound could not control. Heyward's polite retorts and the foggy noncommitments by the other three rendered the Pennsylvanian's quest doubtful.

I drew Mr. Heyward aside after lunch and exposed my soul about Melinda. Then I proffered the yet unanswered question:

"Why" I asked, "why does she feel compelled to marry Bennett when she clearly does not want to?"

"Landon, her family situation is the product of archaic English laws that we should discard like old clothes that can no longer be repaired. And with independence, we will. Her father was hurt financially by the Stamp Act and has not been able to recover since. Melinda was just a thin shy child then with an extraordinary bent for music and learning. I remember well her serious angelic little face as she carefully tied two pence in the corner of her kerchief for a repast at school. Did you know we schooled young ladies in Charles Town? She excelled in learning and, though blossomed into a lovely young woman, she hasn't really changed."

He was being evasive, as evasive as his niece, his wife, the whole lot of them.

He did explain that the elder Watkins and McKees have worked their plantations side by side for many years and are hoping to consolidate the properties by their children's marriage. Ian McKee is grasping for still more and Wheeler Watkins has had some legal and financial problems with Factor Trammel that the marriage would solve.

"I don't understand, sir."

"I really can't go into it; it's a private matter between the families that I'm not at liberty to discuss. Time for the afternoon session now. Excuse me, Landon."

Thus I learned little but hereby record what I did.

This incredible Congress, although avoiding action on independence, has established two committees which are, de facto, the Foreign Ministry and the Ministry of Commerce. The former, cloaked as the "Committee of Secret Correspondence", is Franklin's invention and will negotiate with the French. Bingham says I may be employed by Franklin if interested.

Employment with the Congress? My intellect and my spirit are at war. Possible solution: If I am acting on behalf of Lord Chatham while in the employ of the Congress, do I not remain loyal? I need not favor independence to be employed by the Congress. At least half of the delegates are opposed to it.

Can I postpone my ultimate decision by accepting employment, or do I merely alter which contestant hangs me?

November 19th 1775

Although knowing Duche would likely present a hawkish sermon this morning, I attended morning prayer, the strangest church service I have ever beheld. At first the lovely windows and the beautiful shaft of light from the ceiling to the Bible comforted me. But the peace was not to last.

The Rev. Duche was persuasively preaching for American independence when abruptly he was without voice or motion. The object of his attention was Naomi, absolutely nude Naomi, walking silently up the aisle with a jug of blood in her hand. The congregation was equally struck dumb as this attractive young female, bare of foot and behind, with dark brown hair cascading down her back almost to her waist, walked forward, up two steps, and to the altar. Avoiding the great Bible, she poured the blood on the altar.

Naomi turned toward the congregation, her face lighted in the wildest way and staring straight down the aisle. Her round breasts were in full view and her slim waist brought one's eyes to a triangle of brown hair below. Silently she walked back down the aisle and disappeared.

Duche stammered a dismissal and the service ended. Her silent sermon, not Duche's, will be the one remembered.

November 20th, 1775

Either I'm being tested or just being removed from the city while the Committee meets with the French secret agent. Franklin has me delivering a letter to Dr. Witherspoon. I am delivering the message to Prince Town College regarding the illness of Peyton Randolph and the probability of his being replaced as President of the Congress.

Naomi's startling escapade is known to all now, but Franklin diverts that she should appear at every service to increase attendance.

November 21st, 1775

Back in Philadelphia. When I delivered the letter to Witherspoon, he invited me to stay overnight at the college and join in a supper honoring Saint Andrew, the Scots' patron saint. It was a symbolic feast of poverty and featured Haggis, the rankest dish I have ever attempted. They took a fresh-killed sheep's stomach, filled it with a mixture of the animal's organs ground up with oats and cooked it into an unpalatable state. Fortunately it was served up with a plenteous supply of dark ale and I followed every mouthful of the smelly mixture with the ale to avoid tasting it—and to avoid offense. But alas the combination inebriated me and about midnight I gave it all back to the sheep pen.

Watching again the monastic life of those lads, I committed myself to avoiding service in the Presbyterian clergy as well.

Upon returning, I coursed the port for any new ship that might have brought the French agent, saw none likely.

Militia patrol the city at night now.

November 22nd, 1775

To inquire about freeing his mother, Nick and I went to the Abolitionist Society, a Quaker-Mennonite organization dedicated to the freeing of all slaves in America. On the office wall was a sign:

Know ye all that slavery is inconsistent
with Christian Principles
February 18, 1688

They are offering every encouragement to the freeing of slaves and, I suspect, even spiriting Negroes out of southern provinces. They aid in publishing books and broadsides against the practice and lobby-walk congressional delegates to aid their cause.

They suggest that in Virginia I try the same statute that I did for Nick. Manumission is permitted in Virginia under special circumstances, as a reward for public service—if it is approved by the Governor. I shall go to Harrison.

Peyton Randolph, President of the Congress, died today.

November 23rd, 1775

Went to Bingham's office to arrange an audience with Mr. Harrison and found the secretive secretary quite amused. His silly laugh nearly brings me to nausea.

"Did you hear, did you hear?" he laughed and covered his mouth as though merriment were forbidden. "When the Congress voted in the reluctant John Hancock to replace Mr. Randolph as President, Mr. Harrison decided to show the bond between northern and southern provinces by encouraging him."

Eyes regularly shining, Bingham gushed, "The big Virginian picked up Mr. Hancock, carried him to the front of the room and placed him in the President's chair. Then he turned to the Congress and shouted: 'We will show Mother Britain how little we care for her by making a Massachusetts man our President, one she has excluded from pardon by public proclamation'"

"Oh, he got applause for that! Is he for independence?"

His hand abruptly closed the conversation and he hurried away saying neither Harrison nor Franklin is available. What transpires? Perhaps French spy Bonvouloir is here.

November 24th, 1775

Now I am as much a spy as Bonvouloir. I spied on both Harrison's and Franklin's houses last night but saw nothing unusual. If caught doing this I am finished.

November 25th, 1775

The news from Virginia is that Lord Dunmore is increasing his raids in the countryside around Norfolk. Mr. Harrison is quite agitated about it.

"You want to buy and free my cook Annie? I don't even know whether she's there or not. She may be cooking for Dunmore and the Ethiopian Brigade by now! My plantation is already in distress and the loss of slaves will finish it. The cost of renting and entertaining here is excessive too, you know. My kitchen is making a pauper of me."

I looked about me at the well-appointed house; I had heard that he was entertaining lavishly and was considered by a disapproving Adams to be of little use in Congress or Committee. An idea struck me.

"Perhaps, Mr. Harrison, you could use your cook right here. She could be near her son, reduce your costs, and at a time convenient to you, be freed to live here with Nick. He has become so valuable to Mr. Dunlap's printing house and stable he has a situation there anytime he wants it."

His eyebrows raised his jaw and then both features dropped in perfect coordination.

"What an idea! Perhaps, perhaps."

He contemplated for a moment, then turned to his desk. He opened a slave ledger which had columns titled Name, Skills, Ages, Value, Remarks. From my position I could see zeros under values and remarks to their right such as mad, infirm, superannuated, crippled, worthless. When I leaned

closer to see if I could spot Annie, he abruptly turned to me
and our heads nearly collided. After a quick glare he leaned
back and pronounced like a magistrate:

"Annie may be brought here. We'll see to her freedom
later. Can you fetch her? That's part of the bargain. You
must bring her here, allow me to have her services in the
kitchen until this Congress is adjourned, then she's yours."

"At what price, sir?"

His vague answer implied a virtual gift.

November 28th, 1775

Spent the last three days and nights prowling about like
a thief, but have learned nothing about any French spies.

Did not return to the Rev. Duche's church Sunday.
Neither did Naomi. Bingham says Galloway has spirited his
niece out to their country seat for "instruction."

I did discuss my uneasy religious faith with Duche again
and cannot but appreciate his moderation and assurances that
I will return to a reasonable state of grace in time.

Oh petite Whippoorwill, I need your thoughts.

November 29th, 1775

The Congress is so beset with disagreement, it
accomplishes nothing. Adams and Jefferson are out of
patience. Bingham says Jefferson is overset with personal
misfortune (death of his little daughter and a sick wife) and is
about to leave.

November 30th, 1775

Tonight Bingham escorted me and my cypher sheets to
Mr. Franklin's rear door by an indirect route. The trembling

shifty-eyed secretary would not let me open the door until we had stood in the cold darkness for several minutes and watched for any witnesses to our entry.

After lengthy questioning about my loyalty and my method of encoding messages, he offered me a position as clerk and messenger for the Committee of Secret Correspondence. My salary, twenty Congress-invented dollars per month plus expenses.

God help me, I accepted. Then he required that I swear an oath of allegiance to the Congress! Half of its members feel no allegiance toward it whatever, nor do I. But I did so, valuing country and duty over integrity.

Does such an oath portend the future? Should American independence come, would citizens swear allegiance to this body of quarreling egos?

Some form of parliament is needed but a monarch is an essential focus of loyalty. Without such a personage a country could disintegrate.

Franklin then handed me a directive to Lee in London to begin secret negotiations for French and Spanish aid to the rebellion and asked me to encode it. I converted it into shorthand and then rearranged the symbols with my cypher sheets. It was done in twenty minutes. When I finished, he took my encoded shorthand letter and his original fair copy and peered at me.

"Your friend Randolph can decode this for Lee to read?"

"Yes sir."

"Now we have another mission for you, of equal import, your journey to the south. See me Saturday."

Now I am a spy for both the rebels and the Government!

JOURNAL FOR DECEMBER 1775

December 2nd, 1775

This morning Mr. Franklin went straight to the subject, directing that I shorthand the conversation and produce a memoir for his records. He is intrigued with my ability. After the transcription, I pocketed the shorthand for this entry. Am I becoming duplicitous?

"Vickers, we need information from the southern states—Yes, I call them states—and we need to give their legislatures direction. Dickenson and his buzzards are doing everything they can conceive of to gain votes against independence. Both Carolinas may be on the verge of voting against. ˙ Georgia delegates show their disinterest in independence by their poor attendance.

"The disaffection is everywhere. New York has failed to approve the directions of the Congress and many merchants there have refused to follow the non-importation agreement. My own Pennsylvania, Maryland and New Jersey have instructed their delegates to resist every measure that would lead to independence."

He paused and sighed; perhaps at the thought of the Loyalist Governor of New Jersey, his own son? He began to pound on his desk as he spoke.

"Furthermore, and most important, none of the reluctant delegates to this Congress believe the British intend to make war on us. Until the British demonstrate that, this Congress will not consider separation and then it may be too late. We must arm ourselves before the British troops attack but we cannot do it without foreign assistance. However, no foreign nation is going to support us openly unless we first declare independence."

"But I don't see what I can do..."

"What you can do is to go to Virginia and the Carolinas ...and Georgia. You will have an official Letter of Direction from this Congress and a Congressional seal. Your letter from Lord Chatham will stand you in good stead too."

"But what would you have me do, sir?"

"Gain intelligence of any British acts or plans of war and get it to us as quickly as possible. Establish a string of stages, a horseback express to the Carolinas. We must get intelligence from the South rapidly and overland to avoid the British Navy."

"But we have a postal service," I interposed.

"Quite inadequate, especially in the South. After Lexington the Continental Congress assumed control of William Goddard's private service, but it still takes two months to exchange letters with my informant in Charles Town."

"What am I to do?"

"Go to the Committees of Safety to which I am addressing instructions in these messages and see to it that they establish additional staging posts no more than a day's journey apart, half-day at the canter, with at least two horses and two riders and a stagemaster at each one. Send me reports of your progress, both to keep me informed and to test the system. Go by Goddard's office in Baltimore and tell him you are doing this.

"Instruct him to pay these new postmasters and riders at the same rate as the others and to notify us of the cost. We'll get him the funds. You inform him of names and locations of the posts. Call this a postal service but its true mission is military intelligence. We must have it."

He handed me a seal stamp and some envelopes which he personally franked with his signature, then announced: Remember, we want news from South Carolina in ten days."

"Sir, it takes ten days to come from central Virginia."

"News of the British attack on Breed's Hill at Boston came here in five. It can be done. And be prepared to use it yourself. You return here at once with any news of great import. A new British invasion is just such a message."

"Yes, sir." I was incredulous and he knew it.

"Thank you, Mr. Vickers. I'll see you Tuesday and give you the papers you will need."

December 3rd, 1775

Attended church today without incident. The Rev. Duche was more reasonable but I am estranged with my own soul. I am the son of an iron monger, not a descendent of gentility. My religion is of the Established Church because I have known little else, not because I chose it.

Tonight the sky is unfettered, reveals multitudes of stars. There is scientific speculation as to what they are but even more theological speculation as to why they are there. The scientist has an advantage: he may be able to prove his theory is correct, that the earth is round and revolves about the sun. How does the theologian prove his religion is the correct one?

My loyalty? I admit to some sympathy for colonial causes, but I am neither a separatist nor a Republican. Strange, but the only certain loyalty I have is toward a subject that has only just come into my life: Melinda.

Good news from the South. The North Carolina Assembly passed a resolution forbidding their Congressional representatives to vote for independence and South Carolina is likely to do the same.

Watched Franklin's house last night, saw nothing.

December 4th, 1775

This evening Franklin left his house by the back door and walked alone to a house almost a mile away and entered at its back door. I followed discreetly and hid behind a wall until two other figures had entered. Saw nothing inside.

When I turned to slip away, my wanting nerves failed me utterly. A spitting, yowling apparition with glaring eyes not two feet away on top of the wall almost caused me to faint. It was cautiously approaching me when I turned on it, but the cat's fright was no more than mine.

Mr. Biddle saw me return, thinks I am visiting some wench, judging from his sly grin, and I did not disabuse him.

December 7th, 1775

Franklin postponed my departure with no explanation. The divided Congress is erupting again with secret meetings, incessant quarreling and corporate confusion.

Decided to visit Mr. Aitken's book store, known for its treasonable literature. Here in a rear room, away from the general public like lewd French art, lie patriot papers, broadsides and poetry of every description extolling the virtues of liberty and independence. It is a literary whorehouse of penny-dreadful political trash, proposing every deviation from proper government imaginable, Genghis Khan to Republicanism to Anarchy.

One of the poems even attacks the King in a scurrilous manner. Someone named Freneau included in a poem:

> From the Scoundrel Lord North,
> Who would bind us in chains,
> From a dunce of a king
> Who was born without brains, etc.

There is also material here on ancient Greek and Roman politics, writings by Locke, Burke and Ferguson, and translations from the French by the radicals Rousseau and Montesquieu. The Puritan Club discussed some of these authors but I have read little of their works. Aitkens says they are the foundations of the American dream of self-government. More an American nightmare of self-delusion.

A half-hour ago there were two men at a table near me talking fervently. The quiet one was Dr. Benjamin Rush, a secret separatist, says Galloway. His louder companion, a rather unhandsome commoner with pock-marked face and squinting eyes, spewed nothing but vile criticism of British Royalty and society. Portions of his diatribe I recorded:

"In British cities the few wealthy swim in a sea of vermin-laden poor who struggle to survive in a frightful atmosphere of stinking slums under a fog of coal smoke. In the country cruel taxes assure that the farmers struggle only for bare survival.

"From the King to the slave trader, the vulgar cream of society move from house to house in closed coaches without touching foot or scarcely seeing the fetid streets. Their only concern with the colonies, if they are aware of them at all, is how to exploit them for profit."

Dr. Rush finally encouraged him to leave and meet him at his home. Later learned the malcontent's name is Thomas Paine and that he is writing a political tract. Strange fellow.

December 10th, 1775

For three days the nervous Bingham has refused to see me; something must be happening. An encoded and most disturbing letter from Randolph, sent to New Bern and forwarded here by his father. (Attached)

London
27 October 1775

My Elusive Landon:

I have your letter of September 1st and am happy to know you are well. These are tumultuous times and I fear for the safety of both of us.

I have news of considerable gravity. Lord Cornwallis is mobilizing a large army, provisions and a great fleet for transporting them to America. They will embark soon and their destination is the Carolinas.

Mr. Lee is making prodigious exertions to obtain arms and munitions for the American forces, principally through Mr. Beaumarchais. However, he needs specific information as to what is needed and, above all, news of intent to declare independence from Britain. He suggests such details be brought to him as soon as possible.

The French Army has recently acquired many new weapons but the old, now excess, are still effective and available. Beaumarchais proposes that he found a fictitious shipping company which will be secretly financed by the French and Spanish governments.

This company will supply munitions and other necessities to the American provinces for tobacco or other products. Mr. Lee suggests that Mr. Franklin dispatch a special emissary to us with a list of your specific needs, that he memorize this list and bring with him no indication of his true purpose.

Bonvouloir should have arrived by the time you receive this. Take care that he intends you no harm. Treat the contents of this letter with utmost discretion, Landon. You hold our lives in your hands.

Your trusting friend,
Randolph

December 12th, 1775

We leave on the morrow! When I told Bingham I had news from Mr. Lee, he took me to Franklin on the run.

My letter opened both Franklin's eyes and mouth. He told me I knew far too much for my own safety and would not even admit he was in communication with a merchant from Antwerp. But he warned me not to reveal what I did know because spies were everywhere. He gave me the necessary papers for my mission and reminded me he wanted intelligence from the Carolinas within ten days of the event.

Then he wished me good fortune, shook my hand and waved me off.

Sleep will not come; what should Lord Chatham be told, if anything? Randolph's words, "you hold our lives in your hands" haunt me, as does Chatham's trilogy of virtue. Where does my loyalty lie?

December 15th, 1775 - Baltimore

Nick and I arrived here without incident and found the office of Postmaster General Goddard just as he was leaving for the day. I found him to be a large muscular man of 40 perhaps, balding, and more than a little harassed by the Congress. He knew who I was and what Franklin wanted.

My recollection of the conversation:

"Mr. Vickers, six weeks from Charles Town to New York is the best we have been able to do overland. To Philadelphia in ten days is impossible unless you have wings."

When I told him I am to establish additional posts, riders and horses, and to plan for night relays so that the messages move at the gallop day and night he just snorted.

"Impossible—but I wish you well, I wish you well."

Thus, with such encouragement from a professional, I set out to do the impossible.

Amazing; from Quakers to this most capable Jew, people of dissimilar religions and background appear to be working together quite effectively. In Britain neither Jew, Quaker, Catholic, Scot, nor Irish would likely hold Mr. Goddard's position. And he has established his headquarters in a solid Catholic town, the source of most of his local employees.

Sunday, December 17th, 1775 - Alexandria

Followed the postal route to here per Mr. Franklin's instructions. The response at each stage varies from indifferent to sincere cooperation. To cast out the rumor that the British are coming always helps.

Nick is happier, knowing he'll bring back his mother with him, and unfailingly helpful.

December 22nd, 1775 - Williamsburg

Fortune was on my side; my old chamber at Anderson's was available and the stable is well supplied with provender.

Nick is with his mother at the Harrison Plantation and happy. His hated overseer died recently and Mrs. Harrison is most solicitous for their well-being. She doesn't even seem to mind her old cook's departure. Perhaps they have more servants than they can support.

Too late to see Melinda tonight.

December 23rd, 1775

With Melinda once more but chaperoned rigidly. She seemed happy to see me at first, came smiling towards me, eyes regularly shining, with the gracefulness of a young deer and softness of face of a child. Oh, she is a comely lass.

But then she hesitated, offered her hand formally and became distantly polite. I was not able to speak to her privately the entire evening. Perhaps her aunt is bent on diminishing my loyalist influence on her. She did at least invite me to Christmas dinner and gave me a little packet of two nectarines; always has a gift.

Finally excused myself and left. Penetrating cold out.

December 24th, 1775

Called the local Committee of Safety and harangued for Mr. Franklin's cause. They treated me with the greatest civility and were most anxious to have express service to Philadelphia. There is talk of moving the seat of government to Richmond or Alexandria should the British take Williamsburg.

Melinda allowed me to attend church with her and Aunt Elizabeth today but the rector's sermon was again inflammatory. He quoted the sermon of another rector in Virginia, a Lutheran. The latter, Muhlenburg by name, had recently delivered a patriotic farewell sermon for independence and at the end dramatically threw off his ministerial gown to reveal the full uniform of a Colonel. Then he proceeded to recruit for his regiment on the spot. The narrative was actually stirring to hear but I do not know whether to believe it.

Snowing heavily tonight, as thick as I have ever seen. Travelers from the south say a great snowstorm is pursuing them.

Melinda is warming up. Together we decorated Aunt Elizabeth's house for the Christmas festivities tomorrow. At Melinda's request, I went into the forest and stumbled around in the snow collecting boughs of pine and red cedar and also found some holly, laurel, and other weeds of color until I could tolerate the elements no longer. What idiots we men make of ourselves to gain favor of a female.

She took these and displayed them with moonshined fruit and vegetables on the tables and mantels and transformed the entry hall and stairway into a pine and bayberry candle scented room of greenery. An altogether festive scene.

December 25th, 1775 - Christmas Day at Williamsburg

The snowfall is the heaviest I have ever seen, a foot and a half deep. From the distant vistas to the close ones—such as the dried tulip poplar blossoms erect on the trees' fingertips, holding snowball desserts—everything is white. But there many who suffer from it. The postal rider says it is even deeper to the south.

I waded through the snow to Melinda's and joined in the festivities. There were great fires in every fireplace and the table was laden with a fragrant ham from the smokehouse, a turkey from the wild and provisions from the earth cellar. Despite the weather and fear of British attack, guests came for repasts, games and singing. Melinda surprised us all by presenting her re-established school of slave children, dressed in indigo blue as in Charles Town. She entertained us upon the harpsichord while the children sang glees and carols charmingly. Then the indigos retired to a feast in the kitchen. Who will enter Heaven, if she does not?

Noted French professor Mirabeau was among the guests.

The festive scene was bizarre. Despite the appearance of levity, the talk of war and the small number of men present gave the party an unexpressed somber mood. Even Melinda admitted that but for the smuggler from the West Indies, such a feast would not have been possible.

When she played the harpsichord again, we gathered around the instrument to sing and I stood close behind her. Her hands are so delicate and facile on the keys and yet strong enough to make and dye clothes for suffering children. This damsel attracts me beyond my own ability to understand.

December 26th, 1775

When I finally found an opportunity to speak with her privately today, she was in a dispirited mood. Yesterday and today almost anything I did or said, or failed to do or say, was interpreted to mean that I am more interested in my employment with the "wicked Continental Congress" than in her or my country.

As if these aggravations were not enough, she told me Bennett McKee and her mother have both written her the banns have been published. He intends for marriage with her and is demanding a date for the wedding. When I pressed her for a reason for this unholy alliance, she wept, said something about being a sacrifice to Trammel and ran out of the room.

Bennett also wrote her I refused to duel with him and intimates he may shoot me at the first opportunity. To him I am at least a Tory, probably a British spy and deserve no better.

I should be extending the Postal Express to the south, but the snow is paralyzing. It is so soft and deep, horses cannot even pull sleighs.

December 28th, 1775

Bitterly cold yesterday. Melinda is still keeping her singing slave children in a loft above the kitchen. They would not likely have survived otherwise. In my own frigid chamber at Anderson's, the cold made sleep impossible and froze my water pitcher.

Finally abandoned my room and gathered with the other occupants, mostly of a lower sort, in the tavern dining room around a big fire. It was a miserable night; the air was fouled with unwashed vulgars' flatulence and two hounds, one of which was an odorous bitch in heat. The sanded floor was wet with tobacco-tinted saliva, there being no spitting basins. One of the drunken rustics had a lech for the barmaid until she broke a clay pitcher over his head.

We awoke to discover that one hound had emptied himself all over the room and someone had cascaded in the corner. With daylight several began to cough with a consumption and the spitting began anew.

Tonight all are in the same habitation of cruelty again, a little less frigid but no less flatulent.

December 29th, 1775

What a vicious self-perpetuating evil is slavery. When we learned of grievous distress among the Negroes, Melinda and I went out to help. Some have neither adequate clothes nor dwellings to protect themselves from the frost and the deep snow makes it difficult to find firewood and food. We took many into homes and taverns but some not soon enough; several of the older ones died. Aunt Elizabeth found one corpse just outside her gate. Melinda worked with them all night on the Judson Farm, notorious for its abominable care of slaves, and I helped her. The venture exposed me to an unforgettable birthing.

A pregnant slave began to give birth just as we were about to leave the frigid little hut where her broomstick family* huddled. With only our candle lantern for light, her man took two fence railings, fixed one horizontally about two feet above the dirt floor. The other he placed behind it parallel and higher. The laboring female put her knees over the lower rail and her back against the other. She wrapped her arms around the upper and labored with gasps and heaves until she dropped the steaming infant daughter into a blanket Melinda held below. Almost fainting, I had to step out into the night to recover. Then owner Judson came by and offered that the child looked malignant, was worthless. When he added "It costs more to raise them than I can get at auction" Melinda abruptly faced him in seething anger.

"You dastardly blackguard, there is more malignity in your soul than in all the Negroes in America. You are not fit to live with the meanest of them."

In a single motion Melinda scooped up the afterbirth and hurled it into his astonished face. When he raised his arm to strike her I leaped between them, but he began to gag and ran out into the night with a vomit. Thus have I witnessed slavery at its most depraved and unblushing worst—and she at her finest.

We took the three of them to her house where they joined at least twenty other wretched slaves huddled in the cellar.

December 30th, 1775

Escorted Aunt Elizabeth through the deep snow to her mill to assure that the stream will be turned out of the flue

---

Marriage of slaves was not recognized in Virginia but often an older slave would pronounce a few words and the marrying couple would jump over a broomstick lying on the floor to symbolize their union.   R.E.H.

when the snowmelt comes. Melinda remained behind for her French lesson. A pox on Mirabeau.

Captain Marshall is our Christmas fruit smuggler and he is in Williamsburg! His ship is moored off Hampton, but he's reluctant to sail for fear of being seized by the British Navy. I listened to him boast in the tavern how he sails for a French port in the West Indies and takes out French papers. Then he courses to Statia and trades his cargo for munitions and sails here under the French flag. But he knows British patience is at an end.

Melinda absented herself all morning "to perfect my French pronunciation." Methinks the lady doth perfect too much.

December 31st, 1775 - Hampton

Captain Marshall came into the ordinary early this morning, preparing to return to his vessel off Hampton. Needing to get to Norfolk to verify a stage post there, I asked if I might have passage across the bay.

"Aye, if I go myself." Then he postured what I knew was a lie; says he has fifty barrels of molasses for Norfolk.

Molasses indeed; but I decided to risk it and asked if I could join him.

"Aye, but dress warmly. It's still bitter cold out."

Left a note at Melinda's house (Mirabeau there again!) and followed a well-trodden trail in the deep snow to Hampton. We arrived about dusk, left Mysty at a stable and rowed to the ship.

First Mate Fordyce had much fresh intelligence. After a battle at Great Bridge the militia ran the British out of Norfolk and a Colonel Howe of North Carolina is in command there. The British have resorted to chicken-stealing raids because they have no provisions; they're faced with famine at sea. A

British captain came ashore and told Colonel Howe he had best supply them with provisions or Lord Dunmore would bombard Norfolk. This morning he sent word to the loyalists to take their women and children and leave. And this afternoon all his ships deployed close to shore. The First Mate considers the situation an opportunity to slip out behind him.

"Fordyce, one round into our hold........"

"Aye, but stay here and they'll hang us."

Marshall thought a moment.

"Captain Stevenson of the Culpeper battalion is nearby. Tell him I have fifty barrels I can't deliver to Norfolk but I'll turn them over to him if he'll give me a receipt. We'll need all the small boats and assistance he can give us. We're hoisting anchor after dark. What's not unloaded by midnight we take to Alexandria. Promises to be a clear night and favorable wind."

Captain Stevenson put his men to the task but the bitter cold, ice in the water and snow on the shore delayed every motion. I watched for a time, but when the frost had so penetrated my body that I could scarcely find my shriveled phallus for a necessary stop, I retreated inside.

It was midnight before Captain Marshall had the barrels of gunpowder on shore and hoisted anchor. Eerie it was to watch him leave. I saw only the silhouette of the ship, heard the anchor chain and windlass, but no voices. Then he silently ghosted away on the lightest breeze.

Thus a new year begins in America. Unmerciful Creator, let the new year be a happier one than the last.

JOURNAL FOR JANUARY 1776

January 1st, 1776 - Hampton, Virginia.

Cannonfire awakened us this morning at four and all ran to the third floor to behold a frightful scene across the harbor. The British fleet was bombarding Norfolk and fires were starting all along the shore. The cannonade has not ceased all day and now, at dusk, the entire town appears to be ablaze. Has Dunmore gone insane?

To return to Williamsburg is impossible; snow too deep. Adding to this miserable scene is discomforting intelligence from South Carolina. A frozen and exhausted man stumbled into the building saying he had a message for the President of the Continental Congress from Mr. Drayton of Charles Town.

Sensing the significance, I shorthanded:

"We gotta bloody war on and Mr. Drayton wants those in Philadelphia to know it."

His speech was almost unintelligible but I wrote:

"I was told to come north until I found a reliable postal service but they's none to be found. Took me fourteen days to get to Norfolk and I found it on fire. The whole town!"

"How did you get here?"

"Walked the last ten miles when me horse bellied up in a snow drift and died. Colonel Stevens sent me cross the harbor on a smack, said you'd be able to send it on. They was about to give Tory Riddance to Governor Campbell when the Scots in the back country come up with maybe two-three thousand men, and laid siege to Major Williamson's fort at Mile 96. They's going to be a frightful bloodletting—maybe already has been."

I offered to send the message by my just-established postal express, at the gallop all the way to Philadelphia. I showed him my Congressional seal, which impressed no one.

"But," I asked, "have any British forces landed? Any news of reinforcement?"

He knew of none.

Hundreds of people are fleeing Norfolk into the countryside in this cruel cold. A family of six now shares my chamber with me. The woman is heavy with child and they have lost everything.

What an egregious tragedy we are witnessing and all within the British family.

January 2nd, 1776.

Still cannot leave Hampton. More wretched people are streaming in and Norfolk is still ablaze. There is word the patriots are completing the burning to destroy the "Tory base" totally and forcing people into exile in a campaign of Tory Riddance. The pretty little harbor town of shiplap houses and robust commerce is no more.

January 3rd, 1776 - Williamsburg.

Heavy smoke still hanging over Norfolk. Back to the tavern by supper time but too disheveled and exhausted to present myself to Melinda.

Dispatched an express rider for Philadelphia with the South Carolina message and letters I had written to Chatham and Franklin, but I have no idea how long their journey will take—if they arrive at all.

A curious incident at the tavern tonight. I had dressed to visit Melinda and was warming at the fire when two rustic commoners came in, took off their muddy boots, pulled up chairs to the fire and spat at the flames with neither sufficient range nor accuracy. Then these odorous buckskins, having seen me at Aunt Elizabeth's mill and assuming I was the owner, boldly directed me as though I were a servant, to grind their grain when I resumed operations. I responded to them politely enough and suggested they see the mill operator. They had some stout and thumped out.

Anderson noted the liberties they took.

"The spirit of independence," he offered, "is being interpreted as levelling all to a common status. Everyone now considers himself on an equal footing with his neighbors, whatever their station. No doubt those rustics conceive themselves in every respect your equal, Mr. Vickers. It's nothing less than rank Republicanism."

Thus this society disintegrates before my eyes. But would I be one of those rustics, had not Chatham intervened?

January 4th, 1776 - Williamsburg

Called on Melinda only to be turned away; Mirabeau was tutoring her in French! Consumed with the vehement flame of jealousy, I departed only to circle about and re-enter the house from the rear, into the cellar through the storm door. I situated myself beneath the parlor while the "instruction" was in progress. Shorthanded their conversation:

"Oh, Monsieur Mirabeau, enough grammar for today. Tell me more about Paris, as you started to do yesterday."

"Paris? Miss Watkins it is the center of the universe, the focal point, c'est a dire, of great architecture, literature, art and entertainment. And d'amour."

"Sir, whatever do you mean by that?"

"I mean that only a Paris gentleman can properly admire, honor, respect and be affectioned toward a lady of douceur—such as yourself."

"You jest sir. But is it not a center of commerce? Culture has to be supported by business."

"It is the center of direction of trade. The port cities are the centers of action. Compare it to your lovely self. I touch your forehead, the center of direction. I touch your fingers, centers of talent and dexterity, your knees, centers of transportation, your waist, center of graceful motion, your..."

(Could not understand her reply to this lascivious flatterer but she moved across the room.)

"And once we gain independence, should we not engage in commerce with these centers?"

"Indeed, Mademoiselle, you should be engaging now, if independence is your intent."

Oh but sir, it is. And what should be the nature of this engagement?"

"Procurement of the means of achieving independence. Britain is not going to let you out of their grasp voluntarily."

(More walking and low voices. I shall strangle him.)

"M. Mirabeau, I have information regarding the military plans of the British, expressed by Governor Dunmore in a liquorous state before he was exiled, that should indicate the extent of support necessary to make our forces viable. Have you any way to communicate this to your centers of commerce?"

"Oh Mademoiselle, I have no such interest in political affairs. Now I must depart for duties at the College."

(Abrupt was his departure. Is she spying on him?)

I escaped as well. In my hurry fell into the potato bin but emerged, I hope, without being seen.

The news of Norfolk has reduced this town to a state of terror; everyone expects Williamsburg to be destroyed next and Melinda threatens to return to Charles Town. Only the presence of Bennett McKee stops her.

January 5th, 1776.

Still waiting for some improvement in weather. Spent a quiet evening with Melinda. She offered me tea with lemon wedges and Jamaican sugar and played the pianoforte. We talked about the precocious Mozart and earlier composers and generally avoided unpleasant subjects.

She did ask how I move among the rebels so easily. There is nothing easy about it. I am suspected by some despite anything I do. When I told her I mask my true loyalty she startled me by stating she is doing the same, especially with Mirabeau. She is suspicious of her tutor, is attempting to learn his true motivation for being in Virginia. That explains her flirtation but she refuses to believe the danger in such activities and I could not dissuade her. He may be one of the Beaumarchais frogs who will kill any goddam if ordered to do so. Also told her that I gave Lord Dunmore the essence of my rebel troop list and plan to add to it.

January 7th, 1776.

Being Sunday, I went to church to be with Melinda as much as possible this last day in Williamsburg. But what an unchristian service. The rector is nothing less than treasonable. Must agree that Governor Dunmore has given him an excellent example of British Government stupidity.

Another sad parting with Melinda tomorrow and a renewed threat that she may return to Charles Town. She is always unhappy about my leaving, as am I, but she supplied me with some provisions, a scarf she made, and a tearful kiss, in spite of it. So help me God, she will not marry that man.

Williamsburg, Va.
January 8th, 1776

Blessed Cassandra,

Such glorious news that the travail is over and you have a daughter! Mistress Jane Austen will be four months old and I pray you fully recovered by the time you receive this. I have dispatched a little garment wrought for her.

The news here is disastrous. Norfolk was just burned to the ground. Nothing stands but chimneys offering smoky plumes of prayer for mercy. First the Royal Navy bombarded the town of several thousand loyal citizens and set it afire. Then a rebel mob finished it.

We fear Williamsburg may be next. My French tutor is almost irrational about Norfolk—suggests that French intercession would prevent such destruction and we should request their aid. He is a strange man.

I am proceeding with my studies but see little of Landon. He was away nearly three months and I fear both he and Uncle Thomas are becoming infected with independence fever. Landon will not discuss it but I suspect he is serving both Lord Chatham and that despicable Congress. You know where my loyalty lies.

I am both angry with Landon and fear for him. He was here a fortnight for the Christmas holidays and contributed to the festive season in many ways. When we were victims of the worst snowstorm in memory, the slaves suffered terribly and he labored with me to help in every way—to include midwifery! He was my dear helpmate through all of it.

Even so I kept my distance because I no longer know whether I can trust him. He publicly plays the role of American patriot to be safe but may begin to believe that he is one. He has already left for the south.

*I may have told you the banns have been published
announcing my marriage to Bennett—but I will not agree to it.
I have a right to my own destiny.*

*Today is not a good time to write. Nothing but ill news
stalks the land and I am indulging in self-pity. But your good
news cheers me beyond measure!*

> *With warmest affection, my dear friend,*
> *Melinda*

January 8th, 1776 - Isham Allen's Inn.

Melinda stood at the gate as I passed her house this
morning. She said not a word nor waved, just watched me
without expression, then turned and walked into the house. I
ache for fear of losing her.

Nick and his mother were waiting at Berkley. Harrison's
amiable new overseer, Mantor, is driving the coach to
Philadelphia. They will ride with him and I will follow as far
as Richmond.

Nick's mother is pleased with the prospect of freedom but
is a little frightened over such a change in her life. She has
never known anything else but living with the Harrisons. She
leaves dressed in an old prunella gown with her total
possessions in one portmanteau.

The weather encouraged us to spend the night here.

January 9th, 1776 - Richmond, Va.

The Committee of Safety and the Richmond stage is well
organized with four good saddle horses and riders. The
Chairman was no less than George Mason. Well known in
Virginia for writing the *Fairfax Resolves*, the original proposal

for non-intercourse with Great Britain and for proposing the establishment of the Continental Congress, he is also the father of thirteen children.

When I mentioned his N. Carolina friend, Alexander Gaston, he invited me to lunch. Mason is now a member of the Virginia Convention and is engaged in writing a Virginia declaration of rights and a Republican constitution.

I dared to ask:

"Mr. Mason, hasn't this been tried before and abandoned? Are we just in another era of political experimentation that Britain endured under Cromwell? Do we not have Locke's civil rights and religious freedom with the monarchy?"

George Mason eyed me patiently. A mistake to ask; it evoked another lecture not unlike those of Jefferson.

"Mr Vickers, we are not renewing an old idea only to abandon it later. John Locke was for religious freedom for all except Catholics and atheists. We go further, freedom for all. Mankind is slowly groping upward through a maze of ignorance, superstition, and acceptance of status quo."

"But aren't these concepts essentially British? Must they include separation from Britain?"

"They're British in part, but the British Government has forgotten them. Magna Carta, the Great Rebellion, John Locke and others have all contributed and so have Greek and Roman philosophers from ancient times. And the French. Have you read Voltaire, Rousseau, Diderot, Montesquieu? These French philosophers have also influenced political thought, how government ought to serve the people but," and he emphasized each word, "We're the first to dare codify it and try it." (Recorded this dialogue at once while my memory was fresh.)

He agreed to send me a copy of his declaration through Gaston in New Bern. This is a man of exalted sentiments, clearly one of Virginia's elite, yet like many others, he is for independence, Republicanism, distribution of power in government and abolishing slavery. He elaborates on French political thought, Roman law, the English Bill of Rights, on and on until my mind cannot absorb it all. Leaves me sensing only my ignorance and guilt for collecting intelligence on the troops that would protect his experiment. The military ledger and cypher stencils are well hidden but worrisome. Perhaps I should leave them in Jst. Howard's strongbox.

Wrote virtually the same letter to Melinda, Randolph and to Lord Chatham describing Mason's views, gave them to a Mr. Lloyd who is another "quitting the colonies forever." Kept no copies.[*]

Richmond, Virginia
9 January 1776

My Rakish Randolph,

Today I conferred with George Mason, whom you and others have recommended to me and I now understand why. Until now I have heard little but protests and criticism of the British Government, but he has given some form to the revolutionary movement, has proposed what they would substitute. Whether his or any other province would adopt them I don't know, because his concepts, though laudatory, are probably impractical.

Mr. Mason is writing a declaration of individual rights and a constitution for Virginia which appears to codify what many in Philadelphia want. He says his republic would be served jointly by a governor, representative assembly and a judiciary. Each of

---

[*] *Fortunate Reader, I saved this letter and my reply. Both are attached.*   *R.E.H.*

the triumvirate is somehow independent of the others, dividing power. There would be no final authority anywhere. Seems unworkable.

These organs of government would be elected by the common people who would be influenced only by reason. Now Randolph, this is the weakest aspect of the entire idea. The common people here are ignorant, vulgar, vacillating and unfit to judge. Their vote would be influenced by greed and fear, not reason.

George Mason lives in a tempting, seductive dream; his untested theories could produce rule by mobs of disaffected. I confess some affinity to these principles but, like the challenge of religion, they give the human race goals they cannot achieve.

Randolph, am I still a target for murder by a French agent? My employment with the Congress to establish communications from the south aids the movement for independence. But I live in constant fear of ambush.

What say you to all of this? Write to Charles Town, my overzealous "patriot".

Landon

━━━━━━━ ⚬⚬⚬❁⚬⚬⚬ ━━━━━━━

London
18 February 1776

My reluctant Piggy:

Huzzah! I do believe there is some hope for you! You can hide it no longer; you are witness to one of the most worthy experiments in all history and you know it.

I am delighted that you have at last met George Mason. Mr. Lee says he is a wise gentleman, not at all an impractical dreamer. But nothing has convinced me of the correctness of our cause more than what I see in England. There is rampant *corruption and desperate poverty here in London which a Republican government would eliminate. Cities and kings breed these ills; we should avoid having either in America.*

Here there's no reliable process for the people to be heard, for corrupt men to be removed from office. Civil rights are here in theory but the rigid class structure prevents their exercise.

Meanwhile, the greatest fleet assembled yet is nearing your shores with the intention of tearing you apart. The Congress must unite in a declaration of independence and get European aid.

The atmosphere is tense here; I may be suspected of spying. Last week a British intelligence officer questioned me about my activities. Unfortunately, both diplomatic and romantic rendezvous call for discreet movements at odd hours; these have been observed more than I realized.

And you are suspected as well by the French. I have assured Beaumarchais that you are now employed by the Congress and represent no obstacle to independence. But it may take several months for Vergennes' agents to learn that. Lord Chatham's "From whence comes this goddam little frog?" is still quoted by them.

> *I remain your concerned comrade,*
> *Randolph*

January 10th, 1776 - Petersburg

A melancholy day, beginning with tidings from South Carolina. There was a clash between Scottish loyalists and militia in South Carolina in the midst of the greatest snowfall in anyone's memory. Two feet of snow fell in thirty hours. This and the superior strength of the militia shattered the loyalists and averted civil war. Will Melinda be safe in Charles Town now?

I sent this news to Mr. Franklin by express and reluctantly coursed south as Nick and his mother went north. As a parting jest I added a sign to the milepost, reading "Philadelphia 250 Miles", and asked him "What does it say?"

"Freedom, it says freedom," he laughed.

Having parted with my love and then my faithful traveling companion, my disconsolation was aggravated by learning that Josiah, the Judson slave whose woman bore a child on two rails in that hut, had been tried and convicted of stealing food for his hungry woman and infant during the recent snow storm. They punished him by placing a red-hot poker in his hand, in the name of King George, rendering it useless for the rest of his life.

Little did the pitiable fellow know that neither the King nor any representative of his had anything to do with it. This tragedy was wrought by local officials criminally ignoring basic human rights, the very rights Mason had just been discussing.

January 15th, 1776 - Martinborough, North Carolina.

Completed another journal book; having to use newsprint until I draw on my supply in New Bern.

Express stages are established now at Petersburg, Greenville Courthouse, Halifax, Tarborough and here.

Sean Molloy took me in and enthusiastically established a post at his stable in town. His two Indian riders and ponies performed a remarkable demonstration race for my benefit—to include swimming the swollen Tar River.

Do not detect anyone following me. Have waited as long as two hours in hiding aside the trail to verify.

Governor Martin has issued a proclamation to all loyal citizens to assemble and put down the rebellion. Have the British landed? I refer to them as though they were the enemy; what I should do is join them. Damnation—why do I not have Melinda with me?

The town is tense with excitement over the mobilization. Some forty ill-dressed and poorly armed men hurried off to the south just as I arrived. I have identified a multitude of these units in my ledger and their number is increasing.

January 16th, 1776 - New Bern.

Back to the home of Randolph's father. A letter from Randolph awaited me, attached. An earthy epistle, he makes a valid argument that science and invention can be suppressed by church and state. Whether great minds will better perform "in the unfettered freedom of America" remains to be learned.

London
20 December 1775

My Wandering Landon:
And where might you be tonight? I pray this epistle will find you without too much delay.
While waiting in this parlor for my new companion Cynthia, as she makes preparations upstairs, I might as well compose a letter for subsequent encoding. She's a good humored and entertaining wench; her chief fault lies in her endless attention to appearance. We are to attend a ball celebrating the end of the International Meeting of Naturalists and Experimentalists. Such onerous tasks imposed upon me.

M. Beaumarchais has appeared again to assure us of both French and Spanish support. He has the final approval of both governments, but will give us nothing in writing as proof. We have no choice but to accept his word. B. hid the purpose of his visit by the clever device of attending this conference with one Georges de Buffon, the French author of a lifetime compilation of all knowledge of the natural world. ALL! Forty-four volumes in the making. Having some ability with the French language, I acted as interpreter at some of these sessions.

Landon, I must tell you about this conference. Particularly fascinating were the exchanges of Buffon and Erasmus Darwin, eccentric physician of note here. The latter has written a poetical treatise entitled Zoonomia, which points out some continuity and similarity in all life forms and suggests all life may be descended from a simple common source.

Buffon has independently reached the same conclusion though he may have to apologize to the authorities of the Sorbonne. The Great Chain of Being is a common theme at these sessions. We are somehow related to the animals, both in internal arrangements and in our proclivity for lust, hunger and survival.

Darwin quoted the Greek ancient, Lucretius, who wrote that man is part of nature and his origins are savage, even animal.

Cynthia has suggested as much to me, comparing me to the beasts when abed with her. Referring to my healthy frequency and enthusiasm, I presume. But the difference, I reply, lies in my sentimentality and gentleness with her and she appears to enjoy it with few inhibitions. Do you deplore me?

The conference included other astounding features. A geologist delivered an amazing lecture theorizing that the earth is much older than the Bible suggests and an inventor supported him by demonstrating his orrey, a model showing that the movement of the planets around the sun had to have evolved over an incalculable period of time.

Another demonstrated an engine powered by steam, being manufactured at Soho. Limitless possibilities!

I mention these expositions of knowledge and invention because societies tend to resist them as threats to established wisdom, religion, even government. Some elements of the church in both England and France are suggesting participation of the Devil here; I doubt that some of these expositions would have been allowed in France. Imagine these great minds at work in the unfettered freedom of America. Am I too enthusiastic?

Regarding the European aid, Beaumarchais insists it is contingent upon the American colonies declaration of independence. He never fails to mention this.

Cynthia has finally brought her toilet to perfection and is approaching. So off to the ball and, I trust, to a more intimate invitation later.

Good night, friend
Randolph

January 17th, 1776 - Remaining in New Bern.

Transferred my newsprint notes to a journal book. Jst. Howard is in bed with the colic, a dear and gentle man. Found a postal stage here already in existence but only with connections to Charles Town. Merchant Green, who operates it, is pleased to look to the north as well.

January 18th, 1776

Justice Howard up today and feeling more fit, but is a troubled man. North Carolina is divided and at war with itself. Only the lack of munitions on both sides delays the battle. I tried to divert his thoughts:

"What is Dr. Gaston doing?" I asked and shorthanded:

"Oh, he married Margaret Sharpe, visiting from England, last May and then proceeded to devote his energies to this dastardly rebellion. He's as deranged as ever about George Mason's ideas of constitutional liberty. Meanwhile Governor Martin—at sea, mind you—has declared this Province to be in a most horrid and unnatural rebellion and has pronounced the Scots a military force of the King."

"How big a force?"

"I don't know. Several thousand perhaps."

He then asked me why I was in New Bern and I told him of Mr. Franklin's wish for faster communications from the South. When he questioned me as to where my loyalty lay, I confessed to confusion and doubt. I told him I want to live here but under the protection of a more congenial British Government.

"And what do you think the Continental Congress is going to do," he quietly asked.

"I don't believe it's capable of doing anything."

He waved me away so that he could rest and the unhappy conference ended. Poor man. He is virtually my father, as his son seems my brother, yet we both disappoint him.

January 20th, 1776.

J. Howard continues unfelicitous. Dr. Gaston and Stanly talked with me briefly today; they were impressed with my mission and congressional seal and assured me the express would be maintained in North Carolina at top efficiency. What they both wanted to know, but I certainly could not tell them, was how soon and in what strength Virginia could send reinforcements if North Carolina were invaded.

When I cautiously inquired about the whereabouts of Grover, they said they believed he was headquartered in Statia and did not often venture to the provinces any more. But he had been in Savannah recently to establish trade with that province. They may be selling him provisions for the British.

January 21st, 1776.

Justice Howard much improved. Mrs. Howard is solicitous of his health and his spirits are raised, but both fear the outbreak of war. Everyone is expecting an invasion and I leave tomorrow to look for it. Wrote Melinda.

January 30th, 1776 - Charles Town.

Rode here in nine lonely and uneventful days. Thoughts of Melinda and doubts about faith and loyalty plague me during such lonely jaunts. Mysty is sustaining her strength very well and I am learning to use leg and spur control handily. One useful maneuver we still have not mastered yet is Nick's turn-and-kick.

The postal express route is established the entire distance, though not very charged with a sense of urgency. No message will arrive in Philadelphia in less than three weeks.

Mr. Trammel, the factor about whom Melinda made a vague reference, was my first target. Found the man, wearing an intense lined face and greying hair, feverishly engaged with his accounts. Feigning need for a loan:

"Mr. Trammel, I've inherited property near the Orangeburg Township on which I wish to build a home. I see you're busy, so I'll come straight to my subject. Would it be possible to borrow money for this undertaking and what would the interest be?"

"Busy indeed," he snapped back, "my accountant, fearing Gadsden and the Liberty Boys, fled last night. We've both been called Tories and threatened, but he didn't even give notice. May have been kidnaped."

He stopped abruptly, eyed me coldly with: "Didn't I once hold a letter for you? I'm a factor but not a moneylender."

"I had heard you were."

"I don't know you; your speech isn't local. You're from the Committee, aren't you? Marcus Landrum's going to debtors prison was not my doing. Or is it my wife? It was perfectly legal and a necessity that I declare her insane and send her to an institution. No woman with her views could be sane. You live here?"

"No, but I plan to and I'm not from the Committee, sir. But I do have friends here who would vouch for me. Do you know the Heywards, the Watkins?"

His countenance grew even colder. "And who is to vouch for them? You had best borrow elsewhere—although I don't know who would lend to a sandlapper. Really must get to my accounts, to discover whether this former clerk has sconced me. Good day, sir."

This was approximately the conversation. It lasted less than a minute and I gained nothing except hostility when I mentioned the names Watkins and Heyward. That troglodyte would be hostile to a sainted mother.

No one at the Heywards but servants. Melinda's mother is at her plantation, they say, and Bennett's parents probably at theirs. And they do not know where Bennett is. "Mr. Watkins? Why he's in the west."

Fruitless efforts.

January 31st, 1776 - remaining in Charles Town.

There's a war scare here too. The snow campaign discomfitted everyone but left South Carolina troops arrogantly confident. McKee's battalion is to the south on the Georgia border.

Saw Charles Rutledge today in uniform with the rank of captain! He shrugged at my astonishment, said he had no choice but to join the militia. When obliged to tell him what I was doing, he laughed outright. Opportunists?

Received a letter from Bingham today dispatched twenty-one days ago. Franklin wanted it to reach me in ten days!

Bingham's news is that 5000 more British soldiers are on their way to America from Great Britain. Further reinforced by British troops from Boston, they will surely invade somewhere. It's North Carolina, has to be.

But nothing Bingham writes equals the broadside he enclosed, entitled *Common Sense*, published anonymously by some ill-humored mind in Philadelphia. It's an incredible document full of polemic and error, yet will appeal to many.

Common Sense argues that any government is an unfortunate necessity and Monarchy the worst of all. It also echoes Jefferson's idea that all stratification of society by inheritance is unnatural; that no one, by the accident of birth, has a right to be in perpetual preference to others. Nature particularly disapproves of the hereditary right of kings, he writes, otherwise she would not so frequently give mankind an ass for a lion. He calls King George an ass!

He also argues with some logic that a government separated from its people by a vast ocean cannot govern. A half year is consumed conducting the most ordinary business.

My intellect tells me separation could be right; my spirit answers it's wrong. This broadside is the most outrageous polemic on the rebellion yet and it clearly worsens the situation.

Bingham urges me on to Savannah to complete the postal express. Of course; why not? There I may have the good fortune to find both McKee and Grover waiting for me. I have nightmares about dueling with both of them at the same time. In one of these dreams it was Melinda who was killed. Why does the mind conjure up such insane thoughts?

When I confessed my fears to Charles Rutledge, (He knows and dislikes McKee) he accommodated me by drilling me with the dueling sword and pistol. I am adept with neither.

Had a long friendly tete-a-tete with Charles and his Ruth, close friend of Melinda. Both are intimately acquainted with Melinda but are as reluctant as any to explain the family secret that has her entrapped.

Williamsburg, Va.
January 31st, 1776

My Dear Cassandra,

An impatient gentleman who is being forced to leave Virginia for England stands in the parlor whilst I write. He is being expelled for merely supporting the King—the crudest treatment.

I am most grateful for your invitation to remove to Hampshire until the present unhappiness is concluded. I am inclined to accept but I shall to go to Charles Town first. I must face up to my mother and Bennett, defy the banns and then go into exile if necessary. Charles Town is also a safer place to wait and to embark for England.

Landon has become an unknown. He is still away and I am most lonely without him. He does write to me but I fear for both his safety and his rationality.

We fear Williamsburg may also be destroyed by British forces—the town is such a hotbed of fools—and are thinking of leaving. Uncle Thomas' status with the Congress does protect us but broadsides such as Common Sense have inflamed the local blackguards.

I have begun to collect some interesting information I cannot discuss. Much of it is easily available from garrulous braggarts. Even Prof. Mirabeau's tongue is loosening and I am achieving this without allowing him to loosen anything else!

Your shipment of woolens may have been lost at sea. Pirates who call themselves "Privateers" prey on British ships and rob them. I pray the Royal Navy will capture them all and restore civility in America without further destruction.

We shall probably leave for Charles Town in a few days if the weather permits. I will write you and perhaps embark from there. The blackest dreams haunt me; I truly need Landon.

Would that I could talk with you, amiable friend,
Melinda

JOURNAL FOR FEBRUARY 1776

February 1st, 1776 - Beaufort, South Carolina.

Mr. Gadsden passed me on the street in Charles Town this morning just as I was mounting up to ride away. His short legs almost took him around the corner, then returned him with:

"What are you doing here, Vickers? I thought you were in Philadelphia. Where are you going; why haven't you called on me?" he blurted in his usual rapid way.

I explained my mission; "Now I'm en route to Savannah."

"Tell them to run Governor Wright right out of Georgia, just like we did with our governors in the Carolinas. Can't you hold that horse still?"

I dismounted. "Have you any news of a British landing?"

"No, but I wish they would, right in Philadelphia. Then we'd get some action."

"Toward independence?"

"Toward independence. But we won't get it now, not yet. Too many buzzards and not enough hawks."

"You may be interested in this broadside, *Common Sense*, just arrived."

"I have one; am printing a thousand more—convincing!"

"What's happening here, Mr. Gadsden?"

"We may be a target for invasion. At the Provincial Congress on the 10th I'm proposing independence and eviction of all Tories. Well, you had best be on your way." His legs turned and carried him away. Over his shoulder: "Come and see me when you return and watch the Tory Riddance."

"I shall, sir." I rode away contemplating this obstinate heretic evicting all the loyal citizens he calls Tories. Would that include Melinda—me?

The postal stage at Beaufort is well established and ready to ride. The postmaster also offered that McKee's 2nd battalion is on the South Carolina-Georgia border. How to avoid it?

I exercised with both the pistol and sword as Rutledge advised but contemplating a duel renders a dolorous stomach.

February 2nd, 1776 - Savannah, Georgia

Arrived here late after being stopped several times on the road by militia. McKee was not among them but at the Georgia border they searched every item I had. Most are looking for fleeing loyalists. Melinda could be grossly mistreated at such an outpost if found with intelligence.

My lodging is at Tondee's Tavern, in a private room upstairs but no lock. The room being about eight feet wide, I found a small log of equal length, pulled it in my window and wedged it between the door and the opposite wall.

Tondee's Long Room, well known and popular, was full of ignorant jolt-heads tonight. I studied the room through a window for signs of McKee or Grover, saw neither, and entered cautiously. Mr. Tondee himself was eating supper and invited me to join him. This mad-brain rudesby became most friendly when he learned I am employed by the Continental Congress. Convincing him I needed to report the news to Franklin, he allowed me to pencil the following:

"Sit down, Mr. Vickers, it's chicken and turnips and raisin pudding tonight."

I accepted a bowl of the strong-smelling victuals and looked about the cacophonous room.

"Why such high-spirited guests?"

"The Council of Safety arrested Governor Wright," Tondee laughed. "Arrested him for trying to send gunpowder to the Creek Indians. The shipment was in accordance with a treaty, he said, and he pleaded with us to send it on to them and to release the Indian who came to negotiate, to keep the peace. We released the Indian but kept the munitions and his French musket."

"How did you know it was a French musket?"

"There it is over the fireplace. Model 1763, 75 caliber smoothbore, 45-inch barrel. But Wright committed other acts. Four British men-of-war and some supply vessels sailed in to buy provisions and the Governor urged us to let them buy, lest they burn Savannah like they did Norfolk. Well, the Council of Safety refused them, but we hear more British vessels have appeared. They're determined to get provisions for their forces in Boston."

He paused to contemplate that. "And we're just as determined to prevent them. We've got ships loaded with 2000 barrels of rice and other stores off Hutchinson's Island, but they're well guarded. Charles Town has purchasing officers here to buy some of it."

I looked about the room full of boisterous militia in all manner of self-designed uniforms, but none look like the uniform of McKee's battalion. What unthinking clods they are. These events have brought more excitement to these men than they have ever known before. They are swaggering, arrogant, over-confident bawds and ignorant of the tragedy lying ahead. When they became excessively merry and vulgar, one exposed himself to the guffaws of the others and I left.

Exercised with the pistol and sword again.

February 3rd, 1776

Williamson's stable has good horses and appears to be operating an effective and profitable postal service to Charles Town. Posted a letter to Franklin. My Congressional seal had little effect on the dull clerk.

The Council of Safety is occupying the home of James Habersham, victim of Tory Riddance. The place is a madhouse of running messengers, officious militia and puffing older gentlemen, all with earnest faces, making preparations for war. The guard would not let me in. No sign of McKee.

I walked to Governor Wright's home on Telfair Place. Two dunghill militiamen stood guard so I made no attempt to enter. A mistake to go there; now I am being followed.

February 4th, 1776

Last night a note slipped under my door frightened me witless. The missive requests I meet a Mr. Brown, loyalist, tomorrow morning on the field just south of the cemetery. A trap? When I casually asked Mr. Tondee where this was he told me just south of the Oglethorpe Square and added:

"That's the old dueling ground. Convenient, isn't it, right beside the cemetery." Then the daft old man laughed!

Spent the day inquiring discreetly, strolling near the site and attempting to find out who Mr. Brown is, but learned nothing. Meanwhile, some blackguards are following me.

Savannah is frenetically converting itself into a fortress. Cannon defend the waterfront and troops are constructing berms at town entrances. Motley assortments of militia are appearing and people are hoarding provisions. I can see the twenty ships with 2000 barrels of rice aboard, moored tightly together across the river from Savannah.

What can Brown want of me? This is some kind of ambush.

February 5th, 1776 -Aboard the *Scarborough*

Merciful God, I am at sea again. Must record the unseemly day; obliged to use the back of a discarded navigation chart with the purser's pen.

I departed through my window on a rope at dawn, went to the dueling site well-armed and watched from a hiding place in the brush until an older man limped into view, placing his left foot down with the greatest tenderness.

At the appointed hour I cautiously called to him and showed myself. After mutual assurances, this victim of an outrageous tarring and feathering which nearly killed him asked me to assist in the Governor's escape! He wanted me to deliver a message to a John Stuart, aboard the *Liberty* and about to be exiled to the British man-o-war *Scarborough* with other "innocent Tories."

Stuart is to tell the *Scarborough*'s captain to have a longboat ready at Cockspur Pier at midnight, ready to transport the Governor and six others to the ship.

"How can I get it to Stuart without suspicion?"

"Take one of your messages with the Congressional seal, yes, we know about that," responding to my wide eyes. "In the message invite Florida's Governor Tonyn (he spelled it for me) to send delegates to the Continental Congress. You can show that to the infamous Council of Safety and they'll give you a pass to the *Liberty*. You can walk right aboard, hand it to Stuart and give him the message."

"But this is dangerous and I'm losing time..."

"Do you realize what Governor Wright is losing? Eleven plantations totalling 24,000 acres and 500 slaves and now he has to escape like a criminal. You must do this."

I fled through the brush willing to help but wanting in nerves to do so. Returned to my chamber, composed a letter to Governor Tonyn, forged Franklin's signature and sealed it with the congressional seal. Then I called on the Council of Safety.

The letter ruse worked. An hour later I was on the Liberty and made the rendezvous with Stuart. He repeated my message clearly and assured me he would deliver it.

Then dangerous complications. As I started to disembark, a disheveled militia officer and some Sons of Licentiousness I recognized as my recent followers stopped me and ordered the *Liberty* to depart immediately. With a freshening wind and favorable tide, the captain was more than willing.

I showed them my Congressional instructions but the idiots refused to let me off, called me a spy and threatened to hang me if I stepped ashore.

My protests created no effect but derision and more threats by those common asses, so I was obliged to remain aboard with no belongings except my cloak, pistol, and dagger. I had become a victim of Tory Riddance.

At the *Scarborough* I delivered the message to Captain Barclay myself and now await a boat back to the mainland.

Barclay sent the longboat to meet Governor Wright but that is a diversion to the real action tonight. He is sending crews to Hutchinson's Island to seize the twenty rice-laden vessels and turn them over to a private shipowner.

I will go with the raiding troops to get ashore but will take no part in the rice stealing.

February 6th, 1776

Another nightmare now embedded in my memory.

A platoon of raiding parties lowered into longboats about three this morning and rowed for several hours in a smart windy rain to the north shore of Hutchinson's Island.

To avoid this action and get across to Savannah, I walked beyond the line of moored ships. The raiders executed their scheme with alacrity. Before I had reached the end of the line, they had captured every rice ship.

Unfortunately for the raiders, a contrary wind prevented their departure and the Savannah defenders had time to react. Rather than to allow the British to take the provisions, the rebels opted to destroy them. Cannon fire proved the shoreline batteries were out of range and a hastily organized assault in small boats was driven off by musket fire.

Then a longboat manned by six oarsmen moved up the line of ships. A figure standing in the stern shouted to the ships crews to come about and sail with the wind around the other side of the island.

I found a leaky bateau and two ancient oars and pulled for Savannah. The bateau had scarcely moved out into the current when one rotted oar broke. Meanwhile the current carried me directly toward the first rice-laden supply ship.

Even as this was happening, I realized a much larger vessel was drifting after me and it was afire. Accompanied by other boats guiding it, they obviously intended to ram it into the uppermost ship, the one I was helplessly approaching, and set the entire line afire.

With the bateau badly leaking, I had little choice but to board the supply ship when I came up against it. Just when I reached the deck, the longboat with the standing figure approached the same ladder. When he mounted it, the boat crew saw the approaching fire vessel, abandoned their passenger and rowed frantically out of the path of the approaching flames. The newly arrived ship's crew, screaming "There's gunpowder aboard," jumped into the river on the port side and swam for shore.

The abandoned figure on the ladder came aboard, hurried to the bow, seized an axe and began to chop the mooring lines free so that the ship would float away and escape the fire vessel. I was about to assist when the unmistakable voice of Bennett McKee came from another boat drawing alongside.

"I know you, you God damned traitor; get off our ship or I'll kill you."

The silhouette turned and our eyes met. God Almighty, it was Grover, the most profligate, artfully wicked and thieving wretch I have ever known. He was the merchant who was about to sconce this cargo for the British. Thinking I had challenged him, the murderer snarled like an animal when he recognized me, drew a pistol and fired at me. I felt the ball graze my left leg, cutting it without entering, but the impact downed me.

McKee came on deck at that instant and, not seeing me, started for the garrulous Grover. They drew swords and began to fight savagely while I dragged myself into a sitting position.

The cursing Grover soon proved himself to be an excellent swordsman and forced McKee into a desperate defense. The latter retreated to the stern, parrying Grover's attack as best he could. The burning ship was now less than fifty yards away and I had to do something. Choosing the foul-mouthed Grover as the worst of two scoundrels I tried to discharge my pistol at him but the rain-soaked weapon misfired. I managed to get to my feet, draw my dagger, and limp toward the antagonists.

McKee stumbled backwards and accidentally stepped into the uncoiling stern hawser which trapped his foot.

Grover seized an abandoned musket and raised it to shoot McKee. At the instant I charged Grover, intending to knock the gun aside, he fired and struck McKee in the upper leg.

I threw myself on Grover, bore him to the deck and tried to stab him.

He maneuvered on top of me, still rasping verbal abuse, clawed at my eyes with the long nails on his thumbs and first fingers. I parried with arms and shoulders while he grooved my face brutally and avoided the dagger. I thrust it into his side but he kept clawing. Just as I strained to get the weapon to his chest, he stiffened abruptly and fell on it. McKee had freed himself, crawled over to us and thrown himself on Grover's back. McKee's eyes met mine and then he collapsed also. Together we had killed the most venomous villain in America.

McKee's companions could not stop the fire vessel and returned to rescue us. They got us over the side just as it struck and spilled burning firewood on to the supply ship deck. Frantically they rowed for the Savannah side, shouting for a doctor, while I tried to stop McKee's grievous flow of blood.   He was barely conscious but looked up at me quizzically.

"What are you doing here?"

"In service to the Continental Congress. It doesn't matter now, just be still until a doctor comes."

"I have no feeling in my leg. Is Melinda well?"

"As far as I know."

"Do you know she responded to the banns with a written refusal to marry? Her mother burned it, told me to ignore it. But I'm finished anyway...and so is her father. I could have saved him." Do not remember what I said but his last remark is verbatim.

We lifted him out of the boat and laid him on a blanket under a huge moss-covered oak. With that he fainted but the doctor managed to stop the bleeding and then turned to me. Though covered with blood from the three of us, I was not in danger. As he dressed my wound with a searing ointment to prevent fester, I looked around at the grave faces seeing the results of war for the first time. The bloodletting here and the destruction across the river slowed time for a moment.

As the freshening wind spread the fire to all four ships and cremated Grover's body, the running figures abandoning the vessels appeared to be moving in molasses, slowly, like one in a foul dream of being pursued. Even the flames writhed skyward slowly, reminding me of the flames of Norfolk and suggesting the flames and death yet to come. Around me great oaks waving beards of gray moss added a hellish prospect to the wind.   Irrationally I imagined moss-covered Grovers leaping out of the trees to set me afire too.

But I regained my senses and saw the unconscious McKee to the hospital, where they said he would recover, limped unmolested to Tondee's to wash my sanguinary clothes. There's still some firing across the river; Tondee says the British are stealing some 14 or 15 vessels.

I have some respect now for McKee. He at least knows what he stands for and is fighting for it. Would that I were equally certain, but I will still not permit Melinda to marry him. And what did he mean that Melinda's father is finished?

Tondee agreed to send reports to Charles Town on McKee's condition. My leg is aching fiercely but I am riding out in the morning.

February 9th, 1776 - Charles Town.

Returned to Holliday's Inn after a discomforting trip not worth recounting, but there is no letter from Melinda. Had a doctor look at my leg and he says the wound is healing without fester.

About to go to my chamber when Gadsden came into the tavern. He looked at my clawed face.

"Vickers, whither ye been, wrestling with a catamount?"

"With a pirate, sir, who tried to condiddle grain in Savannah for the British Navy. He nearly clawed my eyes out."

"No matter, it will heal. But this action portends a bloody drama."

Gadsden went to a table and dropped into a chair.

"Don't just stand there Vickers; sit down and have an ale with me. Listen carefully; shorthand it if you like for posterity. Shakespeare wrote all the world's a stage, did he not? Let me describe a drama for that stage.

"The scene opens with the most powerful nation in the world taking an interest in a string of provinces across a great ocean. This nation and others have been exploiting the area for many years but the people don't want to be exploited any more. They have radical political and religious beliefs. Most of all they have a nationalistic spirit and they want independence. So they rebel."

"You're speaking of this situation?"

"Just listen, Vickers. Legions of reinforcements pour in to put the rebellion down. Now the drama really begins. The invaders establish a series of small forts from which they sally forth to control the countryside. They recruit local troops to help but they are not very effective.

"The invaders rarely lose a battle but they cannot control the countryside. The natives just fade before them and come back. And they are getting copious assistance from the unconquered north.

"So the invaders build a defense line on the northern border of the provinces they do occupy. This is an elaborate defensive line including the latest features of military art.

"Are you suggesting the southern colonies...."

"Vickers, you interrupt too much. Neither the defense line nor the efforts to pacify the lowlands work. And the ever-present threat of other powerful nations assaulting the homeland inhibits the invader's commitment. The losses become unacceptable and the people clamor to get out.

"The leadership is so discredited it is deposed and the faraway provinces have their independence. Did you study history at Oxford, Vickers? What am I describing?"

"The outcome of an American revolution?"

"I am describing the attempts of the Romans to conquer Britain.

"Despite their overwhelming military power, system of forts, Emperor Hadrian's wall to keep the northern hordes out, they could not defeat the spirit of the people. Maximus and his successors withdrew.

"Vickers, the British Government refuses to learn from its own history and will repeat the disaster. They will attempt to occupy the southern provinces and then strangle the north by attacks and blockade. To do this they will attack Charles Town first. They will avoid war with either France or Spain, mind you, but that will inhibit their campaign. Eventually the British people will rebel against the useless slaughter, the Government will fall and our independence will be accepted. It's human nature to fight for independence from foreign subjugation. It's happened throughout history, will be repeated here and our descendants will witness it again.

"Too noisy here. Come and be my house guest."

I accepted in spite of his historical nonsense.[*]

He also invited me to attend the meeting of the Provincial Congress tomorrow, as an observer in the balcony. *Common Sense*, the broadside profaning the King and demanding independence, has turned the man wild.

---

[*] *ENLIGHTENED READER, Gadsden's prophecy was remarkably accurate. Britain was the great world power but could not pacify a string of provinces thousands of miles across a great ocean. The British Government feared a political philosophy called Republicanism and could not cope with American nationalism. It dispatched thousands of troops, organized native forces, imported mercenaries—Hessians—and controlled most of the major cities but failed to defeat General Washington's elusive forces.*

France discreetly provided massive aid to the Americans but Britain did not dare attack France for fear of another major war. Finally the British people demanded peace, the Prime Minister resigned and the next administration ended it. R.E.H.

My facial scars and leg are healing, but the greatest relief is freedom from Grover or McKee. Only the French to worry me now.

Must get Melinda out of Williamsburg.

February 10th, 1776

The Provincial Congress met today and nearly resorted to violence. Gadsden was masterful but someday he may be hanged.

In the midst of a chaotic interlude when everyone was shouting and disagreeing, he leaped up and plummeted down the aisle to the speaker's stand. Even before he got there, he was roaring like a lion until every other voice was silenced. Then he scolded the group, read extensively from *Common Sense* and demanded the "absolute independence of South Carolina and America."

The delegates, British after all, were astounded and denounced him and the rascally author of the broadside. One man called Gadsden's speech treasonous, him a traitor, and offered to ride at the gallop to Philadelphia to present South Carolina's vote against the separation. (I wish he would try it; I would be interested to know how long it takes.)

Gadsden was out-voted and they retained their provincial status, but he was persuasive. He almost convinced me!

He is calling from downstairs...

Tis a letter from Melinda; came by packet boat a week ago to the Heyward House. She and her aunt are coming to Charles Town by carriage and hope to be in New Bern by February 20th. So do I!

February 12th, 1776 - Georgetown, South Carolina

A late start and delays at the ferry made for a poor day. Lodged at *The Silent Woman Inn*, the words on a sign in the shape of a headless female. Had a meatless supper and the innkeeper warned me of even more scarcity of provisions to the north.

February 22nd, 1776 - New Bern

Arrived after a dangerous and impoverished journey through bands of rebel marauders, calling themselves militia, who challenged me at every turn in the road. Most are moving south under orders and their loose tongues generously provide more intelligence for my ledger. Looting off the countryside, they are exhausting food supplies and both Mysty and I found little sustenance this week.

Melinda not here yet but Jst. Howard welcomed me with a handsome supper of neck of lamb, beans and a good rich raisin pudding with a bottle of Lisbon. Rumors of imminent British attack are plentiful and wild. A British "ghost patrol" of four horsemen is roaming the land stealing provisions. Sgt. McDowell?

No signs of McDonald's force or an invasion, but all activity points toward a confrontation.

Spent much time tending to Mysty and saddle repair. Leather is becoming hard to find and the old saddle is coming apart. I miss Nick's aid and companionship.

February 23rd, 1776

Unsettling news from the cellar. A footsore neighbor, Harry Merrill, deserter from McDonald's "army" fearfully descended last night and is hiding there lest he be arrested.

Harry says McDonald was advancing toward the coast with about 1500 men to meet with a British landing force but had arms for only a third of them. When a few began to desert, he formed up his command, harangued them in a patriotic speech and ordered those not ready to die for the King and the salvation of British America to leave at once.

Harry decided his courage was not war proof and did so with several others, to the jeers of those remaining. The command's cavalry patrol, led by Sergeant McDowell, chased them and lashed them with whips until they ran into the swamps. When one of the others tried to fight back, McDowell shot him.

Then he said McDonald reversed his march and withdrew to await more favorable circumstances.

Melinda has still not arrived. Decoded an ominous message from Randolph, burned it as he asked, but saved the original encoded.

London
23 December 1775

Christmas Greetings, Landon:

I hope you will be in New Bern soon; father will safely hold this letter until you arrive. Mr. Lee has secret intelligence he dares to transmit only through this route. His source is a member of Parliament I cannot name but French money got him elected.

You must get this information to Mr. Franklin's Committee of Secret Correspondence. General Howe, in Boston, has proposed to London that he be sent 20,000 additional troops. With these he will abandon Boston, occupy New York, and commence military operations to invade Massachusetts from the west. The Government has secretly approved this plan.

The other significant intelligence is that Mr. Lee has Monsieur Beaumarchais in his pocket. Beaumarchais is proceeding with his false business venture in France to sell arms and munitions without the apparent knowledge of the French Government. This activity may, in fact, be secretly financed by the French and Spanish governments, whose goals are probably nothing less than the destruction of the British Empire.

There is much public disagreement here as to what the Government should do. Some MP's advocate overwhelming military suppression. There are others, however, who would send peace commissioners tomorrow to keep the colonies British. But Lord Chatham's influence is so diminished that I cannot imagine you to be in any danger.

It is more than tedious to encode all of this. I pray you are able to read it. I miss you, old man, and I wish we were playing whist together at Barney's again. Pray treat this information with dispatch and utmost discretion. Burn the decoded version.

Your enduring friend,
Randolph

February 24th, 1776

Melinda is here and we must expedite. When I told her about my encounter with Bennett and his injury, she received the news calmly, perhaps even numbly, but would not discuss her situation. Neither would Aunt Elizabeth. They appear grimly determined to get to Charles Town and resolve the matter before they discuss it with me.

They did discuss the aberrant actions of her former French tutor. He abruptly became hostile and resigned as her tutor just before the ladies departed. Elizabeth believes Melinda asked too many perceptive questions about his presence in Virginia.

Bingham interferes again from Philadelphia. An express rider delivered his urgent message to the New Bern Committee of Safety. Bingham had mentioned me so I soon found myself standing before the Committee.

Dr. Gaston, speaking for the members:

"The dispatch warns that General Clinton has departed Boston with at least 1000 men and is sailing for North Carolina. He plans to rendezvous at Cape Fear with a large fleet from Britain which will have several thousand aboard. They intend to join up with the loyalist forces in North Carolina on the Cape Fear River and reestablish British control in the Carolinas and Georgia.

"Vickers, Mr. Bingham requests that we inform the Congress at once, should this invasion occur and he suggests we use you as courier if you can be found."

I was thinking fast.

"I'll go south myself, sir, to be in a position to leave at once if the British appear. There'll be advance indications, a small landing force or patrols, and I'll watch for these signs. Charles Town may be the British objective, sir, so I could also look beyond Cape Fear."

Gaston thought about that for a moment and agreed that I should go as far south as Charles Town, then return here. Thus I obtained permission to get Melinda through the danger area without delay. I left and recorded the conversation.

Did not dare to tell the New Bern committee the content of Randolph's letter but I put the essence of it in a sealed message to Franklin and entrusted it to the postal express. I harangued the first rider about the urgency but that direction is unlikely to be forwarded.

What am I doing? Lending encouragement to a war of independence? Do I want that? Perhaps now is the time to take Melinda and escape to Britain through Florida. Whatever we do, we'd best get out of North Carolina.

Leaving early tomorrow if we can repair the coach front axle. Her driver just called me to help.

February 25th, 1776 - Jackson's Inn on the New River

The fragile machine made it this far but it's ailing. The front axle is split and the suspension shows trail damage. But we must get south of Cape Fear before we stop long enough to replace it.

This afternoon, while the horses rested and the driver tightened the splints on the axle, Melinda and I walked up to a pleasant grove of trees overlooking the countryside.

I was anxious to be proper (she had chided me to do so) and would not touch her as we walked. Finally I pinched the smallest possible fragment of her skirt and held on like a child clinging to his mother. When she laughed at this, I picked her up, stood her on a rock outcropping and teasingly called her my Charles Town whippoorwill. What a relief it was to break the spell of gloom on her face.

It was a congenial day. Despite the chill, the sun was warm and the air was still. The tall tulip poplar trees, walnuts and oaks were devoid of leaves but their trunks and limbs painted long shadows on the ground. Beneath the trees a squirrel rustled in the dead leaves looking for leftover nuts. A female deer down in the draw below stood motionless, watching us but did not flee.

Then we saw the reason she did not. At our feet not more than a rod away lay her spotted fawn in a thicket, hoping not to be seen. It was curled up as instructed with white tail down, head and ears flattened and eyes not moving.

"Bless his heart. Oh, it's beautiful here, Landon."

"It is at Whippoorwill too. Living there with you would make it perfect."

She was abruptly melancholy again.

"It's not for me, Landon. I shall never live there. Only God knows what will become of me, but I believe you will stay in America and support independence." She touched my lips with her finger, would not let me speak. "Your property and your "obligations" will keep you here, but not with me."

My protests were in vain and the mood was dark for the remainder of the day.

The excellent horses did well today in spite of some high water and the axle did hold. The news here is that both McDonald's force and the militia are marching for Wilmington and may clash there by morning. A traveler here, with the same destination as us, knows a route to the west of Wilmington and Cape Fear to avoid the fight.

He drew a sketch of the route to follow. I know not what to do but follow his suggestion.

Cannot get Melinda's premonition out of my mind.

February 26th, 1776 - Moore's Creek Bridge

We made it here by noontime but were prevented from crossing the river by an arrogant Colonel Lillington and his 2nd Regiment. They are throwing up earthworks on this side of the bridge with the greatest urgency and other troops are doing the same thing on the other side. Where do these colonels get their titles?

Do not know why they are here making such preparations. We are staying in the little house of Widow Moore, who kindly offered us her spare accommodations. I am in the hall outside the door where Melinda and her Aunt are sleeping.

February 27th, 1776

It's dawn now but I'm unable to sleep. The digging around the bridge on the left bank and ripping of lumber from the bridge has not ceased all night. From this vantage point, not two hundred yards away, on a little bluff, I can see the fires of the troops on the other side but they are not attended. A ruse? Do they expect an attack here? Perhaps I should awaken the ladies now and leave.

I hear a few gunshots. Something is happening on the other side. Just beyond the fires cheers are sounded. Merciful God, a line of troops is approaching the bridge!

Wilmington; the Harriot's house.

Two o'clock in the morning, the great clock in the hall chimes, as I write of yesterday's tragic events in the detail that Mr. Boswell would have me do.

In the first light of dawn, an officer led his Scottish Highlanders to Moore's Creek bridge and started across. The militia had torn up the planking and presented the attackers with only two logs on which to cross.

At that instant a frightful volley of musket and cannon fire erupted and ripped into the attackers. The leader fell but rose and started forward again.

A second volley hurled him backward, lifeless, and hit everyone on the two logs as well. The few who made it across were shot before they could reach the earthworks. Those behind, seeing certain death before them, fell back.

Their officers tried to rally them but the momentum and spirit was gone. A few sought cover and fired but many appeared to have no weapons other than swords. They began to retreat and the retreat turned into a rout. As they ran into the woods, the militia rose from their positions with an exultant roar and rushed to the bridge with replacement planking. In less than a minute they were crossing and pursuing the routed attackers.

The battle was over but the results were just beginning. Melinda had joined me and was weeping uncontrollably. At her insistence we went to the bridge to attend to the wounded.

Two visions of those next hours are intense in my mind. One is the carnage. The dead were frightful enough with bodies torn open and ripped apart. One torso had received cannon blasts that removed both head and legs. Another dead youth lay on his back with his stiff arm holding high a handful of grass.   Still another smooth-cheeked boy appeared untouched until I saw the natural opening in his ear had enlarged slightly where the ball had entered.

The agony of the wounded was even worse. First they were screaming, then groaning, then quiet, then dead. Two militia doctors and several others tried to help but there was little they could do for most. Before we left I saw more than two dozen bodies laid together for burial. At least another dozen are in the river, killed or drowned.

An equal number of wounded, mostly Scots, fill Widow Moore's barn and many of them will not live to see morning.

My other burning vision is that of Melinda, dearest Melinda, tending the injured men. While she bound their wounds or gave them water she talked to them, prayed with them, sang to them, wrote a letter for one.

Melinda had a tenderness, a compassion, a love for the wounded beyond my ability to describe, and she demonstrated a cool resolve in the face of all that gore that amazed me. After blooding her skirt, she tore it apart to bind wounds.

But now I hear her crying continuously in the next room and Elizabeth cannot console her. Morality, reputation be damned; I'm going to her.

Nearly dawn now. I did go to Melinda and what a revelation it turned out to be. With her aunt present I held the sobbing girl for at least an hour. When she quieted, we discussed leaving British America together. The coastal schooner *Rebecca* sails regularly from Charles Town to Saint Augustine with loyalists returning to England. She made no decision, but this raised her spirits somewhat and she fell into exhausted sleep.

Elizabeth took me by the hand, quietly led me from the room and presented THE REVELATION. She told me that in addition to exposure to horrible slaughter, Melinda believes she is witnessing the destruction of British America and her personal life as well. Her father is deeply in debt, so much so that trial and debtors' prison is a certainty if he returns from the west. At the insistence of Craig Trammel, the factor who lent him the money, a court case is pending.

Ian Watkins' trouble began a decade ago when the Stamp Act put him at a disadvantage. Then because both his rice and indigo crops failed in '74 and the Yellowjack killed many of his slaves, he could not pay his debts. He borrowed more to invest in western land, is out there now trying to sell it and cannot. If he returns, he'll be arrested.

But if this marriage takes place, the McKee and Watkins lands will be consolidated, 9000 acres. Bennett's father has promised to assume all of Melinda's father's debts, dispose of them after the wedding and operate both plantations thereafter. Bennett would eventually control everything.

"And Melinda was to sacrifice herself for this?"

"Landon, Bertha Watkins is a proud and ambitious woman. She put her daughter in the unendurable position of having to marry Bennett to save her father, their home and plantation. It's deeply embarrassing and sad for all of us."

I was stunned, speechless.

"But Melinda finally had the good sense to act in her own behalf and write a refusal. Her mother destroyed it, accusing Melinda of sending her father to prison."

"Now they lose everything?"

"Trammel has already taken their town house," she continued, "but my husband is making some interest payments on the country property to hold him off a few months. Meanwhile, Melinda's mother has returned to the plantation to plant a rice crop and start anew. And she was obliged to sign publicly the Association and favor independence.

But nothing suffices to meet the debt in time except marriage to Bennett. It's a humiliating experience for her and for Melinda. They did not want you to know. You say Bennett is recovering?"

"The doctor said he would. When can her father return?"

"I don't know. If South Carolina goes for independence, maybe new laws will eliminate this archaic procedure."

"You want independence too, then?"

"We're probably going to have it whether I want it or not. The world in which Melinda grew up is collapsing. People are either fleeing or turning rebel and she feels increasingly isolated from both her relatives and her friends."

The above is as I recall it. I retire scarcely knowing what to think....or do....or say to her.

February 29th, 1776

Two long days of unspirited rest have changed little; Melinda has been silent the entire time. I have not tried to discuss either the battle or her personal affairs. In the meantime, Gaston has sent word that I must remain in the area to watch for the British fleet and has reminded me that was Franklin's directive as well. But how do I get her to Charles Town?

There's jubilation and revelry everywhere, which we are unable to share, as the news of the defeat spreads. And they are defeated. General McDonald, sick abed, is imprisoned in

New Bern with his surviving officers. His command no longer exists; only Sgt. McDowell's mean-spirited patrol escaped. However there is new intelligence, from a fisherman named Harvey. He says there is a British fleet off Cape fear, but I cannot get anyone else to confirm it.

Charles Rutledge is here! Leading a reconnaissance patrol from the south to search for British forces also, he's about to return to Charles Town. Taking advantage of this, I asked him if he would take the two ladies with him. He readily agreed but I opened a hornet's nest when I revealed to Melinda I had to remain in North Carolina to look for an invasion. She is convinced I am for the revolution and abandoning her to Bennett. She is deeply angry with me; I have never before seen her like this. When I told her, she burst into tears—actually cursed me—and ran out of the room. Deciding to leave, I finally called to her that I would return to Charles Town as soon as possible, probably later this month, and departed to the sound of lamentations that could be heard throughout the house.

There's no pleasure in this for me either. Franklin is giving me irksome tasks and Chatham is suggesting that I quit and return to England. Either course is distasteful.

The atmosphere is so bitter in that house, I am staying at this miserable inn which does not even have a name. I vow it's a former stable; the smell is unmistakable. There is such demand for lodging, any clod can hang out a shingle. Or perhaps the odor is that of the occupants.

The ultimate absurdity of this day was that two ignorant religious dissenters were arguing in the ordinary over which day it is. One stated that today is actually Sunday, February 18th, (old style) and that we are all violating the Sabbath. He maintained the British change to the Gregorian calendar was a Popish conspiracy born of Satan and that he has been denied eleven days of his life. What an ass!

The other insisted the change had to be made and this day, the 29th, is added to February every fourth year because a year is actually 365 and ¼ days long. He claims, however, we should be observing a truce and worshiping on the last day of the week, starting tomorrow evening at sundown, along with the Jews.

I cannot imagine that the Creator of this little planet and the foolish human beings on it (which has to be a Divine error in itself) has the least interest in which day we stop killing each other, if we stop, to observe the Sabbath.

For what purpose did those men slaughter one another? It has accomplished nothing except to create widows and orphans. And why did I deliver the message which caused McDonald to attempt this campaign? My soul is sick beyond measure.

JOURNAL FOR MARCH 1776

March 3rd, 1776 - Wilmington

Back from reconnaissance and Melinda is gone. Perhaps gone out of my life too.

Oh God, British forces are now off Cape Fear. Witnesses reported two companies came ashore two days ago while I was to the north of Wilmington. Apparently seeking only fresh victuals and water, they stripped the countryside of young cabbage palms and other wild plants and retreated to their ships.

What does this mean? Do they know of McDonald's defeat? Should I fear them or welcome them?

I sent an express message to Franklin with this intelligence. Tomorrow I shall go to Cape Fear myself.

March 10th, 1776 - New Bern

After a week of reconnoitering where the invasion is expected, I quit and returned here. A small fleet is anchored offshore but evidences little interest in establishing on land. Waiting for others?

Many of the North Carolina militia have returned to their fields and are making prodigious efforts to prepare for the planting of tobacco seedlings and corn. The mobilization has badly delayed the building and dunging of the thousands of little hills of soil needed for planting.

March 11th, 1776

Dr. Gaston has just arrived with his comely wife, Margaret. He wants to discuss with the regimental commander here the forming of another volunteer company. Mrs. Gaston came along to visit her brother, Herbert Sharpe.

Gaston had two epistles for me. One was a message from Bingham telling me Franklin is dissatisfied with the express. Twenty days from Charles Town to Philadelphia is too slow; an urgent message must come in half that time! He wants a miracle; I can scarcely even get their attention at some of these postal stages. I have little authority and they have little incentive.

The other, a letter from Randolph (attached), bodes no good. His spies inform him the Government is sending both emissaries of conciliation and fleets of invading troops at the same time. Not very plausible intelligence.

London
8 January 1776

My Unlettered Landon:

I am learning little from you or anyone else regarding the events in America. Can you not write more than this message from Mr. Franklin to begin serious negotiations with the French? We have already begun, two months ago. Beaumarchais has returned to France and awaits specific requests from us regarding supplies and travel routes. Why aren't they forthcoming?

There is a persistent rumor here that some twenty British commissioners (I would call them spies) have been sent to the individual colonies and to the Continental Congress to negotiate for peace. I cannot confirm this but I fear, if true, the independence movement will be jeopardized. Vergennes will not tolerate their presence or yours if they believe you are participating. Take extreme care, Landon.

The King has announced that he will "compel the colonies to absolute submission," and has hired 18,000 Hessian troops to reinforce the British. Meanwhile, Sir Peter Parker sailed ten days ago with a huge fleet of troop ships and the Carolinas may be his destination.

Moreover, we believe General Howe will abandon Boston soon and operate from a base in New York. Other troops under General Cornwallis may have been ordered to do the same in the south.

Landon, I hear no more of your maiden, Melinda. Has she jilted you for taking liberties? I for one am scheming to break out of my monastic existence. Cynthia is not always available but there's a good humored young woman, Bertha, in the neighborhood to whom I believe I offer some appeal. Having a narrow vulgar soul, I am cultivating her acquaintance.

And I remain your impatient friend,
Randolph

March 12th 1776

Is my head being turned toward favoring the revolution? Dr. Gaston invited me over to Herbert Sharpe's tonight. Suspecting his brother-in-law's loyalty to Britain, he took me aside in the garden, feigning interest in the mulberry trees there, planted to support a failed silk industry.

He had in his hand a truly remarkable document that George Mason had sent him, the draft Virginia declaration of rights that Mason was writing when I talked to him. Upon reading it, I was obliged to agree that observing the principles therein would correct virtually all of the abuses that I have witnessed in America, by loyalist or rebel. What a happy, if impossible, prospect, to live in a country whose laws would be based upon a written constitution including such ideas. Gaston's enthusiasm is infectious.

Gaston also wants to go across the Cape Fear River with Mrs. Gaston and Herbert Sharpe to see the latter's newly acquired property and he wanted my opinion as to whether or not it would be safe.

I could only answer that since McDonald's defeat, the entire area appeared to have returned to peace and normality. The few British ships off Cape Fear seem to have little interest in invasion. Furthermore, I was returning to Charles Town and perhaps we could travel together as far as Cape Fear. He was agreeable to that and we leave in the morning.

March 13th, 1776 - Cape Fear River Crossing

We finished what must have been a twenty-five mile route today; Alexander Gaston pressed hard. He has an excellent coach and four healthy matching black Hackneys, each one sixteen hands in height, which can trot for hours. My Mysty, tied to the coach, came along nicely as well. Alexander

Gaston wears the uniform of a captain now. He's resigned from the Committee of Safety and aims for the command of a company. I cannot but admire his actions and the principles he stands for. He shows Mason's declaration of rights to everyone and promises to lend it to me to make a fair copy.

Margaret Gaston, a pleasant young lady, has been a very agreeable companion. We are tenting for the night, with her brother providing the means. Supper was two fresh-killed turkeys roasted and young cabbage palm centers, boiled and tasting somewhat like artichokes.

Just saw Alexander and Margaret retire to their tent. What must it be like to bed with a lovely lady every night? Would I ever sleep? My imagination becomes indecorous thinking of being with Melinda. Would we undress before one another? Imagine lying beside her, hearing her as she sleeps, reaching over and touching

(Bottom half of page torn off. R.E.H.)

March 14th, 1776 - Wilmington

With heavy heart, bloody head, and bitterness toward the British Government and its brutal troops, I record today's tragic events.

It was a beautiful morning when the ferry arrived and everyone was in a jovial mood. Alexander wore his uniform and proudly displayed his coach and four to all. We approached the ferry and as is the custom, everyone dismounted until Alexander put the coach and horses securely aboard. I went back to a tree where Mysty was tethered.

But just as he motioned for us to join him, a British Army patrol of four horsemen led by that red-moustached Sergeant McDowell galloped up from nowhere.

Seeing Alexander's rebel uniform, they demanded he surrender his horses for their use and himself as a prisoner of war. Instead, he released the ferry from the dock and shouted to the oarsman to start rowing.

The sergeant dismounted, ran out on the dock and aimed his musket at Alexander, then hesitated as Margaret screamed at him not to shoot. As Alexander moved to the bow of the ferry to hide and I ran toward the soldier from behind, she fell to her knees before him, pleading for her husband's life.

But the vicious blackguard fired directly into Gaston's back, pitching him forward in instant death. When I threw myself on the cruel brute, intending I know not what, another soldier struck me on the side of my head with his musket butt. I lost all consciousness and woke up hours later.

Herbert tells me the soldiers fled at once; he retrieved the coach and horses and returned to Wilmington with Alexander's body and me, for all appearances dead also. Remembering my interest in Mason's declaration of rights, he handed me the bloodstained and torn draft.

What a melancholy situation. My head aches, the hearing in my left ear is dulled and my cheek is bleeding. Both Herbert and I are in mental agony for having contributed to Alexander's senseless death. Margaret cannot be consoled.

May God damn the British! I am finished with them.

March 17th, 1776

It is St. Patrick's Day but not observed here. The murder has created a new fever of war preparations. Delegates to the Provincial Assembly at New Bern departed this morning to consider North Carolina independence and two militia companies marched through town to occupy Cape Fear. I would go to Melinda but my head aches too fiercely for me to even leave my bed.

March 18th, 1776

My hearing remains dulled, the cut on my face smarts and the headache persists despite taking powders of willow bark. Worst of all, my soul is in torment. I wrote Lord Chatham with heavy heart, fair copy attached, another to Randolph and one to Melinda telling all of my decision.

⸻

Wilmington N.C.
18 March 1776

The Right Honorable Earl of Chatham Hayes, Kent, England

Sir:
I have long considered your letter suggesting I return to England. I agree with you, sir, that circumstances make reconciliation unlikely. Enmity between Britain and America is in the extreme; e.g.:
The Provincial Congress of South Carolina has just established an independent government and adopted a temporary state constitution with the caveat "until an accommodation of the unhappy differences between Great Britain and America be obtained." South Carolina is mobilizing, fortifying Charles Town and preparing for war.
The news from Georgia is that naval skirmishes off Savannah have sent loyalists fleeing to East Florida. In St. Augustine, Governor Tonyn threatens to invade Georgia with

Florida Rangers and murderous Indians by land and privateers by sea.

Governor Martin's insertion of some British Army officers and a band of murderous raiders into the Scottish Highlanders of North Carolina has led to cruel misfortune for many. General Clinton's threatened invasion may cause the North Carolina Assembly to declare a state of war with Great Britain.

Governor Dunmore has totally destroyed the largest city in Virginia in midwinter; the alienation is equally total. I have in my hands Virginia's bloodstained answer, and I predict America's answer, to such dastardly acts. This document, Virginia's Declaration of Rights, is so damaged, I shall write only its essence:

It states that all men are by nature free and independent and have certain inherent rights, the enjoyment of life and liberty, property and pursuit of happiness and safety. All political power shall be invested in the people; those in authority are their trustees and servants.

Thus by free elections and choice, not heredity, do all men determine who occupies public office, how they should be taxed and which laws should govern them.

The declaration protects an accused person's rights in matters of law, prosecution, and in particular, reasonable punishment. It puts an end to the wicked practices now all too common. The military is strictly subordinate to civil power and freedom of the press and religion is guaranteed.

I must emphasize, sir, that none of these provinces has voted for permanent separation from Britain. But they are so close that any further hostile acts by British forces will break the fragile threads of connection that remain.

As for myself, sir, I have made a decision that gives me excruciating pain to inform you. I am casting my lot with the American provinces in the hope and belief that they will declare *themselves independent. I do this with great reluctance and heavy heart, for I have endeavored to abide by your admonition to do my Duty, maintain my Integrity and serve my Country.*

But where is my Country? Which is my Country? My memories of your guardianship, of Gresham and Oxford, of London and of England are warm and abiding. I have many friends there and, no doubt, could find a reasonable career with my training and experience. Moreover, I have utmost respect for your sensitivity to the mistreatment of America, but my people, my land and my spirit are all here. Thus I must go with them.

I beg your forgiveness, sir,
Landon Vickers

March 29th, 1776

The express rider brought an immediate response from Melinda today, so bitter and accusatory that I burned it in a rage. This miserable fortnight just completed has been one of headaches, hearing loss and emotional torment. God must be punishing me for my desertion of his calling.

How can I free myself of this idea?

Melinda is distraught over my decision to support the independence movement. She is not only heartbroken but utterly disappointed in me as a person of integrity. She accused me of having lied to her in the past, of having intended treason from the beginning.

She accused me of rejecting her, abandoning her to Bennett, bringing her nothing but pain. She reminded me (a reminder I did not need) that unless she marries Bennett, the court will consider her father's case early in June and surely commit him to debtors prison. She even suggested in bitter words that there must be another woman in Philadelphia seducing me; certainly the Continental Congress was doing so.

I had tried in my letter to explore ways to avoid both marriage to Bennett and debtors' prison for her father, specifically by a Provincial Assembly voiding the law, or even offering my own property to that avaricious Trammel, but she did not respond to those proposals.

She is LOYAL and will not hear of any proposal, not from a government parasite turned into a bifurcated traitor, a congenital liar, a heartless philanderer like me, etc., etc.

March 30th, 1776

My primary talent appears to be an ability to hurt others. No illness of the mind is so difficult to cure as that which is aggravated by guilt.

Even Mysty dislikes me. While I was tending to her, she kicked me in the shin and it's complaining fiercely tonight.

I should go to Melinda but to ride there and return will take a fortnight. Do I dare? And what can I accomplish? How can I convince her that she and her loyalist friends are about to be exposed to every kind of indignity and perhaps even expulsion from the country. I can do nothing with her.

Post Script!

Oh miserable Chichester! The express rider was just leaving for Charles Town when he recognized me and pulled a letter from the pouch, a rude message from that ass Bingham. This prince of prevarication accuses me of amorous escapades! I'll crown him King Liar with my chamberpot.

Why must I course to Williamsburg now?

His billet-doux attached.

THE CONTINENTAL CONGRESS
Committee of Secret Correspondence

March 5, 1776

Mr. Vickers:

I assume you are in Charles Town as I write. There is urgent news.

We have suspicions that Virginia is to be the object of a major British assault for the purpose of seizing the southern colonies and then defeating the north separately. The Congress has placed Major General Charles Lee in command of a new Southern Department, headquartered in Williamsburg, to thwart this attack.

Mr. Franklin directs that you go immediately to Williamsburg, reconnoitering the Carolina coasts en route, for a conference of most critical import. Use the express horses. I and other representatives of the Congress will be there conferring with General Lee and you should report to me when you arrive. I will have instructions for you from Mr. Franklin.

He is highly disturbed that no message has arrived from Charles Town in less than twenty days. He threatens to replace Mr. Goddard with another postal director and to end your situation as well if service does not improve. This frail Congress is about to disband for lack of evidence of British malicious intent. The buzzards are dismissing Norfolk as an accident and are about to dismiss themselves as a deliberative body. You cannot imagine the atmosphere here. I suggest you abandon your amorous escapades and attend to your duty.

With urgency,
William Bingham
Secretary

Charles Town S.C.
April 7th, 1776

Oh my dear Cassandra,

Disastrous events encompass me and I am sorely afflicted with melancholy. First I was a witness to the fearful slaughter of loyal young men in North Carolina. Now I must report the loss of both my suitors, Bennett in death and Landon in treason.

With respect to Bennett, there are sympathetic condolences about the house in deference to my loss, but few realize the sensation of relief in my breast. The melancholy event has freed me. Do not believe I rejoice in his death, but the disparity of our purposes and characters were such that I could never have conceded to an alliance with him.

Landon has foully abandoned both me and his country. His treasonable attitude is beyond understanding and I am disappointed in him as a person of integrity. He has not been truthful, may have intended treason from the start. He now espouses the cause of that contemptible Congress and has the effrontery to suggest that I join him in this "dramatic moment in history for the rights of man." I confess that I yearn for him, weep in the night to be with him again and yet detest him when morning and reason return.

He is not alone in this madness. Many of my friends are opting for separation from Britain. My friend Ruth is following Charles' obvious bent for independence. All expect them to marry soon. Ruth urges me daily to marry Landon and argues almost convincingly in his behalf. Certainly Ruth's and Charles' devotion to each other is a joy to observe.

Even my own mother has abandoned me. She has signed the "Association" and declared for independence. Aunt Elizabeth is silent on the subject and only God knows what Uncle Thomas is doing in Philadelphia.

I do not know what I should do but prepare to flee. Secretly I have collected my meager resources and some possibly useful intelligence. I dare not include it here but from Mirabeau I learned that massive French aid will be coming to support the rebellion. I am prepared for departure, should the necessity arise.

Praying that you may never experience the hopeless wretchedness of

Melinda

March 31, 1776

Merciful God, the express rider from Charles Town told me Bennett McKee is dead! The poor man succumbed to wound festering and gangrene after the skirmish at Savannah.

Contrary emotions afflict me. I am relieved that Melinda cannot marry this man, but does this mean that her father goes to debtors' prison?

Pitiable Bennett, he died serving what he believed to be his country, honoring what he believed to be right. What is right and honorable for me?

Damnation, I dread this diversion to Williamsburg. The British may take Charles Town or the court Melinda's property before I can return.

Herbert's doctor says I should not go anywhere for another week. I do admit to difficulties, but my hearing has returned despite an unbalancing dizziness when I try to rise.

Fortunately Mysty is in good flesh and well accustomed to my directions. When properly agitated, she can now execute the "Nick Reverse" like a wild animal. Pray I will never have to use it.

JOURNAL FOR APRIL 1776

April 7th, 1776 - Wilmington.

There were two Easter services at St. James Church but I entered between them to pray alone for Melinda. There is purpose in my life now; to serve my new country and to protect Melinda from harm. Perhaps these worrisome concerns will free me from so much self-examination and guilt for past actions.

Coastal sentries from Cape Fear northward have nothing to report. The danger is southward, perhaps Charles Town itself. But I am ordered north, will leave tomorrow.

April 10th, 1776 - New Bern.

Reluctantly staying with Justice Howard again. The dear old gentleman is distressed with events, his son, and me. He has a strong sense of duty and integrity but it is to Britain that he maintains his allegiance. He should go to England until the conflict is resolved.

A startling letter from Randolph, within a gift for his father, is his last; he flees for America. British intelligence intercepted one of my coded letters to him and, despite their inability to read it, came to arrest him. He fled to France, where he wrote he was coming.

I gave Jst. Howard the essence of Randolph's letter and burned it, but the news did little to cheer him.

I fingered my recent journal entries. When I asked him if he would continue to keep them in his strongbox, he agreed to do so and encouraged me again to keep it up. I almost destroyed the military ledger, now listing forces in all thirteen colonies, then decided to keep it.

I am leaving despite the rain.

April 12th, 1776 - Hallifax, N.C.

This town is a bedlam of excitement and celebration. The Provincial Congress meeting here instructed its delegates to the Continental Congress to vote for independence, but only if proposed by others. The hawks will welcome this.

April 16th, 1776 - Williamsburg

Found both chamber and victuals at Raleigh's Inn but the sullen serving maid was constantly scratching flaking skin. When she handed me a pitiable shin of beef with deposits from her scratchers on it, I settled for ale and a remnant of bread I had in my pouch.

Mirabeau, Melinda's former tutor in French and archery, lives in the Inn now. Why?

Major General Charles Lee is indeed in command of the "Southern Department" and is responsible for defense of the southern provinces. He has posted recruiting broadsides and established a headquarters, but has done little else.

New and remarkable intelligence on the invasion! A few days ago Privateer James Barron captured a British mail packet on the Chesapeake with a secret communication from Lord Dartmouth to Governor Eden revealing the whole British plan of military operations. Barron brought it here and in Bingham's hands was a fair copy of the entire document. The Carolinas are indeed their objective, not Virginia, and Charles Town is the probable point of invasion.

Merciful God, let me reach Melinda first. Poured out my heart in a letter to her; kept no copy.

April 17th, 1776

The worried Bingham gave me his full attention this morning. He listened intently as I told him of everything I had experienced and learned. I even told him of Randolph's departure from England and my resignation to Lord Chatham.

When he asked about my "Tory lady" I sharply retorted she is not a Tory lady and I wish to return at once to remove her from danger. Charles Town is about to be destroyed as Norfolk was.

He ignored my request and called two Philadelphians, Mr. Deane and Dr. Bancroft, and required me to repeat everything. They are en route to France on a secret mission to obtain French military aid.*

Never have I seen such a solemn-faced, secretive trio of men. Nothing I told them disturbed them more than the news that peace commissioners may be on the way from London.

"We've already heard this," said Deane. "That false tale has been deliberately placed among us to confuse us. It is the primary reason why the Congress refuses to vote for independence."

"Only North Carolina and Massachusetts are even half-inclined," Bancroft added. "The other delegates remain in Philadelphia only for the most fragile reasons."

Then that ass Bingham proceeded to chastise me in front of everyone for my "pitiable progress" in establishing a fast postal express; my last epistle took twenty-two days to get to Philadelphia. I explained that the motivation varied with

---

* *UNINFORMED READER, Bancroft was the first traitor and spy in American history. He accompanied Deane to France, reported all secret negotiations, and flow of arms to the Americans, to the British Government.* R.E.H.

stages, that I was not taken seriously at many of them. I discovered coming north that at three stages there were not even any horses.

"What if we commission him?" mused Deane. "Yes, make him a captain, Bingham, make him a captain. I'll recommend it to Mr. Franklin."

Then Deane leaned forward and peered at me, or into me, as though he were examining the back of my skull, on the inside.

"You are now to be a military aide to this committee of the Congress. You answer to no one else. But you give us a ten day express service from South Carolina or we'll revoke your commission. Do you understand?"

"Yes sir, but I'm not sure its poss..."

"If someone waving a conciliation covenant from London," retorted Deane, "walks into the Congress, I doubt that even Massachusetts will vote for independence."

The agitated Deane began to pace the floor and pound one fist into another. He turned to me. "We need news of another military encroachment on our shores, a serious one. Only that will turn the majority for separation. Get yourself a uniform."

I shorthanded the conversation and hurried for a tailor to be fitted for the uniform. It took a month's pay for two uniforms.

This tailor is also making Grand Union flags similar to the one Washington adopted, and I purchased one. If these thirteen red and white stripes with combined crosses in the corner on a blue field are to represent a national flag, why not equip myself with one?

Found myself surrounded by Virginia Assembly delegates at Raleigh's tonight because I had just come from the south. I withheld only what Bingham told me to, but some of their ashen faces took me aback. Their stark, worried, even frightened exchanged glances reminded me again of the men of the *Sophia* when some tried to launch a lifeboat in the hurricane to escape to shore. Some of these gentlemen are seeking escape too. They would take a chance in the open sea to get back to the homeland and they're as uncertain of the form of government they want as they are of independence.

One of them who is not frightened, (though somewhat frail from a winter illness) named James Madison, is probably the youngest delegate here. He cannot be a day older than myself, yet quietly displays more wisdom than any about him. I pray he recovers.*

The arguments are endless. Meanwhile, the location of the British fleet remains a mystery and so does Mirabeau's presence at Raleigh's.

April 18th, 1776

An inquisition I experienced today. I was directed to appear before new arrivals from the Congress, Braxton of Virginia, Livingston of New York and Boucher from Annapolis, and endure lengthy questioning about foreign trade.

Bingham warned me to say nothing of Lee in London or Beaumarchais but it is most discomfitting to be in this role.

The subject soon switched to a possible British invasion. I predicted an assault on Charles Town within a month but the cold element clearly tried to entrap me and discredit me. With

---

AMUSED READER, you know full well he recovered to be the author of the United States Constitution and our fourth president. His concern for his health was greatly influenced by his mother, who has never admitted to a well day in her (thus far) 94 years of life. R.E.H.

acid tongue Braxton accused me of inventing the intercepted Dartmouth letter for want of real intelligence. When Bingham showed him the captured message, he conceded, but behaved very much unlike a gentleman. In the future I shall have nothing to do with him.

How am I going to escape this assignment? Melinda may be in considerable danger.

Mirabeau approached me today and inquired of her health, asked questions obviously pointed toward determination of where her loyalty lay. This man bears watching.

April 26th, 1776

A full week has passed and little has happened. Reports from the Carolinas do not indicate any British action but these messages are most unreliable.

The ill-tempered and profane General Lee refuses to believe the danger is to the south. This lanky fellow struts about in tight green breeches he calls "serry-vallies." He is more concerned with the welfare of his hounds and refuses to move until one of his pungent bitches has pups.

When I am commissioned and have a uniform, neither Bingham or anyone else will prevent my departure.

Damnation, Bingham just presented me with a task which intolerably delays my departure. The silly ass crept up to my door without a sound and knocked very lightly.

When I admitted him, he looked about the room for eavesdroppers, closed my window and curtains, and approached me with hand over mouth. Another secret coming, no doubt.

He whispered that I must go to Norfolk to meet Goddard, the Postmaster General. He has a message of utmost sensitivity. A French vessel is there with a secret agent I am to escort here.

Told him I could not, would not, but his cant was so intemperate, I decided to oblige, but only if in uniform. Too dangerous otherwise.

The cringing nuisance finally agreed and left.

April 27th, 1776

Sixteen days it took to deliver the last intelligence report from Charles Town to here. It will take another five to reach Franklin.

Bingham ordered me to be on my way. Went straightaway to Johanson, the tailor, and found my first jacket nearly complete but a finger too big and only temporarily stitched. However, I took it and a military hat he already had. I leave in an attire which, with my own breeches and dress boots, passes reasonably as an officer's.

April 29th, 1776 - Norfolk

The city is gone; only a few wharves remain. It is a graveyard of ashes with chimney tombstones. A few pitiable souls have built shelters near the harbor and one grieving man was carting his wife's fetid remains from a temporary burial site to a cemetery without the environs.

The new captain greeted William Goddard this afternoon in a manner not intended. Deciding to use military demeanor and bravado to get his full cooperation, I marched into his newly built log postal office and gave him a smart military salute. Unfortunately, the temporary stitches, already strained by the ride could not tolerate another pull and gave way on the right shoulder. When I dropped my arm and the sleeve fell off, Goddard burst out laughing.

Do not wish to remember this scene.

When he could stop laughing, we discussed the express route, the riders, the managers of stages, pay and other costs such as maintenance of stables, etc., in detail. Meanwhile a dutiful servant sewed my sleeve on and repaired other seams sufficiently for me to wear it back to the tailor.

When I inquired about my mission, he hushed me as though I were a child. In a low voice he asked me to wait here until morning and when the man appears, escort him to Williamsburg. He handed me the agent's business card, innocent in appearance but laden with intrigue:

Roderique Hortalez et Cie
Importations et Exportations
24 Blvd. St. Germain
Paris, France

I turned it over and there were the handwritten words:

Disponible maintenant:
200 canon
200,000 lb. poudre de fusil
20,000 fusils
Et Cetera

This was the message I was sent to receive. The company is Beaumarchais' fraudulent business and they have available now 200 cannon, 200,000 pounds of gunpowder, 20,000 muskets, etc.

Mr. Goddard has offered me overnight lodging. I find that as his guest I am most welcome and comfortable. We even discussed his Jewish faith for a time and it is quite interesting. The Christian faith is based solidly on his. Jesus was quoting a long-established Jewish creed when he said "love the Lord thy God" and "thy neighbor as thyself." I cannot but imagine that there are many rooms in the House of God for good people of differing conceptions of our Creator.

JOURNAL FOR MAY 1776

May 1st, 1776 - Williamsburg

Mr. Vingtcinq, he mysteriously introduced himself (which simply means twenty-five in French), so I introduced myself as Mr. Twenty-six, which did not amuse him. He came dressed as a Virginia militia private (must have sconced the uniform) and asked to play the role of enlisted aide for concealment of his true purpose. We traveled to Williamsburg in that fashion, neither of us knowing the name of the other. Probably I was just another goddam to him.

At Farnsworth's Inn without the town he said he would take a room and hope for visitors soon.

I found Bingham, handed him the business card, and retired to my room hoping to hear no more of it. Wounded leg aches tonight.

May 2nd, 1776

Bunghole Bingham will not release me until my commission is confirmed. So tonight after dark I was obliged to escort him to Vingtcinq and shorthand the conversation.

We met in a coach on a lonely trail beyond the inn where the Frenchman was staying. There I recorded, after swearing an oath of secrecy, to the most incredible conversation. Our visitor spoke English hesitantly but his meaning was always clear.

Vingtcinq began: "Monsieur Beaumarchais' establishment d'affaires has 2,000,000 livres to buy military necessities for the American colonies. By June premier, he will have an agent in every major French port who will be prepared to load vessels with whatever you need.

"You may pay for it eventually in tobacco and grain but we need to know what you want. We have available now, 200 cannon, 20,000 muskets, 200,000 pounds of gunpowder, clothing, shoes and other necessities."

Bingham produced a paper which apparently duplicated Deane's itemized list of necessities, vessels that might be coming and ports to which they were sailing. He also discussed the use of French ships to Statia and a transfer there to American bottoms.

Vingtcinq repeated emphatically, "Monsieur, the French Government cannot officially assist the American colonies, or even secretly allow this commerce in any meaningful quantities, until you have declared your independence."

When he finally offered his name, Dumont, I thought his eyes would leave their sockets when he heard mine.

"From whence comes this goddam little goddam? You are the agent of Chatham?"

"No longer, sir. I am a military aide to the Congress."

He left us in some disbelief. At parting I exchanged a stare with the coldest eyes I have seen since Grover. We returned to the city with coach lanterns unlit but near the tavern I am certain I saw Dunmore's Indian, Pitch.

May 4th, 1776

Obliged to remain abed these two days until the swelling in my leg subsided. It did not until a doctor bled me two ounces, very rich and therefore needed. Paid him 2/6.

My second uniform is ready to wear and I do not look too badly. With this costume, the scar on my cheek (from the rifle butt at Cape Fear) could be taken for a saber cut and I see no reason to correct the assumption.

The French goddam, Dumont, (if that be his name) is worrisome. He was overheard talking to Mirabeau and inquiring about me and about Melinda. If he is even thinking about harm to her I will kill him.

Startling news today. Massachusetts authorized their delegates to vote for independence but had no more courage than North Carolina to initiate it in the Congress. Braxton departed for Philadelphia at the gallop, determined to prevent the Virginia delegation from making the proposal.

The thought of independence is exciting one moment, dreadful the next. I lie abed fretting about it and what might happen to Melinda until my stomach aches. Wrote her a letter warning her of Dumont's mysterious interest in her.

Merciful God, let me go to her!

May 5th, 1776

Sunday brought me to church but my heart was not in it. What does one pray for, the dissolution of one's country, Britain, or the birth of one's country, America? United Free States of America, some call this land now. Suspect I am being followed again. Both Dumont and Mirabeau have disappeared.

General Lee, having learned of my shorthand ability, has dictated to me orders for various commanders. These messages tell me he sees no immediate threat but he is having great difficulty organizing any defense of the south.

May 6th, 1776

I am a captain in the Continental Army! Now I belong to a group with a personal interest in victory; defeat would mean a mass hanging. The Earl will be distressed to learn of my commission.

Went to Bingham for permission to leave. Instead he assigned me to another spy mission. With his usual furtive demeanor, he told me Jonathon Boucher, an unbending loyalist from Annapolis, is in Yorktown with a strange companion. He may be one of the English agents sent here to entice the colonies to remain loyal to Britain. I am to accompany them to Williamsburg and note whether they attempt to influence members of the Assembly to vote against independence. When I started to protest,

"Vickers, these two come from Maryland, a province about to withdraw from the Continental Congress and they are an abomination to our cause."

"They're not going to let me follow them around and observe their lobby walking."

"Just stay with them as much as possible without arousing suspicion and discreetly observe."

I record this to later prove that he ordered me to do this. Thus do I remain in Virginia trapped on another dangerous mission of folly.

May 7th, 1776

Jonathon Boucher and Donald Yardley, an officious Londoner, awaited me just without Yorktown. We returned without incident, though a lone rider did follow us at a distance. His silhouette reminded me of the Indian, Pitch.

As expected, they thrust themselves into every clutch of delegates they could find. But when Yardley ordered me to bring him some grog, I suggested he get his own and left.

Dispatched another pleading letter to Melinda.

May 8th, 1776

Yardley and Boucher sat in the balcony and listened all day to the Assembly's bitter debate over independence. Tonight they entered Farnsworth's to join a gathering of delegates. I followed them discreetly but discovered I was not the only one following. A cloaked figure stood in the rain outside the window and watched them at length. Something is amiss. Told Bingham and went to bed.

May 9th, 1776

Oh the Devil visited from hell last night. Someone put an arrow into Yardley's back, mortally wounding him. Boucher never saw the assassin, but the next morning the militia found Mirabeau's dead body a quarter of a mile away with a black arrow in his back. Boucher was completely unnerved and hurriedly returned to Maryland.

Bingham and I conjectured into the night about these murders. One possibility is that Dumont directed Mirabeau to kill Yardley to prevent his influencing Virginia to remain loyal to Britain. Then Dunmore's Pitch assassinated Mirabeau because he was a French agent. Dumont has departed.

May 10th, 1776

The overbearing and foul-mouthed General Lee is at last thinking that South Carolina may be the British target and departs for Charles Town Sunday with his staff and hounds. I plan to follow.

May 12th, 1776

Mr. R.H. Lee rode in from Philadelphia this morning on a frothing mount and, despite his fatigue, began agitating at once to get the Assembly to propose separation. He says the atmosphere in Philadelphia is more uncertain than ever. Pennsylvania, New York, and Maryland all threaten withdrawal over the independence issue.

Even the Virginia delegation is disintegrating. Harrison and Braxton are preventing the Virginia delegation from proposing separation. Lee also presented an appeal to the Assembly from Mr. Jefferson that he be allowed to withdraw from the Congress and return home. Jefferson states the Congress is getting nowhere and his wife is gravely ill.

No news of either a British conciliation offer or an invasion. Either would tip the balance just now.

I prayed for Melinda in church today; do not know the value of it. Miserere mei Deus.

May 13th, 1776

Intense debate in the Assembly today. George Mason pleaded with them to propose independence. At one point, when the opposition could think of no further argument, one of their group said contemptuously of George Mason, author of the Declaration of Rights:

"It's well known his mind is failing." The brilliant old patriot turned on him and replied:

"Sir, when yours fails, nobody will ever notice it." They tabled the sensitive issue until tempers calmed.

Still no permission to leave. I may desert.

May 15th, 1776

Nothing from Melinda. Left for England or just finished with me? Straightaway to Bingham's office I marched to obtain permission to leave at once. His unfeeling response: permission denied. If the Assembly votes for independence, he might send me to inform Franklin. Damn them both, stupid asses.

Franklin writes in a new letter that in spite of his efforts, the Pennsylvania Assembly is voting against separation and others are resisting it too. Maryland delegates are preparing to withdraw from the Congress entirely. They're actually packing their belongings. If they leave, at least four other delegations will follow and independence will be a dead issue.

The Congress declared May 17th a "Day of Humiliation, Fasting and Prayer" for the Revolution. They had best do something; Adams' political tactics are not working.

Midnight

After a stormy session the Assembly voted late tonight to propose independence to the Congress; a Colonel Nelson galloped off into the night for Philadelphia shouting "Virginia free and independent!"

They also refused to accept Jefferson's resignation from the Continental Congress.

May 17th, 1776

I go southing tomorrow! A great British fleet has been sighted and Bingham is anxious about it. He is anxious!

I am to be paymaster at the various express stages as I travel south but I do not savor it; prefer not to carry bags of newly printed Continental dollars of doubtful value. An indication of their value came when I tried to pay my lodging charge to Anderson with some old Spanish coins.

"They're not worth a Continental."

Bingham's final admonition: "Remember, ten days!"

May 19th, 1776 - Richmond

Paid the Stage Master and riders. They want money for better mounts but I told them to go to Goddard for that.

Much rejoicing in the streets tonight over Virginia's independence and the election of the rustic Patrick Henry as the first Governor of the free state.

For a cavalry lance I paid five shillings and tied my Grand Union flag to the blade. With the lance lashed vertically, the flag rides high, prompting cheers.

There is a conference room full of Methodists here, representing all the colonies, they say. How lustily they sing. They're dressed quite beyond their station and... "And what is your station, Landon?" asks my conscience. I retract the thought....and they do serve the poor.

May 25th, 1776 - New Bern

Almost midnight when I arrived. Mysty is holding up well, but the packer is not. Bearing perhaps too much load.

First journal entry in a week. A strange sick feeling has permeated my body for as many days. What are we doing? If independence succeeds, will we be annexed by France? If it fails, will we be drawn and quartered like the wretched wagoner? Switching one's patriotism is not easy but there is something awesomely right about what America is doing.

Jst Howard says every militia unit has mobilized to meet the threatening invasion and the effect on spring planting is serious. Farming is being done poorly or not at all and they need the crops.

The Howards are well but resigned to events. He is so highly regarded, no one molests him, despite his coolness to independence. I shall remain here only until first light.

May 31st, 1776 - Cape Fear

From a coastal watch tower I observed at dawn a huge British fleet moving to the south.

Charles Town
June 1st, 1776

Blessed Cassandra,

   This epistle may well be my last to you and I dispatch it secretly with the loyal Freneau family. They embark for St. Augustine in a few hours and thence to London, being deported with virtually no warning. The vulgar "Sons of Liberty" term it Tory riddance.

   They encouraged me to join them but I do not want to surrender our fair city to the Republican rebels yet. Moreover, by merely walking the streets, observing the troops and defenses and listening to conversations, I collect information which should be useful to my country. Some members of St. Cecelia are quietly doing even more but I should not dwell on that here. I am under suspicion myself. I often feel cold glances when out.

   Am I in grievous error? There are moments when I could destroy all such intelligence and run into Landon's arms. When he writes such as: "Oh that I were gloves upon thy hands that I might touch both cheeks" I am vulnerable! His letters say he is coming.

   A significant loyal populace remains and we pray for rescue by British forces. The harbor is rife with rumors of a great fleet approaching but I know not where the truth lies.

   Even Charles has joined the militia. He and Ruth plan to marry soon and invite Landon and I to join them.

   I am prepared for departure should the necessity arise and I accept your gracious invitation to stay with you until I make permanent arrangements. However the thought of leaving this fair land, my parents and Landon wrenches my soul.

I am your disconsolate friend,
Melinda

JOURNAL FOR JUNE 1776

June 10th, 1776 - Charles Town

Nervous soldiers challenged me as I approached a barricade erected across the road into town. It was dusk and raining and they were fearful of being attacked. My Grand Union, atop the lance not only saved me from being shot, they cheered when they recognized it.

The lieutenant commanding the outpost vows there is a British fleet offshore, and some troops have landed on Long Island, but there is no fighting yet.

My uniform and the Grand Union managed to get me past two more guard posts and I was in town. I went forthwith to Mr. Gadsden's house to take advantage of his standing offer to stay there but it was not to be. The energetic old widower had married a third time to one Anne Wragg. She met me at the door in neat kerchief and stomacher and was pleasant indeed, but his absence, commanding Fort Johnson, made my occupancy awkward so I vainly sought lodging elsewhere. Too many troops in the city.

I finally approached Melinda's house about nine o'clock and presented myself as a wet soldier simply seeking shelter until I could make other arrangements.

An old servant ushered me into the parlor and fetched Melinda. I had changed to my fresh uniform at the stable and assumed a dignified military stance before the window, thinking I might impress her.

Then I could hear her running overhead, but when she came into view on the stairs, her pace was quite casual. When she saw Captain Vickers of the Pennsylvania Regulars, she hesitated.

"Miss Melinda, I've been in Charles Town several hours and cannot lodging Would it be possible for me to use the coachhouse or any other place you would allow me for tonight only?"

She hesitated again, then actually stammering:

"Why, why....yes, Landon, of course. The coachhouse guest room is available but you'll probably find soldiers sleeping below in the stable. They come in every night and sleep there without even asking permission."

"Are they threatening or disturbing you?"

"No, not really. But you'd think their commander would have made some provision for them. They're often hungry and ill-dressed, too. There are thousands of men here now and the number grows daily. I would estimate 8500."

She paused and looked at me. Communication was tense.

"I've been so worried about you Landon; I've missed you, thought I would never see you again. What are you doing here and why are you wearing that uniform?"

I explained the circumstances and added, "You must believe that I had no other choice."

"Well I don't believe it. You could have left on the *Rebecca* for England and I would have gone with you."

"Left for what purpose? Live in wretched exile the rest of our lives? We've discussed that before."

I paused and changed the subject.

"Melinda, I did not come at this hour to debate or plead for anything but a night's lodging. Dear lady, will you grant me that?"

She did and here I am recording her words, contemplating her lovely manner of speech, even when angry.

June 11th, 1776

Melinda invited me to breakfast and we dined in silence. But it was not silent outside. The militia is tearing down buildings on the waterfront and converting them into defenses and barricades.

Finally Melinda volunteered that the preparations are all in vain. She does not believe the British are coming here. The troops landed on Long Island are just a feint. Meanwhile, every day more of her friends leave forever. Some are being evicted, expelled as Tory Riddance.

But those who left recently included Trammel and the entire court. They abandoned properties, legal cases, everything. She believes her father's case is a forgotten matter and that President Rutledge thinks the new constitution will eliminate such laws.

Excellent news! And she sees some virtue in the new government!

She looked at me again sharply.

"And I suppose you're going to leave for Philadelphia if they attack?"

"If I go, I'll take you with me. I'll not leave you here to be victimized like the women of Norfolk."

"You're a fool, Landon Vickers and you're lying to me. You stay here in that uniform and you'll be killed. But if you leave again, we are finished, you and I. You show no more intelligence than Bennett McKee."

With that she went into a fit of weeping. I took her into my arms and tried to comfort her. She did not resist but neither did she cling to me as she has in the past. There was a numbness, a passive despair in her demeanor. Finally she regained her control and told me the coachhouse room was mine as long as I wanted it and asked to be left alone.

I left the house and found General Charles Lee's headquarters. The foul-mouthed man was on reconnaissance but his assistant adjutant, none less than my friend Captain Charles Rutledge, was there and greeted me warmly.

"And what are you doing in the uniform of the Pennsylvania rebels?" he laughed.

I explained the nature of my employment and looked about the harbor. What I saw was a sense of urgency not unlike that of the defenders at Cross Creek, but on a larger scale.

The work is relentless to turn the city into a fortress with outlying forts protecting the approaches. Charles says a frantic effort is now underway on Sullivan's Island to defend the harbor entrance. That fort was begun some months ago but apparently is not completed.

Within the city several thousand men are at work. Soldiers, militia, hundreds of Negroes, even some gentlemen are laboring with impressive perseverance. Neither rain nor mosquitoes nor station exempts anyone.

Along one street they are tearing out window sashes and lead weights to make musket balls. They're not only building barricades and artillery emplacements but removing buildings, trees and thickets for fields of fire. Women and children are bringing food and water to the sweating workers while others are carrying provisions into central supply houses for storage and later issuance.

Charles Rutledge explained to me that his uncle, President Rutledge, who is also South Carolina's commander-in-chief by virtue of his elected position, fears the British will try to sail past Fort Sullivan and assault the city directly. But he reasons that if the fort on Sullivan's Island is strong enough, they'll pay a terrible price.

He also confided that he and Ruth are to be married.

I returned for supper with Melinda and her aunt, supplying their kitchen with a side of salt pork and a firkin of oranges from a British sloop seized off St. Augustine.

Melinda is rather contemplative; I won't press any sensitive subject just yet. To bed in the coach house.

June 12th, 1776

Melinda invited me to breakfast again. We tried the oranges but they were sour. I was told they were grown experimentally in Florida. If so, Floridians will have to find some other crop.

Melinda let me kiss her when I left the house, whispering, "Please be careful." She may be reconsidering my marriage proposal but I dare not mention it yet. Went straightaway to a goldsmith to order a pendant to be made for her birthday, June 16th.

Unfortunately, he was a victim of Tory Riddance too, deported to St Augustine. Only the young apprentice and some disks of soft brass remained. He is a calligrapher and I asked him to finish the surface of one and inscribe on it:

A Mon Petit Engoulevent
Que J'aimerai Toujours

(To my little whippoorwill, whom I will always love.)

At General Lee's headquarters I saw the man in action. Charles Rutledge was there and told me neither Lee nor his imported staff nor half-a-dozen hounds are much appreciated. The local commanders have been organizing the defenses since January and Lee's arrival contributes mostly disagreement.

General Lee is energetic, rash, cursing and obscene, indefatigable, and a little frightening. Only President Rutledge seems to be able to influence him. They were arguing when Charles escorted me into the office of his chief of staff, Colonel Baldwin. This Baldwin is obsequious with the general but overbearing with others.

Baldwin listened attentively as I explained my mission to inform the Congress of a major attack on the mainland.

"With your permission, sir," I concluded, "I'll send a message to Philadelphia now describing the situation."

A mistake to ask; to assert himself he had to refuse.

"Not until we're better informed. We don't know yet how big the British force is or its intentions. It's being so obvious with its presence that we suspect a feint. Couriers will come from New Bern and Savannah if there is any indication of attack at those places. And we're commencing a reconnaissance here."

Baldwin suddenly raised his eyebrows and looked at me anew. "Gadsden told me about you, an emissary of Chatham?"

"Yes, sir, I was..."

"And do you still have his written orders directing you to this duty? Ah, this gives us an opportunity to gain intelligence, solid intelligence directly from the British."

"I don't understand, sir."

"With your papers, man, you could row out there in a bateau and ask for sanctuary, claim you're escaping from us. Gain all the information you can and then slip away and come back to us with it."

"No, sir, I cannot do that," I answered, even surprised at my own bluntness.

"What? Why not? Are you afraid? I can order you to do so, you know."

The room grew tense and quiet. I gulped and took a defiant stand.

"Colonel Baldwin, my commission and my orders place me directly under the authority of the Congressional Committee of Secret Correspondence. I am specifically directed to carry out only this mission, to respond to no other orders. I have this in writing. But there's another reason..."

"Cowardice, that's the reason I see," he shouted.

I could feel my face reddening, my entire body tensing.

"Sir, I have resigned from my situation with Lord Chatham and I have committed myself to a free America. I cannot abuse my integrity to go lying to the British."

"I don't believe you. Let me see your orders."

I did so; Secretary Thompson's handwritten instruction and signature were unarguable.

"If you say you're for the revolution, let's see you prove it. I think you're just a pusillanimous shirker!"

I was so angry I couldn't speak—until I had an inspiration which gave me control of myself. I shouted back:

"May I suggest, sir, that we go together, in uniform, to reconnoiter the British and gather intelligence? Not hiding behind lies and dishonor but acting in a straightforward discretionary manner as any patrol might."

"You're presumptuous and insubordinate, Captain."

The wide-eyed Captain Rutledge retreated. I did not.

At that moment General Lee walked in and, noting the shouting, demanded an explanation. My knees grew weak; I feared a court-martial for refusing to obey an order.

To my amazement and relief, General Lee said:

"Good idea, Baldwin. You know British order of battle, he knows the terrain and waters here, don't you, Captain?"

"I can find someone who does, sir." Baldwin's face turned pale but he said nothing.

"Well, that's settles it. We can spare you for a couple of days, Baldwin, and we need the intelligence. You two can go tonight to see what's on Long Island, tomorrow night to scout the fleet. Get a small boat and a local pilot for that." The colonel started to protest but Lee interrupted.

"I'm going out to Fort Sullivan now, Baldwin. That obstinate ass, Colonel Moultrie, insists that his spongy palmetto log and sand fort will prevent a British landing and President Rutledge won't let me withdraw him.

"Get word to the Engineers to collect every bateau, longboat, raft, anything that floats, and build a floating bridge from Sullivan's Island back to the mainland. They're certain to be overrun and must have a way to escape. Get to it."

"Yes, sir," Baldwin answered like a proper soldier, but he would not look at me. I found myself actually embarrassed for him in spite of his grievous accusation of cowardice. But now he has to go with me to avoid being accused of the same unmilitary flaw.

He turned to me and stiffly said:

"Get a map, Captain, and come up with a plan for this. I can't leave now; have to get the floating bridge started. I'll join you about three. Will that be soon enough? "

I assured him it would. (This conversation not recorded verbatim but contains the essence of the exchanges.)

I arranged for a boat to take us to Fort Sullivan and called on Melinda. I told her I would be gone for two days only (which she doesn't believe), changed to my workaday uniform, and now wait for Baldwin at Gadsden's wharf with somewhat less than full courage.

June 14th, 1776

Colonel Baldwin and I sailed to Sullivan's Island on a cargo sloop and immediately departed at dusk for a long row around Long Island. It's separated from Sullivan's only by a narrow tidal creek.

We had a small sailing bateau with muffled oar-pins and rowed with mast down. The owner, one Calvin Jones, came with us; his knowledge of the waters and strong arms on a third pair of oars were invaluable in the darkness.

On Jones' advice, we covered our hats and faces with mosquito kenting and painted our hands with turpentine to ward off the pesky insects. The dark gauze also made our faces less noticeable, but seeing more difficult. On one occasion, when we landed on Long Island, I stepped off the bow and my right leg sank in the mud up to my hip. But for the other leg outstretched I would have gone even deeper into the bottomless slime.

We made our way easily to the north side of Long Island and followed a hunting trail Jones knew until we could hear the voices of the British troops. But in the dark we could see nothing.

Baldwin proposed we hide in the brush, observe by day, and have Jones meet us the next night. Jones volunteered to hide the bateau and himself in the swamps nearby and wait for us.

What we discovered through the day was that the British have several hundred soldiers on the island and two batteries of artillery. Their preparations indicate an assault across the creek on to Sullivan's Island and thence to the Fort.

Jones says the creek separating them from Sullivan's is more than seven feet deep even at low tide. They will need boats or floating bridges and seem to have neither.

What I noticed was miserable boys (some cannot be more than sixteen) enduring heat, mosquitoes, hard labor, poor victuals, and overbearing sergeants. These young faces, picked up off the streets and farms of Great Britain and pressed into military service, looked more bewildered and fatigued than anything else.

The atmosphere was quite different from that in Charles Town where a decade of smouldering bitterness and fear has energized them like a disturbed Carolina ant hill.

The British troops are sons of the commoners, who have no quarrel with anyone, people I saw daily in London and elsewhere. Now I suppose I will see them hurl themselves into the fearsome fire of equally young men whose parents or grandparents came from the same country. Why cannot these differences be resolved in some way other than slaughter?

Last night we completed an encirclement of the island and with the little sail moved silently and undetected with the tide straightaway through the anchored British fleet back into the harbor. We counted eight men-of-war we could see and twice that number of provision and troop ships. No way of knowing how many were beyond our vision.

One fact is clear; they have the power to penetrate the defenses and take Charles Town directly if they choose. The guns at Fort Sullivan, however, will make them pay a high price. They may choose to reduce the fort first.

Returned to the coachhouse guest room by early morning, after a day and two nights of rowing and walking in the mud. I am exhausted. Having shaved and bathed (and made this Gentleman's Entry, Mr. Boswell!) I can no longer resist sleep, though it be nine in the morning.

Ten o'clock in the evening now and all is well. Oh, it is with me, it is with me—and I must add to the journal.

I awoke at twilight after a too-warm day of sleeping. Unclad except for a sheet I abruptly realized Melinda was sitting on the edge of my bed watching me. I was so startled at her presence and my state of undress that I nearly overset the tray of food she had.

"It's all right," she smiled, and held a fresh shirt for me so I could sit up and put it on.

"Stay right where you are and have something to eat," she whispered, "but I had best go."

"Please don't. Who will know you're here? And what if they do? Then you'll have to marry me."

She laughed, leaned over and kissed me, and started for the door. I leaped off the bed with the sheet about me, and intercepted her with a kissing embrace. That lasted several minutes and I was becoming less of a gentleman each minute.

I picked her up, losing my sheet, carried her to the bed and laid her there as gently as my aching muscles would allow. When she offered no resistance, I knelt beside the bed and began to kiss her.

There was no stopping for a while. When I partially disrobed her and exposed her sweet bosom, she did not resist. But I knew I must stop. I just closed my hands on her sweet loveliness as her eyes searched my face. This was really happening; she was allowing me to see, to touch, to kiss her intimately.

My passion was intense but I knew I had advanced beyond propriety. If I continued, she might dismiss me later for having taken advantage of her in this fiery moment. She put both of my hands on my chest and covered them with hers.

"Do you love me, Landon?"

"Yes, you are my beloved. Why don't we marry?"

"In the Song of Solomon are the words 'My beloved is mine and I am his.' I am yours," she whispered, "but I will come to you after we are married."

She covered herself and the mood changed.

"Landon, my only concern is the change that has come over you regarding this terrible revolution. I don't understand you and I don't think you know what you're doing. British America will remain British; The rebellion will fail and I'm afraid you'll be killed."

The tears flowed again. Then she regained control of herself and left. Only then did I realize my sheet had dragged the breakfast tray off the bed and I had stepped on it and broken it.

June 15th, 1776

Should destroy the last entry except that I like to read it, to savor it. An exquisite time, even if abruptly ended. Interrupting an assignation thusly is comparable to preparing for the ultimate banquet, sitting down before it, savoring it, then leaving before the eating begins.

And she is willing to marry! The agreement is most tenuous and so is the date, Saturday, June 29th. She is in consultation with her friend, Ruth, about their marrying at the same time. I am just beginning to grasp that Ruth has been my most valuable ally. Her aunt is quite happy about it but her mother probably does not even know about it yet.

Now if the British will just postpone any military action for two weeks, we can return to Philadelphia together. She agreed to do that but still resists the idea of American independence. Sometimes on a sleepless night I do also.

The military intelligence is confusing. The courier from New Bern says a man-of-war put a large patrol ashore near Cape Fear two weeks ago but the reconnaissance appeared to be more for water and provisions than any other reason. Could that activity be to hide the real reason?

From Savannah come rumors of Admiral Parker's fleet joining another from St. Augustine to seize Georgia.

Still another rumor from a privateer is that General Howe is enroute to Philadelphia with an offer of reconciliation. His source: British seamen on a sloop the privateer captured. Then why is this fleet here?

Nothing will turn the head of General Lee, however. He discounts these reports and fiercely presses everyone to greater efforts. I have reported the British presence.

Meanwhile I am a temporary and very junior member of Lee's staff. He knows I have no military experience but who below the rank of colonel has? I am useful as an aide, scrivener and courier. Colonel Baldwin grudgingly leaves me alone and I stay as distant from him as I can. On the other hand, Charles Rutledge and I are becoming close friends as our marriage plans converge.

I saw Melinda briefly this evening, in the presence of her Aunt. She is clear-eyed, happy, openly affectionate in her language, and shows not a sign of guilt regarding our lapse of restraint. But our political differences I dare not mention. To bed now, to imagine the experience again.

June 16th, 1776 - Sunday

Today is Melinda's twenty-fourth birthday and it turned out to be far more intimate an anniversary than I had intended. I am bold to be writing this but I must.

I took her to church with Charles and Ruth at St. Michael's but did not tarry after because everyone is laboring on the defenses. The four of us did obtain the services of the Rev. Fletcher for the wedding on the 29th.

These headstrong damsels are happily engaged in preparing wedding dresses, reception to follow, concert the night before, etc. squarely in the middle of this preparation for a great battle. Charles and I have used every argument we can muster to advance the date, but they will not entertain it. Relatives need time to get here.

I reluctantly left her at home and spent most of the day around General Lee's headquarters preparing messages. He enjoys dictating instructions to the various commanders. If I could only convey to the recipient the irritation and impatience in tone, the cursing, the pacing and gestures, the reader would quake.

But tonight Melinda consented to an assignation with me! After supper I discreetly took her to my coachhouse room to give her a birthday gift, the brass disk with the French words artfully inscribed.

She accepted it sweetly, teasingly promised to wear it at the wedding. She shared with me some Portuguese wine, which I poured into her Jefferson cups, and we toasted our coming marriage—but avoided the unresolved political schism. After the second cup, however, there didn't seem to be any schism. Verily I lost control of myself and she yielded totally to my embrace.

"Oh, Landon," she whispered, "I want to have you."

"What?"

"I didn't say anything," she retracted but too late.

We looked into each other's eyes; all differences of the past were gone. As I fumbled at my clothes, she disrobed before me in the fading light. Without any apparent embarrassment or shyness she revealed her lovely self to me. I was in a dream looking at a beautiful painting that had come to life. As the Song also sings, thou art all fair, my love; there is no spot in thee.

When I came to her, clumsily, but determined to be gentle, she just sought my eyes, looking for trust and love and commitment.

I am scrupulous about truth and always intend my innermost thoughts in this journal, but what followed is too intimate to write. It was not a matter of the flesh overcoming the spirit; the flesh and the spirit became one and we became one in a mutual surging climactic act of love.

Then in the next moment she pushed me from her, burst into tears and wept uncontrollably. She quickly dressed, ever weeping, and ran from the room without explanation.

Strangely, I don't feel the least guilty. She is a lovely, darling maiden and I adore her.

Charles Town
June 17th, 1776

My Dear Cassandra,

I delight in your letter of May 1st with the sketch of Jane. She is six months old today and surely the ultimate joy. Steventon Parsonage will never be the same.

I must describe the tumultuous events of the past two weeks climaxing last evening. May God forgive me not only for my sins but for my enjoyment of them.

Landon is here and he profoundly influences me. This swain has a grip on my soul that is beyond description. Even now as I would write, I enter into a reverie about him until I can scarcely continue this epistle. He claims to have the same symptoms! It must be a disease peculiar to lovers.

Cassandra, I confess in closest confidence that concupiscence overcame me and I yielded to his passion. Dare I write I wish to repeat the lovely experience? But only within marriage. And there must be marriage lest an issue from this liaison precipitate disgrace.

Landon has been steadfastly loyal to me and wants to marry. I know that he is in torment over his decision to switch national loyalty and, having done so he is even more lonely than I. Yet I sense his love is sincere and he needs me—even as I need him.

All kindred about me insinuate trust of him into my doubtful mind and I have conceded—reluctantly one moment and excitedly the next. We are to be married on June 29th in a double ceremony with Charles and Ruth. You must not think of me as unsteady—more correctly as uncertain.

Now I must end my obsession of several months to collect all possible intelligence about the rebels to thwart this horrid revolution. I turn the outcome over to the mercy of God. Having absolute faith in the bearer of this epistle, I will admit I was astonished to find the St. Cecelia group has been conspiratorial for the past year.

Though presenting to most a false image of shallow unconcern for events about us, they have produced, for example, a detailed map of the Charles Town defenses and are looking for a way to get it to the British fleet. This is only hearsay, mind you and you must reveal this to no one. I do not know what to do with intelligence I have already collected but will have no further part in such things. I do not want to become a victim of "Tory Riddance" kidnapping.

Unfortunately I am under suspicion simply because I have been so outspoken against independence in the past.

Just now it does not seem that I will come to Hampshire but who knows what the future may bring? Uncertainty is now the utmost sensation in the breast of

Your Melinda.

June 17th, 1776

Learned with relief the wedding is still to take place. As a wedding gift Aunt Elizabeth is offering us her coach to travel to Philadelphia! But my horses may not suffice. Meanwhile wedding preparations continue as feverishly as war preparations.

Now we have no rector to marry us. The Reverend Fletcher fled to Florida last night with his wife and child. Despite his moderate views and efforts to serve all parishioners, he was labeled a Tory and was forced to leave. Must find someone else to marry us.

Wrote to Bingham and told him of plans. Did not see Melinda all day but left a message that Fletcher is gone.

June 18th, 1776

Colonel Moultrie sent a message that the British have now landed about 2500 men on Long Island and he is deploying a skirmish line to resist them.

General Lee left for Fort Sullivan at once, allowing me to accompany him. It is a crude fort; a square enclosure is surrounded by two parallel walls sixteen feet apart, built of soft palmetto logs. The space between the logs is filled with sand. The palmetto tree, peculiar to these southern shores, grows to 30 or 40 feet, shedding branches below a large tuft of palm leaves at the top.

Colonel Moultrie had his men felling these and stacking them to contain the sand. The west wall rises very slowly.

At opposite ends of the fort stand two flags; one is the Grand Union devised by General Washington, the other a blue South Carolina flag with a silver crescent and the word Liberty on it. Inside are palmetto leaf-thatched shelters to shield the men from the fierce sun and intermittent rain.

Meanwhile, Colonel Thompson at the east end of Sullivan's Island has about 800 men opposing the British landing force. Mostly riflemen, but including a two-piece artillery battery, they expect to be "highly incommoding" (as Thompson expressed it) to the British attackers before they fall back to the fort.

Colonel Moultrie is the essence of confidence and self-assurance. He is virtually ignoring General Lee (who wants the whole project abandoned) by insisting President Rutledge has ordered him to conduct the defense there. He has on the island altogether perhaps a thousand men, 30 cannon and about 500 pounds of powder. More artillery is being landed daily in the face of General Lee's frustrated orders that the number of cannon be reduced.

We returned to the mainland at Haddrell's point, seat of another defense under General Armstrong. There was Colonel Muhlenberg, Lutheran minister turned soldier, directing the artillery emplacement. He was the gentleman who preached his last sermon in a uniform hidden under his priestly robe so that he could dramatically shed the latter at the end of the harangue and ride off to the war. Perhaps he could marry us, dissenter or not.

I had supper with Melinda and her aunt. Our primary problem is that no proper clergy is available. The parsons are all gone, either because they are "Tories" or they are military chaplains elsewhere.

I mentioned Colonel Muhlenberg and the little chapel at Haddrell's Point as an alternative and they are willing.

Melinda gives me long looks, I pray of affection, but we have had little opportunity for private conversation. I am fearful she may have dark afterthoughts about our passionate rendezvous or my declaring for independence and dismiss me. Her tender loving on Friday was a lifelong commitment for me.

June 19th, 1776

Bought two harness horses today for the coach, for forty Continental dollars. They are supposedly a cross breed of Yorkshire and American Standard but the reckoning is outrageous. Now I am nearly penniless. However, with these and Mysty, I should be able to make it to Philadelphia. I wrote Bingham to find us a temporary place to live there until I find something more permanent. Difficult to believe all this is transpiring. Her recent willingness to accept me, a treasonable person, remains a mystery. She does not discuss it and I am wont to threaten the fragile engagement we have.

June 20th, 1776

Charles and I escorted Melinda and Ruth to Hadrell's Point today and arranged for Muhlenberg to marry us on the 29th. He too is reluctant to wait, does not believe the British will accommodate us. It is rather unconventional and awkward to turn to a Lutheran rector but we have no choice.

June 21st, 1776

Old George awoke me this morning and asked me to hurry to the house before the mob broke in. I guessed the difficulty and threw on my uniform coat, breeches and boots.

Entering the rear, I ran to the front door and saw, as forewarned, perhaps thirty "Sons of Liberty" chanting for the door to be opened in a search for St. Cecelia spies deserving Tory Riddance. I knew that Melinda might be suspect and I decided on a risky course. George opened the door quickly and closed it behind me as I stepped out. The unruly gaggle was surprised by my appearance and quieted down long enough for me to remind them that the owner of the house was for independence and was a delegate to the Continental Congress. I told them the Heyward's niece was betrothed to an officer fighting for liberty until his death, their lead window weights had already been given, etc.

They accepted my harangue on behalf of the Heywards but when one of the hoydens mentioned Melinda by name I promised to run him through if he ever came near her. They moved on to harass some other household.

I finished dressing and ran down to Lee's headquarters for help. Charles sent a platoon to disperse the mob.

Melinda is not a little impressed with me, a situation I do not mind. But she was genuinely frightened. When I held her in my arms, her entire body was quivering.

June 22nd, 1776

Melinda's mother has returned from the plantation and accepts the situation. We have given her little choice and there is hope that her husband's situation will be resolved.

Since we are leaving for Philadelphia immediately after the wedding, the many ladies fussing about Melinda like bees around the queen have decreed that there should be more festivities prior to the wedding. To watch them at work, one would never guess Charles Town was under siege. Starting tomorrow there is to be a series of teas, dinners, concerts and a reception, all of which I would prefer to miss.

No news from Philadelphia other than a plea from Bingham to bring them word of any invasion at once. He's no longer giving me a choice; I must bring the intelligence myself. And Franklin wants it, of course, in ten days!

He writes the Congress is as divided as ever and any report of an attack is sure to break the deadlock. An offer of peace by General Howe (who is known to be sympathetic to the colonials) might do it too, writes Bingham, but in the wrong direction.

June 23rd, 1776

A British deserter just reported that the British fleet plans to begin its naval bombardment today. The intelligence is taken seriously; the pace of preparations is frantic. But those who know the harbor say the winds are not in Admiral Parker's favor, that he cannot attack until they change.

Charles promised to send along messages after me by the express riders, should I depart before the attack.

We must have the wedding at once and depart. I reminded Melinda that she has been threatened with Tory Riddance, some of her friends have already been kidnaped and thrown aboard departing ships and if the British do attack the wedding will be impossible.

She was convinced and went to Ruth, whose grandmother is coming from somewhere in North Carolina and has not arrived yet. Each day Ruth asks for another day of delay.

The first tea honoring the brides-to-be took place today and Charles appeared briefly. Alternately frowning and smiling ladies looked we two men over thoroughly, as though we were about to be put on the auction block, while someone played a flute in the parlor across the hall. Both sides of the political issue were represented and Melinda was gracious to them all. A tense truce is in effect.

June 24th, 1776

Still no evidence of enemy action but I dispatched more orders for General Lee. Another inspection tonight. Charles and I and our ladies enjoyed an elegant dinner of fine sirloin of beef, legumes and plum pudding. From whence came these ingredients? One elderly lady wanted to know my ancestral roots beyond my parents and was appalled when I could not answer her.

A pleasant evening but we were watched from the street by two Sons of Liberty until I ran them off.

I am in a profound dilemma. Melinda has turned over to me detailed intelligence on the defenses of Charles Town, to include a map of fortifications, location of artillery and reserves, etc.—all collected by gentlemen of St. Cecelia! One of them thrust it into Melinda's hands just before the Sons of Liberty seized him and she passed it on to me.

My own military ledger is a nearly complete resume of numbers and locations of American forces in all thirteen colonies. The two collections would be of enormous value to the British. I know Melinda would rather go to England until the conflict is resolved and we could do that by boarding the *Rebecca* after the wedding. (It sails for England.) As an Englishman I could give this intelligence to my country or as an American I could burn these papers and aid my country.

Where does my loyalty lie? Am I witnessing "a most horrid rebellion," as King George termed it, or "the most noble experiment in the history of mankind" as George Mason described it? This vast land and its people have such awesome potential; how can I not be a part of it?

June 26th, 1776

General Lee took Col. Baldwin and me with him to the new fortifications at Haddrell's Point where Col. Muhlenberg commands the artillery. When I asked Muhlenberg if he could conduct the wedding, he offered to preside only at Haddrell's Point and no later than Friday. So the wedding is Friday.

June 27th, 1776 - Haddrell's Point Chapel

Charles and I brought the coach here, with my Grand Union flag on a cavalry lance waving above it and Mysty trotting behind. We're spending the night here.

Melinda and Ruth will arrive at ten o'clock and the ceremony will begin at once. They will come by a lesser used route—and well escorted, says Charles—to avoid those clods who might attempt Tory Riddance. I should have stayed back and come with her.

I have offered to Randolph, in the event of any tragedy befalling me in these hazardous times, my journal for transcription and have asked that it be dedicated to Melinda:

A Mon Petit Engoulevent
Que J'aimerai Toujours

With these last words I end my journal, at least for a time. My soul is at peace, whatever the future may bring, for I have found love and I have found purpose in life, but I leave to Posterity whether I have adhered to Lord Chatham's charge regarding

Duty, Integrity, Country
Landon Chichester Vickers

EPILOGUE

Faithful Reader, despite the appearance of a joyous event pending, an undercurrent of premonition existed in the hearts of the wedding party. The bloodshed about to occur, the price of independence, would be increased manyfold throughout the thirteen provinces.

The following letters found with Landon's journal reveal the traumatic experiences of Landon and Melinda, not unlike those of many before the war ended.

Randolph Ewing Howard

———— ⋙⬤⬤⬤⬤⬤⋘ ————

Aboard the Rebecca
At sea off Charles Town
June 28th, 1776

Oh my dear Cassandra,

What hath God wrought! With heavy heart over today's tragic events and fear for the future I compose this sad epistle. Both Ruth Craig and I have been married to, and then torn most foully from our husbands. How shall I relate such an incredible tale? This day began pleasantly enough. Captains Vickers and Rutledge were the handsome uniformed bridegrooms and Ruth and I the brides at a double wedding in the chapel at Haddrell's Point.

Not wishing to compete with apparel, Ruth and I were dressed quite similarly in white lustering, little white hats and white gause-flounced coats. There was some decolletage but the pit of the bosom was covered with a modesty piece of lace. In our preparations this morning we teased and laughed and even wept a bit with excitement.

As we entered the chapel to join our waiting bridegrooms the light breeze gently tugged at Ruth's hair and coat and she was lovely indeed. Then my eyes met Landon's and I could see little else, sensing reassurance in his gaze.

Charles and Ruth first exchanged vows, then Landon and I. The ceremony was such as to touch the feelings of even the most insensitive. Colonel Muhlenberg covered his uniform with his priest's robe and was earnest and kind. When Ruth expressed her vows, looking at Charles with eyes shining and face aglow, I was inclined to tears. When I expressed mine, it was with tears.

But oh Cassandra, when the ceremony was over and Charles and Ruth walked out of the chapel ahead of us, a catastrophe unfolded. Five British cavalrymen, a mounted patrol, galloped out of the woods immediately adjacent to the chapel with such alacrity that none inside could do anything.

A red-moustached patrol leader reined up, shouted "Rebel, shoot him", and aimed his musket directly at Charles. At the instant he fired, Ruth stepped in front of Charles with her arms raised in protest and perhaps also in sacrifice. The ball struck her squarely in the breast.

Men ran for their weapons and rushed outside firing but the patrol escaped. Colonel Muhlenberg ripped off his robe, leaped on a horse and rode after them with saber drawn. Landon and several others followed.

Charles went berserk. He ran screaming after the patrol for a few steps, returned and gathered Ruth in his arms. He wept, cried to her to speak, attempted to revive her but to no avail. She looked at him, tried to speak, but only blood came. As a great stain of red spread across the white lustering and into the lace at her bosom, she raised one hand toward him, then expired. My dear friend of a lifetime was gone. I can scarcely continue for tears.

This frightful scene was interrupted by a massive volley of cannon fire in the harbor. A line of British men-of-war was hurling volley after volley of fire into Fort Sullivan.

Charles did not hear the cannonade or see anything but Ruth. He held his lifeless bride against him and rocked to and fro like one soothing a child. He talked to her, prayed to and cursed God with fearful language, cursed the British even more fearfully, and shouted incomprehensible things.

Colonel Muhlenberg returned from a fruitless pursuit and dismounted. He told me Landon and others were still looking for the murderers but that when Landon returned, he would have to leave for Philadelphia immediately with news of the battle. The colonel then knelt beside Charles and talked quietly to him with compassion and tenderness. But Charles could not be consoled, just held her body to him.

Colonel Muhlenberg helped him to his feet and began talking to him softly.

"Duty calls us all now. I must go to Fort Haddrell and tell them we may be attacked overland, outflanked from the rear. You must warn General Lee at Charles Town and Vickers must go to Philadelphia. He is under orders to do this, only he knows the entire route."

Charles started toward Ruth's covered body again but Colonel Muhlenberg restrained him. He turned and walked numbly to his mount, leaned against the animal's neck and wept. Once more he returned to Ruth and no one stopped him. He uncovered her face, kissed her cheek, stroked her hair and recovered her face. When he stood up, the colonel said that Ruth would want him to be strong now and do his duty. To fight for independence is the only hope for liberty.

Charles seized the colonel's coat lapels and stared at him with the fierce eyes and contorted face of a man gone quite mad.

"Liberty? Ruth is dead. That's the liberty they have given her. What else matters? Liberty doesn't matter." Then shaking him, "Nothing...else...matters!"

Without another word the pitiable man mounted up, slowly turned toward Charles Town and was almost out of sight before his mount broke into a canter. Colonel Muhlenburg whipped his stallion into a dead run for Fort Haddrell. All the men were gone.

Then misfortune became my lot. When we women placed poor Ruth's body in the coach and I took the reins to return to Charles Town, the accursed British patrol reappeared, its escape apparently cut off. The red-moustached fiend leaped aboard, put a pistol to my head and ordered me to drive at a gallop to the harbor. The blackguards were desperately trying to reach the British landing force which should have come ashore by then.

They mistook the ship Rebecca, engaged in "Tory Riddance," for a British landing ship and ran into American militia instead. In a fearsome exchange of fire one of the patrol and two militiamen were killed and I threw myself on the ground to avoid being shot.

In the confusion the remainder of the patrol escaped and the Sons of Liberty believing I was a spy who had come voluntarily with the patrol, dragged me and my trunk aboard the ship with other loyalists and ordered the vessel to depart at once under a white flag of truce. They chose not to believe anything I said.

Perhaps this is God's will—I cannot know. The Rebecca is sailing for Rhode Island but will transfer us to a British ship returning to England. I am now a married woman and have a certificate to prove it, but soon an ocean and a war will separate me from my beloved misguided husband. Whatever his or my flaws, we belong together. He is my Landon and I am his

Melinda

28 June 1776
Charles Town

Randolph,

A brief memoir of today's tragic events. Melinda and I are married but Charles' bride was killed by the blackguard McDowell! Oh God, it was his worst deed yet. We gave chase, could not catch him, and upon return I found he had doubled back to the chapel and had taken Melinda to the harbor. With Mysty at a dead run I followed only to find the coach with Ruth's body and three others dead on the ground. Melinda was on the Rebecca, now sailing out of sight, of her own free will, declared the lying bystanders.

Randolph, you cannot imagine the agony of the moment. Here lay Jones' sailing bateau which could have taken me to a British ship and thence to join Melinda. The packet of military intelligence I held would have earned me full passage. But there on the other side of the harbor the little fort was taking a frightful pounding and responding in kind. With the knowledge of this attack, a wavering Congress would surely vote for independence.

The agony was that I had to act at once, for fear of being trapped in Charles Town by a besieging force and for the urgent necessity of getting the news to Philadelphia and continuing immediately to Rhode Island in the slim hope of intercepting the Rebecca.

I hurled the precious intelligence into a nearby smithy's forge and lashed my lance to Mysty's saddle.

Randolph, the heat of that forge cannot exceed the heat of rage boiling up within me. If I knew who banished Melinda I would kill him. And may God damn that Sgt. McDowell for what he has done to Ruth, to Melinda and to me.

The remainder of my journal and this note I shall leave in your father's strongbox en route if I have not gone mad by then.

Landon

Baltimore, MD.
(date illegible)

Mr. Benjamin Franklin
Chairman, Committee of Secret Correspondence
The Continental Congress, Philadelphia, Penn.

Mr. Franklin:

I am obliged to bring to your attention a series of violent acts and abuses of the Postal Express System perpetrated by Captain Landon Vickers. Henceforth is a summary of his unseemly actions.

The felonies began on June 28th at the Georgetown, S.C. Stage in a most violent way. First, a British mounted patrol appeared and proceeded to take all four of the fresh horses at gunpoint. They had just remounted when Captain Vickers rode up on a frothing mount displaying a Grand Union flag on the tip of a lance. The British sergeant, appearing to recognize Vickers, shouted "kill him" and they turned on him, firing as they came. Instead of fleeing, the captain drew a pistol, lowered the lance and charged straight into the group, screaming like a maniac. Before they could react to this unexpected maneuver, he shot one directly in the face and ran the lance through the sergeant's chest so deeply the point protruded from his back. The impaled soldier's shocked face turned white, then lifeless.

Vickers unsheathed his saber and turned on the remaining two. Rider and mount acted as one; the horse was charging, halting, turning, even kicking, while the saber slashed, thrust and riposted. The two soldiers fled.

Stagemaster Jamison acknowledges that he had never seen such horsemanship or swordsmanship. But skill in combat does not forgive transgression.

Vickers dismounted, went over to the dead sergeant, withdrew his lance and plunged it into the corpse again and again, like one gone mad. Then he attached the lance to the horse the sergeant had taken, mounted and whipped him into a dead run to the north without so much as to ask permission.

At New Bern, Stagemaster Biggleston reported that this young officer, distraught and dressed in a much abused uniform, arrived on another worn animal. He asked that it be returned to Sean Kirkpatrick, fifteen miles to the south, where he had abandoned a stagecoach.

Then Vickers seized a wagon with two hitched bays and driver, tied his bloody Grand Union lance to the seat and at gunpoint drove off into the night. He forced the driver to gallop the horses most of the night, though he lay down on the wagon bed half asleep.

At Tarborough he rode up on a horse from Allen's Stage like a Lucifer out of Hell and, because the bridge was washed out, ran the poor animal directly into the swollen stream. When horse and rider became separated, Vickers came ashore, still holding his Grand Union flag, ran to the stable like one lost to all reason, took a fresh horse and rode off.

The Hallifax Stage reported he left another ruined mount and took the stagecoach to Richmond in a state of collapse. There he took to the saddle again (tied himself to it) for Fredericksburg and rode all night to the ferry at Alexandria, exhausting two more horses in the process.

At Newcastle, Mr. Van Der Meter, a stable owner, reported that an uncouth man in tattered uniform and displaying a bloody flag galloped in at noon on July 4th. When he reined up, his spent horse collapsed and fell on the man's left leg. Injured, he could not get up. When he demanded, lying there on the ground, the best mount available, his agitated demeanor and waving pistol encouraged Mr. Van Der Meter to give him what he asked. He had to be lifted on the horse.

Vickers and Van Der Meter's prize mount raced to the north and neither has been heard of since.

Sir, I must protest these criminal demeanors, demand that Landon Vickers compensate for his odious actions and that he be denied further association with the United States Postal System.

I remain your obedient servant,

William Goddard
Postal Administrator

———————<small>⟶••••◉••••⟵</small>———————

Philadelphia, Pa.
July 5th, 1776

Mr. Randolph Howard
Office, Justice Martin Howard
New Bern, North Carolina

Dear Mr. Howard:

As rector of Christ Church and sometimes counselor to Captain Landon Vickers, I dispatch at his request this memoir of a remarkable event. He is indisposed with injuries to his hands and one leg which fortunately he will overcome.

After the Congress voted for independence yesterday Mr. Dunlap the printer and Landon's Negro friend, Nicholas Harrison, worked all night to transform the Declaration of Independence into a printed broadside. At noon Mr. Bingham turned copies over to three express riders to distribute the documents to the thirteen new states. Meanwhile the word had spread throughout the city and the crowd before the State House was so large that a militia company had to clear a lane and hold it open for the riders to depart.

They were just placing copies in the pouches when a frightfully disheveled man, displaying a bloody Grand Union flag, rode up the lane at a full gallop. He dismounted, shouting for Mr. Franklin, but fell to the ground, quite unable to stand. Nick carried him into the room, laid him down where we were working and began to attend to his injured leg and hands.

His eyes wandered like one demented. When he asked "What's happening here?" I recognized Landon and told him they were preparing the Declaration for distribution.

He glared at me unbelievingly. "They've voted for independence already?"

He began to breathe rapidly, obviously in great pain, and told us between breaths that the British began their assault on the 28th of June.

Mr. Bingham did not believe him, not in seven days could he have come from Charles Town. Besides, he told Landon, the British had just landed ten thousand troops on Staten Island and we had all the justification for independence we needed. I bent over the miserable fellow, heard his tragic story and mutterings about going on to Rhode Island, an impossibility in his condition.

As the riders loaded their saddlebags, we gathered at the windows to watch their departure. When Landon was unable to rise, Nick picked him up in his powerful arms, laid him on a large table before the window as gently as if the captain were a child.

The three horsemen galloped abreast down a lane through a cheering crowd and separated to deliver the news to all the states. Bells began to ring throughout the city and it was an emotional experience for all of us. Landon just lay there with tears running down his face while Nick comforted him.

To regain control of himself, Landon tried to read the small print of the Declaration, finally thrust it at Nick with:

"What does it say?" (A cruel thing to do to an ignorant Negro, I thought.)

But Nick took the paper and, with eyes fairly shining, began to read the glorious words. Against a background of cheers and church bells outside, we were transfixed by his ability to read them with such inspiration. When he reached "We mutually pledge to each other our lives, our fortunes and our sacred honor," the room broke into applause and Landon closed his bandaged hands over Nick's.

Then, in the midst of the celebration outside, a young lady in a white dress and white hat came up the lane the riders had just used. Captain Vickers started up, hallucinating she was his poor wife, and began calling her:

"Melinda! Melinda! Oh my God, Melinda!"

When she came closer and he realized his error, he burst into piteous weeping. I bent over him and offered:

"You have done your duty, son, you have kept your integrity and THIS is your country."

Landon nodded, tears flowing, and turned his face to the wall, his lips repeating "Melinda, Melinda, Melinda...."

I am overcome and can write no more.

Your servant, Sir
Jacob Duche, Rector